# WICKED DELIGHTS

With stories by

Kate Hill
Adrienne Kama
Lisa G. Riley
Kimberly Kaye Terry

Harmony™
Erotic Paranormal Romance

New Concepts Georgia

Be sure to check out our website for the very best in fiction at fantastic prices!

When you visit our webpage, you can:
* Read excerpts of currently available books
* View cover art of upcoming books and current releases
* Find out more about the talented artists who capture the magic of the writer's imagination on the covers
* Order books from our backlist
* Find out the latest NCP and author news--including any upcoming book signings by your favorite NCP author
* Read author bios and reviews of our books
* Get NCP submission guidelines
* And so much more!

We offer a 20% discount on all new Trade Paperback releases ordered from our website!

Be sure to visit our webpage to find the best deals in e-books and paperbacks! To find out about our new releases as soon as they are available, please be sure to sign up for our newsletter (http://www.newconceptspublishing.com/newsletter.htm) or join our reader group (http://groups.yahoo.com/group/new_concepts_pub/join)!

The newsletter is available by double opt in only and our customer information is *never* shared!

Visit our webpage at:
www.newconceptspublishing.com

Wicked Delights is an original publication of NCP. This work has never before appeared in book form. This work is a novel. Any similarity to actual persons or events is purely coincidental.

New Concepts Publishing, Inc.
5202 Humphreys Rd.
Lake Park, GA 31636

ISBN 1-58608-828-9
Tamed by the Tiger © copyright May 2006, Kate Hill
Forsaken © copyright May 2006, Adrienne Kama
Unparalleled © copyright May 2006, Lisa G. Riley
Pleasure Principle © copyright May 2006, Kimberly Kaye Terry
Cover art (c) copyright 2006 Dan Skinner

All rights reserved, which includes the right to reproduce this book or portions thereof in any form whatsoever except as provided by the U.S. Copyright Law.

If you purchased this book without a cover you should be aware this book is stolen property.

NCP books are available at special quantity discounts for bulk purchases for sales promotions, premiums, fund raising, or educational use. For details, write, email, or phone New Concepts Publishing, Inc., 5202 Humphreys Rd., Lake Park, GA 31636; Ph. 229-257-0367, Fax 229-219-1097; orders@newconceptspublishing.com.

First NCP Trade Paperback Printing: June 2006

Other NCP titles in print by Kate Hill:

The Chieftain's Bride
The Mad Knight's Bride (Coming Soon)


Other NCP titles in print by Adrienne Kama:

The Chronicles of Stella Rice


Other NCP titles in print by Kimberly Kaye Terry:

Love's Redemption

This anthology is dedicated to Andrea and Madris. Thanks for handing us the ball, and allowing us to run with it. You chicas rock!

> Much love,
> Kim, Lisa, Kate and Adri

## TABLE OF CONTENTS

| | |
|---|---|
| Tamed by the Tiger | Page 7 |
| Forsaken: Immortal Surrender | Page 73 |
| Unparalleled | Page 125 |
| Pleasure Principle | Page 201 |

# TAMED BY THE TIGER

## Kate Hill

### Prologue

"This is an emergency. We need to see you right away."

The panic in Kesi's voice alerted Raine because her friend rarely overreacted to an assignment. She'd always sweat the small stuff, but when it came to business, she had everything under control. Whatever happened to Kesi's unit must have been horrible for her to call at midday, when she knew Raine would be sound asleep, and demand a meeting.

"Just keep calm and tell me what happened," Raine said, cradling the phone's receiver between her shoulder and ear while rubbing sleep from her eyes.

"I told you. We were attacked. The operation was planned to perfection. We cornered the weasel and Saloni was beating the hell out of him when this *thing* attacked us and escaped with the target. You know I've seen a lot of shit, Raine, but this guy was like nothing I've ever dealt with before."

"What do you mean?"

"In the past, Saloni and I have both mixed with weretigers, but never one this powerful. And it was black. To my knowledge there are no black weretigers."

Raine's brow furrowed in thought. What Kesi just told her didn't sound good. "Well the target is a weretiger, too. Makes sense that another of his kind would try to save his ass. Just because we've never seen a black weretiger doesn't mean one can't exist. I do agree we need a meeting to figure this out."

"No shit."

"I'll ignore that."

"As long as you don't ignore the problem, that's all I care about."

"None of you are too injured to travel, right?"

"Right."

"Then come to my place. We'll be safe here while we figure out what's going on. I'll get someone back on the target and his mysterious rescuer so we can get the job done. All good?"

"It's a start. We'll get there ASAP."

A click on the other end of the line told Rain that Kesi had hung up. She switched off her cell phone and placed it back on the night table, then glanced toward the window. Sun bled through the space on the sides of the drawn shade. Usually she slept through the day, but the discussion with Kesi had her too wound up. It had been literally ages since anyone had interfered with one of their jobs. Knowing a male had stopped them irritated her even more. She could only imagine how Saloni felt, since it was *her* chance for vengeance. Not to mention that Kesi, known as the best fighter in the sisterhood, was absolutely beside herself.

Over two thousand years ago Raine's grandmother, along with two other magical women, had formed the Wakened Veils. Many of the original members still existed, depending on what type of supernatural powers they possessed. Vampires, Succubae, and some were-creatures for example, lived very long lives. Tired of being subject to the whims of men, they banded together and used their powers for vengeance against any man who brought harm to a woman. Their secret society grew and their legacy continued through generations until units of the Wakened Veils patrolled each continent. Raine was in charge of the units that secured the United States east of the Mississippi. Her duty was to listen to cases presented by her warriors, bring the most important ones to the three founders known as the First Wraths, and see that the cases assigned to her units were carried out with stealth and efficiency. A problem such as the one Kesi reported must take top priority. Neither she nor any of the warriors involved could rest until their target--and the bastard who had the audacity to rescue him--were punished.

## Chapter One

The tiger's muscular body pushed through the lake's churning waves, the weight of the man-beast on his back scarcely hindering him. He tried to ignore the taste of blood in his mouth and the lust for battle pulsing through him. At the moment his most important concern was reaching safety before those demonic women regrouped and tried to complete the job they'd started.

Nearing the riverbank, the tiger took the man-beast gently by the scruff of the neck and dragged him out of the water. He glanced toward the dirt road, noting the car still parked to the side of it.

Closing his eyes, he drew a deep breath, feeling his powerful chest expand. With the utmost control, he released the breath, his body changing. Bones reshaped, muscles compacted, his spine shifted, and his face molded into its man form. Wet black hair retracted, leaving rivulets of water trailing over smooth flesh and drenched tendrils of thick human hair hanging past his shoulders.

Sanjay glanced at his son sprawled on the muddy ground, still halfway between human and tiger. Blood ran from several wounds on his back and legs, but they had already started to heal. He hoisted the youth onto his shoulder and carried him to the car where he propped him against the hood and lightly slapped his catlike face.

"Rahul, come on. Wake up. You need to change back so we can get out of here."

The man-beast stirred, and then growled. Sanjay pulled his hand away before savage fangs sank into it. The man-beast's eyes focused on him, recognition flashing through them, before they slipped shut. With several measured breaths, Rahul changed to his human form. His battered body sagged and if Sanjay hadn't caught him he most likely would have hit the ground.

"Get in." Sanjay shoved him into the car and reached for a first aid kit. He started cleaning the rapidly healing injuries but Rahul shoved his hands away.

"Father, why did you follow me?"

"Good thing I did or else you'd be dead."

"I could have handled a bunch of women."

"Highly unlikely." Sanjay continued tending Rahul's injuries. "And before you lose your temper again, it's those particular women who would give you difficulty. Did you happen to notice their ear cuffs?"

"I was more interested in avoiding their weapons than admiring their jewelry."

"The engraved silver ear cuffs they wear are a symbol of their sisterhood, a way of identifying themselves to each other. They kill men, Rahul. In particular, men of a magical nature."

"They wouldn't have killed me."

Still excitable from repressing the urge to destroy enemies in battle, the tiger in Sanjay was in no mood for Rahul's obstinacy. Grasping the youth roughly by the jaw, he snarled, "Killing is *all* they do, Rahul, but they never kill without reason."

"What is that supposed to mean?"

"It means keep your silence, boy, until I'm finished aiding you."

Rahul's chest rose and fell with each furious breath and he glared at Sanjay yet kept his silence. He must have sensed his father had been pushed to his limit and any further provocation would end quite badly.

Sanjay worked quickly, knowing it was only a matter of time before those she-devils recovered enough to follow them. Crossing the river would have thrown them off their scent temporarily, but the women were vampires and when it came to tracking, few creatures surpassed blood drinkers. They needed to get out of the area and to the hotel room Sanjay booked two states over. It would mean driving all day, but he had little choice.

Moments later the men, now dressed in jeans and T-shirts, drove down the dark country road.

"May I ask a question, Father?" Rahul asked, his voice haughty. At Sanjay's nod, he continued, "If you were certain those women wanted to kill me, why did you leave them alive?"

"You know it is not our way to harm women. No self-respecting weretiger would do such a thing. Not only that, those particular women never kill without reason. I want to know which one of them you angered enough to warrant a death sentence."

"How is it you are so familiar with them?"

"I've had all I will take of your insolence. I want an answer to my question. Now!"

"And if I don't want to give it?"

A growl trapped in Sanjay's throat. He would have been within his rights to punish Rahul for his insolence, but no matter what the situation, his son was usually respectful and collected. This uncharacteristic rebelliousness combined with tonight's attack told

Sanjay something was drastically wrong. He needed to uncover the problem before he lost Rahul, and not simply to death.

"Why don't you want to talk to me?" Sanjay asked, trying to keep the demand from his voice. As leader of their clan, he was accustomed to his men responding immediately when asked a question.

"Because this is not something you can understand and I don't want you to interfere. What happened tonight is between Saloni and me."

"Saloni? She's a vampire." Sanjay recalled one of the women from tonight's attack.

"Yes."

"Who is she exactly?"

"No one you would know about."

"I realize that. I only know about, Nidhi, the girl you're to marry."

Rahul's jaw tightened visibly and he held up a defensive hand. "Father, don't do this."

"One of us must do something, Rahul. If this Saloni woman has called upon the Wakened Veils, they will not stop hunting until you are dead."

"The Wakened Veils?"

"They are a group of women--all of magical origins--that formed two thousand years ago to seek revenge against any man who dared harm one of their own."

"And no one has stopped them? Surely it wouldn't take much--"

"No one has stopped them because not only is their secret kept safe from everyone outside their group, but they are intelligent and well trained. Assassins comparable to Thugs and Ninja, except these females have various powers far beyond the realm of mortals."

Rahul snorted. "It sounds as if you're afraid of them."

"Your attempt to goad me is weak--as weak as whatever actions led you to be marked for death by this powerful group of women."

Rahul growled and shifted position to glare at Sanjay. "You know nothing about what happened between me and Saloni."

"Not if you don't tell me."

The younger man sighed deeply, his anger fading to an expression of sadness that affected Sanjay more than he wanted to admit. From the moment Rahul was born, Sanjay had loved him in a way he never imagined possible. He had felt little for the boy's mother, and she even less for him, but both parents had adored Rahul, even if Sanjay had stupidly wasted many years playing the part of clan leader instead of father. He had been harsh with Rahul for the boy's own good. Theirs was a savage world and to keep the respect of his men, Sanjay needed to maintain firm control over everything and everyone, including himself. Sometimes he worried that he had learned too late that power tempered with understanding made a better leader--and a far better father--than he had often been.

"Do you remember two centuries ago when you went to South America?" Rahul asked.

"Of course."

"During the months you were away, I met a woman in a village not far from our clan's meeting place. Saloni. We were very much in love."

Sanjay glanced at Rahul, noting a gleam in his eyes that wasn't there when he spoke of his fiancée, Nidhi. Not a good sign.

"Why did you never mention this woman to me? Tell me she was not engaged to someone else." *Or worse, married.*

"I wanted to marry her, but her family would not accept me."

"Why not?" Sanjay snapped, irritated. Not only was Rahul a successful businessman more than able to comfortably support a family, but he was a fierce protector. Women would like the idea that he was handsome and kind. "You didn't tell them about your shape shifting, did you? Because you know that cannot be discussed until after the engagement--"

"Only Saloni knew."

"I will refrain from mentioning how stupid it was to tell anyone outside of the clan, except your *wife*."

"You just did mention it. Now do you want to hear this story only so you can lecture me on my mistakes?"

Sanjay drew a deep breath and released it slowly. "Go on."

"Her parents had already arranged her marriage and she refused to go against their wishes, so I left. I had to get as far from her and India as possible or else I thought I might lose my mind."

"That's why you were gone when I returned from South America."

"Yes."

"I see. But I still don't understand what you did to provoke the Wakened Veils. It seems to me that the woman was the one in error, not you."

"When do women ever make sense?"

Sanjay shrugged, unable to argue with that bit of reasoning.

"She probably wants revenge because she and I slept together."

"Ah." Sanjay smirked. "Now the proverbial plot thickens."

"It was only one time ... maybe two."

"Maybe?"

"Father, I would rather not go into detail."

"How about going into detail about how she became a vampire?"

"When I returned from abroad, I went to her village, just to make sure she was happy with her new family--"

"Or to see if she wasn't so you could pick up where you left off?"

"Since you already know the story, you obviously don't need me to continue," Rahul said sarcastically.

"Just go on."

"Saloni had died in childbirth, or so I thought."

"So now she's a vampire and seeking revenge on you. Why?"

"I have no idea." Rahul gestured helplessly with his hands, and then added softly, "Except that tonight she mentioned something about Nidhi."

"She's jealous."

"But she refused me."

"It doesn't matter. She refused to disrespect her parents' wishes but at the same time wanted you to remain faithful to her. Love can be a double-edged sword, one that females wield with untouchable skill."

"You speak like an expert."

"I'm much older and more experienced than you." Sanjay fell silent for a moment, concentrating on merging with the speeding highway traffic. The road was a long stretch, with cars rushing by on both sides. It had been quite some time since he'd traveled outside of rural areas. He spent most of his time in jungles or open country. His very nature demanded the freedom only available outside the city. Rahul had inherited much of his mother's human nature and was, for the most part, well able to deal with the confinement of city life.

"I don't think they intended to kill me, Father," Rahul said quietly. "At least I won't believe Saloni meant to."

"Do not underestimate any member of the Wakened Veils. When we get to the hotel, I want you to stay there. If you don't hear from me within twenty-four hours, I want you to return home. I've alerted the clan to this problem and they are ready to defend you. I pray it will not come to that. If it does, many will die on both sides of this battle."

Rahul paled a bit, though Sanjay didn't think for a moment it was out of fear for his own life. In spite of his recent rebelliousness, the clan meant everything to Rahul and he would not wish to put them in danger.

"Where are you going, Father?"

"To see if I can put a stop to this situation before it gets out of control. If these women will simply see reason, there need not be any more bloodshed on either side."

\* \* \* \*

Raine awoke at dusk after a restless day plagued by worries about Kesi's report. Standing in the shower, her face tilted toward the faucet, she allowed the water to soothe her. One of the greatest pleasures of the modern world had to be the shower. Raine loved the sensation of fresh hot water running over every inch of her while she rubbed scented soap or gel over her skin. Nothing got a woman in the mood for seduction like this marvelous invention. The only thing missing was a man to share it with her, but tonight she'd rectify that problem. She'd been so busy with work that she'd neglected her hunger for the past few nights. Tonight, she would seek out a strong young male and gorge herself on his every essence. Her nature demanded she feed off the energy of others-- human males being her prime target.

Like her mother and grandmother, Raine was a Succubus. Not all offspring of a Succubus and her chosen mate were lucky enough to inherit the power. Since her father wasn't mortal, but a vampire, Raine had a stronger inclination toward magical tendencies than most. Thankfully his disgusting blood drinking habit hadn't passed on to her.

Reluctantly, she stepped out of the shower and dried off with a thick, oversized towel. After smoothing on perfumed lotion, she slipped into her lacy black bra, matching panties, and robe, which she left unbelted. She strolled to the kitchen and set a tea kettle on the stove before walking to the fridge to find something to cook for breakfast. In spite of how her stomach rumbled, her thoughts focused more on her *other* hunger, the one that made her heart beat faster and her nipples tighten with anticipation. Tonight some unsuspecting man would get more pleasure then he ever bargained for.

First she needed to wait for Kesi and Saloni who she expected to arrive at any moment.

"Miss Santangelo, forgive my intrusion but--"

Raine let loose a scream loud enough to waken any zombie within ten miles. Grasping the butcher's knife that hung from a nail on the wall, she spun and found herself facing a tall, dark-skinned man with raven black hair that hung to his elbows.

"Please, don't be alarmed. I mean no harm and only want to talk."

"How the hell did you get in here?"

A smile played around his full, rather sensual lips. If she'd met him under other circumstances, Raine would have been thrown by his stunning good looks. His face was angular but without the half-starved look common to many models and actors considered handsome in this modern age. Five o'clock shadow dusted his sturdy jaw, further accentuating his raw masculinity. Most fascinating of all were his eyes. They were large, wide set, slightly tilted at the corners and such gleaming black Raine was certain if she stepped closer she could see her reflection in them.

"A funny question from a Succubus who spends her nights slipping unnoticed into men's beds." His voice was deep yet smooth as warm caramel. It poured over her, soothing, yet at the same time arousing. For a man such a voice was more than an asset, it was a weapon that drained a woman's strength, much like Raine used her Succubus physique to drain energy.

"How do you know me?" Raine demanded, not liking this man's calm collectedness that bordered on arrogance. She stepped closer, the knife poised to attack.

He stood his ground, his sleek body relaxed yet at the same time she felt the power radiating from him. If she struck, no doubt he would be ready. The question was, why hadn't *he* attacked yet?

"I have come to discuss last night's attempt by your Wakened Veils to execute Rahul."

A cold feeling swept through Raine. How did he know about the Veils?

"You have many questions," he continued. "Please allow me time to explain."

"I'm listening."

"Perhaps you would like to clothe yourself first." His gaze swept her body in a manner that reminded her of how hungry she was. Actually, if he wasn't a damn intruder she wouldn't mind seeing exactly what was under that black tank top and those jeans that hugged every inch of his long, well-muscled legs ...

She shook her head slightly. This was crazy. He was an intruder in her house and she was thinking about screwing him until his eyes crossed. That's what she got for allowing the hunger to last for days. Her mother always warned her to feed at least every other night or there was no telling when or with whom her control would snap.

"If you know I'm a Succubus then you also know a state of undress doesn't bother me," she sneered, not taking the knife from its defensive position. There was no way she was going to relax her guard until she heard more. "Move to the table slowly and sit. Now!"

He did as she requested, his obsidian eyes never leaving her. Good lord, his every movement was like a smooth, masculine dance, so graceful yet powerful. He settled into the chair and placed his hands on the table, palms down.

She sat across from him. "Who are you and what do you know about Rahul?"

"I am Sanjay. I am Rahul's father and have come to ask your sisterhood to spare his life."

"How do you know about the Wakened Veils?"

"I knew your grandmother, Miss Santangelo."

"Apparently you were on her good side, or you wouldn't be alive. Still, I can't believe she would disclose our secret to you."

"I discovered the Wakened Veils by accident."

"And she allowed you to live with this knowledge?"

"She trusted my discretion."

Raine curled her lip, her hand tightening on the knife. "If you really knew my grandmother then you would know she trusts no man."

"Why don't you ask her? That is what I want. A meeting with her."

"Why not go to her directly?"

His eyes widened in an innocent gesture that roused her suspicion even more. One thing was for certain, no man who looked and talked like him was innocent. This was a master of seduction if she'd ever met one, surpassing any incubus or vampire she'd ever met.

"Is this not the proper channel within your society? I must go through you before reaching her. And are you not the one in charge of my son's execution? You may stop it."

"No, I may not," Raine said. "I don't have the power to overstep a decision made by the First Wraths."

"But you can postpone it and arrange a meeting with them for me." He leaned closer, his expression even more intense. She thought she heard something resembling a growl rumbling deep in his chest.

"You're the one who stole him last night, aren't you?" she asked.

He nodded. "I am."

"The black weretiger," she murmured.

"You realize I could have destroyed your warriors, but I

refrained."

His attitude irked her, but he did have a point. "Why did you?"

"Because it is against our ways to harm women. We serve our goddess and respect those made in her image. That is why I prefer to negotiate for my son's life--"

"Your *son* does not share your respect! A woman suffered and died because of him. She will have her revenge."

His brow furrowed. "I'm sure they both suffered over their separation, however that was her doing, not Rahul's. As for her unfortunate death, I do not see how my son is at fault. And she did not die. As you know she is now a vampire."

"*Her* doing? Not *his* fault? He promised her eternal love then abandoned her, pregnant, so she was forced to marry somebody else. If it had not been for a vampire, she would have died in childbirth along with her son. *Your* grandson."

Sanjay's hands curled into fists and he sat back in the chair, his broad chest expanding with a deep breath. He released it so slowly that Raine marveled at his control.

Finally he said, "That cannot be true."

"Why?"

"Rahul told me he proposed to her and she refused, saying her parents had already arranged her marriage. The child she lost was her husband's, not my son's."

Raine raised her eyes to heaven and shook her head. "Typical. One man lies, another man swears to it."

A muscle twitched in his chiseled cheek. "My son is many things, but he is not a liar."

"Says you."

"What makes you so certain this woman is not lying?"

"We have known her for over a century. She is one of us."

"Then why did she take so long to seek him out for vengeance? Why did she wait until he is engaged to be married before asking your sisterhood to strike? Could it be for jealousy instead of revenge?"

"I've heard all I care to. You have ten seconds to get out of my house before you regret coming here in the first place."

They stood simultaneously and she thought he might actually obey her.

One moment he stood across the table and the next he pinned her to the wall, one massive furred paw pressing to her throat, the other trapping her wrist until the knife dropped to the floor. His handsome face elongated, covered in gleaming black hair, something between tiger and man.

"I will not harm you, but you must listen to me," he said, his voice deeper, more animalistic but no less beautiful. "Please."

Raine's teeth clenched and her heart pounded, yet beyond her rage and fear, something else stirred. She had the feeling this man had never begged for anything, yet he was pleading with her for his son's life. His gaze, still fixed on hers, seemed to reach into her soul.

No matter what emotions he roused within her, she couldn't let him think he could use force to sway her. Her eyes closed halfway as she summoned the power that lay coiled and waiting within her. She wrapped her legs around him, squeezing tightly, and leaned her head closer in an attempt to kiss him.

He turned away and released her so abruptly she might have fallen if the wall hadn't been directly behind her. Before her eyes, he returned completely to his human form.

"I know too well the results of a Succubus' kiss," he said, his voice rougher than it had been.

"Then keep your paws to yourself." She belted her robe and bent to pick up the knife, but his booted foot closed over it.

"Leave it. We could kill each other without weapons if we want to. I need you to help me stop the violence that will ensue if your sisterhood continues stalking my son."

"Since when does a weretiger give a damn about stopping violence?"

He took a step closer, his broad chest inches from her face. Raine swallowed hard. Damn he was sexy as hell but incredibly frustrating. "We are not what you think, Miss Santan--"

"Will you quit with the Miss Santangelo stuff already?" She ran a hand through her hair and sighed. "Just call me Raine."

"Raine, I know the Veils will keep tracking Rahul until they are given the order to stop. Neither I nor my clan will allow him to die for a crime he didn't commit. For all our sakes, arrange a meeting for us with your First Wraths."

"It won't matter what you say. They have made up their minds."

He placed his hands on her shoulders, his gaze fixed on hers with such intensity that she longed to look away but couldn't. It was as if he had her under a spell. No man had ever made her feel like this. The sensation was heady.

"Do you have any children, Raine?"

"You mean there's something about me you don't already know?" she quipped.

"*Do you have any?*" he repeated.

She detected an edge to his voice that hadn't been there before.

"No, thank goodness." The last thing she wanted was a kid tying her down.

"Then you don't know what it is to hold a child in your arms, see your future in his eyes. To take him into your heart. If my son dies, part of me dies, too. You have the power to help me. That probably means nothing to you, but at the very least finding the truth should. By executing a man before determining his doubtless guilt, you are becoming like those the Veils seek to punish."

Raine stared at him for a long moment. After so many centuries of living, few things reached her heart. Looking into his eyes she was certain of one thing, he believed every word he spoke. He believed in his son's innocence and something told her he even bore some respect for her sisterhood.

Sighing deeply, she closed her eyes and shook her head. "Fuck. All right. I'll talk to my grandmother and see what I can do. How can I reach you?"

"I will give you the phone number of the hotel where I'm staying."

She walked to a drawer and removed a pad and pen. Their fingers brushed when she handed them to him. His were long and slim. She couldn't help imagining how they would feel on her body, stroking and teasing in warm, wet places. Desire flooded her, making her ache with need. Damn, she didn't want to reveal her arousal. Too late. His dark eyes flickered in her direction and she knew his sharp, weretiger senses detected the aroma of her lust, perhaps even heard the quickening of her heartbeat.

Using the tip of his tongue, he moistened his full lips before placing the pad and pen on the countertop.

"Thank you for your cooperation, Raine."

"Don't thank me yet. Instead of a meeting the First Wraths might command your execution, too."

"It is a risk worth taking."

"Your son is lucky to have such a loyal father."

He didn't reply, merely held her gaze with those penetrating eyes.

"By the way," Raine continued, "how did you get in here?"

"You left your bedroom window open."

She curled her lip. "It's on the second floor."

Smiling slightly, he shrugged. "Just a little stretch of the legs."

"Well this time use the front door."

He nodded, allowing her to guide him down the stairs to the foyer. Once he'd gone, she hurried to her room and closed the window, muttering under her breath, "Damn were-creatures."

Though she had planned to hunt, it was far more important that she contact her grandmother and think of a way to pacify Kesi and Saloni who were bound to be furious if they couldn't track Rahul immediately. She expected the women to arrive at any time and was glad they hadn't showed up when Sanjay was here. That would have been utter disaster. Before introducing him she needed to make preparations or Kesi would probably try to skin him alive, in either human or tiger form.

\* \* \* \*

Once outside Raine's house, Sanjay drew a deep breath of crisp New England air, hoping it would do something to soothe the scarcely controllable lust racing through him. When he'd come to bargain for his son's life he had no intention of feeling such attraction to Raine. Still, he should have learned his lesson about Succubae, especially one related to Vidonia. Raine, with her brown hair and eyes the color of dark chocolate, had not only inherited her grandmother's beauty, but her spirit. Something about passionate, independent women aroused Sanjay more than anything. For a man of his nature and position in the clan, such women were a guilty pleasure.

Furious at himself for being attracted to a woman who had labeled his son a liar and a cad, he stalked through the city. He struggled to tune out the obnoxious noise and neon lights that in his agitated state seemed even more annoying than usual. If only he could go off to the country for a few hours and stretch his tiger's limbs in open field or through winding forest. Glancing around at the skyscrapers and crowded streets he wondered why anyone chose to live in such a place. Of course he was looking at it from a tiger's perspective. To a Succubus like Raine, the city was perfect for stalking the mortal men she preyed upon.

While he hurried through the streets, miserable in the urban surroundings, she was probably dancing in a club, her breathtaking curves exposed, and a string of pathetic mortals drooling after her. Perhaps she had already found one to sate her demonic lust. The image of her straddling her prey, her sleek thighs clasping his hips, had his cock pulsing in a way he didn't want to think about. Sex was the last thing that should be on his mind, but he couldn't help himself.

The woman's power had infected him and would overtake him if he let it. When she'd stepped into the kitchen wearing nothing but her underclothes and a silk robe, it had taken him a moment to control his arousal enough to announce his presence. Though not especially tall, her gorgeous body could set a man's blood on fire. She didn't have that emaciated look so many women in the modern world strove for, but healthy curves he longed to touch. Even the sound of her scream had sent an erotic thrill through him, reminding him of how a female weretiger might sound, if one existed. Her large dark eyes had fixed on him with strength and pride befitting her high rank in the Wakened Veils. At first he expected her to fully rebel against hearing him out, but she'd proved surprisingly diplomatic. Perhaps her attraction to him had influenced her. Women often found weretigers compelling and Sanjay was considered a master of seduction among his kind. Females, even magical ones, usually couldn't resist him and he had a rare talent for handling Succubae.

In spite of her collected manner, the seductive, musky scent of Raine's lust had betrayed her feelings for him. That was something he could use to his advantage, providing he kept his passion for her under control. He had no choice. His son's life was far more important than lust.

He paused at a payphone where he dialed the number to Rahul's hotel in the next state and quickly briefed him on the night's events.

"Once I hear from the woman I will contact you again," Sanjay said.

"Did you find out exactly why Saloni is mad at me?"

"We'll discuss it later."

"Father--"

"I said later." Sanjay slammed down the receiver. A telephone conversation was not the right way to ask his son whether or not he was a liar. Knowing the mood Rahul had been in lately, he'd most likely get angry and complicate issues by running off.

Sanjay continued down the sidewalk. Upon reaching his hotel room, he undressed and shifted into his tiger form. If he couldn't enjoy the outdoors then he could at least relax in the shape he found most comfortable. Feeling the great cat's powerful muscles ripple, he yawned wide then stretched his long body, his front legs extended. He arched his back and growled before stepping onto the bed where he sprawled on his side, listening to the sound of traffic outside. Hopefully he would hear from Raine soon. He hadn't slept in days and though tired, he couldn't rest soundly until Rahul was safe.

Raine's accusations also plagued him. Not that he didn't trust Rahul, but he realized there were two sides to every story. When it came to Saloni, his son hadn't exactly been forthcoming in providing information. It was as if he wanted to keep the affair from Sanjay. Was this out of rebelliousness or did he truly have something to hide?

He growled, angry at himself for doubting Rahul. The younger man was stubborn and had certainly inherited a good portion of Sanjay's arrogance, yet he had never been a liar and he had always respected women. He couldn't imagine Rahul treating a lover so callously.

Sanjay stood, pounced onto the floor, and paced, feeling caged both physically and emotionally. If the Wakened Veils were men it would have been so much easier to deal with them. He and his clan would have fought to the death without a moment's compunction. When dealing with females, he was bound by the laws of his clan to negotiate. Destroying them was a last resort, and even then he risked punishment from the goddess they served.

Aside from his basic beliefs, he didn't like the idea of killing first and questioning later. His youth had been spent wallowing in power, bathing in blood. The tiger's strength intoxicated many young men and being among the first of his kind, Sanjay was no exception. He had taken many lives, often without thoroughly investigating whether or not his victims deserved death. Many centuries and thousands of regrets later, he had tempered his power with mercy. He had fought hard to make his clan see the error of their ways, but eventually they had listened. Only Rahul seemed to have been born with the desire for true justice, something rare for a mortal let alone a weretiger. That was why he couldn't accept Raine's story of him impregnating and then abandoning Saloni, no matter what the Wakened Veils wanted to believe.

He wasn't sure how long he paced the room before he became aware of Raine's scent of natural musk combined with sandalwood perfume. Passion rippled down his spine. Closing his eyes, he filled his lungs with air and synchronized his shape shifting with the release of breath. By the time she knocked on the door he was back in his human form and pulling on his jeans. He zipped them, not an especially easy task since her delectable aroma had him semi-erect. If the situation hadn't been so grave he most likely would have been pole hard and ready to seduce the gorgeous Succubus.

## Chapter Two

Raine stood outside Sanjay's hotel room door, her heart pounding with anticipation of seeing the handsome weretiger again. She had spent close to an hour on the phone with her grandmother and no sooner had she hung up than Kesi and Saloni arrived along with Bo, the third member of their unit. If convincing her grandmother to allow Sanjay to meet with the First Wraths had been difficult, it was nothing compared to breaking the news to Kesi and the others….

\* \* \* \*

Before opening the door to Kesi's agitated pounding, Raine closed her eyes and counted to ten. She hadn't been looking forward to this meeting with Kesi, Bo, and Saloni, even if the three vampires were her friends. No doubt Kesi would be angry, Saloni emotional, and Bo trying too hard to keep everyone in good humor.

"Girl, what the hell took you so long?" Kesi strode into the foyer, Saloni and Bo behind her.

"She's wicked pissed," Bo said.

"You bet I'm pissed. Do you know how long it's been since somebody knocked me out cold? When I get my hands on whoever it was who stole our target I'm going to skin him alive and give Saloni the coat."

Both Saloni and Bo glanced at Raine and wrinkled their noses in disgust.

"That's okay, Kesi." Saloni held up a long, slender hand, her dark, almond-shaped eyes narrowing. "All I want is Rahul."

"You'll get his ass. Don't worry about it."

"Ladies, we need to talk," Raine said.

Kesi froze, giving Raine the stare that meant trouble. "Ladies? Whenever you start out with "ladies" it means you're going to say something we're not going to like."

"No. It's not something you won't like," Raine said. "It's something you're going to hate. Come and sit down."

"Sit down?" Bo said. "What does she mean *sit down*."

"Forget the sit down, Raine, and tell me what you found out."

"Well, the good news is I know who attacked you the other night."

"Who?"

"Rahul's father."

"So it *was* a weretiger." Kesi struck her fist into her palm. Her brow furrowed and she glanced at Raine. "And the bad news?"

"The First Wraths have delayed the order for vengeance upon Rahul."

"What?" three voices demanded and three pairs of eyes glared so hard at Raine she thought she might go up in flames.

"That cannot be," Saloni said, her chest rising and falling with each agitated breath. "After what he did to me ... this cannot be!"

"Sanjay--Rahul's father--was here earlier."

"I knew I smelled something familiar," Kesi said. "Damn. I thought it was psychological because I've been obsessing about that fucking black tiger since the attack. Where is he now? You got him chained up somewhere?"

"No."

"Why not?" Bo asked in her calmest voice.

Somehow the lovely Chinese woman's soft, yet accusing tone got to Raine more than Kesi's ranting. Whenever Bo used that unnaturally calm voice, she was at her most dangerous. Still, Raine was in charge and she needed to let these women know that while at the same time showing them the respect they deserved. Sometimes she really hated her job.

"Everybody come in and have a seat," Raine stated and before anyone could protest, led the way to the kitchen. "Coffee? Tea?"

"Forget the damn coffee and tea. Tell us exactly what's going on with these weretigers!" Kesi snapped.

Raine could practically see the flames shooting out of the vampiress' nostrils. Tall with smooth ebony skin and a body an Olympic athlete would envy, Kesi easily took charge of just about any situation. She and Raine had been close friends for a millennium. They had both been up for leadership of the northeast U.S. units, but Kesi had decided she preferred fieldwork and training recruits to paperwork and direct dealing with the First Wraths. She was the one person in the Veils who was Raine's perfect balance, but at times like this Raine disliked working with her. Sometimes Kesi hurled herself so forcefully into the kill that she lost sight of justice.

Sighing, Raine carried a tray of refreshments to the table and sat.

"Sanjay asked for a meeting with the First Wraths because he feels Rahul has been unjustly accused."

"What does he know?" Saloni snapped. "He wasn't even in India during the time Rahul and I were together."

"I find it difficult to believe the First Wraths agreed to a meeting with him," Bo said. "It is against our laws to allow a man to speak in defense of another."

"That still holds true," Raine stated. "I have agreed to speak for him."

"What?" Kesi glared. "I can't believe you'd do this, Raine."

"You didn't speak to him, Kesi. I believe he is sincere in his beliefs and in his desire to find a peaceful solution to the problem."

"Peaceful? He knocked me out for an hour."

"And me for two," Bo added.

"I want my revenge," Saloni said, her face taut.

"Most likely you will get it." Raine held each woman's gaze in turn. "The First Wraths have only agreed to meet with him if he brings Rahul with him. They will be at our mercy and killed immediately, if the First Wraths wish it."

"Why are you doing this?" Kesi demanded. "Are you hot for him? Is that it, Succubus? Have you fed lately?"

"You're out of line, Kesi." Raine stared hard at her friend.

"No, I'm right, aren't I?"

"The First Wraths have agreed to this. I merely brought the man's proposal before them. I understand that you don't like this decision, but as members of the Veils, learn to live with it."

"Maybe she's right." Bo held Raine's gaze. "Our first law is to seek justice. I'm sure the men will get exactly what they deserve."

\* \* \* \*

Sanjay's door opened and Raine's breath caught at the sight of him, barefoot and shirtless, wearing faded jeans with a hole in the knee that clung to his long, muscular legs. His shoulders were broad, his chest lean and arms powerful. She had the sudden urge to lick every inch of his six-pack abs. A few sparse dark hairs dusted his chest and the flesh around his navel.

"Raine," he said, that deep sexy voice bringing her gaze to his face. His obsidian eyes captured hers, refusing to let go. "Please come in."

He let her inside then closed the door behind her.

"I'm surprised to see you here."

"I wanted to bring the news in person."

In truth that was only part of the reason. Because of him she had wasted a night of hunting, and as Kesi suggested, she was growing quite desperate to feed off a man's energy. It was only fitting that if she suffered because of him, he should repay her efforts. After she informed him of the First Wraths' rules for their meeting, she intended to give in to her urge for this man's sinfully gorgeous body.

"Well?" he asked.

"Aren't you going to offer me a seat?" She stared at him with her most seductive look.

He lifted his chin toward the breakfast table in front of glass doors that opened to a balcony.

Raine sat and crossed her legs, exposing a good deal of her shapely thighs. She knew a certain brand of man found her type of body--muscular yet with womanly curves--irresistible. By the way Sanjay looked at her, she knew he was that kind of man. As a Succubus, she was skilled at using her body for seduction. After placing her small black purse on the table, she folded her hands on her lap. She tilted her face in his direction as he approached and loomed above her, radiating the energy of a great cat even in his human form.

Folding his arms across his chest and fixing his dark gaze upon her he said, "This is not a joke."

"Tell me about it. You have no idea the hoops I had to jump through to convince the First Wraths, not to mention the unit assigned to your son, to hear your side of the story."

"But they will listen?"

"Under certain conditions, yes."

"What conditions?" Though his voice remained calm she detected annoyance in his eyes.

This was *not* a man accustomed to taking orders from anyone. She could tell *he* was the one who usually established conditions rather than bow to someone else's. Since he was also quite old, she didn't doubt it galled him even more that women were in control of circumstances so important to him. She couldn't help feeling a perverse satisfaction knowing this. She'd met too many men like him throughout her life. Her own father had been such a controlling swine that the Veils had eventually staked him. She couldn't even say she missed him.

"First, both you and Rahul must be present at the trial."

"To ensure an easy kill if he is still found guilty."

"You did attack three of our women, Sanjay, and also admitted that if Rahul isn't set free there will be further bloodshed. We must take steps to ensure our own safety."

"How can I be ensured of a fair trial?"

"You can't. But you are the one who came to us. Of course you're free to leave right now, but don't doubt we'll follow you. I know several members of the sisterhood who would just love a black tiger coat."

His lip curled slightly and she heard a low rumble in his chest. A thrill of fear and arousal darted through her. This SOB was more virile than any man had a right to be, and deep inside she had to admit the beast in him turned her on. Watching him shift to a half man-half beast earlier that night made her long to see him in complete tiger form. She didn't doubt he'd be magnificent.

"What are the other conditions?"

"The meeting must be held at my grandmother's home in Cascais, Portugal. I have already arranged for plane tickets." At his nod, she continued, "Last, you will not be allowed to speak without a sponsor from the sisterhood. Needless to say, you haven't done much to win any popularity contests among us."

"The meeting is a farce. No member of your sisterhood will speak for our benefit."

Raine drew a deep breath and released it slowly. "I will. I'm your sponsor."

"You believed what I told you?"

"I believe in your feelings for your son and will see that he gets a fair trial."

For a long moment he held her gaze, as if deciding whether or not to believe her. Something told her he didn't trust any easier than she did. Finally he nodded.

"Fine," she said. "You and Rahul will meet us at the airport tomorrow evening at five and we'll travel together. My friend Kesi will be accompanying us. She is one of the warriors you attacked. Just a warning, she's not happy with you."

"I don't imagine she would be. I put a stop to their amusement."

Raine's brow furrowed. "You think our work amuses us?"

"Doesn't it?" He bent and placed his hands on the chair arms, caging her with his sinewy arms and broad chest, his face so close she detected the faint gray ring surrounding his obsidian irises. His lips were near enough to hers that she need only lean forward and they would touch. "Tell me the truth, Succubus. You're all so twisted by hatred that you enjoy causing others to suffer."

"Only those who deserve it."

"When was the last time you sought out a man for pleasure, not simply to quicken you with his energy, but for companionship? For love."

"Love?" She smirked. "I'll tell you what I know about men's love. My grandmother and the other founders of the Veils were slaves to men. She tried to warn my mother not to trust them, but she wouldn't listen. My mother fell in love with a Roman vampire who made her life and mine hell. He was an evil, torturing bastard--my father--as are my brothers. Mother was so ashamed of her decision to *love* that it took her literally ages before she confided in the Veils who avenged her by staking my father during his daylight sleep. I had to content myself with spitting on his cremated remains, but to tell you the truth, I would have gladly killed him myself. Unfortunately I was locked away at the time as punishment for my nature. Can you believe a bloodsucking vampire would condemn me for draining a little energy?"

She wasn't certain if a buildup of hunger made her weak, but as she spoke long buried emotions rose within her--rage, fear, sadness. The urge to hit something or cry almost overcame her, but she knew a better way to pacify herself. Besides, Sanjay owed her not only for complicating her life but for representing him to the First Wraths.

His gaze held hers with sympathy she both craved and despised.

"I'm sorry," he said, his deep voice shockingly gentle.

In reply she grasped the back of his head, loving the sensation of his silky hair running through her fingers, and covered his mouth in a harsh kiss. Her lips pressed hard against his. For a moment he didn't move, but allowed her to vent her emotions. Her tongue plunged into his mouth and swept against his, savoring his warmth and taste. Clasping the back of his strong neck she pulled herself closer to him. His hands remained braced on the chair arms, rock hard and immovable.

Then his tongue met her strokes, engaging in a hot, sensual battle. He explored every inch of her mouth and gently bit her lower lip before licking it. Damn, this man could kiss!

Hunger, both for energy and pleasure, almost overwhelmed her. She resisted the urge to moan for a whole two seconds before the raw, passionate sound escaped her throat. Running her hand over his broad back, she relished the sensation of hard muscle beneath smooth, warm flesh.

Her nipples tightened and tingled, desperate for his touch. The flesh between her legs ached to feel him buried deep inside her. She wanted--no needed--his energy flowing through her. Not wishing to succumb to her mother's fate, Raine had always avoided bedding magical men. Human males were far easier to control, but too delicate for her to drain enough energy from one to truly satisfy her hunger, unless she wanted to kill them. Execution was one thing, but out and out murder was another.

Sanjay was not a mortal man. His weretiger strength beckoned her. Most likely even he wouldn't be able to completely satisfy her, but he would certainly come closer than anyone she'd ever been with. Even more, she wanted to enjoy him not as a Succubus, but as a woman. This emotional attachment to him that she was developing annoyed her, yet she was unable to resist it. Perhaps if she gave in and got him out of her system….

"Umm," she purred as his large hands stroked her ribs. His fingers lightly traced the sides of her breasts before he took her face in his hands and thrust his tongue possessively into her mouth. When he slipped an arm under her legs and his other around her back, she clung to his neck, allowing him to lift her. His mouth still locked with hers, he carried her to the bed, only breaking the kiss when he placed her on the mattress.

She opened her eyes and gazed at him through her lashes, pouring her energy into a passionate look that never failed to draw men to her. The soft expression had left his beautiful eyes, replaced by a look of raw lust that sent her heart racing out of control. A slight smile touched her lips. Apparently this powerful weretiger was no more immune to her charms than mortal men, even if he had managed to resist her earlier that night.

Actually, from the moment he'd pulled away from her after pinning her to the wall in her house she'd wanted to conquer him.

"Unzip me," she said in a breathy whisper and rolled onto her front.

He brushed aside her hair and placed a firm hand to her bared neck. A shiver darted through her. Weretigers were known to kill by snapping the neck or strangling their victims. Did he get a thrill from seeing her in a vulnerable position? What had she been thinking? Slowly he unzipped the back of her tight black dress. His hand slipped inside, caressing her back. She felt him unfasten her bra, completely exposing her back to his touch. His hand moved from her neck, replaced by warm lips. He pressed kisses down the length of her spine, and then ran his tongue up it, making her quiver with pleasure.

When he slipped the dress and bra down her shoulders, she turned to him with a sultry smile, removed the garments, and tossed them onto the floor.

His eyes seemed to burn into her as he straightened and unzipped his jeans. Raine drew a long, slow breath of anticipation. Her heart thrummed at the sight of his thick, beautiful, dark skinned shaft, the bulbous head flushed with desire. She moistened her lips and imagined taking him in her mouth, running her tongue over his ultra sensitive flesh, drawing his energy, his very essence, inside her. He tugged off the jeans, exposing long, steely legs lightly dusted with black hair. Raine's hands flexed with the need to touch them.

Placing a knee on the bed, he grasped the sides of her satin panties, pulled them over her hips and down the length of her legs. After casting aside her shoes and underpants, he grasped one of her feet and kissed the arch. He kissed and caressed his way up one leg. Upon reaching her inner thigh, he licked with slow sensual motions.

Raine's eyelids fluttered. She floated on a sea of passion, calm on the surface yet with a killer undercurrent. He moved to her other leg and gave it the same attention. By the time he'd licked and kissed every part of it, her eyes were closed and her breathing deep while she stroked her breasts. She rolled her thumbs over her taut nipples then pinched them gently.

Sanjay placed a hand on either side of her waist and kissed her belly. The tip of his tongue dipped into her navel before he licked a sensual trail up her stomach and between her breasts. He took a nipple into his warm, wet mouth and laved it before sucking it hard.

"Ah!" she cried, instinctively clutching his head nearer and arching against him. "Yes, oh, yes."

He purred--a deep rumble in his chest--which she felt as well as heard. While he sucked and licked one nipple, his hand caressed her other. The pad of his thumb teased its tip then circled the areola. Raine wove her fingers through his long, silky hair and wrapped her legs around him. Their bodies moved sensually against one another. He felt so good--big, hard, and warm. His scent, that of musky male and woodsy cologne, filled her.

She tightened her grip on him and felt some of his energy pour into her. Crying out, she grasped his head and tugged it toward her face, starving for his kiss.

With a growl he covered her lips with his and plunged his tongue into her mouth, thrusting while he pressed her deeper into the mattress, his hard staff trapped between them. He reached down and gently used a finger to prod her sheath.

"Yes, oh, yes," she panted, opening her legs to his exploring hand. Two fingers slipped inside where she was so wet and yearning. He withdrew them and rubbed one digit, now slick with her lust, over her engorged nub. Circling the sensitive flesh with his finger, he continued plunging his tongue into her mouth.

Raine moaned and rocked her hips to the rhythm of his finger and tongue. Though she had been touched by men before--what

Succubus hadn't?--none had ever stirred her like this. She wanted more than just his energy. Never had she imagined that there *could* be more.

"You're so beautiful," he whispered close to her ear before tickling it with his tongue. He took the lobe between his teeth, nibbled it gently, and tugged upon it.

"So are you," she breathed, her eyes closed and feet sliding up and down his hair dusted calves. Damn, she wanted him so badly! "Sanjay, I want you to take me. Fill me."

He paused in kissing her, a hand braced on either side of her head, and commanded, "Look at me, Raine."

She opened her eyes and met his gaze, thrilled by the desire in his expression.

Grasping his face in her hands, she whispered against his lips, "Do it. Take me."

His eyes half closed, he rubbed his nose against hers in a gesture that reminded her of the cat in him. One long arm reached across to the night stand where he opened the drawer and removed a condom. Instantly her respect for him rose several notches. Though she regularly used a pregnancy protection potion supplied by a member of the Veils who was a skilled witch, she was impressed by a man with enough intelligence to take responsibility for his actions. That was rare among humans, let alone immortal beings who had little chance of being infected by disease.

He broke contact with her for a brief moment to roll on the condom. Raine watched, fascinated by the sight of him handling his staff.

"Stroke it," she said, sitting up.

He glanced at her sharply, his brow furrowed.

"Please," she continued, surprised to plead with a man in this situation. Usually she took the lead and made the demands in bed, without question from her partners. Even in his aroused state this man remained in full control of himself. This both irritated and aroused her. She'd deal with that later. Right now the woman in her wanted to be appeased. The Succubus could wait. "Please, let me watch you stroke yourself."

He tilted his head to one side for a moment, as if in question, and then slowly ran his hand up and down his staff. She fixed her gaze on it, her breasts rising and falling in breathless desire. The engorged flesh swelled even more beneath his caress.

Without warning he pushed her onto her back and used one hand to pin both of hers above her head. The tip of his staff prodded her.

Inch by inch he filled her with a slow, controlled thrust. By the time he reached the hilt she was almost crazy with desire. She wriggled beneath the marvelous weight of his hot, sinewy body. It had been so long since she'd lain beneath a man. Usually she preferred to be on top, taking complete control when she drained a man's essence. He must have bewitched her because at the moment this was exactly where she wanted to be, trapped beneath him as he pumped into her in a steady rhythm that pushed her closer and closer to ecstasy.

Wrapping her legs around him she met him thrust for thrust. She tugged against his grip, but he was far stronger than she was and refused to let her go. When she tried covering his mouth in a kiss powerful enough to draw his energy into her, he avoided her lips.

With a wicked smile, he panted, "Not yet, Succubus. Neither of us is ready for that."

"I'm ready," she stated. Good lord, she was far beyond ready. Her entire body burned with desire for him. All she needed was one more thrust and--

He stopped moving and lowered more of his weight onto her, not allowing her to so much as wiggle.

"In a hurry, are you?" he teased, though she knew by the gleam in his obsidian eyes and the cadence of his breathing he was just as aroused as she was. "Haven't you heard that patience is a virtue?"

"Not one of my virtues." She lifted her head in an attempt to kiss him, but again he eluded her. She wrapped her legs around him in a fierce hold. His eyes slipped shut and he groaned, a sound of pleasure-pain. In spite of his resilience, he wasn't immune to her power.

Again he thrust into her with that frustrating rhythm that stirred her yet never allowed her to reach the blissful place she so desired. He paused, burying his face between her neck and shoulder.

Using her internal muscles to squeeze his rigid staff, she writhed beneath him. He was completely possessing her, turning her into a desperate mass of out of control hormones. *She* was supposed to be driving *him* crazy, yet here she was on the verge of begging him to release her from this unendurable tension.

After three more teasing thrusts, she moaned, "Please, oh, please, Sanjay. I can't wait any longer."

He made an incredibly seductive sound, a cross between a deep chuckle and a growl of passion. Releasing his hold on her wrists, he drove into her fast and rough, exactly how she liked it.

"Yes, yes! Oh damn, you fucking gorgeous beast, yes!" she cried and buried her fingers in his hair. She dragged his head closer and kissed him.

Sanjay's mouth opened to her probing tongue. His tongue met it with demanding strokes. Filled by his energy and pleasured beyond her wildest fantasies, she came. The force of her release shook her from head to toe. Her eyes tightly closed, she clung to him and felt him come long and hard. He groaned, his body straining against hers until he finally collapsed atop her.

She rested there, her legs still wrapped around him, and felt their hearts pounding in unison while she languidly stroked his hair. Then reality struck. This *man* had *fucked* her, a Succubus! He had taken control and--

"Umm," he purred against her throat and licked it with long, tender strokes. "That was remarkably pleasant."

"Pleasant?" She curled her lip and tried to shove him away. "Get off me you big--"

"Fucking gorgeous beast?" He grinned, his dark eyes glistening with humor and far too much male pride.

"More like you arrogant asshole."

"What upsets you more, Succubus? That I am the one in control or that you enjoy it?"

"Control?" she snorted. "I let you think you were in control."

A patronizing smile touched his sensual mouth. "Of course. Come here. It's nearly daylight and we both need to get some sleep. We have a full schedule ahead of us."

"What do you mean come here?"

"I mean *come here*." He wrapped an arm around her and held her close to his side.

"Uh, if you're asking me to spend the day, this isn't the most polite way to do it."

"Forgive me," he said, brushing a stray lock of hair from her face. "If you would like to spend the day here, I will not object."

God, this man irritated her! Why in the world did she find him attractive?

Her teeth clenched, she slipped from his embrace and went to leave the bed, but he caught her hand and squeezed it gently.

"Raine, I would like you to stay."

"Why?" she demanded, meeting his gaze. The tone of his voice made her heart flutter. Raine made a point never to sleep with men she had sex with. Sanjay should be no exception. On the other hand, she had never had such a desire to sleep with anyone--until now. The bastard was obviously a master of manipulation. He got her to plead his case to the First Wraths and took control in their lovemaking. Now he was probably trying to butter her up so she'd fall for him and somehow ensure the Veils left his son alone. "In case you think I can pull some strings because my grandmother is a First Wrath, you're wrong. There is no favoritism among the Veils."

"You think I would use lovemaking for that, especially after what you told me about your past experiences with men?"

"I think you'd do anything to help your kid. Don't get me wrong, in a way I admire that."

"Then I change my mind. I do not want you in my bed after all. You may go."

Raine stared at him, stunned. "Not want me in your bed, you egomaniac? My god, you are the most arrogant, obnoxious--"

"Let me see, I am a rude, manipulating sex fiend with an overblown ego. Why, then, are you here with me now?"

"Good question." She reached for her clothes and started to pull them on, but he sat up and wrapped his arms around her.

"Let me go."

He growled softly and licked her ear, then murmured in it, "Come back to bed. I bedded you because I desire you, Raine. No other reason. I think you are the one manipulating me, using your Succubus powers, because it has been a long time since I've wanted a woman this badly."

Tugging the dress from her hands and tossing it aside, he covered her neck and shoulder with soft kisses.

Raine's eyes closed halfway and she smiled, a little quiver running through her as his stubbled jaw tickled her tender flesh. "Damn, you have a hell of a good line."

"No self-respecting weretiger uses lines."

"Yeah. Right." She grinned and turned in his arms, allowing him to pull her back into bed. He tugged the sheet over them and held her close, her cheek pressed to his chest and his chin resting against the top of her head.

## Chapter Three

Raine wasn't sure how long she lay awake in Sanjay's arms before the warm, fuzzy feeling started to fade and anger set in. She couldn't decide if she was angrier at him for seducing her or at herself for allowing him to.

She was a Succubus, ruler of the bedroom, yet she'd surrendered to him like a mortal submissive bowing to her master. For the first time in her life she had gained more animal pleasure than life force.

*All right, weretiger. It's time you paid up*, she thought, moving away from his side, careful not to wake him. Simple enough since, in his sleep, he'd moved his arm from her shoulders and raised it above his head.

Raine knelt beside him and gazed at him for a moment. He was so handsome with his face utterly relaxed in sleep. His long, lean body draped the bed like a cat in repose. Raine smiled slightly, noticing how long and thick his eyelashes were, how kissable his sleep-softened lips appeared.

*Damn it, Raine. Get a grip.*

She closed her eyes halfway and summoned her power, feeling it roll through her in hot, passionate waves.

Sanjay stirred a bit. His nostrils flared slightly as his finely-tuned sense of smell detected her Succubus pheromones. She needed to act quickly before he woke. It galled her that she feared staring him down, at least before she had him under proper control. Something in the man's expressions made her go weak all over.

She straddled him and covered his mouth with hers. Her tongue thrust between his lips and she drew upon his energy while clasping him with her thighs. Almost immediately his cock hardened and he moaned with pleasure.

Raine concentrated on his heartbeat and the rhythm of his breathing, keeping hers in perfect sync while rocking against his erection. It pressed against her soft, aching flesh, making her wet and ready to claim him, take everything he had to give.

Her mouth still fused with his, she shifted position and grasped his cock, relishing the feel of velvet over iron. She flexed her strong leg muscles, lifting herself a few inches higher, and placed the crown of his erection against her damp feminine lips. She broke the kiss and lowered herself onto him, fully impaling herself upon his swollen flesh. Her hands clutched his broad chest, kneading the steely muscles and relishing his pure, virile perfection.

Sanjay's eyes flew open and met her gaze, his expression unfocussed. His eyes were too black for dilated pupils to show, yet she knew if she could see them they would practically fill his iris, so lost was he in her Succubus' spell.

"Ah!" he gasped, his hips bucking in time with her furious pace. His neck arched against the pillow, tendons straining beneath the smooth, dark skin.

Raine could scarcely control her excitement at the incomparable high of being filled with his energy. He was so strong, this weretiger. By all that was sacred, she could probably survive a month on his life force without a bit of hunger.

His eyes closed halfway and his hands clawed the air for a desperate moment before gripping the headboard so fiercely that she actually heard the wood creak.

Moaning, she rode him faster, her internal muscles clamping around him almost painfully, draining him of his very essence. It felt so good to have him buried inside her without the stupid condom. Somewhere in the back of her mind, Raine thought she would have to remember to thank her witch friend.

Raine's entire body throbbed with orgasm, yet combined with such savage feeding the sensations grew stronger with every moment rather than diminishing. Her power sustained his erection while at the same time keeping him in a relentless state of climactic pleasure. Usually mortals lasted only moments before either passing out or forcing her to cease her actions before killing them entirely. This weretiger possessed far more stamina.

His head thrown back and hips thrusting in a ferocious rhythm, he spoke to her in his native tongue, too lost in sensation to translate his thoughts to a language she understood. Beneath her caress, his chest grew slick with sweat. His heart slammed against her palms, powerful, immortal--a weretiger heart.

For the first time ever she began to tire, burning off energy as quickly as she took it in. Her legs trembling, she clamped her vaginal muscles around him tightly then released him. Gasping, she collapsed atop him, her entire body throbbing. For several moments she didn't move, but lay still, listening to his heartbeat slow and enjoying the sensation of their sweat slicked bodies pressed so close together they were like a single being.

Finally gathering her strength, she sat up and glanced at Sanjay.

He was completely unconscious. If he had been human, she didn't doubt what she'd done would have killed him. This man challenged her yet fulfilled her in a way she never imagined possible.

A chill swept down her spine. Her almost uncontrollable attraction to him terrified her. Was this what the beginning stage of love felt like?

Of course not. This was lust. Her area of expertise.

*Then why are you shaking, Raine?*

Her head spun. She had to get out of this room. Away from this man. She needed to collect herself before traveling with him to Portugal. If she didn't regain control of herself, her grandmother or Kesi would notice her attraction to him. They knew her almost as well as she knew herself, perhaps even better. She didn't want them to think she had agreed to speak for Sanjay because she had *feelings* for him.

She dressed quickly, left the hotel, and drove off as fast as possible without risking a speeding ticket.

* * * *

The following evening Raine and Kesi stood in the airport waiting for Rahul and Sanjay to arrive.

"They're not going to show," Kesi said, her arms folded beneath her full, firm breasts that strained against her red tank top tucked into snug jeans.

Kesi was about the only vampire Raine had ever trusted. She found most of them to be self-centered gluttons like her father, but Kesi was the exact opposite. If more vamps were like her, they'd have caused a lot less trouble for themselves throughout the ages.

"They'll be here," Raine said, though a tiny voice inside her kept murmuring that Kesi might be right. "If their intention was to run, why would Sanjay make the effort to arrange a meeting?"

"We should have stuck a guard on Sanjay like I suggested last night."

"I told you I kept an eye on him."

Kesi cocked an eyebrow and said, "I don't even want to think about how. Did you leave him with enough strength to even get to the airport?"

Raine glanced at her friend for any sign of suspicion that she knew Raine was on the verge of emotional involvement with the weretiger. Nothing. She was doing a fine job of keeping her private thoughts just that.

"I said he'll be--there he is." Raine lifted her chin toward the door through which Sanjay just stepped. A thrill of desire shot through her just from seeing him again. He wore black slacks and a black collarless shirt. Sunglasses concealed his eyes and his hair was tied at his nape. A younger man, not quite as tall and with a slightly darker complexion, strode beside him. Rahul. She recognized him from a photo taken by a member of the Veils who had tracked him just before they attempted his execution.

"So the weasel and his daddy showed up," Kesi sneered.

"We're supposed to keep this civil, remember?" Rain said.

"All I remember is him knocking me the fuck out a couple of nights ago."

"Kesi--"

"It's fine." Kesi held up her hand adorned with several silver rings. "I know how to do my job."

"Raine." Sanjay nodded as he joined them.

He looked calm and collected. Rahul, however, wore a tense expression, his brown eyes alive with fury. Raine nearly smiled. The boy obviously had his father's spirit but a lot less experience in keeping it under control.

"Sanjay. This is Kesi."

"We met," Kesi snapped, taking a step closer to the men, her stance relaxed yet powerful.

Sanjay turned to her and removed his glasses, his dark gaze fixed on the vampiress. "I offer my sincere apologizes for any harm I caused you the other night."

"Yeah. Right."

"You must understand the necessity of my actions."

Kesi curled her lip and said, "They just called for us to board. Let's get on with this and the less talk the better, get it?"

"I told you, Father. They are completely unreasonable." Rahul glared from Kesi to Raine and back again.

"And I told you to be either silent or polite," Sanjay said in a quiet yet deadly voice.

Rahul looked ready to argue, but refrained. He glanced past the women toward the enormous windows facing the runway.

"I'll take junior," Kesi said sarcastically and motioned for Rahul to follow her so they could board.

Sanjay and Raine walked behind them. She noticed that other than when he'd first greeted her, he hadn't so much as glanced in her direction. He pocketed his sunglasses and kept his gaze fixed straight ahead.

"So you decided to drain me and run last night," he said very quietly so no one else could hear. "Not that I should have expected any courtesy from a Succubus."

"What's that supposed to mean?"

"Nothing of importance."

"I don't recall either of us making any promises last night," she continued, unsure of why she felt the need to defend her actions. "You got just as much out of it as I did. Probably more. When was the last time you had an hour-long orgasm?"

His expression stiffened and he cast her a disgusted look. "Have you any pride? We are in public, not a hotel room. Or perhaps your kind can't tell the difference."

Raine's first reaction was anger. She was prepared to slap him with a nasty comeback but stopped, a realization dawning on her. An uncontrollable smile spread across her face. "You feel used? I hurt your pride a bit, Sanjay? I'm sorry."

"No you're not."

Under normal circumstances he would have been right, but not this time. "No. I am. I thought it was just a way for us to pass the time."

"Another lie." He turned to her with such intensity in his eyes that she felt heat rise in her face. "You didn't really take me the first time. I took you. That tells me many things, Raine, most important of which is last night was not simply a way for you to pass the time."

Before she could think of a satisfactory reply, it was their turn to board. Once seated with Kesi and Rahul there was no way they could continue the conversation.

Frustrated, Raine gazed out the widow and thought about Sanjay's accusation. Unfortunately, he was correct. Last night meant far more to her than she was willing to admit. She thought for sure she had been in control--if not before then at least after she'd drained his energy. Usually if she took a man like that, she had no desire for him again. Rather than sate her hunger for Sanjay, making love with him and taking his energy had only increased it. To her dismay it wasn't really his energy she craved, but *him*. The sensation of his kiss and touch, the sound of his voice in her ear and his scent mingling with hers.

Sighing deeply she prayed for a fast trial. If she was forced to spend any length of time with Sanjay, she would be lost. A proud Succubus tamed by a tiger.

*But not just any tiger*, she thought, glancing at the handsome man beside her. A clan leader. One of the first of his kind and probably the only black weretiger in the world. He was beautiful, wild, passionate and quite possibly meant for her.

No. That thought was too frightening. Yet even as she told herself that she could not surrender to him again she knew she would. Already her most sensitive places ached for his touch. She shifted in her seat, her pulse quickening and her nipples growing stiff beneath her T-shirt and bra.

Sanjay glanced in her direction, her lust reflected in his eyes. She turned back to the window. It seemed Rahul wasn't the only one facing a trial. In some ways Raine's was even more difficult. How could she possibly defend herself against the only man who had ever managed to stir her soul as well as her body?

\* \* \* \*

The group arrived in Lisbon in the morning where they took a rental car to Cascais. Raine was at the wheel, Sanjay was beside her and Kesi and Rahul were in the back seat. They drove in almost complete silence, except for a necessary word or two. Tension filled the car, particularly when they entered the lovely seaside resort town that had been home to Raine's maternal family for generations.

Throughout the ride, Raine's thoughts spun, focusing mostly on the trial ahead but also on her feelings for Sanjay. Part of her actually wanted him to be right about his son's innocence. One thing she didn't doubt was his love for Rahul. She wondered if he would have felt the same way about a daughter. Probably not. Focusing on that grounded her a bit.

"We're here," she said, stopping the car in the circular driveway in front of her grandmother's villa.

It was a beautiful home of tan brick surrounded by trees that danced in wind blowing cool from the nearby beach.

As Sanjay stepped out of the car, she saw him gaze longingly toward the seemingly endless stretch of sand lapped by frothy waves. She didn't doubt he wished to run free down the beach in his tiger form, stretching his powerful feline legs. One thing she knew about all types of weres, they hated being trapped in their human bodies for any length of time. She almost sympathized with him. Rahul was a different story. He had not only nearly ruined a woman, but was dragging his father down with him.

*Unless he's innocent*, she reminded herself. *Doubtful, but possible.*

"Move," Kesi ordered, shoving Rahul toward the house.

"I've had enough of you." The young man glared, but Sanjay's hand fell heavily on his shoulder and he kept silent.

"Enough?" Kesi curled her lip. "I've got news for you, pussycat, everything has just *begun*."

"Kesi." Raine glanced at her friend.

Kesi flashed her fangs a bit and motioned for Rahul to lead the way toward the house. Raine and Sanjay followed behind. By the time they reached the door, two tall women in semi-wolf form stood to greet them. Covered in hair, their faces slightly elongated, they retained their human bipedal position but with heavier muscle and more flexibility. Much like when Sanjay had stopped his shifting halfway between tiger and man.

The loup-garou warriors carried guns and kept wary yellow eyes fixed on the men.

"Fifi. Angelique." Raine nodded at the guards.

Rahul curled his lip. "Fifi? She looks more like Fido."

"Enough." Sanjay hissed, his hand clamping around Rahul's throat. "It's as if you *want* to die."

"Break it up!" Kesi shoved her way between father and son while the wolfish guards each grabbed one of them and yanked them inside.

"Wait," Raine called, following the guards down the corridor she knew led to secret holding cells in the basement. "They're to come with me. I want my grandmother to--"

"Raine."

She spun at the sound of her grandmother's voice.

Vidonia stood at the top of the wide spiral staircase. Like most Succubae, she was very beautiful and aged so slowly that she looked more like Raine's sister. Slightly above average height with long black hair, dark eyes, and delicate lips painted red, she exuded charisma that most men found irresistible. Many people told Raine she had inherited that magnetism, but at times she doubted it.

"I had hoped for you to speak with Sanjay before the trial," Raine said, walking toward the staircase. She paused at the base.

"Sanjay, how long has it been?" Vidonia asked, a slight smile on her lips.

"Long enough for many things to have changed."

At his reply, Raine's brow furrowed. What was he talking about? She didn't like the way her grandmother was looking at him, and vice versa.

"As long as your respect for the Wakened Veils has not changed."

"If it had, we would not be here," he stated.

Vidonia held his gaze for a moment longer, then motioned for the guards to take them away. She looked at Raine. "Come with me."

"Excuse me," Kesi said. "Have Bo and Saloni arrived yet?"

"Yes," Vidonia said. "They're having breakfast by the pool. Feel free to join them. My granddaughter and I have much to talk about and will meet with you later."

Kesi nodded and disappeared through a door to her left while Raine walked upstairs and followed her grandmother.

In the master suite, Vidonia took a seat at the breakfast table. "Come sit with me, Raine."

Raine joined her grandmother. Though filled with questions, she waited respectfully for the First Wrath to begin the conversation.

"When we spoke on the phone you made it clear that Sanjay believes he is telling the truth about his son," Vidonia said.

"Yes. Even though Rahul is most likely guilty of the crimes he is accused of, Sanjay has faith in him. Of course, it is not unusual for one man to have faith in another. If Rahul were a daughter--"

"Sanjay would hold her in the same regard," Vidonia interrupted. "Unlike many males, especially from his time, he has respect for women. If any man could raise a son to have such respect, it would be Sanjay or one of his clan. Weretigers serve a most powerful goddess. Sanjay is descended from the first clan created many thousands of years ago. Through the ages, the clan divided. Some no longer retained their respect for females, but Sanjay and his clan are still loyal to the old ways--to their goddess. Unlike many were-creatures, he has mastered his power, not the other way around. That is why I convinced the other First Wraths to allow him and his son to be brought to trial."

A question had been burning in Raine's mind since Sanjay had disclosed his acquaintance with her grandmother. "How is it that you know Sanjay? He would not go into detail about that. I can't understand how you could let a man, no matter how good, know of our existence. If you didn't believe he should die, then you could have at least used one of our psychics to erase his knowledge of us."

Vidonia sighed deeply, her gaze shifting past Raine to the picture window. Finally she said, "Sanjay's mind would not accept the hypnotic suggestion. You've met him, so I'm sure you've felt his strength."

*In every way.* Raine shook her head. She couldn't think about the lovemaking she and Sanjay had shared. Not in front of her grandmother.

"Yes. He is powerful."

A slight smile touched Vidonia's lips and she nodded. "He is probably the first man I ever trusted and he has never betrayed that trust. For over two thousand years he has kept the secret of the Wakened Veils. I believe, and the other First Wraths agree, he has *earned* the right to this trial."

"But how did you meet him?" Raine pressed.

Vidonia stood and walked to the window. She gazed at the beach in silence for so long that Raine grew a bit annoyed. Sometimes her grandmother got this way, sinking into an almost peaceful state of utter quiet.

"You've taken him, haven't you?" Vidonia finally asked.

"His energy?"

"His energy. His body." Vidonia turned, still wearing that slight, knowing smile.

Raine stiffened. "If you think, Grandmother, I would arrange a meeting with the First Wraths because I'm lovesick--"

Laughing, Vidonia returned to the table and rested a hand on Raine's shoulder before sitting. "Of course I don't think that. You're not a child or a fool. I know you sensed his integrity and part of you trusted him. I'm not talking about that, however, but *him*."

"Yes," Raine said quietly. "I've taken him."

"Have you?"

"Yes."

"Or did he take you?"

Thinking back to those final moments before she'd broken away from him, Raine recalled how her energy had seemed to drain away. It was as if she needed to expel what she'd just taken in order to match his strength.

"I've never felt energy like his," Raine admitted. "But I'm accustomed to human males."

"Magical ones are much stronger," Vidonia said, "but even among them weretigers are powerful."

Raine was starting to lose patience. "Will you answer my question, Grandmother?"

"Sanjay was the first and only man ever to overcome my powers."

The meaning of her grandmother's words struck Raine like a fist. She wasn't sure of the reason why. Her grandmother was a Succubus. It probably wasn't the first time they had taken energy from the same man.

"Were you and he--?"

"Lovers," Vidonia admitted. "For a short time. I couldn't accept the power he had over me. After killing my husband, I vowed never again to let a man have control of me in any way. Had I allowed it, Sanjay might have commanded my heart."

Raine felt a little sick. The idea of her and Vidonia in love with the same man was somehow *wrong,* even if they were Succubae.

"You're falling in love with him, if you haven't already," Vidonia stated.

"Of course not. I told you I'd never--"

"But you have."

"Are you? Still in love with him?" Raine almost didn't want to hear her grandmother's reply, yet she had to.

"No." Vidonia held her gaze steadily. In her eyes, Raine saw only the truth. No jealousy, no competitiveness. "Anything between us ended long ago. I have retained a measure of respect for him and, if you choose to continue exploring your feelings for him, I will support you."

"Providing we don't put him and his son to death."

Vidonia nodded. "Providing that. If Rahul is found guilty again, he will be executed and the First Wraths have decided that Sanjay must be destroyed with him. Otherwise he would be too great a threat to us."

"You should have followed your own advice, Grandmother. It seems no good comes out of a relationship with any man."

"You're still young, Raine. Eventually you will learn there are exceptions to every rule."

## Chapter Four

Sanjay and Rahul were guided to the basement of Vidonia's villa where they were locked in cells. While all weretigers hated the thought of imprisonment, Sanjay had a particular loathing of bondage. Long ago, when their original clan had divided, many wars were fought among weretigers. Severely wounded in battle, Sanjay had been captured by rivals and locked in a cage so small he could scarcely turn around. Eventually his warriors freed him, but since then had been unable to completely overcome his hatred of enclosed places.

His current cell wasn't as small as that horrible cage, and included the comfort of a bed and toilet, yet to Sanjay it was almost unbearable. No sooner had the guards locked him inside than his heart began pounding and he had to remind himself to breathe.

"Father, are you all right?" Rahul called, his voice laced with concern. Though unable to see one another since their cells were on opposite sides of the same wall, Rahul knew about Sanjay's hatred of small spaces. Apparently the anger he'd been harboring for his father hadn't completely overcome his affection.

"Fine." Sanjay closed his eyes and concentrated on taking several slow, even breaths.

"You shouldn't have interfered in this," Rahul continued. "I could have handled Saloni."

"They were going to kill you."

"Now they'll probably kill us both. You shouldn't have struck a bargain with these she-demons."

"If what you told me is true, there is a chance justice will be done."

"If?" Rahul snapped. "You doubt me? You think I could do the things they say?"

Sanjay growled, not in the mood to argue with his obstinate son. "If I thought that, the Veils wouldn't have to kill you. I'd do it myself."

Rahul fell silent, mostly likely guessing Sanjay had just about reached the limit of his patience.

After a moment, Rahul continued, "I don't know why she refuses to speak to me. I know we could work this out if she would talk instead of fight."

"There are two reasons she would not want to talk. She either hates you and wants to see you executed--"

"I told you--"

"Or," Sanjay's voice rose above his son's interruption, "she still has feelings for you and fears that speaking to you will weaken her resolve."

"I like that thought better. And what about you? How did you convince these women to hear you out? Don't think I didn't notice how you and Raine looked at one another."

"I just met her on the night I rescued you."

"That doesn't matter. Love strikes like an assassin's dagger-- without warning and without mercy."

"I am not in love, Rahul," Sanjay stated, though somewhere in the back of his mind he knew that if he spent any length of time with Raine he would be lost to her. "Besides, love is what got us into this situation to begin with."

Rahul sighed so deeply that Sanjay heard him from his cell. "That is true. I thought Saloni had already gotten her revenge on me by rejecting my proposal. Just when I've finally gotten over her and am ready to settle down and start a family, she does this to me."

Sanjay gripped the bars on his cell door and allowed his head to drop to his chest as he continued fighting the panic welling inside him. He reminded himself this was not a cruelly small cage, nor was the situation permanent. His grip on the steel tightened and he felt it bend. His eyes flew open and he straightened, bracing himself more firmly. Pulling on the bars while at the same time shifting into man-beast form, he felt his muscles burn and a light sweat break out over his body. The bars bent a bit more. He relaxed his hold, panting slightly, and smiled. *Definitely* not a permanent situation. Still, it was best to play along with the Veils and allow them to find justice, if possible.

"Are you sure you're all right?" Rahul asked.

"I'm sure," Sanjay replied, his breathing once again under control. He walked to the bed and sat. Knowing he could break out helped him to relax, though he still hated being cooped up.

He and Rahul fell silent for a time. By the occasional hum of a mantra coming from Rahul's cell, he guessed the youth was practicing relaxation techniques and stretching to pass the time.

Sanjay's thoughts spun out of control, swinging from the trial to Raine and Vidonia, then back to the cage again. He knew they would be trapped at least until the trial a few days hence.

In an attempt to center himself, he sat cross legged on the floor, closed his eyes, the backs of his hands resting on his knees, and breathed slowly, evenly. If he couldn't shift shape and run through miles of open country, yoga was the next best thing.

He wasn't sure exactly how much time passed before he caught the scent of sandalwood perfume.

*Raine.*

He opened his eyes, straightened his legs, and shook them out a bit before rising to his feet in a single fluid motion. Seconds later, Raine approached.

For some inexplicable reason the woman seemed to become more beautiful each time he looked at her. Yes, he found her physically attractive, but her inner strength and compassion shone through, making her even more desirable. In many ways she was like her grandmother. Though as lovely as ever, Vidonia had never touched him the way Raine did. He had enjoyed their brief affair but hadn't been terribly disappointed when it ended. Even now, he rebelled against the thought of never having Raine again. He resisted the urge to reach for her through the bars and pull her closer for a kiss.

"I came to see if you need anything," she said. "Kesi and the others feel you must be kept under close watch, but the First Wraths agree you should be made comfortable."

"How can weretigers be comfortable in a cage?" Rahul demanded.

Raine glanced at him. "My comments were directed at your father. If not for me speaking for you, you would be held in a rat hole a level below this one."

"Saloni would like that, I bet," Rahul said. "Another torment for the crime of offering her love."

Raine held Sanjay's gaze for a long moment before she walked out of his line of vision to Rahul's cell. She said, "Since you seem to feel like talking, now is a good time for me to hear you out in preparation for the trial. As you know, I will be speaking for you and your father."

"You have my thanks," Rahul said. "But I still believe the most efficient way to end this would be for Saloni to speak with me. I'm sure if we had the chance to work this out--"

"You will have a chance to speak with her during the trial, under the First Wraths' observation. In the meantime, tell me everything from the moment you and Saloni met."

\* \* \* \*

Five days later Rahul still awaited trial because the third First

Wrath had yet to arrive. With family business to attend in Egypt, she sent word that it would be another three days before she could get there.

Other than brief trips to the shower, Sanjay and Rahul remained locked in their cells. Sanjay had been escorted to the phone one time to make contact with the acting leader of his clan. His distress at being imprisoned was beginning to tell on him. Though he communicated with his usual calm, the shadows beneath his eyes told of sleepless nights. The guards confirmed that for the past several nights he had been relentlessly pacing his cell, often in tiger form. Rahul seemed better able to cope with captivity.

Raine spent several hours a day with them, preparing for the trial, and couldn't help worrying about Sanjay. She had to free him from cell, even for a few hours. Several times she told her grandmother and the second First Wrath, Lani, she would take full responsibility for him if they would allow her to take him out. Finally they agreed.

More eager to spend time alone with him than she wanted to admit, she hurried to the kitchen to pack a meal. She had promised the First Wraths they would stay near her grandmother's property, so she intended to take him to the private stretch of beach behind the villa. There he could safely expel some energy in tiger form. She tried telling herself she chose the beach only for his benefit, but deep inside she fantasized about making love with him on the moon-kissed sand.

She was in the middle of fixing sandwiches when Kesi and Bo stepped into the kitchen. By the look on Kesi's face she hadn't come for food, but for an interrogation.

Without prelude, Kesi asked, "Are you sure it's a wise idea to take Sanjay out?"

"He's going nuts in that cell," Raine said. "It's not right."

"Hello!" Bo waved a hand in front of Raine's eyes. "Neither was attacking us."

"He was trying to save his son and if you put your hand in front of my face again, lady, I'll break it off at the elbow."

"What a grouch." Bo folded her arms beneath her breasts and leaned a narrow hip against the counter.

"All right, Raine. What the hell is going on with you and this guy?" Kesi demanded.

Raine glared at her friend. "Excuse me?"

"You heard me. We've only know each other for what, a thousand years? You get this *look* in your eyes when you mention the tiger. I saw it the first time you talked about him and it's been there ever since."

"At first I didn't agree with Kesi, but now I do," Bo said. "I think you have got a thing for the weretiger."

"First of all, even if I did have a thing for him, I would never let it affect my judgment. I trust this guy, and so does my grandmother. They've met before."

"Well that makes me feel a little better," Kesi said. "Your grandmother is one member of the Veils no guy is going to make a jackass out of."

Raine paused in wrapping sandwiches and hurled Kesi an angry look. "Meaning I am?"

"I didn't say that."

"You were thinking it."

"Raine, you know I *say* what I think. I don't fucking bite my tongue for anybody, even my friends."

"Guys, let's not fight among ourselves," Bo said quietly. "We're not trying to gang up on you, Raine. We just want to know what's going on."

"Nothing is going on. You want to know if I took his energy? You want to know if I fucked him?"

Kesi and Bo leaned closer, their eyes wide with anticipation.

"Too bad. It's none of your business." Raine smirked.

"Not funny." Kesi glared.

"So not funny," Bo agreed.

"Don't you think it's only fair for us to know--?"

"Okay, Kesi. I like him. As I told you before, I think he's telling the truth as he sees it and I believe he wants a peaceful solution to this problem."

Kesi raised an eyebrow, reached for an olive, and popped it into her mouth. Winking, she said, "You think he's sexy as hell and you've already done it with him how many times?"

Raine shook her head. "You two are unbelievable."

"I'm right," Kesi stated.

"He's off limits to me. I'm not in to sleeping with the same guy my grandmother had, even if it was literally ancient history." Raine knew she was lying to herself. She wanted Sanjay again, regardless of who he had been with in the past.

Kesi, who had been steadily munching olives, paused with one halfway to her lips. "Huh?"

"You mean you and your grandmother both slept with him?" Bo curled her lip. "Did I say yuck already?"

"Nope," Kesi said.

"Yuck. Triple yuck. That's sick even for a Succubus."

"What do you mean, even for a Succubus?" Raine demanded, almost sorry she'd mentioned the whole mess to them. She felt as if she was somehow betraying Sanjay, but the situation had her mind reeling and she needed to talk to somebody. Kesi and Bo were her closest friends and she could trust them to be discreet, unless they thought she was jeopardizing the Wakened Veils. Though they might not agree with her view on Sanjay, they knew her well enough to realize she would never do anything to harm their sisterhood.

"Okay, Bo, give her a break," Kesi said. "I doubt she knew he and Vidonia had done anything when she went to bed with him."

"I didn't."

"Okay, let's say by chance Rahul is set free. What happens then? If you feel for this guy you can't just forget about him because granny had an affair with him ... how long ago?"

"Two thousand years."

"Two thousand years?" Bo chuckled. "Then don't worry about it, woman. Obviously there was no great fire between them if they went this long without getting back together."

"I know you, Raine. You've never gotten close to any guy, other than to drain his energy." Kesi placed a comforting hand on her shoulder and held her gaze. "If you like him, and he and his son aren't the assholes I think they are, then go for it."

Raine nodded. "I'll think about it. Thanks, ladies, but I need to go before Sanjay loses his mind."

"Be careful."

"Don't worry. With Rahul still in the cell, he won't try to escape."

Kesi winked. "That's not what I meant."

"All right." Raine smiled slightly. "I'll be careful."

* * * *

Sanjay stopped pacing when Raine and Fifi, in semi-wolf form, approached his cell. The loup-garou carried keys in her hairy, clawed hand. Her yellow gaze fixed warily upon him as she unlocked the cell.

"What's going on?" Sanjay asked, looking to Raine.

"We're getting out of here for a while," she replied. "I thought you could use a little exercise."

Sanjay heart soared at the thought of even a bit of freedom. It would be wonderful to breathe fresh air and look at something other than the cell. He stepped out, noting how strange it seemed not to have guards' weapons trained upon him.

"How did you arrange this?" he asked.

Raine merely gazed at him through her lashes and smiled before heading for the door.

His brow furrowed, Sanjay stood rooted in the same spot. He glanced over his shoulder toward Rahul's cell. "What about Rahul?"

Pausing, Raine turned to him then walked back. She tilted her head slightly to meet his gaze. "I'm sorry, but they'll only allow me to take you."

"Then I won't go." He stepped back into the cell.

"Father, are you crazy?" Rahul called. "Go."

"Not while you're stuck here."

"You hate being locked up," Rahul said.

"And you enjoy it?"

"No, but I can deal with it. I want you to go. Have a run for both of us. Please."

The sincerity in Rahul's voice touched Sanjay deeply, yet he couldn't in good conscience enjoy freedom while his son was still caged.

"You're not helping him by staying," Raine said. "If you think you're hiding how much this imprisonment is affecting you, you're not, Sanjay. The trial will be in a few days and if you're not rested and emotionally prepared, it won't improve your chances of helping Rahul."

"Father, you know she's right," Rahul continued. "If you don't go for your sake, then go for mine."

Sanjay held Raine's gaze. He drew a breath and released it slowly before stepping out of the cell.

"Are you going?" Rahul called.

"Yes."

"Good. Enjoy it."

"He will," Raine said, offering another comforting smile. "I'll make sure if it."

Torn between the excitement of being free and guilt over leaving Rahul behind, Sanjay followed Raine out of the basement and to the foyer.

From a small table by the door, she picked up a basket covered in blue cloth. "I made some food."

"Where are we going?"

"The beach. It's private and I thought this time of night might be safest for a black tiger to be out running."

"Sounds good."

"Carry that." She used the toe of her sneaker to nudge a blanket folded on the floor.

Sanjay picked it up and they left the house. No sooner had he stepped outside than a thrill rushed through him. It felt wonderful to be out. He could scarcely control the urge to change into the tiger then and there, but he needed to wait for a more appropriate time and place.

It took only moments for them to arrive on the beach, but Raine continued walking down the long stretch, putting some distance between them and the villa.

"This is a beautiful country," he commented. "I wish we were here under better circumstances."

"So do I. And it is beautiful. You've never been to Portugal?"

"No."

"I thought you might have when you and my grandmother--"

"You know about that?"

"She told me you were once lovers."

"That was long ago."

Raine glanced at him, her lips twitching in a smile. "She told me that, too."

"She's a very beautiful woman. You look much like her."

Raine lifted an eyebrow. "At least your taste is consistent."

He detected a hint of sarcasm and realized she might feel a bit uncomfortable, even jealous, about his past relationship with Vidonia. He hadn't expected a Succubus to be possessive. Usually after draining energy from a victim, they cast him aside. Raine's continued interest in him inspired hope that maybe, once they got through this dilemma with Rahul, they might have a chance together. But not if she thought, no matter how wrongly, he was comparing her to Vidonia. While they shared some similarities, they were two very different people. He had respected, even cared for, Vidonia, but never loved her. Raine, on the other hand, he could see himself loving deeply.

"You have her spirit," he continued. "Yet at the same time you're nothing like her."

"What do you mean?"

"She would not have allowed a second trial for Rahul."

"But she's the one--"

"At *your* urging. You convinced her. Vidonia is a strong woman, but I remember her being so embittered by her experiences that she would never give a man the satisfaction of hearing his side of a story. That you were able to convince her proves how much she trusts your judgment."

Raine shook her head. "You're only partially right about that, Sanjay. She has a lot of respect for you. I've never heard her speak so highly of a man."

"Raine--"

"Now isn't the time to talk about these things. We're supposed to be relaxing."

"Forgive me if I find it difficult to relax until the trial is over."

"Well, we can try." She stopped and glanced around.

With the villa far behind them and no other homes in sight, they were free to do as they pleased.

"This is a good spot," she continued.

Sanjay spread the blanket and Raine knelt upon it, placing the basket aside. Drawing a deep breath of marvelous seaside air, he gazed longingly at the stretch of beach. The tiger clawed inside him, growling for freedom.

Raine glanced at Sanjay, noting the gleam in his dark eyes that hadn't been there for days. Relief washed over her. She'd been worried about him for the past few days. It seemed this reprieve was exactly what he needed before the trial.

"Why don't you change?" she suggested, eager to see the black tiger in full force.

He started to shed his clothes, then paused, the zipper of his jeans halfway down, and fixed his gaze on her.

"I'm sorry," she said. "Would you prefer I turned away?"

A smile flickered across his mouth. "No, actually. Do you want to watch me change?"

"Yes." Her heartbeat quickened. "I do."

With a slight nod, he kicked off his shoes and pulled off his jeans. Raine fought the urge to lick her lips at the sight of his gorgeous body. Every night she'd thought about making love with him, of feeling his hardness pressed where she was so wet and wanting.

His eyes closed and his chest expanded with a deep breath. As he released it, his body changed, muscles and bones reshaping and hair sprouting from his smooth, dark skin. Within seconds she faced the most beautiful were-creature she had ever seen. Other than the expression in his piercing eyes, there was little difference between the weretiger and a real tiger. A stunning black coat marked with slightly paler stripes covered his long, powerful body. Enormous paws sank into the sand as he took a step closer to Raine.

Her pulse racing, she remained still, torn between awe and fear, yet she need not have worried. In his tiger form, Sanjay retained all his memories. Though immersed in his wild nature, the core of his being remained the same. He would not harm her.

The tiger's face hovered inches from hers. He moved a bit closer and sniffed her cheek. She chuckled, his whiskers and nose tickling her. Slowly she lifted her hand and touched his neck. The fur was rough, the muscles beneath thick and hard. Rising on her knees, she ran both hands over his shoulders and back, watching her fingers sink into the cushion of black fur.

"So beautiful," she murmured. Other than a ripple of muscles, he remained still beneath her exploration. Gaining confidence, she rested her cheek against his back and closed her eyes. She inhaled his scent--a stronger, wilder version of Sanjay's natural musk.

With a low grunt, he moved away, apparently eager for a run.

"Go ahead," she said. "Have fun."

One powerful leap carried him halfway toward the water. With another he splashed into the waves breaking on shore and took off at a run. His long legs stretched as he tore down the beach, moonlight gleaming on his black coat.

When he grew tired of running, he waded into the ocean, swimming so far out that Raine lost sight of him and nearly panicked. How the hell could she save a drowning tiger? Standing, she ran toward the water, and then stopped, breathing a sigh of relief when moonlight reflected off his gleaming eyes. He swam back and jogged out of the water where he shook off and approached her.

If a tiger could smile, he definitely would have been. Black eyes glistened, his expression more alive than it had been in days. Then those eyes closed and several breaths later, Sanjay the man stood in front of her. Wet black hair clung to his shoulders and arms. Slightly breathless from the vigorous exercise, his broad chest rose and fell.

With a suddenness that stole her breath, he pulled her into his arms and buried his face between her neck and shoulder. Being in his embrace felt so wonderful she didn't even care that he was getting her wet with seawater.

"Thank you," he whispered.

"You're welcome." She clung to him for a moment, then ran her hands over his back, relishing the sensation of hard muscles beneath smooth skin. "Are you hungry?"

"Starving."

"Then let's eat."

"Let's eat a little later," he said, his voice husky, and licked her ear.

A quiver of desire ran down her spine. She gripped him harder, pressing even closer to him as he began kissing her neck. "Umm, Sanjay, I've missed this."

"So have I," he breathed before covering her mouth in a passion filled kiss. One steely arm wrapped around her waist and he buried his hand in her hair, his fingers gently stroking her scalp.

Their tongues met, greedily thrusting and tasting. They fully explored each other's mouths while their hands touched every inch of skin they could reach.

Apparently as annoyed by the barrier of clothes between them as she was, Sanjay tugged her T-shirt up her body. Raine lifted her arms above her head so he could remove the shirt completely.

His gaze fixed on her breasts. Generous cleavage swelled above a lacy red bra. He bent and kissed the plump flesh while at the same time unhooking the bra. Raine breathed deeply, enjoying the sensation of his warm lips on her skin. Her nipples tightened with anticipation. As she shrugged off the unfastened bra, he cupped her breasts and rolled his thumbs over her berrylike nipples.

"I have longed for this," he said, his deep voice raw with passion.

"So have I," she breathed.

With a coquettish smile, she folded her arms across her breasts and ran to the blanket. He chased and caught her around the waist. Tumbling onto the blanket, he cushioned her body with his as they struck the ground.

"Oh, Sanjay," she said between kisses. She kicked off her sneakers and he pressed her onto her back.

Rising to his knees, he trailed his long, slender fingers between her breasts and down her belly. He tugged off her pants, then her socks.

For a brief moment she hoped they wouldn't get caught. If Kesi and Bo followed them out of nosiness, they'd feel her wrath, friends or not. Her doubt faded when he settled between her legs and ran his warm, wet tongue where she ached for his touch.

"Sanjay!" she panted, weaving her fingers through his damp hair.

He growled and continued licking, teasing her to the brink of ecstasy. Several more long, rhythmic strokes and she exploded, every muscle in her body straining with pleasure, magnificent pulsations rolling through her.

Panting, she relaxed completely, her hands releasing his hair and falling to her sides. She felt him stretch out beside her, his warmth seeping into her. Finally she opened her eyes and smiled at him.

"That was so fantastic," she said.

He nodded, his eyes gleaming with passion, and stroked her face. "You look so beautiful lying here."

"Oh right. Sand all over me. My hair sticking up everywhere."

"You look wild. Very, very sexy."

"Yeah?" She ran a fingertip over his lips.

"Oh yeah."

"You're on the sexy side yourself, weretiger." She swept her hand down his side, over his hip, and then curled it around his swollen staff. "I want you inside me again, Sanjay."

In spite of his obvious state of desire, he shook his head. "I have no protection. I cannot risk giving you a child--"

"That's sweet of you, tiger, but I've got it covered. One of the Veils is a witch and she supplies me with a very strong contraceptive potion. Besides, in case you don't remember, this isn't the first time we've made love without the condom."

His brow furrowed. "What do you mean?"

"It's not your fault. Most guys have trouble remembering when I drain their energy."

"You mean you were using the potion that night, too?"

She nodded.

"Why didn't you tell me? I could have made love with you the first time without it."

"Would you have really believed me?" she asked, unable to keep the knowing tone from her voice.

He cast her a half annoyed-half amused look. "Probably not."

"But you do trust me now?"

"Yes." He cupped her face in his hand and stared at her with such faith that her heart fluttered. "I trust you, Raine."

"Sanjay?"

"Yes?"

She was about to beg him to make love to her, but refrained. Why did she always go to pieces around him? The man made her feel so damn girly it was pathetic, yet she *liked* it.

"What do you want, Raine?" His voice became even more seductive, as if he knew exactly what she desired but wouldn't provide it unless she asked.

"What do you think?"

"Tell me." His hand moved from her face to her breast where he languidly stroked the nipple, making it even harder and more sensitive. Each time his thumb rolled over the taut bud, she felt a pulsation of desire between her legs. The man was going to destroy her. A Succubus ruined by passion. The irony was laughable. "Tell me."

"Why? You seem to know what I want."

"And I will enthusiastically provide it, but I want you to tell me your desires."

"Why?" she repeated, her breath deepening as he gently pinched her nipple. His hand moved from the warm sphere and swept down her back to her buttocks. He kneaded the globes, then pressed a fingertip to the delicate flesh between them.

Raine gasped, almost overcome by lust. Suddenly his hand moved away.

"Tell me," he murmured against her lips.

"Kiss me." She had intended to sound demanding, yet the plea in her voice betrayed her desperation. At that moment her fondest desire was for him to claim her body like he had on the night they'd met. She wanted to be overpowered, filled by his hot, throbbing flesh. She wanted to be loved by him.

He covered her mouth in a breath stealing kiss, his tongue plunging between her lips. Her tongue met it with fervor. When he broke the kiss, both were panting. His gaze fixed on hers with such intensity that she felt dizzy with lust.

"What else?" he demanded. "Ask and I will give."

"Here." She glanced at her nipple and brushed her fingertips over the pert flesh.

He moved lower and took her nipple between his lips. Licking and sucking the tender bud, he cupped her other breast in his hand and squeezed gently.

"Yes, oh, yes," she breathed, closing her eyes and surrendering completely to pleasure.

His teeth lightly worried her nipple before he circled it once more with his tongue.

"The other one, too," she panted.

Immediately he switched to her other breast. Raine clutched his head closer and arched against him, encouraging him with lustful whispers.

"Ah!" she cried sharply as he sucked hard. Her entire body burned with need. Unable to wait another moment before feeling his shaft, stiff and demanding, between her legs, she said, "Please, Sanjay, now."

"Now what?" he purred and ran his tongue from her breast to her neck where he pressed feathery kisses.

"Take me now. Now!"

His body covered hers completely. The crown of his erection prodded her slick passage. Inch by delicious inch, he filled her with his thick staff. Raine moaned with pleasure and wrapped her arms and legs around him.

Teasing her with long, slow thrusts, Sanjay growled, a bewitching sound somewhere between tiger and man. Several times she tried to kiss him, but he avoided her lips, unwilling to give himself over to her Succubus power. She sensed he wanted to claim her first. Show her he could again be in control. At the moment she was too aroused to fight him. She merely held him tightly, urging him on in throaty whispers until the speed of his thrusts increased, the marvelous friction hurling her into an orgasm so intense she felt pleasure from the roots of her hair all the way to her feet. She opened her eyes, surprised that he was still rock hard inside her.

"You're ruining me, tiger, but I won't go down without a fight," she panted, bracing her hands against his shoulders and pushing, though he was too powerful for her to move. Still, he rolled onto his back and watched her through half-closed eyes that glimmered with desire.

His thighs parted so she could kneel between them. Clasping his staff in both hands, she bent and took the flushed head into her mouth. While she stroked the shaft she licked and sucked the crown. Her tongue teased the underside and rolled over the tiny eye, tasting the first droplet of his essence.

"Raine, ah!" he gasped, clutching handfuls of her hair. His hips thrust slightly and she knew he was restraining himself from lunging hard.

Arousing him rekindled her excitement. Already she longed to feel him inside her again, but she didn't want to rush. After the way he teased her, he deserved payback.

She used her lips and tongue on him until she knew by the sound of his breathing and the tension in his body he was on the verge of climax.

She mounted him swiftly, guiding his staff into her quivering pussy. Her breathing ragged, she rode him like a demon.

Sanjay's eyes closed, his neck arched and hips lunged upward, meeting her thrust for thrust. His animalistic groans and growls spurred her passion. She gasped with pleasure when his long, slender hands clutched her waist, steadying her as their motions became even more frenzied.

"Yes, yes! Oh, Sanjay! Sanjay," she gasped, her entire body trembling. She struggled to hold back, wanting to feel him come first, though she wasn't sure how much longer she could keep her orgasm at bay.

With a primal cry he bucked and came, his body hot and straining beneath her. Raine burst with pleasure, pulsations rolling through her as she collapsed atop him.

For several moments they lay wrapped in each other's arms while their breathing and heartbeats slowed to normal. Finally Raine shifted onto the blanket beside him. He still held her close. Neither spoke, though many emotions hung between them.

God, she was falling in love with this man. She didn't want to think about what would happen if Rahul was found guilty at the trial.

Once they'd rested, she and Sanjay ate the meal she'd packed.

"Thank you for bringing me here," he said.

"You're welcome. You seemed to be going crazy in that cage, not that I blame you."

"I have a problem with cages," he admitted. "A very long time ago, before even your grandmother was born, there was unrest among my kind. Many battles. I was captured and held in a cage without food and scarcely enough water to stay alive. Since then I have not been able to abide small enclosures."

The idea of him being tormented in such a way made her sick.

"If there was any way for me to convince them not to lock you up--"

"I'm fine. I just wanted to share that with you because you were kind enough to do this for me."

Raine nodded and reached for his hand. She squeezed it gently and he responded by tugging her a bit closer for a kiss filled with tenderness rather than passion. It actually made her feel good knowing there could be more than sex between them.

While she cleaned up the remains of dinner, he changed into his tiger form and had another long run down the beach. The night had grown chilly, so Raine wrapped the blanket around her. She warmed up quickly when Sanjay rejoined her and lay beside her. Cuddling close to his warm, furry body, she closed her eyes and stroked his beautiful tiger's face. His gaze, wild yet affectionate, fixed on her. When they'd first met, they'd been enemies. Now she couldn't imagine him as anything but a friend and lover. The only way to save their relationship would be to clear Rahul's name. Unfortunately, if he was telling the truth it meant Saloni had lied. The Wakened Veils couldn't be used for petty jealousy, only as vengeance against evil.

Raine never would have thought she would want one of her sisters to be in the wrong when it came to revenge, but better that than have Sanjay and Rahul sentenced to death.

## Chapter Five

Raine sat between Sanjay and Rahul at the large triangular table in the meeting room of her grandmother's villa. Across the table, Kesi and Saloni stared hard at the men.

The First Wraths--Vidonia, Lani, and Masika--sat along the table's third edge, their expressions calm, not betraying their thoughts. As representative for Saloni, Kesi was allowed to speak first.

"We are here to prove this *man*," Kesi sneered the word while tossing Rahul a scathing glance, "is guilty of wantonly seducing one of our trusted sisters, impregnating her, and leaving her with no other choice but to marry a man whose abuse led to the death of her child and nearly caused her own death. We are also here to seek justice for his father's violent attack on our sisters as they attempted to carry out their duty. Both these men have already twisted the truth with the hope of avoiding their well deserved punishments. By the end of this trial, you will see that in order for justice to be served, both must be sentenced to severe penalties."

Listening to Kesi, Raine knew she would have her work cut out for her proving Sanjay and Rahul's innocence. After talking to Rahul, she believed he spoke the truth. To her annoyance, she found herself liking the seemingly forthright young man almost as much as his father.

Vidonia nodded in Kesi's direction, and then turned to Raine. "You may speak."

"Our primary reason for being here is not to dole out punishment, but to seek the truth," Raine began. "The Wakened Veils originated because women found no justice in the laws of men. We created our own justice system with the goal of improving upon men's unfair methods. Unless we have become as petty, cruel, and narrow minded as those we learned to despise, I plead with you to listen, unbiased, to what these men have to say."

"We have heard your opening statements and now ask you to present the proof you have gathered," Masika said. "Kesi, you may proceed."

Kesi turned to Saloni with a sympathetic expression. Had the situation not been so grave, Raine would have smiled. Kesi could really lay it on thick when she had to. "Saloni, I realize how difficult this must be for you. When you came to us in good faith and asked for vengeance against Rahul, we promised that justice would be served. Now you must again be forced to relive the past to remind the First Wraths about why they had, just weeks ago, given the order for Rahul's execution."

"It's all right," Saloni said, casting her gaze down to her hands folded on the table in front of her. She hadn't once glanced in Rahul's direction, even to fling him a look of hatred. Very strange.

"Saloni, please tell us how you first met Rahul."

"We met at the home of a friend--a married couple with whom we were both acquainted. Rahul later approached me while I was shopping in the marketplace. He seemed very sincere."

"Only sincere?" Kesi pressed.

"And somehow ... irresistible."

"Irresistible." A slow smile spread across Kesi's face and she turned to the First Wraths. "I'd like to take a moment to remind you that at this time Saloni was a mere mortal with none of the vampire powers later given to her. Rahul is a weretiger and such creatures are known for their sexual magnetism. If Rahul desired Saloni in his bed, it would be simple for him to lure her."

"Objection," Raine said. "It has never been proved that weretigers have any special seductive powers like vampires or Incubi."

"Excuse me, but I personally know of at least two women who have been lured by the sexual magnetism of weretigers," Kesi stated, narrowing her eyes at Raine.

Anger surged through Raine, but she kept it under control. During a trial, friendship meant nothing. By goading her using what she knew of Raine and her grandmother's affairs with Sanjay, Kesi was only doing her job.

"This trial is not about how many weretigers have seduced any number of women," Lani stated. "It is this particular were and woman we must focus on."

Kesi bowed her head slightly in deference to the First Wrath before continuing, "Saloni, please tell us how you felt when Rahul began pursuing you."

"Flattered. He is very handsome and from a good family, but it was more than that. He treated me with tenderness I have never felt from any man. I wanted to please him."

"And he made it clear that bedding him would please him?"

"Yes."

"What man wouldn't?" Rahul said. "But I never pressured her."

"Silence!" Vidonia ordered. "It is not your time to speak. Another outburst from you and this trial will be over."

Sanjay cast his son a furious look and Raine sensed his concern. Though this trial was as important to the Veils as it was to the weretigers, the First Wraths would not allow what they considered insolence from the men.

"During this courtship, did he propose marriage to you?" Kesi asked.

"Yes," Saloni said. "He said if I slept with him he would marry me."

A muscle jerked in Rahul's cheek and his teeth clenched visibly, though he refrained from speaking.

Raine glanced at Sanjay and noted the tension in his expression as well. Fear of what might happen to him, should the trial go badly, curled inside her.

"How long did your affair last?" Kesi's voice forced Raine out of her thoughts and back to the trial.

"Close to a month."

"And then?"

"He broke it off. I can only assume he was bored with me. Soon after I learned of my pregnancy."

"Did you tell him?"

"Yes."

Raine glanced sharply at Rahul, fearful that he might lose control of his temper, but he remained silent.

"What did he do?" Kesi continued.

"He denied that it was his. After that he left India. My family didn't know about my situation, so when they arranged a marriage for me, I pressed for a quick wedding. I needed to make a home for my child."

"What kind of home was it?" Kesi asked in a soft, compassionate voice.

"My husband beat me often. It was because of that my baby was born prematurely and died. If not for the midwife who gave me the gift of vampirism, I would have died giving birth to him." Throughout the trial, Saloni had scarcely lifted her gaze from the table. Tears dripped down her face and she wiped them away.

Kesi offered her a tissue and placed a hand on her shoulder. "Thank you, Saloni. That is all."

Masika turned to Raine. "You may proceed."

"Saloni, I apologize because I know this is difficult for you," Raine began. "However, I must ask you some questions."

"Of course." Saloni dabbed at her eyes with the tissue.

"How long ago did you and Rahul meet?"

"A little over two centuries ago."

"Two centuries." Raine paused significantly. "Not long for many of us, but according to the mortal world it is quite some time ago. Sexuality wasn't nearly as free back then, even in the most liberal places."

"No." Saloni smiled tremulously. "Things were quite backward."

"I understand how difficult it is to refrain from getting closer to someone you care about--one to whom you're greatly attracted--but didn't you think about the risk you were taking in having sexual relations with a man who wasn't your husband?"

"I ... I was very young and foolish," Saloni admitted.

"Objection!" Kesi snapped. "Surely you can't be insinuating that a young mortal girl could have any chance of defending herself emotionally against a weretiger with a couple of centuries behind him?"

"I'm not insinuating anything. I'm stating that during that time, during *any* time, a woman, just like a man, must be held accountable for her actions," Raine said.

"He told me he loved me." Fresh tears spilled down Saloni's face. "I believed him."

"I have no further questions for Saloni," Raine stated, then turned to Rahul. "Please tell us how you first met Saloni."

"Like she said, it was at the home of a mutual friend," he stated.

"Did you later approach her when she was alone?"

"Yes, but not to seduce her."

"Oh, right," Saloni muttered, for the first time meeting Rahul's gaze.

Raine was almost taken aback by the emotions raging between them.

"Silence." Vidonia glanced at Saloni. "I must remind you not to speak out of turn."

"I'm sorry." Again Saloni lowered her gaze.

"If you didn't want to seduce her, then why did you approach her?" Raine asked.

"Because I liked her and wanted to know her better."

"Did you ask her to sleep with you?"

"Not right away, and I didn't exactly ask her."

"Please explain."

"It sort of just happened."

Raine nodded. "I see. And after it happened, did you ask her to marry you?"

"Yes, and she refused."

Saloni glared. "He is a liar."

"I never lie," Rahul said through gritted teeth.

"Order!" Lani demanded. "Saloni, this is your second warning. One more and we will be forced to reprimand you."

Raine turned back to Rahul. "Did she give you a reason for her refusal?"

"No."

"Did you stop seeing her?"

He sighed deeply and his gaze flickered downward. "No."

"Why not?"

"Because I hoped she would change her mind."

"When did she tell you she was pregnant?"

"She didn't. When she finally confided that her parents had arranged her marriage and she would not go against them, I left India."

"I have no further questions," Raine said.

"Kesi?" Vidonia asked.

Kesi held Rahul's gaze. "You claim that you didn't ask Saloni to sleep with you, that it sort of *just happened*. Could you explain how something like that could *just happen*?"

"Not really, no."

"I see. So the two of you were walking through a crowded marketplace and a lustful spirit leapt into your body, forcing you to have sex with her and it was completely beyond your control?"

"No." Rahul's eyes blazed.

"Then you were someplace private?"

"Of course."

"Why would you, in that day and age, take a woman to whom you are not engaged, someplace private if not to seduce her?"

Rahul's jaw tightened even more and he seemed at a loss for words.

"I withdraw the question." Kesi smiled slightly. "I think we get the picture. Do you agree, Rahul, that your affair with Saloni lasted about a month?"

"Yes."

"And during that time you were just begging for her hand in marriage, but she continued to refuse, even though she admits you were a great catch?"

"Yes."

"Did you use protection of any kind?"

"It was not common at the time."

"So for a month you had unprotected sex with a woman, then just left the country without sticking around long enough to see if any children came out of it?"

"She was marrying someone else."

"Oh yes, there's that. How do you feel knowing your baby died because she was forced into the home of an abusive man?"

"Terrible, if you must know." Rahul's eyes gleamed with such genuine emotion that Raine actually felt sorry for him.

"Do you admit that if you had remained in India where Saloni could have confided in you about her pregnancy your child would probably have lived?"

"Objection! How could he possibly speculate about something that is in the hands of nature itself?" Raine interrupted.

Again Kesi smiled. "I withdraw the question, and I have no further questions for this man."

The First Wraths exchanged glances, and then Vidonia said, "You are dismissed until seven o'clock this evening when we will meet back here and question Saloni and Rahul in private."

Raine sighed, closing her eyes for a moment. Her grandmother's statement proved that both she and Kesi had failed to sway the three founders of their sisterhood. She had hoped for a fast trial. Now there was no telling how long it might take.

Sanjay rested a hand on her shoulder. She turned and gazed into his dark eyes.

"Thank you," he whispered.

"I hope I helped a little," she replied.

"Regardless of the outcome, I will always care for you, Raine, and I will always be grateful."

*Even if it's war between our people.* He didn't have to speak the words, the threat hung between them like an impenetrable curtain.

There was no doubt that if the Veils sentenced the men to death, they would try to escape. With their power, there was a chance they could actually get away. If they did, the Veils wouldn't rest until they were hunted down. Raine flinched to think of the gory battle between the Wakened Veils and the weretiger clan that could last for ages. She and her lover, a man she had grown to respect and care for, would be trapped in the middle of it.

\* \* \* \*

Two days later, after intense questioning and deliberation, the First Wraths had yet to decide Rahul and Sanjay's fate. Both Saloni and Rahul seemed equally sincere, and while the First Wraths admitted they would like to condemn Rahul, they could not accuse him without being certain of his guilt.

Again the group sat at the triangular table where Vidonia announced the solution to their dilemma.

"We have decided that to best serve justice we will seek the assistance of one who projects thoughts."

Lani continued, "Since this is a rare gift, there is only one woman who we fully trust to project the untainted truth."

"Word has been sent to Panya, a daemon with the power to read and project thoughts," Masika said. "It will take her another week to arrive."

Raine exchanged glances with Sanjay. Another week in the cage. She cringed at the thought of what he must be going through.

"May I speak?" Sanjay asked and Lani motioned for him to go on. "I know a daemon with the same power currently residing in Spain. He can arrive much sooner and help put an end to this trail."

"He?" Kesi demanded. She looked at the First Wraths. "For something this important we cannot trust an unknown male to interfere. How can we be certain he will show us accurate projections and not manipulated images?"

"Please, I don't understand what you mean by projections," Saloni said. "And can we trust any demon, male or female, to act justly?"

"Not demon. Daemon. A demigod. Not necessarily evil," Raine told her. "As for the power to project thoughts, it is exactly as it sounds. They can read minds and create images for others to see, like a hologram."

"You mean, I must look upon exactly what happened to me?" Panic glistened in Saloni's eyes.

"Of course you may refuse to participate," Vidonia said. "However, using the daemon will facilitate the process."

"Are you afraid they'll see the truth?" Rahul demanded.

"Are you willing to reveal yourself so completely?" Saloni retorted.

He lifted his chin. "Yes."

"For your father's male daemon or one of our choosing?" Kesi asked.

"Either one."

"Then we will wait for Panya to arrive. Also, we have decided that if the man is found guilty, he and his father will be executed immediately by beheading."

A sick feeling weighted Raine's belly. How could she possibly stand by and do nothing while Sanjay was sentenced to a horrible death?

Saloni looked up sharply. "Isn't it customary to beat the guilty party first, and allow his accuser to decide if she wishes to follow through with execution?"

Vidonia nodded. "It is, but we tried that the first time and he managed to avoid his full punishment. This way there is no chance for escape or survival."

"This is what you want, Saloni?" Rahul asked quietly.

"It's what you deserve."

"Look at me when you say that."

Raine's heart pounded in anticipation. A glance around the room revealed everyone else staring at Saloni, anxiously awaiting her reply. Perhaps Raine was not the only one who had begun to doubt her reliability.

"Look at me," Rahul demanded again.

"Objection--" Kesi said.

"Overruled," Lani interrupted.

Saloni turned her gaze to Rahul, then looked to the First Wraths. "I would prefer he not be executed."

"But he is responsible for the death of your child," Vidonia prodded. "And would have been the cause of your death, as well, had it not been for your vampiric creator. For these crimes, which the daemon will confirm, the man must pay to the fullest."

"Wait," Saloni murmured. "Perhaps there has been a slight exaggeration."

"Exaggeration?" Masika asked. "In what way?"

"He did propose to me, but if I accepted my family would have disowned me. They were adamant about me marrying the man they had chosen."

"Anything else that might have been *exaggerated*?" Lani asked.

"And he might not have known about the child."

"Might not?" Vidonia snapped. "Explain."

"I actually never got around to telling him."

"What?" Kesi raised in an eyebrow at Saloni.

"But even if I had told him I doubt he would have done anything about it."

"That's not true," Rahul said. "If I had wanted to marry you before knowing you carried my child, I would have wanted you even more after."

"You wanted me so much that you've decided to marry someone else!"

"Is that what this is about?" Rahul stared at her. "I can't believe you would send assassins after me out of petty jealousy when *you* rejected *me*."

"You knew my situation!" she snapped. "I had to do what my family wanted. You knew that from the first."

"Did you know that?" Sanjay asked Rahul. "She told you she belonged to someone else and her family would disown her, but you seduced her anyway? And slept with her unprotected?"

"You know it wasn't as common back then to--"

"What about common sense?" Sanjay demanded.

Rahul glared. "Father, whose side are you on?"

"The side of truth."

"I loved her."

"You lusted after her," Kesi accused.

"Yes," Rahul shouted in exasperation. "Yes, I lusted after her. She was young and innocent. I wanted her and took her, knowing it was wrong."

"And I wanted him," Saloni said quietly. "When I realized I was pregnant, I wanted to change my mind about marrying the man my family had chosen. I wanted my child to know his real father, but you were gone, Rahul."

"I'm sorry." He held her gaze and Raine saw his hand jerk, as if he had intended to reach out to Saloni across the table.

"So you are telling us you were as much to blame as Rahul," Lani said. "And you used your position in the Veils to satisfy your jealousy instead of punishing a truly guilty man?"

"Damn," Kesi muttered under her breath and flashed Saloni an angry look.

"We need to figure out where to go from here," Vidonia said. "The First Wraths will discuss this matter privately. You will have our decision within the hour."

The three leaders left the room.

"What do you think will happen to me?" Saloni whispered to Kesi.

"I have no idea," Kesi replied. "And don't even talk to me, Saloni. I am so mad at you right now."

Raine turned to Sanjay. They exchanged relieved looks.

"It's safe to say you and Rahul are no longer in danger of execution," she said.

"Then why don't they just let us go?" Rahul asked.

"Don't look quite so happy." Sanjay cast his son a stern look. "You might not have been as bad as Saloni described, but you did not act honorably."

"What?" Rahul looked stunned.

"You placed a young girl, not to mention your own child, in a terrible situation. You did this knowing she was promised to another man."

"But--"

"Silence. I am disappointed in you, Rahul."

"You would be," Rahul snapped. "What did you ever know about love? You married my mother with no love between you."

"That is not your business, boy."

"Then why is my life your business?"

"Stop it, both of you!" Raine snapped.

Beneath the table, she reached for Sanjay's hand. He squeezed hers gently and offered a strained smile. He might be upset with his son, but at least now they would have the chance to work out their problems without the threat of death by assassins hanging over their heads.

A short time later, one of the loup-garou warriors stepped into the room and called for Sanjay whom the First Wraths wished to speak with in private. Raine watched him leave the room, her heart pounding as she wondered what they could be discussing. Moments later, he and the three women returned to the table.

"First, Sanjay will be freed with no punishment for rescuing his son," Masika announced.

Raine couldn't repress her sigh of relief.

"It seems Rahul and Saloni are equally at fault and the only one to have suffered was the child they created," Vidonia said.

"For that you both deserve punishment," Lani added.

"We have decided, and Sanjay agrees, that Saloni and Rahul will serve a month-long prison term during which they will share the same cell."

"What?" Saloni and Rahul shouted in unison.

"Father, how could you allow this?" Rahul demanded.

"You must face responsibility for your past actions and also come to terms with your true feelings for this woman," Sanjay stated.

"But I can't stay away for a month. I have a business to run!"

"And I am your partner, so I grant you the time off. I can run the business along with our vice president who has been handling it very well since we've been away dealing with this issue."

"It's not only the business. I'm engaged to be married. What will Nidhi think?"

"As of this moment you no longer have my approval for that marriage."

"What? Father, even without your approval Nidhi and I--"

"Isn't it bad enough you ruined one woman without doing the same to another?" Sanjay glared.

"What?"

"You do not love Nidhi because you are still in love with Saloni."

Rahul looked horrified. "I am not."

"You are becoming a compulsive liar, Rahul," Sanjay continued. "As leader of your clan, I order you to fulfill the punishment set for you by the Wakened Veils."

"I still have to speak to Nidhi. What will she think if I just don't show up for the wedding?"

"I will speak to Nidhi. After you have served your time, you will have the chance to personally offer her your apologies. End of discussion."

"I will not be forced to live with him!" Saloni glared at Rahul.

"You will do what you're told," Vidonia said. "In our long history no member of the Wakened Veils has ever used the power of this organization for such a petty thing as mere jealousy."

"You're lucky they didn't throw you out entirely," Kesi added.

"I am sorry," Saloni said. "But if you must punish me, at least put me in solitary confinement."

"For you to bear such jealousy for a man even after so many years, you must still have deep feelings for him," Lani said. "Use this time to come to terms with him and with yourself."

Fifi and Angelique, in their half-beast shape, approached. One grasped Saloni while the other took Rahul's arm. He shoved her away, his face and body shifting into its tiger form. Sanjay also shifted. Part black tiger, part man, he grasped his son in an unbreakable hold and dragged him out of the meeting room, following the wolf women and Saloni to the cells below.

* * * *

Later that night, Raine and Sanjay strolled down the beach, eager to spend time together without worry now that the trial was over. His arm draped around her, he held her close to his side. She leaned against him, one hand caressing his chest.

"I almost feel sorry for Rahul and Saloni," she said.

"It will do them both good. There are many unresolved feelings between them. Perhaps now they will be mature enough to handle them."

Raine laughed. "I wonder."

He chuckled and squeezed her gently. "What about us? Are we mature enough to admit that perhaps there is more between us than incredible sex?"

Raine's pulse quickened and she drew a deep breath. She had vowed never to surrender her heart to a man. Never to love. But never suddenly seemed like a long, lonely time.

"I have come to care for you deeply, Raine," he said quietly. "I don't want this to be the end for us."

"Neither do I," she admitted. "But I need to move slowly--at least on an emotional level."

"I understand."

"What about you? As a clan leader, aren't you restricted on which women you can marry?"

"I have already married for my clan and produced an heir. I have learned the hard way that it's wrong to commit to someone you don't love. From now on I want to choose the mate of my heart. I believe I have found her."

Sanjay stopped walking and she turned to him. He gently grasped her chin and tilted her face toward his. A thrill of desire coursed through her as she stood on tiptoe and accepted his tender, yet penetrating kiss.

"Do not refuse me, Raine."

"I won't," she whispered against his lips. Burying her fingers in his hair, she kissed him again, her tongue meeting his with warm, passionate strokes. When the kiss broke, both were slightly breathless. Meeting his obsidian gaze, she offered a slight smile. "But there are conditions."

"Ah yes." He grinned, taking her hand and continuing down the beach. "With the Wakened Veils there are always conditions. Can I bribe you into forgetting about the conditions and just enjoying life?"

"Bribe me with what?"

"I don't know. A shopping spree. A year's supply of chocolate."

She wrinkled her nose. "It's sickening the way the whole world, especially men, seem to be under the impression all women think about are things like chocolate, chick flicks, dieting, planning weddings--"

The shocked expression on his face nearly made her laugh. "You have no interest in weddings?"

"My interest is in the wedding *night*. Forget about the flowers, gowns, and other crap."

Sanjay curled his lip. "What kind of a woman are you?"

"Sometimes, weretiger, your archaic chauvinism boggles the mind."

"Archaic? I saw talk shows about these things and women like chocolate and weddings. End of discussion."

"Like hell. I--" He cut short her sentence by covering her mouth with his.

She weakened instantly and melted into his arms. Damn, the man got to her like no one else.

"Does it bother you that I don't like the things talk shows say I should?" she asked.

"I couldn't care less, as long as you like me."

"I more than like you." She took his face in her hands and kissed him. "But I still haven't forgotten about the conditions. A woman can't be too careful, you know. Especially when she's falling in love."

"You would think I am the one who must be careful considering I have just handed my heart to a Succubus."

She poured all her affection into a single look and said, "I'll be careful with it, weretiger."

Wrapping an arm around her, he held her close as they continued down the beach.

"You don't even want a little wedding?" he prodded. "I'll take care of all the details. Even the menu."

"I didn't think guys liked planning weddings."

"Now who's being archaic? Have you not heard of metrosexual men?"

"What?"

"Don't you watch any television at all?"

Raine laughed and slipped her arm around his waist. With Sanjay beside her and the burden of the trial over, she felt a completeness she had never experienced before. Maybe, just maybe, she had been wrong about love after all, or perhaps she had simply gotten the only decent man left in the world. Either way, she wasn't going to question her luck. For the first time in her life, she intended to simply enjoy it.

The End

# FORSAKEN
## *Immortal Surrender*

Adrienne Kama

"Do not judge me by my flaws, though they are many"
-*Umberto Pena*

### Chapter One

Ambrosia Kennedy's fingers glided over the sleek neck of the guitar. She reveled in the feel of the taut length of it beneath her fingertips. With a languorous rocking, she rotated her hips, losing herself to the emotions humming through her body.

She was totally enthralled.

With a soprano howl she opened her eyes, yanked the mic stand close with her left hand and used it to play eight bars of a bluesy slide guitar riff that ran counterpoint to Kyle's thumping bass.

She watched Kyle swing his blond mane in time with the music. He ran to the edge of the stage and dropped to his knees. The nine security guards standing within the flimsy barricade between the stage and audience released a simultaneous shout of warning when the crowd surged forward and a group of teenaged girls tried to scramble over the wooden partition, grasping for Kyle.

Her band, Maven, had ended the show like this every night for the last five weeks, and every night the crowd went wild. It didn't matter what city they were in or that they were the opening act, the primer for the main event. Every night the crowd cheered them on and every night Ambrosia reveled in the adoration.

If the Talhari Council knew how thoroughly she was enjoying this assignment they wouldn't be pleased. This was her first real mission after all.

Her apprenticeship had been far too long and more arduous than anything her male counterparts ever experienced. Doubtless, even with her extensive training she'd never have been given this opportunity to take part in the slaying of the vamp-goth band, Forsaken, if not for the fact that she was the only hunter who could play lead guitar and sing while working an audience into a frenzy. But even at that the council had only agreed to send her after she'd assured them she wouldn't question the decisions of Kyle and Nick, two veteran hunters. Kyle, of course, was the CHI, Certified Hunter In-charge. Nick was second in command, and then there was her.

It grated.

Still smarting at the indignities of the setup, she leaned into the mic to sing the last notes of the song before her final guitar solo. A sea of aggressive twenty-something males raised their fists in the air and screamed for more.

Indignities aside, this was one sweet assignment. It'd be hours before her performance high waned, hours before she'd be able to settle in bed and sleep. She was too worked up, too jazzed. Maybe Kyle was onto something when he arranged for the kill to go down at sunrise. Despite all of the preparation that had gone into this plan, she'd originally thought five weeks was too soon for a takedown. But she supposed that's why she wasn't the CHI.

Her fingers danced up the neck of the guitar for the last time. She spun away from the mic, shook her leather clag rear end at the audience, and leapt into the air for the final note. A flash of pyrotechnics erupted from center stage, lighting her in bright orange light for several seconds, then the stage went black.

"Maven! Maven! Maven!" the crowd yelled.

Grinning in the near darkness, she disconnected from her rig, slung her guitar over her back, and made her way to the stairs at the rear of the stage. Kyle and Nick moved on ahead of her, walking at a trot. At the bottom of the stairs Trevor, one of their roadies, was positioned with an armful of towels. "Great show, guys. You're really giving those guys in Forsaken a run for their money."

Kyle took his towel and grinned. "You bet your ass we are."

Ambrosia clasped a towel then drew it over her damp face. She nodded as Bill, another roadie, unhooked her guitar strap and took her guitar from her. "You've got one sweet ass, Ambi, and you know how to move it. What I wouldn't give…."

She bit back the sour response that perched on the tip of her tongue and forced a smile to her lips. "Dream on, Billy."

Behind her, Trevor snickered. "I'd watch it if I were you, Bill.

Umberto's already laid his claim. I don't know about you, but that's one guy I wouldn't wanna piss off."

Again, she had to swallow the automatic response hovering on her lips. The day she allowed herself to be claimed by a bloodsucker was the day she lost her mind.

Bill grimaced. A visible shudder vibrated through his obese frame then he stepped away from her. "I didn't mean no harm, Ambi." He held his hand up, as if to stave off an attack. "It was just a compliment. You're not going to mention I said anything to Umberto, are you? I mean, I was just joking around."

For the last five weeks, she'd cultivated a relationship with Forsaken's lead singer. She'd dressed sexy, shoved her body into scanty little dresses and all but thrown herself at the sinister vampire. She was supposed to adore the bloodsucker, least that's how her story went. Truth was, and this grated too, she was finding it harder and harder to be offended when someone remarked on her relationship with him. If he were human, if he weren't a vampire, she'd allow the relationship to develop into the sexual one she knew he craved, but she couldn't. Umberto wasn't a man. He was a killer.

She gave Bill a coy smile and winked. "We'll see."

Kyle tugged her arm. "Come on."

She finger waved to Bill, then followed Kyle away from the stage area. Nick led the way through the labyrinth of cinderblock hallways toward the hole in the wall that was their dressing room, twirling a drumstick between his fingers as he walked. He smiled absently at the groupies milling around the backstage area, "all access" passes hanging like badges of honor around their necks and the sickly sweet fragrance of drugstore perfume heavy in the air around them.

"Sons of bitches." Kyle rubbed at the thick line of kohl eyeliner under his eyes. His blond hair was saturated with sweat and clung to his scalp like a skull cap. "They fuckin' loved us. They wanted a second encore. You're fuckin' brilliant, Ambi. You've got these guys eating out the palm of your hand ... *Umberto included.*" He said the last part through the cerebral communications unit wired through each of their frontal lobes. The CCU was necessary because it allowed them to converse silently, and silent communication was essential when a kill was going down.

Nick glanced at Ambrosia over his shoulder, his green eyes flickering with displeasure. She knew what he was thinking, and she didn't care. She couldn't afford to care. What had happened to Tom, her predecessor, hadn't been her fault. She refused to feel guilty for being glad about her good fortune. Hell, she hadn't even known Tom. "*This is only a temporary assignment for you, Ambi, try to remember that. All that showing off you're doing isn't going to kill the perps any faster.*"

She draped the towel over her bare shoulder and shrugged. "I'm just playing my part."

Nick flicked his chestnut mane and turned away. "And loving every minute of it."

"Shut up, Nick. I think Ambi's performance has been right on target. *I'm going to recommend to the council that they let her join the band full time. She's a real asset.*"

Nick shoved the dressing room door open with a boot then sauntered inside, speaking loud enough for half the world to hear him. "Do you even care about Tom? We don't know shit about how he died or how she operates, never saw her do a kill. All we know is that she was trained by Gaia Knight. The Council may think the sun rises and sets on Knight, but I say big fucking deal."

"Shut up, Nick!" Kyle waited for Ambrosia to enter, then shut the door and set the lock in place. "*All I'm saying is the setup seems to be working. Ambi fits the bill more than Tom, we can take out more bloodsuckers with Ambi than we ever could have with Tom. She looks like a lead singer.*"

Eyes narrowed to thin slits, Nick collapsed onto the worm-out brown sofa in the far corner of the small blue and gray room and regarded her with cool appraisal. "Big tits, round ass, and a pretty little doll face. Yeah, I guess you fit the bill, but you wanna know something, Ambi?"

As usual, Nick was getting on her nerves. Too annoyed to speak with anything that remotely resembled respect, she nodded instead.

"When you put on all that brown, skin-tight leather it's hard to tell where your skin begins and the leather ends. Makes you look like a whore. More like a groupie than a singer, if you know what I mean. Umberto's groupie, if you get me."

It was a challenge to keep from flipping him the bird every time he cut her down. Nevertheless, she turned from Nick, clapped Kyle on the shoulder, and headed for the bathroom. "I'm gonna shower."

"I'm heading over to the hotel now. You and Nick are going to the mansion at midnight, after the show. You're riding over in the bus with Forsaken. I'll be arriving with the team at three; we'll scan the area then enter the house thirty minutes before sunrise." He and Nick exchanged a look. "If anything happens, if anything changes, if they do anything that gives you pause, contact me immediately.

Understood?"

Nick nodded. "Yeah, I got you."

Ambrosia sucked in a breath. This was her first slaying. Everything had to run as smooth as silk or it would be her last. "Understood," she agreed.

Kyle focused on Nick. "You know what you're supposed to do while I'm prepping the team?"

"Recon the house one final time, make sure the layout matches the blueprints we made five weeks back. Check the crypt, make sure there are still four coffins inside. Check the crypt for personal paraphernalia--"

"Ambrosia?"

Unlike Nick who had respectable duties to perform tonight, she found her own tasks to be an insult to her training.

"Ambrosia?" Nick demanded from the sofa.

"You know, Kyle, I think I'd be more use if I helped Nick and--"

Kyle shook his head. "What is your assigned duty, Ambrosia?"

She exhaled. "Distract the band so Kyle can perform his duties without interruption. I'm to stick close to Umberto, because he's the one the others look to for leadership."

The edge of Nick's lip curled into what she could only assume was a grin, though it looked more like a snarl. "Umberto seems to have taken a liking to you so I don't think you'll have any trouble keeping him occupied until sunrise."

"Agreed," Kyle said. "Make sure the band enters the crypt before sunrise. If they don't, contact me. It won't do us any good to go down for the kill if the bloodsuckers aren't even there."

She nodded. "Understood."

"Good. I'll see you both at sunrise."

She stepped into the bathroom, shut and locked the door.

Sunrise tomorrow. It would be the most important day of her life.

## Chapter Two

Ambrosia was standing at the edge of the stage, grateful that Forsaken's security hadn't given her grief about wanting to get a backstage view of the show. For the first three weeks they hadn't let anyone who wasn't part of Forsaken's personal staff in that area during their performance. Only recently Umberto gave Wolf, the head of security, the OK to let her through.

At the moment her plan was to make herself as visible as possible, let Umberto know she was there and waiting for him to get offstage at the end of the show. She only wished keeping her eyes on him wasn't as pleasurable as it had been of late.

She was shivering in the backless, red latex dress she'd squeezed into after showering. Latex was good because it was sexy enough to ensure Umberto would remain focused on her, but she also had her full range of motion. She'd need to be able to move--and fast--come morning. She'd left her hair loose and could feel her curls brushing against her bare shoulders. Though she would have preferred to wear it up, Umberto liked it down. Tonight was all about keeping Umberto's focus on her, by any means necessary.

She was scared ... and excited.

Her first slaying.

But could she kill Umberto? Could she drive a stake through his heart? She'd spent so much time with him these last weeks. Maybe too much time.

"Get off your ass!"

Pulled from her musings, Ambrosia looked toward the stage. Umberto stood at the center of everything, fist raised in the air, his lips pulled into a snarl. To the left of him, Dario, the lead guitarist, whipped his sable mane back and let his fingers dance up the neck of his Washburn guitar.

It was watching Dario that had convinced her that, indeed, the members of Forsaken weren't human. Dario, the golden-skinned, South American vampire whose fingers moved over the guitar fret board faster than even the most talented human hands could manage. Dario wore his vampirism boldly. Unlike the others, he made no attempt to hide what he was. His hair was black as midnight and it glimmered with an unnatural luminescence no human hair could attain. Like an actor playing the part of vampire, he painted his nails a deep shade of ebony, he even let his fangs show when he was onstage. Fans thought he was a Goth kid, an eccentric that fell into character whenever given the chance. Nobody realized he wasn't playing a role. The fangs weren't pretend, and he'd killed countless people with them.

On the far right of the stage was Erik, the bass player--another blood sucker. As pale as Dario was dark and brooding, Erik was the polar opposite of Dario. He seemed more an elfin figure, a character from a Tolkien story. Save his pale complexion, he looked too gentle to be what he was ... and what he was, was a killer. His serene, elfin features were rounded and prettily made. As she watched him he crouched on his knees and bent forward, toward the crowd. His pale blond hair swept the jet black stage like a thousand strands of platinum silk. Erik was beautiful, disarmingly beautiful, yet he was deadlier than Dario, had killed more people. Erik was young, barely a hundred years old, so the blood lust was strong in him.

The youngest of Forsaken, and the most human to the eye, was the drummer, Mathias. He was the only American. The file she'd read on the band said he'd been made in 1957 in--of all places-- New Jersey. His short, spiky hair was pure white in color. Mathias had been a tall man when he was alive. His six-and-a-half-foot frame towered over her five-foot-four-inch body. In addition to being tall, he was mean. Mathias had the disposition of an alligator shark. And although his blood lust was strong, reports showed that he didn't take as much pleasure in the kill as Erik.

Then there was Umberto.

She closed her eyes and exhaled.

Umberto was the oldest, but had experienced the shortest human existence. He'd only had twenty one human years when he'd been made into a bloodsucker three hundred and eight years ago. A Spaniard and son of a noble, Umberto had the disarmingly sweet features of a boy of twenty. He was tall, slender, and artfully unkempt. His wavy, shoulder-length, brown hair was as prettily disheveled as any other disgustingly rich lead singer's hair would have been half way through a performance. There was nothing remarkable in the jeans he chose to wear onstage, or the faded Harley Davidson T-shirts he seemed to favor. From the sterling silver ring on the middle finger of his left hand to the simple pendant he kept dangling from his neck, Umberto seemed very ordinary. But Ambrosia was willing to wager that more than the others, Umberto's look was the most contrived. Though she'd never heard him say it, she knew enough about Umberto to know he'd more than likely spent days creating the most unremarkable look he could manage ... and he'd failed miserably. Unexceptional clothes, rumpled hair, there was nothing in his façade that could hide what he was. At least not to her eyes. His finely muscled frame was too extraordinary to be hidden under clothes. His hair shone with the same vampiric luminescence as Dario's raven locks. And Umberto's eyes....

A low moan escaped her pursed lips, surprising her. She suddenly needed to see him, needed to watch him stalk the stage like the predator he was. Slowly, she opened her eyes ... then jumped back a step. Her heart swelled and she yelped. "You!"

"What were you dreaming about?"

Standing so close that she could crush her lips against the taut nipples tenting his Harley T-shirt, Umberto gazed down at her. His maple brown eyes were fixed to her face and one brow was arched in question.

He was anything but ordinary. He was the most extraordinary man--bloodsucker--she'd ever seen.

"Were you thinking of me?" The edge of his lip rose into a faint smile. It was a smile that said Ambrosia didn't have to answer the question because he already knew the truth.

"I wasn't dreaming. I was watching the show."

"With your eyes closed?" His voice was like molten cream, richly decadent and deliciously intoxicating. If she didn't put her guard up, and fast, she could easily be seduced by the soft Spanish lilt of his voice and the slight moistening of his lips that happened whenever he spoke.

"Umberto, you should be on stage." Damn, she sounded as breathless as she felt.

He stepped forward, closing the distance she'd put between them. "Guitar solo. If Dario didn't need Erik and Mathias to keep the beat for him, they'd have to leave the stage. You know how Dario is."

Her mouth was dry. A potent cocktail of lust and desire surged through her, accompanied by a betraying warmth on the skin. Heat gathered between her thighs, and as always happened whenever she was near Umberto, her neglected sex gave a hungry tug. Nevertheless, she worked her lips until she could make them form words. "Guitar solo, that's right," she agreed. "His time to shine."

"Spoken with the honesty of a true guitar player."

"Guess I can relate."

He moved forward, advancing until her bare back was flush against the warm, dry surface of a pocked, plywood wall. Her breath spilled free on a gasp of surprise. She suddenly felt like *she* was being stalked.

He lifted his arms, set his palms against the wooden wall and caged her within the chill of his vampire's body. She quickly resisted her impulse to fall into his arms, and then had to fight a nearly overwhelming urge to fall into battle stance to fight him off.

He was a vampire, a bloodsucker, a murderer.

He nuzzled her neck, her cheek, her ear. "I've spoken with Nick." His lips glided over the sensitive skin of her lobe.

She shivered. "Oh?"

"I've told him to be ready to leave the arena after the show. My band and I will shower, dress, and then make our leave. I've reserved a spot in the bus for you at my side."

"With your groupies?"

"I don't entertain groupies. I never have. They're too young, too tedious, and too desperate to draw my attention. They're boring. But if you're asking if Dario, Erik, and Mathias are bringing *friends* tonight, the answer is no. It'll be the six of us." He ticked off names, accenting each was a luscious suck on her earlobe. "Dario, Erik, Mathias, Nick, you, and me."

Moving slowly enough to make her tremble, he licked the inside of her ear, letting his tongue dip within then glide out to lave. He panted against her, his breath peppering her cheek.

Umberto was too good at stimulating her.

When she felt the edge of a sharpened tooth, she jolted.

Umberto stood back, gazed at her. His face was flushed pink, his lips blood red despite the fact that she knew he hadn't drunk in days. She knew this because they'd spent every night together for the last nine days. They hadn't had sex--any form of sex was impossible for a vampire who hasn't drunk--but they'd come as close to having sex as two people could.

And damn her treacherous heart, she'd enjoyed it.

The thought that she shouldn't have been assigned to watch the band assailed her again. Staying close to the band should have been Nick's job. She should have gotten surveillance, but nobody ever listened to her.

Umberto let his hands fall to his sides. She couldn't see if his fangs had extended because his lips were pressed into a firm line. "Are you all right?" she asked.

He looked toward the floor, immediately his face was cast in shadow. When he spoke all she could see of him were his eyes. "I'm preoccupied with thoughts of the evening to come, considering various sacrifices I could make to ensure you won't change your mind."

The evening to come. Carnal heat oozed through her.

In an effort to distract Umberto from the night's true events, she'd promised to give herself to him. It was a safe promise to make because she knew that as long as he didn't feed he wouldn't be able to perform. "I won't change my mind."

"You've mesmerized me, Ambrosia, do you know that? I've been enchanted, enthralled, made helpless, and put at your mercy. Never has a woman been more aptly named. There's nothing I wouldn't do for you. Do you believe that?"

She moistened her lips. "I ... I don't know."

"You were made for me; does it frighten you to hear me say so?"

Frighten wasn't the word she'd use. To her considerable shame, hot desire and need was running rampant in her. Lust, pure and simple. Clearly she'd spent too much time with the alluring vampire. "No one's ever said anything like this to me before."

He tilted his head to one side, looking for all the world like an innocent instead of the deadly fiend he was. "I find that hard to believe."

"You're just being nice because I've agreed to sleep with you."

"Perhaps, or perhaps I've waited centuries for a woman like you."

"I didn't know you were so old. What does a girl say to that?"

"You've no need to say a thing here, now. Save it for later." Moving gracefully, he glided close again and slid his arms around her waist.

His lips traced a path along the crown of her head, and she could hear him inhaling the scent of her hair, as though it were the best aroma he'd known in his three hundred years.

An unexpected and disturbing realization came to her. She couldn't be the one to stake Umberto. She'd always thought she'd have the strength of character for such an action against any bloodsucker, but she wasn't so sure now. Worse, she couldn't say if she could stand by and watch someone else stake him.

This night was to be the last of Umberto's life. In twenty-four hours he would no longer exist. He'd be a pile of ashes and a memory, and nothing more. At least that's what would happen if she didn't step in, didn't do something to save him.

But saving him, protecting him would go against everything she'd learned these last years. It would go against who she was.

"My love," he murmured against her ear.

She shivered and another wave of doubt washed over her.

Being assigned to Umberto on this first job was more than likely the true test for her on this mission. No doubt the council was aware of the old vampire's charms, knew how seductive he could be. No doubt Kyle and Nick were prepared for her to act on the sensual vampire's behalf ... and if she did, she'd fail this assignment and be cast away from the Talhari forever.

If she was being honest with herself she'd admit that being cast out of the council wasn't the worst that would happen. She'd be viewed as a traitor and a threat. She'd have to be dispatched. She had too much knowledge of the agency for them to let her live if she betrayed them. Already she'd had a CCU implanted. She could open an internal channel with anyone on Kyle's team at any time, day or night, and never be overheard by non-team members. And she'd received her physical enhancements. She was inhumanly strong now, was able to heal from nearly any injury, and was five times faster than she'd been a year ago. While she wouldn't get her psychic enhancement embeds until this assignment was complete, she was still too much of a threat to be allowed to walk away.

She'd come too far.

Either Umberto died, or she did.

Sharp pain caught her by surprise. Her throat was on fire. An inferno blazed inside of her, pulling at her. In reflex, she tried to scream, but a large hand closed over her mouth, effectively muffling her. She tried to jerk away, but was unable to move. There was a vice around her middle, keeping her stationary.

Umberto, she thought, knowing she was close to panicking. Umberto was drinking from her, was killing her.

She beat her fists against his back, darted looks over his shoulder in search of someone, anyone to help her. But even as she took in the murky forms of men moving about behind the stage in the distance, she knew they wouldn't help. They were part of Forsaken's staff. They knew what Forsaken were and served them willingly.

The fire at her throat, the pain of it began to dull and transform into something thick and carnal. It pulled at her, lengthened until a searing shudder vibrated through her breasts, distending her nipples until they were hard and sensitive.

She sighed at the sudden pleasure.

Umberto rocked against her. He moved his hips in a sensual cadence, rubbing against her and moaning as he drank.

He drew on her and the pull deepened. Her chest tightened, her stomach tingled, and the flesh between her thighs began to perspire. She closed her eyes against the erotic onslaught, but couldn't escape it. Need, unlike anything she'd ever known, descended on her, blanking out everything but that delicious tug.

She sagged against him, too weak to fight and steadily becoming too aroused to want to fight.

"Yes," Umberto murmured, then lifted his head to look at her. "You like that, don't you?"

She blinked at him. There was no stain of blood on his teeth or lips, no visible sign of what he'd just done.

Out of breath and suddenly too fragile to stand for much longer, she braced her hands against the wall and tried to remain steady. If not for his arm around her waist, she probably would have slid to the floor. "What have you done to me?"

His arm flexed as he drew her away from the wall, leaving her no choice but to rest her weight against him. Umberto's eyes had always been mysterious, but just now, seeing them narrowed, blood red, and hazy with lust, she didn't have to wonder what he was thinking. And if she'd had a doubt, the hardening bulge flush against her stomach would have assured her. Umberto was as aroused as she was. His cock was swollen and throbbing.

He gazed into her eyes, licked his lips. "I've put my mark on you."

Onstage, Dario began the final phrase of his solo. The audience was cheering, but the sound was distant to Ambrosia, as though it were happening in another world. "You're out of time, Umberto. You have to get back onstage."

He lifted her effortlessly, cradling her in his arms. His smile was one the devil himself would have envied. "Bonus song. For the next five minutes, I've nothing but time one my hands."

She opened her mouth to reply, but found she couldn't muster the desire to protest. To her shame, she wanted to be alone with the vampire, longed for him to do things he'd only ever whispered of.

He carried her deeper into their shadowy nook and away from the eyes of security. Holding her in one arm, he pulled the heavy, black stage curtain around them, shutting out the rest of the world.

"I feel drunk, Umberto. What have you done to me?"

"Pheromones. We vampires secrete pleasure enhancing pheromones in our saliva. It helps our victims to be more ... accommodating during a feeding."

Had he just admitted what he was? "You've drugged me?"

"I have." His skin was warm; the chill of his body was gone now that he'd sated himself with her blood. His palms were hot against her bare back, searing a slow path up and down her spine wherever he touched. He slid his hand under her dress, cupped her buttock in his palm, and squeezed.

"I can't do this."

"But you will." He repositioned her, releasing her legs while crushing her breasts against his chest. "Wrap your legs around me."

She was moving to obey even as she fought to regain her common sense. Pheromones. They were the only reason why she was responding to him. If not for his trickery she would have been able to stave off the hunger that had assailed her when he'd taken her throat. She would have been able to control herself instead of encircling him in her thighs, panting for him to carry out all the perverse things he'd promised he'd do to on their long nights together. Perverse things she'd often fantasized about.

"That's it," he crooned into her ear. "I'm going to fuck you, right here, right now. What do you have to say about that?"

"I...." When he captured her mouth, she let her words trail off. The wet touch of his tongue was nearly too much for her. She opened for him, greedily welcomed his sleek heat into her. She tasted him, reveled in the thrill of feeling his lips on hers, his mouth swallowing down her moans.

His knuckles brushed against her ass as he fumbled with the fastening of his jeans, then all at once, he was there, hot and hard and ready. "From this night on, you belong to me."

She sucked in a breath, tightened her hold around his neck, and then allowed herself to be lowered inch by wonderful inch onto his cock. "Oh, Umberto."

She was gloriously stretched to her limits, deliciously filled as no man had ever filled her. In the distance she could hear the cheers of the audience, feel the rumble of bass, guitar, and drums, but it didn't touch her here in her secret hideaway with Umberto.

He set her back against the plywood wall, tucked one arm under her thigh, braced himself with his other hand on the wall then moved inside of her.

She whimpered, and then smiled when he pulled nearly out of her then thrust up. The breath came out of her in a rush. She barely had time to suck in air when he eased out, then thrust again. "Oh!"

"Feels good?"

"Yes."

"Sleeping with three-hundred-year-old vampires has its perks."

Her entire body was alive with sensation; her pussy was slick and tingly with the lush feeling of being so thoroughly filled. The vibrations radiated through her stomach, making her tremble. She threw her head back, lost herself to him.

Every thrust had her bare back rubbing roughly against the wooden wall, but the slight stinging wasn't unpleasant. Seemed every sensation added to her pleasure, every touch had her mindless for the consummation of this joining.

"Fuck, this is good," he murmured against her open mouth.

She clung to his arm with one hand while keeping pace with every frantic possession. She was nearing her breaking point, was steadily coming closer to her climax.

He pounded into her, drawing her release closer. When he spread his lips wide, let her see the flash of fangs, she knew what was coming, but was powerless to prevent it.

The moment his teeth broke flesh, the very instant he began to suckle from her, the dam within broke.

She came hard, bucking in his arms and crying out his name. Ecstasy washed over her in mounting waves as he continued to thrust and suck. She was dizzy with the thrill, heady with the sensation of complete submission.

When the pleasure began to dissipate and Umberto slowly pulled free of her, she felt herself slipping into an abyss. Darkness played at the edges of her consciousness. Umberto cradled her in his arms. He had lowered her dress discreetly and was carrying her back through the curtains. "What's happening?"

Umberto glanced over her shoulder and flicked his head in a "come here" gesture to someone in the distance. When he focused on her again, she knew he was about to return to the stage. It was just as well, she was suddenly tired; too tired to stay awake a minute more.

"You're mine now, Ambrosia," he said, then stepped back so a new set of arms could enfold her. "You're weak. You need sleep."

He was right. Though she fought to stay alert, fatigue was heavy on her. Her eyes seemed to close of their own will. "Release me." She'd meant the order to come out powerful and commanding, but the wispy voice coming from her was neither powerful nor commanding.

It was her first assignment, but already she'd failed the Talhari.

"When you wake, Ambrosia, I'll be there to welcome you to your new life."

Her last thought was of Kyle, the mission, and then all was dark.

## Chapter Three

She was alone.

Her first lucent thought was of waking in a small room, moonlight washing over gray, stone walls. She was in a bed, that much she knew, and someone had piled soft blankets on top her, as though instead of June, it was February. A large window dominated most of the wall to her left, but the view did nothing to enlighten her as to her whereabouts. All she could see was a bright, neon moon, and the swaying tops of trees. With a weak groan she let her eyelids drop and tried to remember how she'd gotten there.

Nothing. She couldn't remember a thing ... at first. Then, as if whispered into her ear, a name rose to her lips. "Umberto."

Opening her eyes slowly and half expecting him to appear in front of her, she shifted under the covers and tried to sit up. Her head swam with the effort. Her arms were too weak to hold her weight, her legs too shaky to risk standing on, and her head throbbed.

But she was still alone.

Exhausted by the small effort, she slumped back and closed her eyes again.

She woke suddenly--she didn't remember going to sleep--when something thudded dully against the wall. She would have jerked upright if not for the fatigue. As it was, all she was able to do was dart glances around the room.

Nothing. She was still alone.

How long had she slept? Before she'd fallen asleep the moon shone brilliantly through the window, filling the room with dim, natural light. Now the room was gloomy with shadows. What time was it? And where was she? More importantly, where was Umberto? Why had he let her live?

"Are you thirsty?"

She went for the blade she kept strapped on her thigh, but was brought up short by the heavy cuff sheathing her wrist and the chain running from the cuff to the sturdy steel headboard of the bed. She gave the chain a yank, expecting it to break easily. When nothing happened, panic surged through her. Despite how tired she was, a shot of adrenaline streamed through her veins, giving her strength.

She writhed on the bed, screamed out, and fought to free her arms.

"I wouldn't do that if I were you."

The voice was familiar, but not the one she'd been expecting. Though it took a force of will, she settled back into the cushions and focused her attention on the man who'd come into the room.

At first, all she could see was the glimmer of the flames rising from matching white, tapered candles. The speaker moved to one corner of the room and set a candle in a narrow recess, then repeated the process on the opposite wall.

The gloom dissolved. The soft orange and red glow from the flames lit the room enough for her to see her visitor. "Wolf?" She blinked, but his form remained.

"Ambrosia." His voice was deep, coarse, almost unnatural.

She opened her mouth to speak, and then shut it. What was Forsaken's head of security doing here?

He was six-feet-seven inches of pure muscle. Solidly built with smooth brown skin, a head as hairless as a baby's bottom, and a goatee, Wolf was enough of a deterrent to keep anyone under control. She'd always made a point of steering clear of him. Unfortunately, it looked as though this night she hadn't been given a choice in the matter. "Wolf," she said again.

He held up his hands, palms out. "No, don't try to move anymore. You've lost a lot of blood."

A memory flashed in her mind of being in Umberto's arms, of his lips on her throat, of the sting of pain and pleasure when he sank his fangs into her.

She got her elbows under her and began to rise, but Wolf pressed her gently back. "You can't go anywhere, even if you had the strength. You've been asleep for two days. I had to chain you to the bed last night ... for your own safety," he added.

She'd been asleep for forty-eight hours? But the raid! The mission! She couldn't have slept through it.

Another look at her wrists, at the wide iron cuffs fit around them had fear descending on her anew. "Let me go!"

"Let you go where? To do what? There's nothing for miles but forest, water and predators. You'd be dead before daylight."

"I'm willing to take that chance. It's better than whatever Umberto has planned for me." She stared levelly at him and enunciated her words carefully. "He's going to kill me."

"You think so, don't you? Ah well, leaving is not an option. You have to stay." He set one knee onto the mattress and bent over her, speaking as he rolled her onto her stomach. "You're marked now. The Talhari wouldn't take you back even if we dropped you off on the doorsteps of the Talhari Motherhouse in Paris."

"What do you know of the Talhari?"

"I know enough about that band of hypocrites. They're a secretive bunch, and they're bent on the destruction of vampires."

"You're wrong."

"There are Talhari scholars who do little more than research immortals," he went on to say. "Talhari hunters--which you strive to be, and Talhari scouts. The latter look for possible Talhari recruits."

His touch was surprisingly gentle, nevertheless, she squirmed. "Where am I?"

"Stay still."

His fingers were in her scalp, not really massaging it, but moving around as though searching for something.

The haze cleared and she realized what was happening.

Her CCU!

She'd managed to activate her CCU in time to say, *Help me, Kyle! Umberto* ... before Wolf located the CCU and pulled the external activator free. Her mind went blank and a film of black screened her eyes. She had to blink once, then twice, to clear the fog before her sight returned.

The absence of her CCU, the loss of it made her blood run cold. She wouldn't be able to communicate with the team. She was completely cut off from the others. Alone. And she was more terrified than she'd ever been in her life.

Wolf rolled her onto her back then stood. "That's better. We can't have you calling your old friends for help, can we? One look at you, one sniff, and they'd kill you as quickly as they'd try to kill the rest of us."

"What do you mean?"

"You're marked. You've got the scent of vampire all over you. Your CHI will scent it the moment he's within a hundred feet of you."

How did he know about her, about The Talhari Council? "You're lying. Where are Kyle and Nick?"

A door shut, soft footsteps sounded on the stone floor.

"I suppose Kyle is trying to figure out why his ambush failed."

"Umberto?" She asked, though she knew the Spanish cadence of his voice well. She also knew the feel of his body, the touch of his lips.

She shook her head to clear it. She would not think of what he'd done to her, what they had shared in those brief moments beside the stage when he had taken her in his arms and ... and what? And made love to her, was what she'd been thinking. How ridiculous was that? What happened with Umberto had been a mistake, a mistake she'd only allowed because he'd drugged her.

Umberto appeared beside the bed, eyes narrowed and brows drawn low on his forehead. He was wearing crisp black slacks and an expensive looking black silk shirt. He was beyond beautiful. His hair glimmered in the orange glow of the candlelight; his lips were so perfectly formed she had to squash an impulse to entreat him for a kiss. Dear God, how she wanted to kiss him. To smell the delicious aroma that permeated the air around him, so sweet and fragrant she could lose herself by simply smelling him.

The drug must still be affecting her. It was the only explanation she could find for her continued attraction to the bloodsucker. She didn't care if forty-eight hours had passed since he'd suckled at her throat, apparently the pheromone in his saliva was very strong.

He edged closer to the bed and smiled at her. "How are you feeling, Ambrosia?"

"Kill me or release me. I will not be chained like an animal."

"You're chained for you own safety. Didn't Wolf tell you? You had a high fever yesterday, it made you ... restless."

"I repeat, kill me or release me."

He didn't move. For long minutes he was silent. Then, tucking his fingers into the front pockets of his pants, Umberto shook his head. "I won't kill you and I'm not releasing you."

"But why? What's the...?" Then, all at once she knew. She could kick herself for not figuring it out sooner. Even with her blood loss she should have known what was going on as soon as she woke. "I'm a hostage, aren't I? You mean to lure my associates to you."

His smile was chilly. It made him look every bit of the vampire he was. Gone was the twenty-one-year-old noble's son, in his place was a seasoned killer of the innocent. "There's no need to protect Kyle and Nick. I know who they are. I've known for some time. Even before your arrival on the scene."

"And all that talk of love and enchantment. Was that part of your game?"

"Was it part of yours?"

Sighing, she gave her cuffs one last, ineffective tug, then turned away and stared at the wall. "They won't come, you know."

He made an odd, grunting noise that had her rolling toward him so she could have a look at his face again. It was probably a bad idea to turn her back on him anyway, after the way he'd sneakily attacked her at the show. "You're wasting your time, Umberto."

"I don't think so." He shifted to the right, looked to Wolf, who was standing at the window, gazing out onto the night.

From where he was standing, Ambrosia knew Wolf couldn't see Umberto. Still, Forsaken's head of security swiveled. "Yes?"

"Are you sure she was asleep while you brought her here? She has no idea where we are?"

"Affirmative. And even if she was awake before I entered this room and in communication with Kyle, she wouldn't have been able to give the CHI a location."

"Is there any way to know for sure if she's spoken with the Talhari at all?"

"Negative. But I know the CHI doesn't have unlimited access to his team. Someone has to initiate a conversation. That's how the CCU works; otherwise there'd be constant chatter through the lines. If Ambrosia was asleep, as I know she was for most of the time, there's no way she would have been able to contact the CHI. He would have to contact her."

How did Wolf know so much about CCU's? What he was saying was accurate, and it made her wonder why Kyle hadn't tried to get in contact with her. Then again, maybe he had and she'd been unconscious and unable to respond. And she hadn't been awake long, before Wolf had confiscated her unit. He'd taken it before she'd had a chance to get her wits about her. But he hadn't taken it while she'd been asleep. If he'd done that, chances were good that she never would have awakened. She would have slipped into a coma. Doubtless he'd known. What she couldn't figure out was why Wolf or Umberto cared whether she lived or died.

Rage roiled inside of her. It was all she could do not to scream in frustration. This was her first assignment and she'd made a mess of it. She'd let herself be seduced by a bloodsucker, captured, and imprisoned. It was too great a humiliation. And the fatigue, the weakness ... it stopped right here and now. She was a Talhari and she would behave accordingly. "If you think I'm going to lead my company into an ambush, you're wrong."

Umberto refocused on her. "You wound me."

"They won't risk themselves for one agent. It's not worth it."

He lowered himself until he was seated on the edge of the bed, not quite touching her but close enough for her to feel the chill rising from his body. Regardless of the coldness radiating off of him, a brief shiver of anticipation lighted through her at his closeness. She wondered if he was going to bend over her, kiss her. Touch her nipples as he'd done before and tease them until they were hard little pebbles, sensitive to his every stroke.

Instead of touching her, though, he rested a hand, palm down, on the pile of comforters and studied her face. "Do you want to know what I say, Ambrosia?"

Despite her mounting desire, she released an unladylike snort and shrugged.

"I say," he continued, clasping her chin and tugging gently until she had no choice but to stare into his eyes, "you're absolutely worth it." Still gazing at her, he added, "Wolf, I think Ambrosia and I would like to be alone for a while."

"We don't want to keep our guests waiting for too long."

"We'll be down shortly."

## Chapter Four

"Are you comfortable?" he asked as soon as Wolf shut the door behind himself.

For good or bad, she thought, they were alone now. Though Umberto wasn't as large as Wolf, she had no doubt facing off with him would be far more dangerous. Especially if he drugged her again, made her into that spineless trollop she had been back at the show.

He still held her chin so she pulled free of him and glared. She shook her arms, setting her chains to jangling. "I'd be more comfortable without the bracelets. Think you could give me a hand with them?"

"Would you like me to unbind you?"

"What do you think?"

"Looks like you're feeling better. You've got that sparkle in your eyes."

Actually, she was feeling better. She wasn't sure when it had happened, but the throbbing in her head had receded and strength was returning to her limbs. "Release me."

"I didn't take a lot of blood." He leaned over her, fiddled with the chains. One arm fell free of the cuff. The next followed shortly after. But before she could draw her arms to herself to massage her wrists, Umberto began rubbing the raw flesh with the tips of his fingers. "Does that feel good?"

It did, but she wouldn't be lulled into a false sense of calm a second time. She had to get out of the house, into the forest ... and she needed her CCU. Wolf had taken it with him when he'd left the room. She needed to get her strength back. Wolf was right. As weak as she was now, she wouldn't last outside for long. She felt stronger than she had upon waking, but she was nowhere near as strong as she needed to be. "So you know what I am, now what?" she asked. "Why did you bring me here?"

"Despite what you might think, you're not a Talhari, Ambrosia. You never were. And now, you never will be."

She shook her head, denying his statement. "What do you know about it?"

"Do you know what a psychic embed is?"

"Of course I do."

He lifted a brow. "Do you now? Why don't you enlighten me then?"

"If I tell you, will you release me?"

He threw his head back and laughed. "Absolutely not. This conversation isn't for my benefit."

"Ah, so it's for me. Nice try, but too bad. I'm not releasing classified information to you."

"All right then, I'll tell you. But before the embeds, let's deal with your enhanced physiology first. You've got Intel S--smart steel--built into your skeleton. The Talhari stole the design from the military, so it's been created with technology the average person won't know exists for at least ten years. They've also manipulated it, added to it. Talhari Intel S makes you stronger and faster than any un-enhanced human. I've seen Talhari who could leap onto five-story buildings, fell a tree with his bare hands, and never break a sweat." He paused to study her face. "You're still with me?"

Irritated that he'd been right, she didn't respond.

"In addition to your enhancements, it's pretty damn hard to kill you. Because your job is to dispatch pesky blood drinkers, your immune system has been given a bit of a boost, just in case a vampire manages to overpower you and suck your precious blood. You heal faster than a normal human, you never get sick, and for every ten years, you age one. Essentially, you're a living, breathing superhuman."

"So you've done a bit of research. Big deal."

"Let's talk about you then. You spent your last three years training under Gaia Knight. You received your CCU one year ago, your enhancements nine months ago—which is why you haven't mastered your new strength yet, and you weren't scheduled to get your embeds until you proved yourself worthy on this mission."

She stared at him, open-mouthed. Her fist clenched at this violation of her private life and rage roared to the surface. "You've been studying me?"

"I know that you grew up an orphan. You spent the first sixteen years of your life in various foster homes. You tried your hand at college for a while, but it wasn't a good fit. During your second year of college you met Alma, the female recruiter for the Talhari that services the New England area. She spent the next year and a half wooing you, slowly initiating you into the order. At twenty, you faked your death so you could join the Talhari Council as an apprentice. Am I right so far? On second thought, don't answer. I know I'm right."

"You pried into my life."

He laughed again. "Are you saying you haven't pried into my life, and Dario, Mathias, and Erik's?"

Ignoring this, she jumped to the central point. "So essentially you're telling me that the vampires have files on the Talhari?"

"The Talhari kill our kind. Why shouldn't we know our enemy?" He leaned forward, pressing her arms into the mattress as he moved. "Did you think you could waltz in and kill us without a fight?"

His hold was strong, too strong to resist, so she remained still, eyes fixed to his face.

"I'm an old man, Ambrosia. You don't get to be as old as me without acquiring a few survival skills over the years."

"And my embeds?"

"Talhari embeds are the crux of the matter. Embeds are the supposed implants that make it possible for you to read the mind of weak vampires."

Right again, she thought, growing more annoyed by the minute.

"But that's a lie. The Talhari embeds are nothing more than a genetic alteration. You'd go from superhuman to barely human at all."

"That's a lie."

"It's not. But you don't have to believe me. I'm going to show you the truth tonight."

She tried to look passive, hoping he'd see her wide eyes and trembling lips as a sign of capitulation.

Chances were good that she'd never get a perfect opportunity to escape. As far as she was concerned, she either acted now or remained imprisoned and at Umberto's mercy. "You're not going to let me go, are you?"

He stared at her for a beat, and then his fingers were light on her again, stroking the insides of her arms and sending lovely little frissons over her skin despite her anger. "No. I'm not."

"I'm not a hostage, am I? Not really a prisoner either."

She felt the edge of his knuckle on her cheek, shivered when he brushed it over her skin. "No, you're not."

"You plan to keep me here and make me into…." She kicked her legs up and wrapped them around his throat, then pulled back so he tumbled backward and off the bed. The movement had been fast, one that was only possible using her enhanced speed. As she'd hoped, she had caught him off guard.

Before he landed on the floor she was on her feet and charging, full speed, at the window that made up most of the far wall. She couldn't pause to think about it, couldn't stop to see if Umberto was getting to his feet. He was faster and stronger; her only hope of escape was what little time surprise had brought her.

She ran for the window, twisting at the last moment so she hit the glass with her shoulder.

Though she feared the panes of glass would resist her, her fear proved unwarranted. The glass shattered under the force of her blow and a moment later she was freefalling toward the ground. The fall lasted mere seconds, a fact she was grateful for. She hadn't known how high up she was, or even if escape would be possible, but capture was not an option. Her only choice was to risk everything or die trying.

She hit the ground with a soft, *oomph*, and then rolled head over heels. In an instant she was on her feet again and running toward the distant forest.

Behind her, she heard the unmistakable sound of impact as another body hit the ground. Then, there was the sound of rapid footsteps coming toward her.

Umberto had recovered and was giving chase.

She pumped her legs over the grassy field, wishing she felt stronger. Trying to outrun a bloodsucker on her best day would have been a challenge, this day, when she was weak from blood loss, she doubted she'd get very far before Umberto caught her.

Was he closer?

A band of clouds shifted in the sky, blotting out the light of the moon and casting the night in nearly impenetrable darkness. She could see the outline of trees ahead, smell the moist earth, and sense the presence behind her that was quickly closing in.

If she could make it to the forest and reach the sheltering of the trees there was a chance she could hide from him. All she had to do was a find a secret spot and wait until daylight. Once sunrise came, Umberto would have no choice but to return to the house and retreat until nightfall. By then, she'd be long gone.

But even as she had that thought a solid wall of flesh slammed into her and dragged her to the ground. She landed hard on her stomach. Umberto fell on top of her, knocking the wind out of her.

Without missing a beat, she twisted to her left and made to roll away, but he snaked an arm around her waist and pulled her tight against his chest. "Are you mad?" he demanded.

She kicked, tried to claw at him. She knew now that they'd

relieved her of all of her weapons. She had no choice but to use her hands.

"You can't escape," he said, then grunted when she landed a knee in his bread basket. "All right, that does it." With a strength that easily overmatched hers, he tossed her onto her back and straddled her hips. He caught her hands, stretched over her, and forced them to the ground above her head.

She bucked her hips, tried to twist. "Let me go!"

"Not on your life."

Though he tightened his hold on her arms, he made no move to retaliate. Hell, he didn't have to. She wasn't at her best and he knew it. She knew this, tried to school herself to stop fighting a battle she couldn't win, but her legs seemed to kick of their own will. For long minutes she tried to break his hold, tried to buck him off, but couldn't. With every thrust fatigue edged closer, every twist brought her nearer to exhaustion.

Easily holding her arms to the ground, he smirked. "You're strong, I'll give you that, but you're no match for me. Give it up."

Shit. Her strength was quickly waning. She gave one more thrust, then collapsed on the grass, gasping for breath. "Bastard!"

"I am at that," he agreed, smiling. Clearly he was pleased with himself. "So are you going to go back with me willingly or do I have to sit here and wait you out?"

"I'm not going anywhere with you."

He studied her, seemed to consider his options, then, unexpectedly, he rocked his crotch against her, deliberately grinding against her clit so hard that a surprised gasp of pleasure exploded out of her.

"Are you sure about that, Ambrosia?" He moved against her again, making her dizzy with unexpected desire. "My taking you has nothing to do with Talhari or vampires." He thrust slowly. Delicious sensations washed over her like warm honey. Need, surrender, ecstasy, all combined to conspire against her. "This is about you and me. Period."

His cock hardened as he continued, and he stroked her until she was panting for more.

Despite her craving to give in to him, she spoke through clenched teeth. "You can't keep me here indefinitely."

"*Au contraire*, I can do whatever I want to do. This is my home and there's no one for miles, save you, me, Forsaken, and our guards."

"I'll escape eventually."

"And you're doing such a good job at escaping now."

She was sprawled on her back. His chest was scant inches above her face and his hair was brushing softly against her bare forearms. Despite the fact that this beast had tricked her, had kidnapped her, desire swept over her. The sultry effect of it had her biting her lip even as she swallowed a sigh of longing. She wanted to embrace him, wanted to touch his luscious lips with her own and taste him.

What was happening to her? Could his pheromones really still be affecting her? Then all at once, he was there. His lips were on her lips, his fingers entwined in hers. She tilted her head back and opened her mouth for him, welcomed his kiss with an eagerness that belied her anger, moaned deep in the back of her throat when he slid his tongue between her lips.

"Umberto," she murmured, as he moved over her, covering her with his body.

His kiss was a slow tasting. Not enough to sate, but just enough to tease. His tongue dipped inside, swirled, feasted. He squeezed her fingers between his, rocked his pelvis against her until she was in a fever for him. "But you haven't drank in two days," she whispered.

"I know. I can't make love to you the way I want to until I drink again."

Then he was kissing her again, sucking in her air and exhaling into her mouth with every taste. She was heady with the sensation of having him breathe for her. When he released her mouth she nearly cried out in protest, but he didn't go far. He nibbled on her chin, made a wet trail over her throat before sucking on her collar bone.

"I want to taste you again, sweet Ambrosia." He licked her skin, and then set delicate kisses on her collar bone. "Will you let me?"

All was sensation. There was the lush touch of his lips, the wet feel of his tongue, and his hands moving all over her body, tugging at her zipper and dragging her dress down. But there remained a tiny voice inside her head, schooling her against going any further with him. "No," she panted. "I can't let you."

"Let me drink, so I can make love to you."

There was a part of her, a secret part that didn't want him to ask for her permission. It wanted Umberto to take what he wanted, to hold her down, set teeth to flesh, and drink until he'd had his fill. She'd lose herself in the new sensation of being overwhelmed and overpowered by a force stronger than her. She wouldn't fight him when he impaled her, but surrender to him more completely than she'd ever surrendered to anyone. But even as she had the thought, Umberto left her throat. He peeled the latex over her breasts then

## WICKED DELIGHTS

sucked one pert nipple into his mouth.

She cried out in surprised delight. Umberto groaned his pleasure. His lips were demanding, his tongue merciless as he licked, sucked, and stroked her until she was feverish with erotic need.

"You like that," he said, moving to torment the other nipple.

She rocked against him, struggled against the tightening in her stomach. She was building to her peak and he hadn't even gotten her clothes off yet.

Gliding lower, he tugged on her dress, pulled it over her hips and down to her ankles. Instantly, the wet grass had her shivering. The tiny stalks were soft as moss, but cold and damp with rain. "Umberto--" she began, but never finished.

He fell on her again, spreading her thighs with his hands and laying full length between her legs. When his lips brushed against her vaginal lips, she whimpered.

"I can't make love to you the way I want to," he murmured, "so this will have to do for now."

She should stop him, demand he release her. But all thoughts of denying him anything evaporated when he hiked her hips into the air and buried his face in her sex.

Her back arched in surprise and she cried out a second time. Then his tongue was on her, feasting as though she were a delectable treat. He slid his tongue deep inside of her. The pleasure was nearly too intense for her to hold onto any shreds of control.

She was edging closer to her peak, nearing delicious release.

When he closed his mouth over her clit and began licking, the last remnants of control shattered. She gasped for breath, screamed for mercy. Without thinking about what she was doing she tangled her fingers in his hair, drawing him deeper into her dripping cunt. She wanted to climax, needed to climax with a desperation that was foreign to her.

He sucked her nub and flicked it with his tongue. Then, at last, release flashed bright white behind her closed eyes. She bucked under the force of it, twisted uncontrollably, and cried his name, not knowing whether it was in praise or if it was a request for mercy.

No man had ever made her feel so good.

She opened her eyes, stared at the cloudy sky above, panting.

Umberto reared up on his hands and knees and swiped the back of his forearm over his glistening lips. She caught a brief flash of white when he smiled down at her, saw the edge of his fangs when he began crawling up her length. His eyes had gone blood red and they were hazy with lust. His entire focus was fixed to her throat. Even as he neared it his tongue slid over his lower lip. Then, just as suddenly as he'd begun moving toward her throat, he stopped and looked over his shoulder. "Someone's coming."

She was so caught up that she almost didn't hear what he'd said. Lust was heavy on her and it nearly blocked out everything else. She had to fight her way up from the heady mist of desire, fight to regain her common sense. It was a battle she didn't think she'd win. Even though she knew he was telling her something important, she couldn't stop herself from tangling her fingers in his hair and dragging his mouth down to hers.

For a moment he fought, then his muscles relaxed and he allowed himself to be drawn down.

When their lips met this time, she nearly swooned at the pleasure. His taste was hot and slick, like peppermint and ice cream. She gloried in his flavor even as she fought to regain her equilibrium.

There was a tiny prick of pain on her lips, and then Umberto was sucking on her again, feeding on her.

"Umberto!"

He froze.

"Umberto!" the voice called again.

With a heavy groan, he pulled away. "Something is wrong. We have to go back."

She gazed at night sky, tried to shake her head to clear it.

"Can you stand, Ambrosia?"

"Stand? Go back where?"

"Back to the house. I think Nick is awake."

Nick's name was like a splash of ice water. She slapped the proffered hand Umberto offered away and snatched at her dress. "Nick? He's here?" she demanded as she squirmed into the tight latex.

Umberto got to his feet, pulling her with him despite her protests. "He is. We caught him and four others at the Talhari raid two nights ago."

"And you're just telling me now?" She'd been lying with a vampire, enjoying his touch while he held her friends captive.

"Umberto!" Wolf came to a sliding halt beside Umberto. "They've escaped."

Umberto swung around. "What? How is that possible?"

"I don't know. But we have to track them before it's too late. We can't let them escape. Our location will be blown."

"This isn't good." Umberto clasped her hand and started forward at a run.

## Chapter Five

She ran down a narrow stone stairwell behind Umberto with Wolf moving briskly behind her. The corridor was so constricted that she doubted she could raise both arms and hold them out without her knuckles smacking into stone. The walls were damp with moisture, seemed to perspire in the sweltering June heat.

A series of dim lights were hung along the ceiling, casting low light around them. It was just enough for her to see the steps and the way they spiraled down, deep into the earth.

"What have you done to Nick?" she asked for the third time, and was unanimously ignored for the third time.

In truth, she didn't know how wise it was for her to be descending an unknown stairway with a known vampire and that vampire's body guard. If the Talhari knew what she was doing right now they'd question her sanity. Still, over the years she'd learned to trust her instincts. When you grow up moving from foster home to foster home you learn to read people. Pick up on their vibes, good or bad. Usually she could tell when someone was out to hurt her. Usually she knew when to back off. She wasn't getting any negative vibes from Umberto or Wolf. Fact was, she'd never felt like she was in any danger when she was around Umberto. That's probably why she'd stupidly let her guard down at the arena. Still, if he'd meant to kill her, he would have done it by now. She'd given him countless opportunities tonight alone.

At long last they reached the bottom of the stairs. The first thing she noticed was that it wasn't much brighter down there than it had been on the way down.

A warm large hand prodded her to the left. "This way, Ambrosia."

She glanced over her shoulder at Wolf who was motioning her toward the left hallway where Umberto had gone. She spied low light at the end of the hall, but beyond that she couldn't see anything. "Is Nick in there?"

Wolf shook his head. "He was in there."

She walked quickly, keeping her eyes and ears open for anything amiss. Though she didn't think she was walking into an ambush, she was poised for battle. The moment she entered the room, though, she came to an abrupt halt. Erik, Mathias, and Dario were there. And they didn't look happy.

The room was alight in candlelight, making Ambrosia wonder what these guys had against electricity. Was artificial light too strong for their vampire eyes?

The room was long, maybe a hundred or so feet, with small chambers set to the left and right at twenty foot intervals. Erik, Dario, and Mathias were standing in a loose semicircle in front of the third chamber on the left.

She twisted around until she could see Wolf. "Was he in there?"

Wolf nodded.

The hand that closed around her bicep made her jump. In reflex she went for her blade, and then remembered it was gone. Confiscated.

"Ambrosia," Umberto said, tightening his grip on her arm and pulling her toward him. "I want you to stay close to me."

The knowledge that Nick and four others had been imprisoned within these walls had cooled her lust as effectively as a bucket of cold water. She would have shrugged Umberto's hand off and pushed past him had the other three not been standing at the mouth of the room, watching her.

Mathias, the tallest of the four, sneered. The sharpened points of his fangs protruded dangerously over his lower lip. Despite his spiky, white hair and the army green cargo pants he was wearing, he looked deadly. His jetty eyes were fixed on her face and he didn't seem altogether pleased with what he saw. "I don't think this is a good idea, Umberto. The minute she gets a chance she'll do whatever she can to help them."

Dario, tapping one raven nail against the wall and holding a large black bag in his other hand, nodded. "I understand she's aroused certain feelings in you, but I don't think it's appropriate for her to be here, either. We need to figure out which way they went, find them, and put them down. We're not here to babysit a Talhari trainee."

"It's like I said," Mathias continued. "We should have put them down as soon as we got here instead of waiting around for her to wake up."

"I want Ambrosia to see with her own eyes what the Talhari really are." Umberto studied the room.

"What do you say, Erik?" Dario asked.

Erik's perfectly formed elfin features were fixed in a disinterested frown. His brown suede pants and loose, beige shirt gave him an earthy beauty tonight. "What could she possibly do? She doesn't have her embeds yet, she's practically human. And the others are gone. I don't see why we're standing around chatting."

Practically? "I am human."

"See what I mean? She has no idea what's going on. She's helpless as a baby."

Mathias mumbled something under his breath, and then said, "She has her enhancements, so don't underestimate her."

As if Mathias had just reminded Umberto that she wasn't completely helpless, he tightened his hold on her arm.

Wolf crossed to Dario and took the black bag, speaking in his rumbling baritone as he moved. "She broke through the tower window and jumped out. Could have been around the time the others escaped." He took what she'd thought were four automatic handguns from the bag and began passing them out to the others.

Erik took his gun, and then regarded her with new interest. "Is that right, Ambrosia? But I thought you were with her, Umberto."

"He was."

"Had to chase her down, did you? Is that why you've got bits of grass in your hair? Put up a fight, did she?" He chuckled to himself and looked away. "Or did you spend some time rolling around in the grass together?"

Ambrosia knew her face would have gone crimson if not for her brown skin. How on earth could she have been intimate with the same vamp who'd kidnapped her in the first place? It was downright stupid.

"She caught me by surprise when she jumped out the window." Umberto studied his gun, nodding to himself as he checked the cylinder, sighted, then tucked the gun away into his waistband.

Mathias stalked toward them, no more amused than he'd been before. She thought he would have advanced until he was chest to face with her if Umberto hadn't been standing beside her. As it was, he'd only left a scant five inches between them. He leered down at her. "Fine, bring her along on the hunt. But if you try anything, sweetheart, I'll vaporize you myself."

That just did it. She was tired of being spoken of as though she were a baby, and she was long past tired of not knowing what was going on. She grasped Mathias by his shirt and shoved. "Try it."

He fell back a few steps, but to her annoyance, remained standing. Damn bloodsuckers were a lot stronger than they looked.

When he seemed on the verge of approaching her again, Umberto edged in front of her. "She never got her embeds. You know that, Mathias."

"Did you check?"

"I've tasted her blood, you ass. It's pure. And Wolf has her CCU."

Mathias continued to leer, then took a grudging step back. "Okay, she's safe."

Erik shoved the chamber door open with a booted foot. "I'm going to start searching the rooms. They couldn't have gotten far."

"They have to be somewhere inside." Wolf turned and started for the stairs. "The lycan would have alerted me if anyone had tried to make if off the property. I'm going out to monitor the grounds."

Ambrosia's mouth fell open. "Lycan?"

Again, she was ignored.

"Fifteen minutes," Umberto announced to the room. "I'm going up to search the main floor. Dario, you do the second floor. Then we meet in the courtyard." Still holding onto her arm, Umberto gave it a squeeze. "Trust me when I tell you that your *friends* are more dangerous than you think."

"Bullshit." She tried to pull free, but he held her firm.

"You're staying with me, Ambrosia. It's either that or I take you back to your room in the tower and chain you to the bed. And you know you won't break free. Those chains were designed with Talhari in mind. Your choice."

She hated this. She hated being at the mercy of others, but if her team was in this house she had to help them if she could. If she got chained to the bed she'd be useless.

Mathias moved past her to the far side of the room and began searching the small chambers along the opposite wall.

Dario started for the stairs and she was ready to follow, but Umberto held her back. "After this, I'll explain everything to you."

"I'm counting on that." She let Umberto lead the way out of the room and toward the stairs, allowed him to transfer his hold from her arm to her hand and mount the stairs in front of her. "What do you plan on doing if you find them?"

He didn't answer.

They reached the main floor, but she didn't get a chance to get her bearings. She caught a glimpse of expensive carpets in hues of beige, maroon, and forest green. All around her was decorated with a touch for the dramatic. Antique furniture, paneled walls, and an overall feel of wealth and privilege. As they moved, Umberto searched the rooms, moving with a preternatural speed she was hard pressed to match. She had a sense he wasn't going as fast as he could, that he'd slowed himself considerably in consideration of her. Maybe if she stumbled she could further slow him. Could helping Nick and the others escape be that easy?

After they'd made a full circuit of the first floor, searching the parlor, living room, dining hall, kitchen, and library, Umberto came to a halt at the main entrance. His eyes were darting in every direction, but he made no move.

She spied the wide doorway leading out to the yard, turned slowly with him so instead of facing the front door they were looking at the curved stairways to the second floor. On the second floor an ornate black and gold railing formed a fancy balcony from which a person could stand and survey the foyer below. The balcony floor was piled with fancy carpets, but was barren of furniture. Beyond the balcony, a hall led deep into the body of the house.

"What's wrong?" she asked.

"Hush."

"What do you hear?"

"I'm not sure." He squeezed her hand. "It sounds like--"

Then she heard it too, the low growl of a dog. A very large dog. "What is it?"

His face was grim. "Your Talhari friends."

She eyed him. "Don't be stupid. That's a dog of some sort, or a ... I don't know what, but whatever it is, it's not human."

"My point exactly." His grip on her hand tightened, and he tugged her close until she was standing shoulder to arm with him. "I think I made a mistake insisting that you see them for what they are. I want you to go out back to the wine cellar. Go to the back of the house, just beyond the deck and you'll see the entrance to the cellar. I want you to go there and wait for me there. There's no internal access to it and I doubt the Talhari ventured outside yet, so they shouldn't know of its existence. You should be safe in the cellar."

His gaze was steady, so she knew he was serious, but she wasn't about to do what he said. "If you think I'm leaving you and your fellow bloodsuckers to kill my colleagues, you've got another thing coming."

The growls were louder now, the source closer.

"Don't argue with me. Just go! What's coming down that hall is not your friend."

She was opening her mouth to refuse again when Dario appeared in the second-floor hall. He was running full out and didn't pause at the balcony. He bounded over the railing and landed in the foyer ten feet from them and ran for the front door. "Found three upstairs," he shouted as he went. "They're coming." He swung the door open, leaned out, and howled, "Wolf!"

Umberto pulled the pistol from his waistband. "Where were they?"

"Behind me," Dario said, moving to Umberto's side, holding his own gun in hand. "She shouldn't be here. They're third stage."

The snarls were coming closer, as the sound drew nearer the noise of heavy footfalls echoed through the entrance hall. She knew from the noise that whatever was coming, there was more than one of them. But what were they? Despite what Umberto and Dario were implying, she knew the approaching creatures weren't Talhari. Whatever was coming was bigger than a human and far more deadly.

"Make her go," Dario was saying. "You know these guns won't do anything but slow them down now that they're third stage, and you can't fight and hang on to her at the same time."

Umberto released her and clenched his hand into a loose fist. When he spread his fingers again she saw his nails had lengthened to fine points. She stared at his fingers, at his hands, but made no move to run. For years she'd been told about the vampire metamorphosis but she'd never seen it with her own eyes. The most she'd ever seen were fangs, red eyes. As she watched, his fangs extended, sharpening until the tips were honed to deadly points. His honey-colored eyes were changing too, deepening until all remnants of brown were gone, replaced by the blood red hue of a vampire's eyes. The transformation she was witnessing should have repulsed her. She shouldn't have seen Umberto the man anymore, but the undead thing that had taken over Umberto's body. Problem was she didn't see a *thing* when she looked at Umberto, even now. He was still Umberto; the lure of him was still too strong for her to want to walk away from him.

"They won't go after her," Dario was saying, "not when they have us to deal with." His voice had changed, had grown deeper. She knew he was changing too, was allowing the vampire to take the reins.

"I'm not leaving," she said, forcing herself to turn from Umberto and focus on the balcony.

The balcony shook with the force of heavy footfalls. Because the growls were louder, she figured the source was likely to appear at any second.

"You don't have a choice, Ambrosia."

She was rounding on Dario, prepared to tell him to back off when the front door crashed in. Wolf leapt into the entrance hall, snatching at his clothes as he moved. He ripped his coat to shreds, tore his shirt down the middle. His muscles rippled with every movement, flexing and contracting, bunching and expanding. He was changing, transforming before her eyes, but not like Umberto and Dario. His nose spread, split, lengthened even as his mouth took on the shape of a muzzle. His eyes darkened until they were as black as a moonless night. Hair sprouted out along his naked back and chest, covering him with tufts of thick black fur.

She took a step toward Dario while reaching for her blade. Her missing blade. "Shit."

"He's a lycan. You've nothing to be afraid--" Umberto began to say, but at that moment, three figures appeared at the top of the balcony.

Ambrosia heard herself whimper, felt her heart turn to ice as she stood, staring. She recognized the three, recognized them, but had never seen them before in her life. "Eddie, Pendleton, Dalton," she whispered.

"Get her out of here," Dario said.

On the balcony, the three figures leered. She could make out the glossy black and green uniforms they'd been wearing, knew it well because it was one she'd get to wear after the successful completion of this assignment when she got her embeds. But where her uniform would fit nice and snug, the three on the balcony had rent the stretchy fabric to ribbons. Muscles had burst through seams, exposing the furry, inhuman skin below. Hair was long and straggly, so unlike the close shorn hair of the men she knew. It was like that had devolved somehow, had reverted to a primitive form of man; Neanderthal meets australopithecine. Their arms were longer, their backs slightly bowed, but the gleam of intelligence in their eyes was unmistakable. She thought despite the simian appearance of the three, their intelligence was entirely human.

Umberto shoved her toward the front door. "Go to the cellar. Hide. I'll find you."

She took a step back, thought about staying. She was a Talhari ... at least she had thought she was. She hadn't been trained for this. Her training had centered on vampires, not lycan and definitely not on whatever the hell was on the balcony.

"Go!"

Gaia Knight had taught her that when the odds were clearly in the opponent's favor, there was no shame in retreating to reassess your strategy.

The figures leapt over the balcony railing, landed on the foyer, and loped forward.

She ran. Ran out the open front door, down the front steps, then skidded to a stop.

There were dozens of them. Dozens of beasts closing in on the house. But they weren't like what she'd seen on the balcony. These creatures were lycan, like Wolf. Wolf had never wanted to hurt her, chances were the beasts rapidly closing in on the house wouldn't either ... unless they knew she was a Talhari.

*Run. Hide. Escape.*

She leapt off the stairs and ran around the side of the house, hoping against hope they wouldn't follow. But even as she moved she realized there might be more of them in the back. Even if she didn't see them right away that didn't mean they weren't there, watching from the forest. Wolf had said they were guarding the grounds, so they could be anywhere.

Lycan.

Gaia never said anything about lycan.

She reached the back deck at a run, had to force herself to slow down and search for the cellar entrance. Umberto had said it was just beyond the porch.

Looking over her shoulder, expecting attack at any second, she moved beyond the deck. So far she was alone. No one had come after her. So she searched. The seconds seemed to tick by like minutes--every one of them an agony. She didn't want to think about lycan, and she especially didn't want to think about what she had seen in the house. Talhari, but not Talhari. There had to be a logical explanation.

Then she saw it. She wanted to howl in triumph. "Get a grip, Ambrosia," she told herself. "It's just a wine cellar."

And it was ... just a wine cellar. From the outside it looked old fashioned. The kind of cellar whose doors had been built into the ground. One look at the thing, shadowed by a large weeping willow, and she had an urge to turn around and run. But run where?

"Shit. Get a grip girl and stop acting like a coward." She'd been to worse places in her life, after all, and had never batted a lash. Going unpleasant places and meeting unpleasant people was the nature of her work. She'd gotten accustomed to that a long time ago. At least she thought she had. Then she'd come face to face with a werewolf and seen her colleagues turned into Tolkien creatures of the night.

"Only a wine cellar," she said in a whisper.

But every time she looked at it she got a flash in her mind of the movie adaptation to Stephen King's "Salem's Lot". She could see the vampire, garbed in black, and looming in the shadows, waiting.

Waiting. The damn cellar was creepy. Why in the hell did Umberto tell her to wait there of all places? But it was just a cellar. No Stephen King monsters there, otherwise Umberto wouldn't have told her to wait for him there.

But could she trust Umberto? Could she trust anyone?

Huffing a breath, she started forward.

The grass around the cellar door was pretty much non-existent, which wasn't odd since the spot would rarely receive any sunlight during the day. She bent and pulled the cellar doors open. They moved easily on their hinges. Immediately she was greeted with the stench of mold and rot. This surprised her. She was entering the wine cellar of one of the richest vampires in ... where the hell was she? Virginia? New York? Was she even in the States anymore?

She gritted her teeth and swallowed the lump in her throat. Either she went down or returned to the foyer. Since wild horses couldn't have dragged her back to the foyer, she figured she might as well get this whole cellar thing over with.

What was the big deal, anyway? Before long Umberto would be there.

Steeling herself, she stepped down into the cool darkness. She was enveloped by it at once and again had to staunch an urge to turn tail and run. She kept her hands braced on either side of the wall as she descended, feeling for a light switch, all the while knowing she wouldn't find one until she reached the bottom, and maybe not even then. So far the only light sources she'd seen had come from candles. Odds were the same would hold true for the cellar. And she didn't have matches or a lighter, or anything with which to start a fire. Fortunately there was just enough light coming in from the moon above to light the stairway. She wasn't going in blind.

She wasn't in the habit of descending into strange dark places if she had a choice.

At the bottom, she found a pull cord and gave the line a tug. Immediately, the cellar was awash in light. "Thank God."

Unfortunately, the cellar didn't look any better in the light than it had in the dark. Much as she expected from the foul odor saturating the air around her, the cellar was in severe disrepair. From the look of the place, nobody had done much restoration here. Unlike the immaculate living space upstairs, the wine cellar was in dire need of renovation. The floor was covered by a heavy powdering of dust and grime. It was so thick she could make out the tracks of foot traffic in the dirt. Every counter top and every window was covered in filth. Around the floor she saw bits of rat droppings. Cobwebs and spider webs were the rule not the acceptance. Save the center aisle between the wine racks and the wine racks themselves, everything in the cellar suffered horribly from neglect.

She stepped back onto the bottom step, climbed up, and pulled the cellar doors gently shut.

"Damn it," she whispered, trying to gain courage from the sound of her own voice. She was terrified. Despite her years of training, she was so scared she couldn't think straight. And she'd thought she knew enough to be CHI. What a load of crap that had been.

Carefully she stepped onto the cellar floor and made her way toward the center aisle, taking great pain not to make any noise. As she moved, she searched the shadows for movement.

She entered the center aisle and turned to make sure nothing had crept up behind her. When she turned back and started forward again she noticed that there was a name at the end of each rack. She didn't know whether the name referred to the wine brand or where it came from, and she didn't much care. But she figured if she occupied her mind with something she'd be less afraid. So she glanced at the wine racks, saw that they were organized by place, name and, decade.

And she was still petrified.

She walked slowly, stopping to look over her shoulder every few seconds, until she reached a plaque with Bordeaux scrawled into it. This seemed as good a spot as any to hunker down and wait for Umberto.

When she entered the side aisle she scanned the dates over each bottle, still trying to busy her mind. She reached the far wall and hunkered low to the ground.

The creatures she had seen on the balcony, those beasts had been Talhari. She recognized their uniforms. But how could that be? She'd been with the organization for years and had never seen anything like that. Gaia Knight, who'd become closer to Ambrosia than anyone else, had never mentioned anything of the sort. There had to be an explanation. Either that or Umberto had somehow tricked her. But that didn't make sense either.

He'd known what she was all along. He'd known all of them were Talhari. Instead of letting the mission go down as Kyle had planned, Umberto had kidnapped her, an action that had the effect of pulling her from danger. He didn't have to do that, but he'd done it anyway. And for the two days that she'd been in his house, he hadn't hurt her. Nobody had.

Something moved. She jerked her head up. Instead of running to investigate, she stayed hunkered low to the floor and didn't move again; only listened.

There it was again. A soft shuffle of ... something. What was it?

Again, there it was.

Someone ... something was down there with her.

She was on her feet in an instant, listening. The sound was soft, wispy, like someone walking. No, that wasn't quite right. It sounded like they were dragging one foot behind them as they came. Step, scrape, step, scrape.

She doubted it was Umberto, or anyone with good intentions. Anyone who didn't mean her harm would have come down the cellar stairs, seen the light was on, and called out. They would have announced themselves, not wanting to scare her and not wanting her to scare them. This person did neither.

She tried to peer through the racks, but that wasn't any good. She couldn't see anything, so she moved toward the center aisle with sure, light steps, careful not to make a sound.

The person was closer now. She could hear them breathing. It was a phlegmy sound, as though they were just getting over a bad cold.

The hair on the back of her neck stood on end.

Step, scrape, step, scrape.

She edged near the end of the rack, held her breath. She needed her blades, her weapons, something. Without second guessing herself, she grabbed a bottle of Bordeaux and held it clenched in both hands, batter style.

Step, scrape, step, scrape.

Her hands tightened around the glass bottle neck. It would have to do. It wasn't a knife, but was better than nothing.

Step, scrape, step, scrape.

Goose flesh stood out on her skin. A shiver moved the length of her body.

Step, scrape, step, scrape.

The mysterious person was closer.

Almost on her. Any second now.

Step, scrape, step, scrape. Then nothing.

Nothing.

They'd stopped.

She had to work to keep her breathing under control and fight not to move. She wanted to run, to escape, to get the hell out of the cellar and far away from the house.

The stranger didn't move. What on earth was he ... was *it* waiting for? But she didn't have to think on that question for too long. She knew what it was doing. It was waiting for her to act, waiting for her to make the first move.

She waited, wishing she knew what kind of threat she was facing. Was it a man or a creature, a lycan, a vampire? Unbidden, an image of Peter Jackson's uruk-hai monsters played across her mind's eye and had her shrinking in on herself. Terror washed over her in waves so debilitating she couldn't have run if she wanted to. And she did want to--desperately.

But whatever it was it didn't move. She knew it was still there though. Not only could she feel its presence heavy in the air around her, she could hear the horrid sound of that garbled breathing.

Not human, she thought, and suddenly she knew with certainty she couldn't face the thing waiting for her, the thing that had tracked her down to this cellar.

She swallowed a nearly insurmountable desire to scream. Shaking with terror, she bit her lip hard until she felt blood oozing over her chin, and forced herself to stay calm. She couldn't very well stay in the cellar forever, waiting this thing out. She had to do something.

*Have to escape*, she thought again. *Have to get out of here. Go back to the house and find Umberto.*

*If Umberto is still alive*, a sinister voice inside her head mocked.

She took a deep breath, braced herself to step out into the aisle. Took one more breath, and then screamed.

The sound echoed off the walls around her. She scrambled back, nearly falling onto the ground. She backpedaled until she hit the wall, crashing so hard into it that her teeth slammed against her tongue. She screamed again.

The figure bounded into the aisle after her, loping forward and baring its fangs. The creature's eyes were huge and feral, its hair long and straggly, its form was similar to the creatures she'd seen in the house. Her friends. There were only two differences. This creature had a blade of some sort sticking out of his left leg. She knew at once it was the blade that made him walk funny. Someone had fought the beast, stabbed it, but it had still managed to get away. Then there was the uniform. Where the uniform the others had worn was black and green, the thing before her wore a rent uniform of black and blue.

Still clenching the bottle of wine in both hands, Ambrosia sucked in a breath and tried to steady herself. "Nick?" She tried to press her body into the wall, but had retreated as far as she could go.

The thing before her slowed as it closed the distance. It seemed to grin at her. "Traitor."

It could speak. Though why shouldn't it be able to? It had been human, after all.

Though she trembled and her legs felt boneless, she forced herself to remain standing and ready to defend herself. "I'm not a traitor. You're a liar. You never told me about this. What are you? What are the Talhari?"

"Knew you weren't dead, knew you'd betray us for the vampire."

"Umberto took me. I didn't go willingly."

He laughed. The sound of it annoyed her. She realized quite suddenly that though the thing in front of her was large, ugly, and deadly, it was still Nick. It had the same grating laugh, the same arrogant stupidity.

Still laughing, he said, "They already think you're dead, Ambi." With a growl, he raised his hands, let her see the black talons rising from the tips of his fingers. "They'll never know the truth."

Though her arms shook, she held the bottle up and at the ready. If she had to die tonight, she would not go down easy. "But I'm not dead, Nick. I'm alive."

The Nick thing bounded forward.

## Chapter Six

In reflex, she fell into battle stance with legs spread, her muscles loose and ready, and her eyes fixed on the enemy. She was no match for the oversized thug so she had to think fast, had to act fast.

He launched himself at her, slicing the air with his right hand. She dropped to the floor a second before he would have made impact. The high *swooshing* sound of his talons swiping the air where she'd been was the last sign she needed that Nick wasn't pretending. If he could, he would kill her. Slice her to bits and laugh as she bled to death.

She kicked out as hard as she could, connecting the heel of her boot with his right knee and winning a surprised cry of pain from him. The already injured leg wobbled, but he didn't go down.

She rolled toward him and made a grab for the blade embedded in the flesh above his knee. She got close, reaching out with the tips of her fingers, then all at once, blunt pain had her curling in on herself.

The beast had kicked her in the stomach. The pain jarred her, was nearly too much to bear. She couldn't scream because the air was driven out of her with such force all she could manage was a weak intake of air. Without her enhancements the blow would have killed her. As it was, she fell back, clutching her injured abdomen with one arm.

He lifted his foot a second time, no doubt to kick her again. She tried to move away, but the small space was too constricted. There was no place to retreat, no way to get away from him.

Keening and mad with blood lust, he brought his foot down. The pain of this second blow washed over her. She thought she heard her arm break, and possibly a few ribs. Despite how desperately she was fighting to maintain her control, she cried out as the intense pain radiated out to her entire body.

Before she could catch her breath, he fell on her. There was the sting of his claws along the side of his face. She cried out again when he dragged the talons over her breasts. The pain of it, the agony was nearly too much. He was too strong and too fast. He countered every move she made before she had a chance to act on it. But he didn't kill her. Though he could have done it quickly, he dragged the torture out.

He wanted her to suffer.

With one hand, he lifted her by the throat, spun toward the aisle, and tossed her, as though she were a rag doll. She landed hard on her back. The air erupted out of her lungs. She'd long since lost the wine bottle, hadn't even had a second to use it.

Then he was on her again, grabbing her by the hair and pulling her to her feet.

"Gaia will be devastated by your loss," he said, laughing manically.

Gaia? What did Gaia have to do with anything?

"Her little apprentice," he went on. As he spoke, he spun her to face him. "I'll tell her you went to the vampires, told them of the mission and caused the death of four Talhari. She'll be heartbroken."

When his hands closed around her throat and he began to squeeze, she was almost glad. He was going to blame the failure of the mission on her, not the fact that Umberto already knew who and what they were. Gaia would be devastated. Gaia was like the sister Ambrosia had never had, and Gaia would never forgive herself for training a traitor.

"How does it feel to know you're going to die, Ambi?"

Gaia would believe Nick because she'd have no choice but to believe him. Ambrosia wouldn't be around to tell her the truth.

"Nothing to say?" he taunted. "All choked up?"

Darkness played at the edge of her vision. She gritted her teeth against it, fought to remain conscious.

"Die!"

She wouldn't die, she couldn't let things end this way.

With her last dregs of energy, she brought her knee up as hard as she could and nearly smiled when she felt his nut sack crush beneath her knee.

He cried out and reared back. To her surprise, his grip loosened enough for her to squirm free. She dropped to one knee and tugged the blade free of his leg. With a high-pitched scream of triumph, she drove it into his gut. Black sludge spilled from the wound, but she knew it wasn't enough. She pulled the blade free and drove it home a second time.

Nick howled, spun on his heels, and disappeared into the aisle.

Had he moved off to another area of the wine cellar to lie in wait for her? She decided she didn't care. At least not enough to remain there. She had him on the run and couldn't back down now.

When she stepped into the aisle and saw Umberto, eyes flashing red and teeth bared, she stopped cold.

A low whine fell from the Talhari beast. "No!" Half in panic and half in rage, it slashed one heavy arm down on Umberto's shoulder just as Umberto was spinning to the right.

Though Umberto stumbled, the blow didn't do much damage. Without losing his momentum, he whipped around and attacked the Nick thing. Instead of using his nails, Umberto slammed the back of his hand into the side of the creature's face. The beast sailed across the room, tumbling head over heels and landing in a heap on the floor. Before he could move, Umberto was on him again.

Low grunts of rage and wails of pain rose from the pair. Ambrosia realized that though the Talhari creature was larger than Umberto, he was no match for him. Umberto was an old vampire, much stronger and faster than Nick, even now. Already Nick's beastly face had been crushed beyond recognition. Black sludge oozed from various rents in his flesh. The thing was hurt, battered, and possibly as close to dying as it could get. The thought that she should intervene somehow, should save him flashed into her mind's eye, then winked out. She wouldn't help Nick. He would have killed her without a second thought.

\* \* \* \*

A loud *crackling* rose from the floor, surprising her. She knew Umberto had broken Nick's neck before she looked down at Nick's battered and bleeding body and saw he wasn't moving anymore.

Umberto quickly got to his feet. "Come on, we have to get him upstairs."

She didn't want to touch it. Nevertheless, she moved forward, crouched and took it by the shoulder with her good arm. She noticed the fur was grimy with moisture a second before she fell backward onto her butt and groaned. Her abdomen burned with pain and her forearm felt like it was on fire.

Umberto looked up. For a moment he was wide-eyed and motionless, then he came forward. "Shit! You're hurt."

"A bit."

"Where?"

"My arm is broken, and I think a few ribs, and he cut me up pretty good."

He eased closer, then began to feel her for injury. He prodded her stomach, winning a fresh groan from her, and gently touched her ribs. "Three broken," he muttered, speaking almost to himself. "Your face, your breasts, your shoulder." He exhaled. "Your right arm, he did more than cut you up some."

"I tried to defend myself but he--" She paused, nearly whimpering when he touched the slash along her face. "--he wanted me dead and he wanted to do it with as much pain as possible. I think he's wanted me dead from day one."

"Why did he want you dead?" As he spoke, he bit into his hand and let blood pool in his palm.

"I don't know. What I think is that it has something to do with my mentor, Gaia Knight. He kept talking about her, saying he would tell her that I'd betrayed the Talhari--what are you doing?"

He'd lifted his hand to her face and began smearing blood on her cheek. "My blood will help you heal."

"I'll heal anyway."

"This will make you heal faster."

She opened her mouth to protest, but already she could feel the tingle of regeneration on her face where he'd tended. Seconds after he'd seen to the rents on her arm, it too began to tingle.

"I can't do anything about the broken bones yet," he was saying, then stopped speaking. He looked over his shoulder and frowned. "He's waking up. I have to get him upstairs. Can you walk or do you want to wait down here for me to come back and get you?"

Hell no, she wasn't spending another minute in the cellar if she didn't have to. "I'll be okay." Nick's legs twitched. "Just hurry up and take care of Nick. I'll be right behind you."

Umberto bent and hiked the body over his shoulder. "It's not dead yet so we have to burn the body."

"You don't need my help carrying him?"

He stood, regarded her with one brow quirked, then shaking his head, turned and started for the stairs. "The rest are dead and burned. He's the last one."

Though it took her a few seconds, she stood and started forward, trying her best to ignore the pain burning in her stomach. "Why the fire?"

"Same reason the Talhari burn my kind. So he doesn't come back."

She followed him down the dusty aisle and up the cellar stairs at a limp. "It's the only way to be sure," she said, half to herself. Gaia had drilled the importance of burning the enemy after a kill into Ambrosia. But it was disconcerting to hear the same tactic being employed on someone she had known.

"Are you all right?"

Nick was dead and she was alive. "Yeah," she said, making her way up the stairs. "I think I am."

## Chapter Seven

Ambrosia stood framed in the window, high above the roiling ocean below. She wasn't sure of where she was, or even if she was still in North America. The only thing she was certain of was that she didn't care anymore. What mattered above all else was the fact that she was with Umberto, that Umberto was alive, that she was alive and whole. Her body had healed within hours of Nick's attack. Her healing was sped along by the small infusion of blood Umberto had given her.

She turned abruptly, shivered as a cool night breeze blew in through the open window, flittering easily through the sheer black gown she was wearing. "Why didn't you kill me, too?"

Umberto, sprawled on his back with his arms folded under his head, raised a brow. Though gauzy curtains of chiffon hung around the large bed, Ambrosia could see every detail of him from his mussed brown hair to his booted feet. She'd had to swallow a reprimand when he'd laid on the white linen, boots and all, but realized that she'd moved beyond the stage of life where she had to concern herself with such things. Tonight, her life had changed forever. She'd left the Talhari, was going to give herself to a vampire. "Are you going to answer me, Umberto?"

He frowned. "That you could ask such a question wounds me. You should know by now that I could never kill you. Nick and the others had to die. They're more deadly to my kind than vampires have ever been to humans. Save a few rogue vampires, the majority of us don't drain arbitrarily."

A grin played at the edge of her lips. "So it really is like Anne Rice says, you only go after the evil doer?"

"Just as Anne Rice says," he agreed. Moving with the languid slowness only a vampire could master, Umberto sat up. "And fortunately for my kind, there are more than enough of those."

"Unfortunately for my kind."

"When the order began, the Talhari did good work. They killed those rogues that were an annoyance to all of us. But as time progressed, they, as all large organizations do, lost their way. The Talhari Council found that even with the enhancements they'd ordered surgically implanted in their hunters, they were still no match for my kind." He smirked. "No great surprise there."

Ignoring his arrogance for the moment, she focused in on what he'd said about the enhancements. "Is this when they came up with the idea of embeds?"

"It is. What they did--"

"What are embeds? Will you tell me, now that I see I was wrong?"

"What they did," he continued, "and this is so stupid it boggles the mind, they set about to capture a lycan and cross its genetic makeup with that of their hunters. And that's what they did. They sent out a group of hunters, scholars, and trappers to search for the deadliest lycan they could find. They wanted one that was large, even in his human form; one that was strong, even stronger than other lycan, and they wanted—"

She couldn't keep from interrupting him again because she knew instantly what they were looking for. "Wolf."

Umberto nodded. "Wolf. Of course they hadn't heard of him before they'd commenced their search, but once it began they heard legendary tales about him. Wolf is familiar to all immortals. He's the oldest immortal, the strongest, and the wisest."

"And he serves as your body guard?"

Umberto's jaw sagged. He blinked for a moment, worked his mouth, then threw his head back and laughed. "You think Wolf serves me? You think he's my body guard?"

"Well, of course. He's the head of Forsaken's security."

He set his palms on his knees, as though her words were so ridiculous he could scarcely hold himself up, and laughed again. "Wolf is my elder. If any immortal served another, it would be I who served him, not the other way around."

"Okay, now I'm lost."

He sat up and took a moment to catch his breath. "Come here," he said, motioning her forward.

"No."

"Are you going to make me come and get you?"

She frowned. "First tell me about Wolf."

He gazed at her with narrowed eyes. His lips were pursed for a moment, then he sat back and nodded. "Eventually, the Talhari found Wolf. They caught him--"

"How could they possibly catch him if he was the oldest, strongest, and wisest immortal? Seems he could have escaped them with relative ease."

Umberto frowned. "If you allow me to speak I'll tell you." He waited for her to nod, then continued. "They located him, waited for him to sleep and used a tranquilizer on him. He remembers entering his cottage on the beach in Nassau, going to bed ... his next memory is of waking in a Brazilian forest."

"But how did he escape if he doesn't remember doing it?"

Umberto rose to his full height. "Are you going to let me tell you what I know or are you going to interrogate me?"

With a sigh, she nodded yet again for him to continue. "I'm listening."

"He's a lycan, so of course he had nothing to fear in the rain forest. For the three days it took him to find civilization he was the deadliest thing within. On the third day he found a small village with a doctor, a small general store, a boarding house, and a beautiful Brazilian anthropologist who was staying at the boarding house. True to form, he made *friends* with the anthropologist and used her telephone to contact me."

"So you went to him?"

"I did, as did Dario, Mathias, and Erik. The five of us searched the forest for an answer to what had happened to Wolf. For weeks we searched, but could never find an answer. We thought the Talhari might be involved, by that time we already had extensive records on them, but we could find no proof to link them to it. Eventually we gave up. Then, maybe three years after Wolf woke in Brazil, we began to hear word of a Talhari beast. It wasn't a vampire, but it was similar to a lycan, but not completely. Immortals who'd seen the thing said it was a hybrid beast, part lycan and part ape."

She'd seen the beast herself and realized that was a perfect description of it.

"As soon as we heard of the Talhari beast, the five of us began to wonder if what happened to Wolf had anything to do with it."

"And?"

"And, there's no way to know for sure. Personally, I believe it does. I'm not sure why they made a hybrid, except that maybe they did it to distinguish the Talhari creature from other lycan."

She supposed she'd have to be happy with that. "So what now?"

"Would you like to know a secret?"

Nodding, she stepped toward the bed.

"As much as the Talhari hated reckless vampires who kill without remorse, vampires loathe such creatures. They make the rest of us look bad."

"I wonder then, how did Forsaken come into their line of fire?" The import of her statement wasn't lost on her. She'd said "their" line of fire, not "our" line of fire.

"We've made it our mission to destroy the Talhari. They've gone on a killing spree to murder all vampires and we're not going to let that happen."

She thought of Tom, her predecessor, and figured she knew what happened to him. "Were you responsible for Tom, the former singer of Maven?"

"Erik dispatched him."

"But what of the files I read on you, the people you killed?"

Umberto shrugged. "The Talhari are liars."

"And me?"

"And you are no longer of the Talhari."

She saw his leg move, then he was beside her, lifting her into his arms and carrying her to the bed. With a flick of his hand, he pushed the sheer curtains aside and climbed onto the soft mattress. He laid her gently on the crisp white linen and gazed at her.

With smooth movements, he gripped the edge of his shirt and drew it over his head. She'd never seen his chest, his swollen nipples. Impulse had her leaning onto her elbows and arching toward him. She longed to feel the pert bud of his nipple against her tongue, was eager to have the taste of him in her mouth. "You're so perfect."

He cupped the back of her head and steered her to him. When her mouth closed over him he sucked in a breath. "And you're so beautiful, my sweet Ambrosia."

Hunger turned her blood to liquid fire. She sucked his erect nipple into her mouth and flicked her tongue over it. He was as sweet as fine wine with a tinge of saltiness.

His grip tightened and he moaned. "Yes, Ambrosia. Lose yourself in me."

And that was precisely what she was doing. Her years of training, her need to be a CHI, all of it was drowned in her desire for him. Maybe this was what her life had been building to all along, what was meant to be. She couldn't know, what she did know was now that she knew the truth about her former brethren she couldn't go back.

A mew of protest slid from her lips when he pulled her away from him. Face somber, he studied her features with rapt interest. "You know what I want."

It wasn't a question, but a statement. Nevertheless, she nodded. "You want me to stay with you."

"You'll rarely see the sun, and you can never see anyone from the

Talhari. If they find out you're not dead, that you've allied yourself with the immortals, they'll stalk you to your death. But if you stay with me, I can protect you. You'll have the five of us to protect you."

If she stayed with Umberto she would be committing an unthinkable breach. It was unforgivable and if she ever crossed paths with any of her former colleagues they would kill her on sight. "I want to be with you."

"For all eternity?"

She nodded. "I want to be with you." He ran his fingers over her shoulders, his touch so gentle that it could have been the brush of wind. She shivered, let her head drop back to expose her throat. "Take me, Umberto."

He made no move to obey, but continued to stroke her. Her arms, the pert tip of one nipple, her stomach, his fingers glided over her as though they were hungry for the feel of her skin.

The linen was soft and fluffy under her, like she was lying in a bed of silken down. With the touch of silk beneath her and Umberto slowly driving her mad, she was quickly losing herself to the thrill of touch.

"After tonight, there's no going back," he said, nuzzling her throat.

She exhaled heavily when his lips brushed the underside of her chin, shivered when she felt the edge of a fang scrape gently over her artery. "Yes. Please."

He covered her and her body sank into the mattress beneath his weight. With a moan, she hugged him closer, arching her head further back to expose more of her throat.

"You want me, Ambrosia?"

"Yes."

"Forever?"

She gazed into his eyes, hoping he'd be able to see into her soul and know this was what she wanted. "Please."

He released her, pushed off the bed, and was standing before she had a chance to tighten her hold on him.

"Hush," he said when she opened her mouth to complain. With a smile that sent a delicious thrill through her, he unfastened his pants, let them slide down his legs, and stepped out of them. She'd never seen him naked, had never known how truly perfectly his body had been formed.

His legs were finely made. They were lean and roped with muscle. Though his cock was flaccid and resting docilely against his thigh, his size was impressive. She had to wonder how large he'd become after he drank from her.

"I can see my body pleases you." He knelt on the bed and gazed down at her.

His skin was flushed, his lips full and red. Though his fangs were clearly visible and his eyes more red than brown, she felt no fear. "You're the one who's beautiful."

Moving slowly, he bent over her and crushed her into the mattress beneath him. "I've wanted you from the first moment I saw you, knew I had to have you, that somehow I had to seduce you." She hiccupped when he sucked her earlobe into his mouth and licked. "Make you mine for all eternity." He made a wet path from her ear to her neck. "Even if I had to capture you and seduce you."

She touched him, ran her fingers over his muscular back, down his spine and cupped his full buttocks in her palms, urging him closer. "Take me, Umberto."

He edged her thighs wide with his knee. The moment she felt his cock between her legs she shivered. "From this moment on, you belong to me."

She cried out when his fangs sank into her throat, closed her eyes when he fastened his lips to her skin and began to suckle.

The pleasure nearly leveled her. What had caused a slow building of ecstasy in her the first time he'd tasted her now had lust and need descending on her in great waves. She clung to the mattress, panted into his hair. Her sex clenched as carnal hunger flowed over her like warm cream. She didn't know whether it was his pheromones, her desire, or both, but she wanted him with a desperation that stunned her.

She felt him ease back, held her breath when he paused for five torturous seconds, then cried out in pleasure and triumph when he thrust his stiff cock inside of her.

He growled, clasped her hands and entwined his fingers with hers, then set a rhythm that pushed her nearer to the edge. He drove into her with a primal need that matched her own desire for him. Every thrust was hard and deep, every withdrawal smooth and slow.

"Yes!" he cried, "Yes!"

She wrapped her legs tight around his waist, bringing another cry of pleasure from him. This was too good, too perfect. This feeling, this connection she shared with Umberto was what she had truly been looking for her whole life.

She clung to him, dug her nails into his hands even as he forced her hands deep into the mattress.

He arched back to stare at her. She should have been terrified by his blood red gaze, disturbed by the trace of blood--her blood--on his fangs, but she wasn't. Desire, need, and surrender were what she felt. She was Umberto's, now and forever.

Still staring at her, he plunged deep, pulled free, then plunged deeper. Each possession felt better than the last. Her cunt tingled with the sensations. Desire moved like molten fire through her core and snaked a path throughout her body. Her nipples were ablaze in sensation, her stomach quivered as she neared her climax.

"Fuck me harder, Umberto," she begged. "I'm so close."

Growling deep in the back of his throat, he collapsed on top of her and captured her mouth. His tongue slid past her spread lips. Protecting her from the deadly points of his teeth, he feasted on her, dipping into her mouth then sucking her tongue between his lips and devouring her.

"Umberto," she moaned. His lips were like fine wine, his passion nearly too much. Every touch, every new sensation brought her to a higher level of ecstasy. She was mindless with passion, drunk with desire.

When he sank into her core and pulsed, she lost the last bit of control and soared over the edge.

She bucked under the force of her release, clung to him and breathed his name into the air. Only when she felt her body dissolving, felt her climax dissipating did she realize that Umberto had reached his peak, too.

Panting, he collapsed on top of her.

The soft pink glow of the sun was visible on the horizon when he began to move again. "It's nearly daylight. I have to find shelter."

"Can I go with you?"

He rose from the bed, damp with her sweat but more beautiful than she had words to describe. With a smile, he held his hand out to her. "Of course you may come. For the rest of my life I want to share every day with you."

And she knew there was nothing in the world that would make her happier.

# UNPARALLELED

Lisa G. Riley

## Prologue

For several millennia the two worlds existed side by side, but didn't know it. In many respects, their worlds were the same. When Cro-Magnons walked one earth, they were walking the other as well; when the death of a single man heralded the spread of a religion in one world, at the same time the death of another man did the same in the other. Similarly, large scale tragedies perpetrated by man transpired in one world at the same time that they occurred in the other. None of these happenings were exactly the same, but they brought the same result: they changed the respective world in which they occurred.

The worlds are similar, but not the same. The people measure time in the same way and are on the same time continuum. Their cities and countries have the same exact names, geographies and languages. And while the histories of these countries in their different worlds are somewhat similar, the people are not duplicates of one another.

The differences between the two worlds are many. One world is so technologically advanced that it is light years ahead of the other. Their technology is the peoples' god and has consumed them for decades. It has precipitated the loss of most of their natural resources and has turned most of their world into an ugly gray landscape. Technology has also enabled them to discover a portal from their world to the other and mimic it in science labs everywhere, so that they may travel back and forth between the two worlds at will. Because they are so far ahead of the other world and discovered the portal hundreds of years ago while the people in the other world still remained unaware of it, the people of the more advanced world call their world Parallel Plus and the less advanced world the Sub Parallel. While Parallel Plus inhabitants do not see people of the Sub Parallel as being beneath them, they do not exactly consider them equals either. This is a story of what happens when two people from the two worlds meet. This is Edris's and Enrique's story.

## Chapter One

*Louisville, Kentucky*
*The Sub Parallel*
*Thirty Years Ago*

"*¡No, hermosa negra! ¡No lo haga!*"
The distressed cry came from the other end of the hall and awakened Dalila Rivera Aponte from a fitful sleep. Her husband liked to say that she now slept with one ear open since Enrique had begun to have the dreams. She could only agree with him.

"No, *mi amor*. You stay in bed. I'll take care of 'Rique." She whispered the words to her waking husband. Putting on her wrapper, she left the room and hurried down the hall. The dreams had started several months before. They worried her husband because their son believed that the little girl in the dreams was real, even though he had never met or seen her anywhere before. The frequency and intensity of the dreams also scared her husband.

Dalila, on the other hand, was not scared at all. She'd dreamed the same way when she'd been a child. She just hadn't been as young as Enrique when his dreams started. She'd been 12 years old when her dreams had started and though she didn't know him at the time and had never even seen him in life, she'd dreamed of the boy, and then the man, who would later become her husband. Her family had called it *el ojo tercer--the third eye.* Dalila had only known that the dreams had at first been fun, but then they'd worried and confused her because he'd seemed so real and yet, logically, she'd known he couldn't be.

She'd begun to think she was *loco*, especially when she'd turned 16 and the dreams had turned quite torrid and had made her--a good, Puerto Rican, Catholic girl--feel hot, sweaty *and satisfied* during the night. In the bright light of the morning, she felt sinful, and terrified she was going to go straight to hell for letting the white boy with the beautiful blue eyes have his way with her. And then she'd met him, the man who was *literally* the man of her dreams-- Jefferson Andre Thomas, her American *gringo*--and she hadn't felt crazy anymore. She'd just felt ... complete, even though he hadn't dreamed of her at all. None of it made sense and she didn't try to explain it. She just accepted it. Her goal now was to spare Enrique as much of the same pain and confusion as she could.

"Oh, poor little darling," she said regretfully with a shake of her head when she arrived at her son's room and saw that his restless sleep had tangled him in the covers.

"*¡Oh, careful beautiful one!*"

Dalila rushed over to the bed at this latest cry from her son. "'Rique," she said as she gently shook him and smoothed back his damp, black curls. "Wake up, baby. It is only a dream. Wake up. Mama is here now." She reached over and turned on the lamp.

Five-year old Enrique Jefferson Thomas Rivera fought his way out of his disturbing dream, opening his eyes to see his mother's concerned face. He considered trying to be a big boy and hiding his tears, but decided it wasn't worth it and flung himself into his mother's arms. "Ah, Mama. It is awful!"

"Hush, little one. It will be all right. *¿Es la pequeña muchacha otra vez, sí?*" She asked in Spanish and automatically translated to English as she held him away from her. His blue eyes were filled with sorrow. "It is the little girl again, yes?"

"*Sí, mama.* The little black beauty is in pain."

"In pain?" Dalila asked in surprise with an arch of her brow. Always before, Enrique's dreams of the little girl had been happy ones. "*¿Que es la materia con ella?* What is the matter with her?" The habit of translating every sentence had started when he'd been a toddler and most of the time she found it a hard one to break.

"Oh, Mommy. She has fallen and there is lots of blood with no one to help her. I have to go to her!" Enrique explained anxiously and translated as well. "*¡Debo ir a ella!*"

He wanted to go to her? Suppressing a smile, Dalila held him still as he actually attempted to leave the bed. "Sweetheart." She tightened her grip when he still struggled. "You are a very brave boy, but you cannot go to her. She is only in your dreams, correct?"

"But she is a real person, Mama! I know she is--I just haven't met her yet!"

"I know, my son," Dalila said patiently. She'd heard this argument from him time and time again. "I know. But think about it, Enrique. How can you help her when we do not know where she is?"

Enrique stopped struggling and huffed out a frustrated breath, his body slumping in disappointment. "Well, damn," he murmured softly and suddenly remembering that this was his mother he was talking to and not his friend, Charles, he hurriedly tried to explain as he studiously avoided her eyes, "I mean ... uhhh ... well ... hmm."

He cleared his throat and gave up. He risked a peek at his mother. The unyielding look on her face gave him little hope and he said, "I am sorry, Mama. I am just so worried about her."

Dalila successfully suppressed a smile and said sternly, "*Sí, pero ése no hay excusa, Enrique.* Absolutely no excuse will do. You know better."

"I know," Enrique mumbled with his chin glued to his chest. On a resigned sigh, he asked, "What is my punishment?"

"We will discuss that later," Dalila said firmly. "First, we must finish with your little friend, yes?"

Enrique smiled with gratitude. "Oh, *si,* Mama, we must!"

"Now tell me again about the blood."

Enrique became anxious again. "Oh, there was so much of it. She hurt her knee really bad, maybe broke it, even, and there is no one around to help her. Not even the robot."

"Robot?" Dalila was shocked. "What is this robot you speak of?"

Enrique smiled excitedly. "Oh, Mama, they have a robot. It plays with her and reads books to her, but mostly it cleans."

"Enrique!" Dalila said sternly. "You must not make things up."

"Oh, but I am not, Mama! There is a robot. It is called Florence."

Dalila frowned. A robot that played and read books? Impossible! "You are certain, Enrique?" she asked him. "Absolutely positive?"

"*Ah, sí, Mama.* There is a robot. I have seen her many times."

"If you are sure," Dalila said with a shrug, deciding to drop the subject. Perhaps it was a toy she just had not seen before.

"Yes, I am sure," Enrique said and there was impatience in his voice. "How will we help her, Mama?"

"She is smaller than you are, your dream girl, yes?"

"*Sí*, Mama."

"Then since she is so small, she is probably screaming and yelling so loud that the whole neighborhood will hear her. Just as you get mad and scared when you hurt yourself, she probably gets mad and scared as well. And just like you, she will scream and scream until someone comes. When you hurt yourself, you scream like what is called 'a banshee,' no?" she finished with a grin. "I am sure she does, too."

Enrique smiled at his mother's teasing and thought about what she'd said, before saying earnestly, "You are right, Mama. She will be fine. *La poca negra belleza será fina,*" he said with emphasis as he lay back against his pillows again.

"Darling," Dalila chastised softly, "you must not call her 'the little black beauty.' She is not a horse, no? Or even a pony, eh?" she teased as she poked him in his belly.

Quickly catching the joke, Enrique giggled and twisted to avoid her fingers. "But, Mama, she *is* beautiful. If only you could see her...." He trailed off as he pictured her face, as he had hundreds of other times since he'd started dreaming of her several months before on his fifth birthday.

Once again, Dalila wondered if a five-year old could truly be in love. This was not the first time Enrique had gotten that dazed look on his face when he talked about the little girl. "Yes, darling, I know she is beautiful, but you cannot call her that. You still have not found out her name?"

Enrique frowned as his mother's voice pulled him away from his thoughts. "No, I do not know her name. And if I can't call her *la poca negra belleza*, then I will call her ... I will call her *mi belleza oscura!*" he said with triumph. "My dark beauty. Is that not pretty, Mama?"

Dalila tried not to be too worried that he already thought of the little girl as his. "I'm afraid you do not understand, Enrique," she said as she straightened the covers around him. "You cannot describe her by the color of her skin. It is not polite."

"But Mama, it is her dark skin that helps to make her so especially beautiful!" he insisted.

"I understand, little one, but you must think of something else. *¿Comprehendes?*"

"*Si*, Mama," he said in a disgruntled voice, recognizing the tone and knowing that further argument was useless. "I understand."

"*¡Excelente!* Good night, my baby," Dalila said as she bent to kiss him. "*Te quiero.*"

Enrique rose from his pillows to hug her around her neck. "*Buenos noches, Mama.* I love you, too."

He made himself comfortable once again and certain his mother was gone, lovingly murmured, "*Buenos noches, mi belleza oscura.*"

\* \* \* \*

Eight years later, Enrique swore in helpless frustration as he dreamt of the unknown girl and watched as she did something reckless yet again. She was always doing what she should not. She was ten years old now and her rashness only seemed to get worse as she grew older. "Oh, little girl, must you be so out of control *all* of the time?" he murmured as he watched events unfold.

*Tall and dressed entirely in black, the girl crept outside into the dark night and paused by an odd-looking vehicle. Shaped like an airplane in the front, but boxy like a car in the back, it was small, gray and had what looked to be wings sticking from the sides of it. The girl gave a furtive look around before she pressed a lever on the side and Enrique watched in fascination as a door lifted straight up. She hurriedly climbed inside the back of the vehicle and lay down, pulling a blanket over herself until she was completely covered. The door lowered and shut on its own.*

"I have to go, Terrence." Enrique's attention was caught by the impatient voice of the woman he knew to be the little girl's mother. She was talking over her shoulder as she walked outside of a small steel and glass structure that Enrique knew to be their home. "I told you that this case is top priority and I can't discuss it. Not with anyone except Clay. And before you say anything we'll both regret, I'm not having an affair with him. He's my partner; it's necessary that we spend a lot of time together. But I can't keep explaining that to you, Terrence," she said. "Just take care of the girls and I'll be home as soon as I can."

"When?" a tall, dark man asked as he followed her. He grabbed her arm and stopped her from going any further. He, too, was impatient and his handsome face showed it when she sighed again. His dark eyes showed clear displeasure. "Look, Carma, I don't think it's asking too much to want to know when my wife will be home."

"I don't know," the woman said and folded her arms across her slender, uniformed body. "It probably won't be until morning. Perhaps even later than that," she finished. Enrique detected both resentment and defiance.

"Well, that's just great, Carma," the man said angrily. In contrast to his wife, he wore cotton pants and a long, flowing, white shirt--a color and kind of material Enrique rarely saw when he dreamed of the girl. "You're hardly ever home anymore. The girls miss you. I miss you." His voice had softened considerably on this last comment.

"It can't be helped, Terrence. I have a job to do." She turned and walked toward the vehicle, climbing in and shutting the door after her. She drove the vehicle for a few feet and then suddenly it took flight and was in the air, joining other such vehicles as they flew over spire-topped steel buildings.

*Upon landing, Carma left the vehicle and approached a building with a sign proclaiming it as Region 22 Security and Regulations Compound. Enrique watched curiously as she pressed her palm to a panel and it flashed a bright green. The doors opened almost immediately. The little girl, having slipped out of the vehicle before the door had lowered completely, waited a few seconds before following her mother, squeezing her body through the doors just before they closed. She stayed well behind, but close enough to still follow her, ducking and hiding when she heard voices or other footsteps besides her mother's.*

*She followed her mother down into the basement of the building, staying out of sight, but watching as Carma moved toward a group of two men and two women who stood in front of a brightly lit doorway that was, oddly enough, in the middle of the room and had no depth to it. The girl's eyes grew big as her mother pulled an odd-looking weapon from her holster. Enrique assumed it to be some sort of gun.*

*"Stop!" Carma yelled, "I'm placing you all under arrest for the illegal traversal of criminals through the portal to the Sub Parallel. Put your hands up."*

*The group turned toward her. They all wore facemasks. One man stepped forward. "Put that away, Carma. You're not going to use it."*

*"Oh, you're wrong. I'll use it if I have to--just don't give me a reason to." A masked man grabbed her from behind and the girl screamed, gaining everyone's attention.*

*"Oh, my God!" Carma wailed. "Run, baby, run!" she yelled as she was dragged across the room, closer to the group.*

*The little girl did as her mother said and ran back the way she had come and was*

*up the stairs and halfway down a second hall before she was caught. She kicked her legs*

*and flailed her arms as she was carried back into the room.*

*The girl's eyes searched the room. "Where's my mother? What did you do to her?" she screamed. "Where's my mother?"*

*"Shut up!" the man who had caught her said and covered her mouth. She bit him. "Ow! You little bitch!" he said and pushed her away from him, so that she fell against the strange doorway and hit her head. She didn't move.*

*"What should we do with her?" the man who had shoved her asked. He bent down to check the pulse in her neck. "The pulse is strong. She'll be fine."*

*"We're going to have to get rid of her--just like we had to get rid of her mother," one of the women said and Enrique's heart thudded painfully in his chest. "We can't take the chance that she'll identify us."*

"No, hold on a minute," said the man who'd challenged Carma. "I don't want to do that. And besides, we're wearing the masks."

"You didn't have those same qualms over Carma," the woman reminded him.

"I know that, but Carma was a thorn in our sides who had worn out her welcome long ago with all of her investigating. She's just a child," the man finished and gestured toward the unconscious girl.

"Well, the only other thing we can do is give her some Oblivios," the other woman said with a shrug. "The last hour of her life will be erased from her memory."

"Perfect," the man said. "And we'll just leave her here to be found later."

\* \* \* \*

Enrique awoke with a jerk, his body covered in sweat and the sound of his heart beating furiously in his ears. "God! You stupid girl! Why do I keep dreaming about you, when there is never anything I can do to help you?"

## Chapter Two

As Enrique matured, the girl in his dreams continued to grow as well. She grew to be tall, smart, determined, arrogant and beautiful. She'd abruptly stopped her tendency to be reckless immediately after she lost her mother. The loss had hardened her and made her more responsible and stoic and Enrique was saddened by the loss of the mischievous, happy, go-lucky girl.

The dreams continued, the tone of them changing when he was twenty-one. The dreams became sexual in nature and he was not watching anymore, he was participating. The first time he had sex with her, he was disgusted with himself because he knew she was only eighteen. He didn't investigate the dreams too closely, preferring not to as he told himself over and over again that they were just dreams and she was not real. He figured he had to in order to keep himself sane.

When his mother would tell him that he was blessed with sight from his third eye, he'd tell her that biologically, everyone had a third eye and his was just as blind and closed as everyone else's.

"No, your third eye is very much 'open' and it is developed, despite your unwillingness to use it," Dalila said one day when he'd dropped by for lunch. "I thank God that you were much more open to the possibility when you were a child, otherwise you would not be so lucky today with the gift. It would be dead."

"I am not just speaking of the dreams of the girl, Enrique," she continued. "How do you explain this intuitiveness you have? This … this … special ability you have to know when something is wrong with anyone you care about?"

"I don't have a special ability, Mom," Enrique said as he spooned up the last of his *sopa de arroz con pollo*. The savory chicken and rice soup was one of his favorites. "It's like you said, I'm intuitive," he said and left the table for more soup. At twenty-one, he could never seem to get enough to eat.

"And was it mere intuition that told you exactly where Butch had wandered off to last year?" Dalila referred to the family dog as Enrique sat back down.

"That was nothing, Mom. The stupid dog was horny and had been trying to hump everything in sight for days before he left. Ow!

I'm sorry." He laughed when she pinched him on the arm at his choice of language. "But really, it wasn't difficult to figure out that he'd be at a house with a female dog on the property."

"Yes, but you knew exactly *which* house it was and it was more than a mile away. You did not even check next door with the Johnsons whose little Petunia is female."

Enrique snorted. "Come on, Mom. Her name is *Petunia*, for God's sake. The name just screams 'I'm prissy.' Can you blame Butch for not wanting to waste his time trying to get what he knew she would never give?"

"Enrique!" she chided him even as she laughed. "I am serious. What do you call what you did when you were sixteen? You urged me to go to the doctor for a check-up and when I went they found the breast cancer. It is because of you that they caught it in time," she finished with tears in her eyes.

"Oh, Mom, don't cry. I was just incredibly lucky, that's all. Now, please. Can we stop talking about this? I need to be firmly grounded in reality before I take my chemistry final this afternoon."

\* \* \* \*

The dreams continued and he continued to fight their significance, telling himself that they didn't have any. He spent most of his twenties trying to banish the woman from his head, living the life of a satyr and indulging in sex with as many women as he could. He ignored the fact that most of them were tall, beautiful African American women with dark skin.

She seemed to mock him. He didn't know her name, so he referred to her as 'beautiful one' or 'dream girl.' He told himself that she didn't exist, but found himself wondering if she dreamed of him as he dreamed of her, despite the fact that his mother had told him that her father had been unaware of everything until she'd met him. Whenever he caught himself falling into the trap of believing that she could be real, he'd tell himself to stop believing in fairy tales. He tried his best to block her out of his dreams, sometimes managing to forcibly awaken himself when she appeared. Despite all of his efforts, she never went away and he resented her for it, while longing for her so badly that he would wake up with the taste of her on his lips and still desiring more.

He dreamt of her at least once a week and found her to be arrogant and self-assured, except in bed. In bed, she was less sure of herself and softer, essentially letting him set the rules. In bed, she was his.

\* \* \* \*

*He walked into the room and she lay there on the big bed. From* her black hair with its shocking swath of white in the front, to her wide forehead and heavily lashed, gray eyes to her slightly crooked nose, dimpled cheeks and full mouth, he thought she was perfect. As always, she wore next to nothing and it was in the usual pink she seemed to favor.

The short, thigh-length, sleeveless, nightgown did absolutely nothing to hide the lushness of her long, dark body and he laughed when she deliberately stretched her strong, slim arms over her head so that the lingerie rose past her hips to expose what to him was the vision of a lifetime. Despite the bold move, he saw the hint of shyness in her eyes and smiled.

She pouted prettily up at him. "Enrique," she said silkily in that throaty voice of hers. "Why do you make me wait?"

"Oh, shit," he mumbled as he stared at her hairless mound with naked greed. "You tease me with your beautiful body, but I do not know your name. Why? Usted me atormenta." He walked over to the bed, stripping as he went. He didn't expect her to answer. She never answered questions about who she was. He didn't think she could. "You have become my tormentor, beautiful one," he said again as he unzipped his jeans.

He knew she knew where he'd been staring when she said, "I shaved it just for you, 'Rique, darling. I know how much you like it when it is clearly visible," she purred as she reached down and slid a finger over her cleft, surprising the hell out of him. Unable to look away, he watched as she raised the finger so he could see. "I am already wet and only for you. It is always only for you. And the teasing ... it has never gone unfulfilled. As for the torment," she said with a shrug of supreme unconcern. "It is just a side benefit."

Arrested for a moment by the sight of the drops of cream sliding down her finger, Enrique had paused in taking off his jeans. Her last two comments, however, spurred him into action again. "No, the teasing is never unfulfilled," he agreed as he stepped out of his jeans. "But as I have discovered, even being fulfilled is sometimes not enough. From you, I want more."

He felt her eyes following him as he walked to the side of the bed. He frowned playfully at her. "And just for that crack about my torment being a side benefit, you're going to turn over on your side," he said as he climbed into the bed.

He watched her gray eyes snap and her forehead crease into a frown. "But, Enrique," she protested as she scooted over to make room for him. "I want to--"

"No buts," he said and resisted the pull of her eyes. He knew what she wanted. It was what she always wanted. "Now," he said, when she was settled with her back against his chest and her head resting on his upper arm as he spooned her from behind. "Give me that finger."

He waited in tense anticipation while she decided if she would or not. He knew she was sulking, but it warred with her horniness and he was hoping that the last element won out, because the truth was, even though it was his dream, he could only bend her to his will to a certain extent. "Beautiful one," he chided her gently, just as she flung her hand back at him with her index finger pointing out.

"Gracias," he said and closed his mouth over the entire finger, sucking it into his mouth as the smell of her arousal filled his nostrils and the taste of it exploded against his tongue. He licked her finger clean, not wanting to miss a drop of the dried juice. Slowly sliding the finger from his mouth, he kept hold of her wrist and licked a diagonal path down her palm.

She gasped and reflexively pushed her ass against his dick. Enrique sucked in a breath, but smiled and released her wrist. "¿Se siente bien, eh, Mami?" He said and felt her stiffen. He knew it was probably because of the satisfaction in his voice.

"What?" he tried to say innocently around his grin. "I know it felt good. Your body told me so." When she remained quiet and still, he tsked playfully. "Shame, shame, beautiful one. You have way too much pride," he finished and pushed her hair aside to press kisses to the back of her neck.

"There is no shame in having pride," she disagreed with him, even as she bent her neck to grant him better access. "And in any case," she said with a shrug. "This is not pride. This is anger. It isn't right that you tease me."

"Umm hmm," Enrique murmured as he let his lips linger right at the base of her neck. He bit down gently and had the immense pleasure of having her grip his hand, her nails digging in like a vice. That particular move always got results for him. He waited and smiled when she relaxed against him once again, melting like warm butter.

"Still angry, baby?" he asked, nosing the nightgown aside to get to more skin. Silently, she rose up and lifted her arms in the air, enabling him to slip the nightgown off her. Naked now, she resumed her former position. Enrique tracked kisses down her spine, making her cry out when he sucked the skin between his teeth and bit down.

"I don't want you in just my dreams," he murmured against her skin. He slid his hand over and under her ass and between her thighs until he was covering her cleft. He held her in place with his other hand when she jerked in response. "If you are not real, how can you make me feel this way?" he demanded of her as he slid a finger in her channel while his thumb gently worked her clit in a circular motion.

"Ah, Enrique," she moaned. "Please do not stop," she begged him, opening her thighs wide and pushing her mound against his hand as her body moved in time with the rhythm of his finger.

He pushed another finger inside of her and watched as her eyes closed in rapture and her hands gripped the sheets to maintain balance. She was beautiful and he wanted her more than he wanted to take his next breath. "Who are you?" he demanded softly, just before he pulled his fingers out and removed his hand from between her legs.

He watched as her eyes opened at the sudden loss. She looked at him, her eyes filled with yearning and frustration. The room was full of the sounds of their harsh breathing and the smell of her arousal. "Please, Enrique," she said softly, not breaking eye contact.

His thick, hard cock poking through the slit in his boxers, Enrique lay behind her again, spooning her as he had done before. When she pushed her bare ass against his cock, he groaned out loud at the voluptuous sensation. Gripping her slender hips in his hands, he roughly pulled her back against him, pushing his erection between the cheeks of her behind. "Maldición, bebé, que se siente bien!"

"Oh sí, amante, se siente muy bueno," she whimpered between shallow breaths, completely agreeing with him that it felt good. Very good.

Enrique halted their movements by holding her hips still. She whipped her head around to stare questioningly at him. He laughed at her impatience. "Paciencia, amante," he chided her. "Have patience, lover," he repeated. "Damn, for a dream girl, you sure are demanding. I only want to finish undressing," he said and slipped off his boxers.

Pulling her back against him, he roughly rubbed his hand up her supple body--over her smooth thigh, past her slightly flared hip and across her flat belly until he reached his goal. He loved her breasts. As he cupped one underneath and pinched the nipple between two of his fingers until it was even more taut and straining, he thought again how they were just the perfect size for his hands.

"Please, Enrique, more," she groaned and he could tell that she was close to the brink.

"Not yet," he said before trailing his hand down to play in her mons again. As he pinched the tiny bud between the pads of two fingers, he simultaneously bit down on the tendon that stretched between her neck and shoulder. The combination almost brought her completely off the bed.

She tried to turn to face him and he tightened his hold on her to prevent her from doing so. "Do not make me wait," she commanded. "I am ready now!"

"No more Mrs. Nice Guy, huh? What happened to 'please, Enrique?'" Enrique barely got out between shallow breaths as he caressed her mound loving the feel of the slick, bare lips against his fingers. Closing his eyes, he slipped two fingers inside her and moaned when the silky muscle contracted strongly around them.

When she lifted one leg and put it on top of his, he slid one hand under her hip, lifting her so he could slide his other leg beneath her bottom one. Holding his top thigh between her two, she began to ride it and his fingers, her behind rubbing against his cock as her clit slid back and forth against his thigh. "That's it, baby," he said against the back of her neck. "You got it, sexy mama, you got it."

As her cream spilled out, drowning his fingers and thigh in her unique essence, he lost control and suddenly flipped her over so that she was lying flat on her back. Rising over her, he lowered himself on top of her, feeling her open her legs wide beneath him. He looked into her eyes and plunged his cock deep, causing her breath to catch in her throat, her nails to dig deep in his arms and her back to arch so far off the bed that her neck hung back gracefully in the air for a moment, leaving only the tips of her hair to touch the sheets.

And then he began to move.

She sobbed out his name. He kept his thrusts shallow at first, loving the feel of her tight, wet channel squeezing his penis. He wanted to prolong it for as long as he could.

After several minutes of this, she begged, "Por favor, Enrique. I would like it faster and harder," she requested on a breathy sigh.

"Not yet," he said. "It is not the time for fast and hard. Now is the time for slow and easy," he finished, though the effort to go slow was almost killing him.

It was more than apparent that she didn't agree. Raising her legs, she wrapped them tightly around his waist, at the same time reaching out to tickle him under each of his arms, so that he lost his balance and fell onto her.

As she wrapped her arms around his neck to keep him in place, she began to pump her hips furiously against him. "Minx *impaciente,"* he chastised with a shake of his head. *"You win,"* he murmured teasingly and chuckled when she gave him one of her patented arrogant looks that told him she didn't know why he would expect anything less.

He couldn't hold out and was pounding into her just as furiously as she ground her pussy against him. *"What's your name?"* he demanded again as she tightened her arms around his neck. *"Where do you come from?"*

*"Ah, Enrique, you feel so good,"* she said after one particularly strong thrust. Feeling his orgasm gain momentum and build quickly inside of him, Enrique tried hard to hold it back. *"Ready, mi querida hermosa?"* he asked, wanting to make sure she found her pleasure before he took his.

*"Ah, si, bebé. I am ... I am ... am ... ah ... ah...."* The rest was not said as she screamed.

As he loosed the reins on his own orgasm and felt it rip through him, Enrique felt a memory tug at him. Ah yes, he thought with a smile. She does scream like a banshee.

\* \* \* \*

*"Will you kiss and hold me now?"* Enrique heard her ask and opened his eyes to look at her. Though she tried to look superior, he detected uncertainty in her voice and he felt regret for not giving her what she wanted earlier. She liked it when they kissed, but she always wanted to be held. She seemed to need it.

*"Of course, baby,"* he said as he opened his arms to her. *"I should have done it earlier,"* he finished with a quick squeeze as she settled against him with her head tucked under his chin.

She bent her head back and raised her mouth in preparation for his kiss. *"Yes, you should have,"* she said haughtily, making him chuckle right before he pressed his lips to her smiling mouth in a sweet kiss.

She climbed fully on top of him and he wrapped his arms around her.

*"What is your name, my beautiful one?"* he whispered into her hair. *"What is your name?"* The question was more urgent now because he could feel himself waking up. *"What is your name? Who are you?"*

\* \* \* \*

"Damn it!" Enrique said and sat up in bed. "Thirty fucking years to the day the dreams started and I'm no closer to knowing now who the hell she is than I was then."

## Chapter Three

*Seattle*
*Region Twenty-two, Parallel Plus*
*The Present*

"What were you thinking, Traia?" Commander Edris Perseveranth asked her sister for what seemed like the trillionth time in their lives. "You could have killed someone." Left unsaid was the fact that she could have killed herself.

"It was one little accident," the younger woman mumbled guiltily before slouching down further into the unattractive gray sofa.

"One little accident? You know as well as I that it takes a delicate hand to pilot one of the new sky huggers, yet you took it without having had any training."

Traia tried hard not to pout as she stared up at her impressive, big sister who stood above her looking as impassive and enigmatic as a sphinx. Traia didn't let that fool her. Edris kept her anger hidden, but from experience Traia knew it was there, just beneath the surface. "I'm sorry, Edris. I was only trying to help. I am a licensed flyer, after all. I could see that Senior Officer Cappy was going to hit the hugger during his landing, so I tried to move it, but--"

"But you hit the one parked in front of it. And instead of SO Cappy blowing it up, you did. Yes, Traia. I was there--remember? I saw everything."

"Well, really, Edris," Traia said with a huffy sigh, "there's no need for sarcasm."

Edris stared at the younger woman in stunned silence for a moment. "You're worried about sarcasm? Christ, Traia, *you freaking blew up a brand new sky hugger!*" She yelled and realizing she had, reigned her temper back in and took a deep breath before saying as calmly as she could, "Sarcasm is the least of your worries. You have put me in an impossible position. I cannot save you this time."

"What do you mean?" Traia's voice was full of suspicion.

Edris sighed impatiently. "This is not like when you were a teenager, pulled a prank, and came to me to get you out of the situation, Traia--"

"Which you rarely did, by the way," Traia interrupted in a disgruntled voice.

"You know what, Traia--" Edris began angrily and cut herself off. She had a nasty temper and she didn't want to say anything she'd regret later. "That's a lie and you well know it. No, forget it," she said and shook her head in disbelief as she paced away from her and came back. "You are unbelievable, Traia, and I am not going to let you sidetrack me. You will have to go before the Punitive and Corrections Board in two days and I will not try to influence them. The most I will do--"

"But, Edris, they will most probably fire me!"

"I realize that and if they do, you will just have to face it. We all must learn to take responsibility for our actions--good or bad."

"You always say that!"

"It is a relief to know that you have heard me," Edris said with a roll of her eyes toward the ceiling. "Yet you do not appear to *listen*. You continue to get yourself in trouble. Is there anyone but me who sees the irony?"

"Edris, please," Traia begged, ignoring the sarcasm this time. "Help me just this one last time. I don't want to get fired. Just like you, all I've ever wanted to do was work as a security and regulation officer. If they fire me, I don't know what I'll do. All of my friends are on the Force. If you help me this one last time, I promise I won't get into anymore trouble."

Edris stared down at her, her heart breaking for her. As much as she wanted to, she couldn't show her any mercy. Traia was twenty and it was time she learned to be more responsible. "I am sorry, Traia, I really am, but I can't do it. You are an officer of the law and, as such, your duty is to uphold the law and the rules, not to break them."

Traia's mouth twisted as her eyes glared resentment and Edris mentally steeled herself for what was to come. When the hit came, it was particularly nasty.

"Not everyone can be as you are, Edris. Now I know why all the other officers call you robot--you are as emotionless and as cold as one. You do nothing without turning it over in your mind a million times before. You don't even speak before you've thought about what you're going to say for at least five minutes. It's no wonder you've had no man in your life. Well, I'm not like you. I can't operate that way."

Edris took the blows without any outward sign that they had landed. Inside, she cringed with pain. She'd heard the same things whispered about her during her entire career--both by peers and subordinates. She ignored them to get her job done. But she never expected to hear those words coming from her sister's mouth. She felt tears sting her eyes, but blinked them back. "Yes, well, then it is lucky that others of us can." She took a steadying breath before saying, "I cannot promise because I have several meetings, but I will try to be at your hearing." She left the room before she completely broke down.

"Shit," Traia whispered regretfully. "I didn't mean it." She knew, however, that she would have to allow Edris to calm down before she attempted to apologize. She sighed. She always felt so inadequate around her sister. Everything about her was intimidating. She was fearless and intelligent, and at thirty-two was the youngest regional Force Commander in the system. When she'd made commander at twenty-eight, she'd been the youngest in the history of the Force.

There were a total of twenty-five regional commands in the system. Edris led the twenty-second one, which was comprised of the states of Washington and Oregon. Every law enforcement officer in the two states was under her command. She was also beautiful with her tall, toned, ebony body and perfect features. In Traia's mind, that only made matters worse.

One of these things would have been enough to intimidate anyone, but all of them combined made Traia feel that she had something to prove, particularly since Edris had adjusted her own life, at twenty-two, to take care of Traia when their father had died. Traia felt that she owed Edris, but could never do enough to pay her back. Instead, she tried to impress her, thinking that at least she could make her sister proud of her. Today's episode had been the result of another one of those attempts to impress. Now her career was on the line, she owed money for the sky hugger and, as Commander, Edris would get flack for having such an inept sister on the Force. Traia let out another sigh. "I can't do anything right."

\* \* \* \*

Edris methodically removed her uniform piece by piece and tried not to think about her latest confrontation with Traia. Jacket. Blaster. Holster. Belt. Right boot. Left boot. Ankle blaster. Ankle holster. Simulated leather pants. It didn't work. With a broken sigh of defeat, she sat on the edge of her bed in her shirt and underwear, buried her face in her hands and let the tears fall. She was so tired of having to be the strong one, the responsible one. Even before her father had died, she had been the one in charge.

Her mother had been murdered one month after Traia's birth and their father's grief had paralyzed him, leaving a ten-year old Edris to take care of her sister, herself, her father and the household. The subsequent passion he felt to find out exactly what had happened to his wife had consumed their father. He'd had no room in his life for practical matters like the running of a household, so Edris had still filled the role of main caretaker for the family.

She was *so* tired. This was not the life she'd envisioned for herself at the age of ten, but it had been impossible for her to choose any other. "Well, that's just too bad, Edris," she told herself in a quavering voice. "This is the life you have and you'll have to live it." She lifted her head and wiped her eyes. Sighing, she took a look around her bedroom to try and cheer herself. It was huge and so unlike the world outside. As Commander, she had first access to the coveted and scarce colored silks, paints and wallpapers that made their way to Region Twenty-two. As a consequence, unlike the majority of the people who lived in Parallel Plus, her wardrobe had some colored pieces in it. She welcomed anything that wasn't the ubiquitous black, gray and white of the rest of her world, often wishing that she'd been born on the other side of the portal where there was color, freshness and bounty.

It was not to be so she made do with what she had and covered her walls and furniture in color. Traia's face and words popped into Edris' mind and broke the peace she was so desperately trying to achieve. "Oh, damn it," she said in a helpless voice when the tears began to fall again. She'd been trying all of Traia's life to take care of her and she was determined not to feel guilty for not rescuing her this one time, out of the hundreds of other times it had been necessary to pull her out of trouble.

Like Edris, Traia had joined the Security and Regulation Force at the age of twenty, after spending two years in the training academy. Unlike Edris, Traia did not rise through the ranks quickly. She was still an SJCO, a Subsidiary Junior Class Officer, the lowest of all the ranks. Most of the class she'd come in with had already been promoted. Traia was one of eleven who hadn't. One foul up after another on her part had kept her an SJCO.

Each time she'd gotten in trouble, Edris had worked behind the scenes to make sure she had only received what amounted to a slap on the wrist. But she couldn't bring herself to do it this time. She hoped that Traia wouldn't lose her job, but she also hoped that going in front of the Punitive and Corrections Board would temper some of her zealousness.

Edris rose tiredly and headed toward the connecting bath. She stood in front of the mirror and studied her face. She liked her eyes, the gray color against the darkness of her face pleasing her. Traia had been wrong, she thought with a frown. She'd had lovers before. None of them had ever really been able to satisfy her and the relationships hadn't worked out, but she'd had them. Maybe a total of two lovers was a small amount for a single woman of her age, but that was her life. Attracting men was a problem for her because too many of them were intimidated by her position and just the sheer strength and command of her presence.

She knew she was attractive and could probably have as many lovers as she wanted if she tried hard enough, but to her the effort she'd have to put forth wouldn't be worth the results. "No one in this world--or even the next, probably--can satisfy me,"

Edris whispered aloud. She did wish, however, that she could meet the man who had invaded her sleep the night before. She didn't use the word 'dream' because she didn't think it was her dream. She believed she had somehow been able to witness *his* dream. "Could that really happen? Am I going crazy?"

She'd never seen the gorgeous, dark-haired, blue-eyed man before, but he'd acted like they'd known one another. She even remembered his name. *Enrique*. Hell, she'd said it often enough during the dream that it was practically imprinted on her brain. In his dream, she'd done things that she'd never do in real life. She'd never give up control like that. Never. But she had to admit that the things he'd made her feel had the power to make her knees feel as boneless as water just thinking about them. She'd never had an orgasm like that in her life! And when she'd awakened that morning, she'd been strangely satisfied and had felt the proof of the orgasm pooling between her legs.

Edris frowned as she remembered something else. She'd known his name, but he hadn't known hers. In fact, he didn't seem to know much about her. "*What is your name?*" she whispered the question he'd asked her over and over again. "Dark beauty." Remembering the way he'd said it weakened her insides and made her emit a soft, deep sigh.

The unfamiliar yearning she felt for him was scary and thrilling in its intensity.

Lying in his arms had felt wonderful, she remembered with a wistful smile that was blissful at the same time. She smiled again as she remembered the play of his fingers through her hair while she'd lain on his chest and how ... cherished she'd felt lying there.

Someone had been taking care of and holding her for a change and she'd had no worries.

"God, he was strong ... and tall," she whispered to herself. He was at least five inches taller than she, and slender, but powerfully built and she had no doubt that he'd have no problem handling a woman of her size. She was a perfect six feet tall and she didn't run into many men like him in her little world.

When she caught herself sighing again, she frowned. She had no room in her life for pining over something that would never happen. "This will not do, Edris. Be grateful you experienced it and let it go," she sternly told her mirrored self.

Stripping completely now, she blew her hair out of her eyes. Thick and wavy, it was a rich black color--all except the shock of white in the center. She'd had it since she'd been a child. It was a stark reminder of her true mission in life. Turning on the water, she forced herself to admit that Traia was correct. She *had* become like a robot. She'd had to. It was the only way she could focus to do what she had to do and track down the ones responsible for the death of her mother.

## Chapter Four

"So, tell me, DC Smith, is everything ready for my traversal next week?"

Deputy Chief Angie Smith rolled her brown eyes at Edris. "I know we're at work, Edie, but we're alone in your office with the door closed and for God's sake, girl, we've known each other our entire lives. Stop being so damned proper!" She adjusted her small frame in one of the chairs facing the desk.

Edris allowed a small smile to escape and turned back to her office window. She always spoke formally at work. She couldn't help it. It had become habit when she'd joined the Force. Slang and informal speech did not garner respect from superiors. Her formal speech had made her stand out from the rest of the young recruits in her class. She'd been taken more seriously and had been seen as more mature and competent than others her age. The habit was so ingrained now that it was also a defense mechanism when she felt unsure of herself. Angie and Traia were really the only two people who didn't let her get away with being formal. They knew her better than anyone else.

With a sigh, Edris allowed her eyes to focus on what they were seeing outwardly. The landscape, barren of everything but gray-and-black steel buildings was depressing under the strong glare of the sun. Except for water, they'd depleted most of their resources and everything was a simulation of the real thing, including their clothing, which was only drab black or gray.

Even their food was simulated, Edris thought with disgust. Only the wealthy and those in positions of power had access to fresh fruit, vegetables or sustenance from an actual animal. Just thinking about simulated meat made Edris' stomach turn.

She would occasionally treat herself and purchase fresh fruit or vegetables, but when she really felt like splurging, she bought chocolate. Creamy, milky, mouth-watering chocolate. "God, I wish I had some now!" she murmured.

"Edie?"

Edris turned. "Sorry, Angie, I was daydreaming."

Angie grinned. "Was it about Enrique?"

Edris almost regretted telling Angie about the dream. The other woman brought it up every chance she could. "No, it wasn't about Enrique. Damn. Can we *not* talk about him?" she asked and sat down.

"Okay, but just one more question. Have you dreamed of him again?"

"No, I haven't." Edris's voice was surly. Every night she went to bed hoping that she would, but in two weeks nothing more had happened.

"Um hmm. No wonder you're so damned salty--you're not getting any, not even in your dreams."

"Angie," Edris said warningly.

"Okay, okay," Angie said. "I'll be serious."

"Good," Edris said and sat up straighter in her chair before she heard a soft, sing-songy:

*"Edris and Enrique screwing in a dream, k-i-s-s--"*

"Oh, whatever, Angie!" Edris said. "That's not funny," she tried to say sternly, but was laughing too hard to accomplish it. Angie was good for her. She counterbalanced her seriousness and could always make her laugh. "Anyway," she said after taking several deep breaths. "Let's get back to work. Is everything in order for my traversal to the Sub Parallel?"

Angie sighed. Playtime was over. "Yes. I have your coordinates right here. This time next week, you will be in the Sub Parallel's Chicago. I have Sub Parallel American money for you, a credit card, an Identification Card naming you as an American police officer from Detroit and a driver's license from that same city."

"Good," Edris said, and reaching across the desk for the items, placed them in her handbag. Traversal--travel through the portals to the Sub Parallel--was another privilege given only to the chosen few, mostly law enforcement officers, politicians and scientists. Traversals were limited in order to protect the secret of the existence of the portal and Parallel Plus.

The main reason for traversals was to conduct research. It would be Edris's third time in her career to traverse. The first two times had been to track down criminals who had somehow managed to get through the portals. This time, however, she would be traveling for her own personal research.

"It is warm in Chicago at this time of the year, correct?" Edris asked.

Angie smiled. "Yes, Edris. When you arrive in Chicago, you will be able to purchase clothing made of the light, airy material called linen. Before you leave, you will be furnished with one outfit made of this material, which you will bring back with you. The others that you purchase there, you must leave behind."

Those who traversed only left with the clothing on their backs to minimize the possibility of failure. They could take a small handbag, but luggage was not allowed. They purchased clothing and other essentials in the Sub Parallel, but not before seekers--people trained for just this purpose--went through the portal and purchased a set of appropriate clothing for the traveler. Upon returning, travelers were required to turn in the clothing and cash so that it could be used again.

"Yes, I know." Edris waved her hand in dismissal, before excitedly leaning forward. "What color is the outfit, Angie?"

"Oh, it is beautiful, Edie. The seeker did a wonderful job. The pants are in the style called Capri and they are of a magnificent blue. Your shirt is of a lighter hue, but still blue. You will look stunning in it."

Edris smiled again. "It will be wonderful to not have to wear the Leathers all the time." Security and Regulations officers' standard uniform consisted of soft, simulated leather in pants and a jacket, worn with a gray or black shirt made of a lighter material underneath. The outfit molded itself perfectly to its owner's body.

"Have you requisitioned a replicater for me?" she asked.

"Yes. It's right here. I will take charge of the receiver myself. Don't forget to leave it on," Angie reminded her. "It's the only way I can contact you."

"Don't worry. I won't."

Angie hated to ask, but felt she had to. "Are you sure you want to do this, Edris?"

"I have no choice. I have to find the ones responsible for my mother's death."

"But, Edris, you are traveling under false pretenses." Every traveler had to file mission papers with the Traversal Committee before undertaking traversal to the other world. Edris's mission papers were filled with lies regarding her reason for wanting to traverse. "If you are caught, you could lose your career, or worse, go to prison."

"I know all of this, Angie, but it is a chance I am willing to take."

Angie hated that Edris's life was filled with so much sorrow. Now that Terrence Perseveranth was gone, Edris--and Traia too, to a certain extent--had taken on the cause of trying to find the ones responsible for the loss of their mother. "Edris, can't you just let this go?"

"No, Angie, I cannot. I have come this far and I am too close to finding out what happened to just stop now. After all of these years, I've found a trail and it leads to Chicago. My mother is no longer here because she tried to stop illegal smuggling between this world and the next. They worked with corrupt people on the other side, and I have some of their names. I also have names of the people who worked it from this side of the portal. I just don't have the proof. My suspicions are that smuggling is still going on. It didn't stop all those years ago with my mother's death. If I'm right and I get the proof, it could bring down a lot of people. Judge Patrickson and Commander Bobson of Region Eighteen are just two of them. I'm just trying to find out for sure," Edris explained.

"My mother was a good Security and Regulations officer, and I loved her. She didn't deserve what happened to her. They did not even leave us with a body to bury. All they left were her shield, her weapon, a lot of her blood and speculation and cruel hope." She stopped to calm herself. She got angry just thinking about it. "So, no, I cannot give up--not until those who killed my mother are captured and punished."

"I'm sorry, Edie," Angie said. "I didn't mean to sound so cavalier. I'm just worried about you."

"I know your only motive is to help. But I have to do this."

"I know you have to," Angie said, "but I thought I'd try one last time to talk you out of it. What about Traia? Does she know why you're going?"

"No. I decided not to tell her. She would only want to come and she does not have clearance, but being Traia, she would sneak through somehow. She cannot afford any more mistakes for a while if she wants to keep her position."

"Are you still mad at her about the whole sky hugger thing?"

"Absolutely," Edris said. "Angie, my heart was in my throat when she crashed. I thought I might faint. She's just so damned reckless."

"I know, but her intentions are always good."

"Still. I love her, Angie, but sometimes I really despair over her future and our relationship. This latest incident has certainly set us back. I can't seem to get past it. Every time I try to, the image of her frightened face as the sky hugger crashed and the resulting fire, remind me of her stupidity and I want to scream."

"I hope you two can work it out. She loves you and is always trying to impress you."

Edris sighed. "I know and I love her. I wish she would just settle down and not try to impress me. I've told her time and time again to just do her job and I'll be happy."

A knock sounded at the door. "Yes?" Edris called.

The door opened and an older man and woman in their sixties entered.

A smile of pure pleasure wreathed Edris's dark face when she saw who it was. "Uncle Clay! Aunt Sue!" She rose to come around her desk to give each of them a hug. "What are you doing here?"

Clay Anderson chuckled as he took his turn. "Can't a couple old fools visit their favorite niece when they feel like it?" As her mother's partner, he'd been such a close friend that he was like family. Edris had been calling him 'uncle' and his wife 'aunt' since she'd been small.

"Hey, don't call my favorite aunt and uncle fools," Edris said as she stepped back in his arms to get a good look at him. His green eyes sparkled and his pale skin showed only a few wrinkles. "I might have to lock you up!" she said before noticing a movement from the corner of her eye. "Oh, I'm sorry. You remember Angie, don't you?"

Sue, a plump lady with a ready smile and a raucous laugh, turned to Angie. "How could we not remember her? There were times when I thought you two were connected at the hip. If we saw one of you, we saw the other. Right, honey?" she said to Clay.

"Absolutely. You two were closer than sisters. How are you, Angie?" he asked.

"Fine, sir, thank you, sir!" Angie said with a smart salute.

"Now, none of that 'sir' business. I haven't been Commander of this region for four years. Your best friend here has that honor now, remember?" he asked with a wink.

Angie blushed. "Yes, sir. It's just that your career here was so stellar and, well ... it's just an honor to see you again, sir."

Edris smiled at Angie's nervousness. If she didn't know Clay as well as she did, she'd be nervous as well. He was the most decorated officer in the history of Security and Regulations, having won several dozen honors for his bravery and commitment. He had met Sue when they'd been in the training academy together.

"So, young lady," Clay said. "I understand you will be taking a trip soon."

"Now, Clay," Sue said chidingly. "Mind your own business."

"She is my business," Clay said firmly. "Well?"

"Yes. I'm going to Chicago." Edris didn't question how he'd heard. He still had friends on the Force. "I have some research to do."

"This doesn't concern your mother does it?"

"Clay!" Sue said in surprise. "Why would you ask a question like that? It's all right, dear," she said to Edris as she rubbed her arm. "You don't have to answer him."

Edris flinched, but didn't dare look at Angie. "No, of course it doesn't," she answered Clay. "Why would you ask that?"

"I ask because I know how obsessed you were about finding out what happened to her. It's why you joined the Force. Promise me you aren't taking this trip through the portal with the crazy notion that you'll find out what happened to your mother?"

"Yes, I promise," Edris lied without a qualm.

"Well, that settles that," Sue said. "I've got to run to the little girl's room and then I'm off to visit Terry in records. Honey bunch?" she addressed Clay. "Will you be staying long?"

Edris smiled. For as long as she could remember, Sue had adored Clay.

"Just for a little while," Clay said. "I want to catch up with our girl here. Do you have a few minutes for me, sweetheart?" he asked Edris.

"Yes, I always have time for you, Uncle Clay."

"Oh, that's sweet," Sue said. "Gimme hug, baby doll," she said to Edris. "I wish I could stay, but I promised Terry I'd visit. Goodbye now. Come over to dinner real soon, okay?"

"Yes." Edris hugged her back. "It was good to see you."

"You too, baby doll. Clay, darling, I'll meet you at the car in a half an hour."

"Yes, dear," Clay said and pressed an adoring kiss to her nose.

Edris pounced as soon as her door was closed again. "Why would you ask me about Mother now, Uncle Clay? You never asked when I went through the portal before."

"Before you weren't going to Chicago, which is the destination the portal was programmed for when we lost your mother. I thought you knew that."

"No, I didn't know that," Edris said quietly, thinking if she had, she'd have saved years of wasted time. "Tell me everything," she demanded and walked around her desk to sit back down.

## Chapter Five

"Now, sweetheart, I don't think that's a good--"

"Uncle Clay," she cut him off. "I need to know."

"All right," Clay said reluctantly and sat down. "For years there had been rumors that prisoners were being smuggled through the portals. Families of these criminals were paying off high-ranking officials to get their loved ones through to the other side. Everyone knew it was true, but no one could ever prove anything. Well, for once, we caught a lucky break. One of the guards at the Seattle Federal Courthouse had heard a defense lawyer discussing an escape plan for his client with the prosecuting attorney.

"The guard told his brother, who just happened to be your mother's and my superior officer. He put us on the case and though we were too late to stop that one illegal traversal, enough of a lead was found that we knew we were onto something big. Anyway, Carma and I worked this thing day and night for years. We spent a lot of sleepless nights following leads, talking to potential witnesses and just doing grunt work at the computer. The case was hush-hush because it was suspected that there were even some people on the Force involved. So, if she couldn't work for some reason, then I did it alone and it was the same for her.

"Well, the night Carma was killed was one of those nights that I couldn't be with her. Sue was in the hospital and I couldn't work. Anyway, your mother had found something that led her to the lab right here in the basement of this building. It turns out that the Commander at the time, Watkins Polar, had been in on the smuggling himself. They were doing it weekly and your mother had figured out that that particular night would be one when they would try to smuggle someone out, so she went to the portal.

"She'd known that there was a possibility that she would be killed, so she left me a recorded message and that's how we knew where to look for her when she didn't show for work and we realized that she hadn't been home. We didn't find her, but we did find you, unconscious, holding her shield and her blaster. That's when that hair there in the front of your head turned white. We figured that you must have been too close to the portal's energy source when they sent someone through."

Edris subconsciously tugged on the aforementioned hair and frowned. She didn't remember a damn thing about that night.

"Anyway," Clay continued. "We took you to the hospital and when you came to, you couldn't remember anything. We couldn't find her, Edris, even in the Sub Parallel. As hard as we tried, we just couldn't find her. I knew she was dead, though. She never would have given up her shield or her blaster willingly. They would have had to kill her first. We also found her blood, a lot of it--right near the side of the portal. Nobody could have survived that much blood loss. And you, you poor little thing, you never did get your memory back of that night. Or have you? Have you remembered anything?"

"No," Edris said, fury rolling through her system at the thought of what had happened. "I've tried and tried, but nothing has ever come back to me."

"That's too bad," Clay said. "Your mother also left detailed notes and with those and other clues, we were able to prove who was behind the smuggling a few months later.

Everyone from the lowliest lab workers to officers to lawyers and judges had been involved. The web stretched from here all the way to Florida. That's just how extensive it was, but we got them. Your mother was posthumously honored for the part she played in bringing them down."

"Why was I not told any of this before?"

"Your father knew, sweetheart. I'd always assumed he'd told you."

"No, he was too wrapped up in his own world to bother to tell me anything," Edris said and, for the first time, there was bitterness in her voice.

"I'm sorry."

"It's fine," Edris said and stood, signaling that the visit was over.

Clay could take a hint and he stood as well. "Don't you go off to Chicago for anything crazy," he warned as he opened the door.

"I won't," she promised, thinking that finding out who killed her mother could not be considered crazy by any measurement.

"Well, what do you think?" Angie asked as soon as he'd closed the door.

"I think that something is up and he's not telling me everything. That's what I think."

"Me, too," Angie said. "But what could he be holding back?"

"I just think there's more to the story, that's all. Why would he suddenly show up here today? I haven't heard from him or Aunt Sue in months."

"Maybe he's just worried. He does seem to care about you."
"I know he does and that's why I think he's holding back. He doesn't want me hurt any more than I already have been."
"Do you think he really thought he could talk you out of going?"
"Yes."
"Didn't work out that way."
"It certainly didn't."

## Chapter Six

"Why do you bring me here? How do you bring me here?" Edris asked Enrique as he walked into the room.

Enrique stopped his progress to look at her in surprise. She wasn't lying on the bed. This time she stood. Again, the short nightie she wore--a purple one this time--barely covered her, but he didn't think he'd be getting any anytime soon if the look on her face was anything to go by. She looked angry and confused. "What did you say?"

"How do you bring me here?" Edris said impatiently. "You will answer me now, stranger."

"Stranger?" Enrique repeated. The word angered him. "What the hell? Sugah, the last thing you should be calling me is 'stranger,'" he said as he advanced toward her. Toe-to-toe with her, he said, "Does a stranger make you scream his name, night after night as he brings you to orgasm?"

Edris breathed his scent in deeply and closed her eyes, her senses on overload from his nearness. Still, she stood her ground. She opened her eyes and looked him in his eyes. "That does not signify. You are still a stranger."

Furious now, Enrique made her back up until she was against the wall. It was either that or have her bare toes stepped on. "Does a stranger make your clit heavy and dripping with need from just one look at you?" he asked as he pressed against her so that she felt his thick length through her gown.

Edris couldn't help it and opened her thighs wide to accommodate him and bit back a moan when he gave a hard thrust of his hips, making her rise on her toes. "Stop ... do not--" The rest of her words were lost as he bent his head to gently suck on her neck. Enrique was still furious. That's how she saw him? As a fucking stranger? "Does a stranger," he breathed between suckling kisses as he trailed them from one side of her neck to the other. He took her hands and pressed them on either side of her head, entwining her fingers with his. "Does a stranger make you want to kiss him until you are completely out of breath?" he asked right before he pressed his lips to hers.

Edris greedily accepted his tongue, moaning as he cut a wide *swath through her mouth. She sucked and bit at him, a frenzy of need overtaking her as he thrust his tongue into her mouth in rhythm with the thrusts of his jeans-covered cock against her cleft. A sound of disappointment escaped her throat when he broke away from the kiss.*

"Does a stranger--" Enrique began, only to find himself unable to resist her seeking lips. He pressed a hard kiss to her mouth, released her hands and continued.

"Does a stranger have the ability to make your vagina weep with gratitude when he does this?" He bent his head and bit her nipple through her nightgown, just as he slid his hands up her thighs and to her hips where he grabbed her by her rear and pulled her hips roughly into his.

Edris threw her head back on her neck and screamed. Lifting one leg, she hooked it around his waist and rode his driving cock as best she could. "Please," she begged when that wasn't enough.

"Please what?" Enrique asked as he lifted her so that both her legs were wrapped around his waist. He couldn't stay angry as he looked at her. She opened her solid gray eyes and looked at him and the pleading in them weakened him. "Please what? Say my name."

Edris stubbornly refused as she said, "Please do not torture me any longer."

"Please what?" Enrique asked again as he raised her gown completely and eased two fingers inside her. The gown fell again as he braced himself against the wall with his other hand. "Hold up your gown," he said to her.

Edris took hold of the end of her gown with both hands and raised it until it was under her chin.

Enrique bent his head and suckled her breast into his mouth, teasing the nipple with stinging little bites and soothing it with licks of his tongue each time she cried out. "Please what?" he demanded.

Edris couldn't take it anymore. She wanted to feel his penis sliding into her so badly she would almost say anything. Almost. "Please, undo your zipper," she said and dropped the gown to do it herself.

Enrique lightly slapped her hands away. "Please what?" He unbuttoned his pants and unzipped his jeans partially so that the head of his penis pushed out.

"Please, Enrique," Edris begged, crying out in relief when he pulled his zipper down, shoved his pants and boxers down and shot his erection deep on the first try. Using her feet and hands, she *pushed his jeans and boxers further down around his thighs and palmed his butt, her hands gripping him tightly as she ground him into her.*

*"There you go, sweetheart," Enrique said and bent his head to gently suck at her lips. "You are so sexy, mi bebé. There is nothing in this world that compares to being inside of you," he said lovingly as he looked into her eyes. "Say my name again, beautiful one, say it."*

*"Enrique," Edris obliged him with tears in her eyes. "And there is nothing that compares to having you inside of me, mi amor," she told him in answer to his tender words as she kissed him back.*

*Enrique moved slowly as he kissed her, bracing them against the wall with his legs, his knees bending and hitting the wall on each downward thrust. He gripped her under her thighs, holding her aloft so that each slide into her was smooth and true. He felt the inferno building from the base of his penis, his stomach muscles clenching and unclenching in preparation. "It's almost time, baby," he said harshly, each word a strain.*

*As she felt her orgasm bubbling up inside of her stomach, Edris whimpered from the force of its heat and power. "Oh, Enrique!"*

*"Say it again," Enrique commanded, slamming into her again and again.*

*"Enrique!"*

*"Enrique!" Each utterance of his name followed a shove of his cock into her grateful pussy.*

*"Enrique!"*

*"Enrique!"*

*"Oh, Enriquehhhhhhhhhh," she yelled when the liquid heat rushed throughout her entire body, making her feel hot and numb at the same time as little pinpricks of electricity danced across her skin. "Oh, yes, Enrique! Yes, yes, yes!" The explosion going on inside her body took complete control of her.*

*As the force of his orgasm slammed through him, he erupted into her, his dick an invading force that plunged fast and furiously into her streaming channel as it convulsed around him. The power of his thrusts slammed her back against the wall again and again until, empty and satisfied, he fell against her letting most of his weight rest on his forearms as he leaned them against the wall on either side of her head. Tiredly, he kissed her, his lips sipping at, and clinging to hers as he renewed his energy. "Pull up my jeans," he told her softly and pulled out of her with a slick sound.*

*Edris moaned at the loss and opened her eyes. She felt completely drained, but it was a good, satisfying draining that was invigorating at the same time. Lazily, she reached down and did as he said, pulling them up so that they rode low on his hips.*

*Enrique boosted her up and pulled her close, smiling when she laid her head on his chest and wrapped her arms around his shoulders. He carried her over to the bed where he lay down with her on top of him.*

*Edris adjusted her legs so that they were caught between his.* "Do you truly find me sexy? Even as tall as I am?" *she asked him when she remembered what he'd said in the heat of passion.*

*Enrique frowned and sighed. It always amazed him that as beautiful as she was she still needed reassurance of her appeal.* "Si, beautiful one," *he reassured her gently and gave her a squeeze.* "You are very, very sexy. Do you not get that your height is an added bonus? Especially to someone who is as tall as I am?"

*She lifted her head to look at him.* "So you are saying that if I were short, like a munchkin, you would not find me sexy?"

"Baby, if you were as short as a munchkin, it would be impossible for us to be together. You wouldn't be able to handle big, bad Bubba down there. One thrust and you'd break in half," *he boasted and grinned when she snorted and laid her head back down, so that it rested on his shoulder and her face pressed into his neck.* "I would find you sexy, no matter what package you came in. You were meant for me."

*She didn't say anything, but he felt her lips press wetly against his neck in a soft kiss. He hated to break up such a tender moment with an argument, but it couldn't be helped.*

"I am Enrique Jefferson Thomas Rivera. I am not a stranger. Say it." *He felt her stiffen, but she stubbornly remained quiet.* "Dream Girl," *he said warningly.*

*Edris did not like being told what to do and she didn't want to argue with him, because despite everything, she still felt that he was a stranger. She closed her eyes tightly, wishing she were out of the dream. She felt his arms tighten around her in warning and she lifted her head, her eyes flashing frustration and confusion at him.* "What would you call a man whom you have only seen two times in your life and those two times have only been in dreams? I call that man a stranger."

*Enrique didn't miss her acknowledgment that she dreamed of him as well and even knowing what an important revelation that was, he still couldn't let go of the insult of her calling him a stranger. The primitive male in him wouldn't allow it.* "I am not a stranger! I *have known you since you were two years old and what we have shared in this room is more than what a lot of people are lucky enough to have in their lifetimes. I am not a stranger. I am Enrique Jefferson Thomas Rivera--your lover and your man. Am I not?"*

*Edris looked at him, processing what he'd said. He'd known her since she was two? How was that possible? But she felt that time was short, so she moved onto what else he had said. Perhaps he was right. She knew that there was no one else in her life she'd ever felt this close intimacy with. "Si, Enrique," she said slowly and bent her head to make amends with a kiss.*

*Enrique started breathing again, unaware that he'd been holding his breath as he waited for her answer. "And I am the best lover you have ever had," he teased.*

*Her smile lit up her face. "Oh, si, Enrique, that is true."*

*"It is?" He was surprised she answered so seriously.*

*"Si, Enrique," she said again.*

*"And the best lover you'll ever have?" he teased her again.*

*She frowned and pretended to think it over. "Now that, I do not--"*

*"Just say, 'Ah, si, Enrique,'" he said warningly.*

*"Well...." She drew the word out so that it had at least two syllables.*

*"Come on, say it!" Enrique said and began to tickle her.*

*She tried to curl into herself to prevent his fingers from doing too much damage. "Ah, si, Enrique!" she said desperately around her laughter. "Si, Enrique!"*

\* \* \* \*

"Si, Enrique," Edris murmured as she began to awaken. She smiled, still caught in the dream, as her eyes slowly opened. The smile disappeared when she realized she was in her own room. "Oh, my God!" She sat straight up in bed, cringing when she felt the sticky wetness between her legs.

Gingerly, she got out of bed and went into the bathroom. She removed her gown and climbed into the shower, trying not to think about what had happened. But as the water beat down upon her head, she leaned against the wall and sobbed. Was she going insane?

She had wanted to dream of Enrique again, yes, but she hadn't actually expected it to be a shared dream that had felt so real and one in which she'd actually confronted him about his ability to pull her in. Was he real? Could he really summon her? How could she possibly dream so clearly of a man who, as far as she knew, didn't even exist?

"Edie? Are you all right?" Traia's worried voice came through the curtain, making Edris jump. "I knocked, but you didn't hear me."

Edris took a deep breath and began to wash. "I'm fine, Tray. I'll be out in a minute." When Traia left, she stepped out of the tub, determined that she'd make an appointment with a psychologist as soon as she was able.

\* \* \* \*

Enrique awoke with the sound of her laughter still ringing in his ears. He smiled and then remembered that he still didn't have any answers and he probably could have had them that time. He just hadn't asked. "Damn it, Enrique. You and your stupid machismo."

Chapter Seven

*Casaba, Kentucky*
*The Sub Parallel*

*"Well? What happened?" The voice was hard and uncompromising.*
*"She hasn't been swayed," a weak voice replied nervously.*
*"Damn it, you were supposed to convince her not to go!"*
*"Hey, don't blame this on me," the voice whined. "I did all I could and it didn't work."*
*"Well, we'll just have to convince her some other way."*
*"No!" The weak voice was suddenly stronger. "We will not eliminate her."*
*"All right, have it your way--for now. But you'd better get rid of her the moment there's any indication she can fuck up this operation!"*

\* \* \* \*

Enrique tried to get the conversation out of his head as he studied the most recent e-mail from Sheriff Johnson of Penster, the next town over. He couldn't stop thinking about it, however, and shoved away from his desk to pace in frustration. "Who the hell is it?" he mumbled to himself. The conversation had come out of nowhere earlier that morning as he'd been sitting at his desk. He'd heard it in his head and had known that it had something to do with his dream girl. He couldn't let go of the sense of foreboding he had. He *knew* that she was in trouble. "God damn it! Even if I knew who was talking, there's nothing I can do to help her--just like all the other times."

It had been the first time he'd heard, rather than saw and Enrique shook his head in frustrated wonder as he thought about this new development. "What the fuck is going to happen next?" He wondered aloud. Being unable to protect her angered him and made him feel powerless, so much so that he'd even called his mother, hoping that she would know something, *anything,* that could help him. He hadn't reached her and he'd decided to search the Internet as he waited for her call.

He'd found nothing substantial in all the information and now he tried to make himself believe that Dalila would have something good for him when she called him back. Sighing, he went back to Sheriff Johnson's message. It was marked priority and Johnson had put "Danger" as his subject. After reading the message, which talked about three teenaged girls stealing purses, Enrique let out a mild sound of disbelief. "Get your rifles, boys, we got us a real crime wave going on, right here in central Kentucky," he mumbled. "*Idioto*," he finished, with a shake of his dark head. Sheriff Johnson always overstated matters. Enrique knew, though, that he had to do something since he was the acting sheriff of the town.

Casaba was a small town of about two thousand people. Its downtown consisted of the Casaba Diner, the Casaba Bank, an ice cream shop, a pizza parlor, a couple of antique shops, a laundry mat, what some people still called a dry goods store, which was really just a small department store and the town square. The town square consisted of two office buildings and two municipal buildings--one that housed the mayor's and council members' offices and one that housed the jail and the sheriff's office. The buildings each fronted a small park

"What'd you say, Sheriff?"

Enrique looked up to see one of his two deputies, Tank Orwell, standing in the doorway to his office. Tank had pale skin, green eyes, a slow-witted mind and was about as big as a tank. "Nothing, Tank. Did you need something?"

"Uh, no, sir. Not exactly," Tank said after clearing his throat several times.

"Just spit it out, boy," Enrique said and leaned back in his chair, stretching out his legs to further accommodate his 6'5" frame. "I won't bite." He said it tongue in cheek, knowing that for some of the people in the small town it wouldn't be beyond the realm of possibility that he would. They didn't know him and they didn't trust him. He was not from Casaba and they didn't much like it. A replacement sent in by the governor's office to straighten out what the old, corrupt sheriff had fucked up; he was an unknown entity. And Casaba Kentuckians, like a lot of people, were wary and suspicious of what they didn't know.

The fact that he was half Puerto Rican, had dark hair, but didn't speak with an accent "like that fella on 'Chico and the Man,'" as he'd been told by one crusty, old resident, only added fuel to the fire and served to confuse the hell out of some of the town's residents. Just yesterday, he'd been told by Tank after a briefing meeting, "You sound just like a regular American--like a good ole boy," he'd elaborated when Enrique had stared at him.

Enrique's only response had been silent surprise that Tank could still sound so surprised at his accent after having worked with him for two months and knowing full well that Enrique had been born and raised in Louisville. He let none of it bother him, however, because he knew that people were slow to let go of long-held notions. As long as no one meant anything maliciously, he was good to go. People's preconceived notions were their own business and he'd only be in their lives for a short period of time, anyway. He was there to do a job and do it he would. They were stuck with him until election time.

"Well, Tank, either you need something or you don't. Which is it?"

"Well, uh, Sheriff," Tank spoke in low tones as he entered the office and walked toward the desk. "It ain't exactly *me* who needs anything."

"Well, then, who is it?" Enrique asked.

"It's Miz. Burkas," Tank said and grinned when Enrique shut his eyes and gave a moan of dread. "She says she has a problem and only you can fix it. She's waitin' outside for you."

*"Madre del dios,"* Enrique said mildly. He didn't have time for this today. He opened his eyes. "And wipe that shit-eatin' grin off your face, Deputy, or I'll make you eat it and after all of that, I'll make you deal with Mrs. Burkas."

The smile disappeared from Tank's face, prompting Enrique to whistle between his teeth in disbelief. The boy really believed he'd do him physical harm.

"Uh-uh, no can do, Sheriff. She only wants you," Tank said and was still able to grin as he thought about all the trouble Mrs. Burkas gave Enrique.

Enrique pushed back from the desk and slowly stood. The woman had been trying his patience since he'd arrived in town. She'd been trying to get at his cock since his very first day on the job. The whole town knew it and she didn't seem to care. Never mind the fact that with her short, petite frame, she just wasn't his type. And never mind the fact that she was at least twenty years older than he, because he didn't have any doubt that older women could get just as freaky-deeky as their younger counterparts. No, his biggest problem was that she was a married woman and she happened to be married to the mayor of Casaba.

He put his dark sunglasses on, placed his sheriff's hat on his head and prepared to go out and face the hot Kentucky sun and the even hotter Mrs. Burkas.

"Woo-wee, Sheriff *Ricky*," a sultry voice called. "You sure do look fine in that uniform of yours!"

Enrique looked over to find her standing against a cherry red convertible that she'd parked in one of the five spaces in front of the building. Barely five feet tall, she was delicate and brunette. Her body was perfectly toned and she may have been short, but she had long legs. She wore a halter-top and a mini skirt. For a woman who was well into her fifties, she could have easily passed for one at least ten years younger than that.

"Afternoon, Mrs. Burkas," he said as she pushed away from the car and sauntered slowly towards them. Enrique heard Tank emit a low, long whistle as he, too, watched her walk. Enrique grinned, his straight white teeth a perfect contrast to his tanned skin. "Thank you for the compliment. What can I do for you today?" he asked her just as she arrived to stand in front of him.

"Why, darlin'," she said flirtatiously as she played with his collar and looked up at him through her lashes. "Anything you want to do *for* me, or *to* me, is perfectly fine *with* me. And I'm not a stickler--it doesn't even have to be within reason." She winked teasingly.

"Well, I might take you up on that, ma'am," Enrique said. "If I didn't know that your husband wouldn't like it."

She moued her disappointment, her mouth moving into a pretty sulk. "Ah, well," she said. "It's just as well because I got serious business here today. I was robbed."

"When?" Enrique asked, surprised.

"Why, just about twenty minutes ago, over there at that little mall in Penster."

"Come inside out of this heat," Enrique said and opened the door for her. Once inside, she sat in a chair in front of one of the two desks in the main office.

"In Penster, you say?" Enrique asked her as he stood and Tank sat down.

"Yes. It was three girls that did it. I was just minding my own business and walking over to the food court to pick myself up one of them drinks from that new Jamba Juice place. Why, they have the best juice drinks you ever did taste," she said, completely oblivious to the men's impatience as she veered off subject. "They give you just the greatest little pick-me-up after a long day. You all ever been to Jamba?"

"I can't say that I have, no," Enrique said. "Could you get back to your story, please, Mrs. Burkas?"

"Oh, right. Well, anyway, just as I was making my way to the counter, I felt this tug on the strap of my purse and before I knew it, my purse was gone. Cut and snatched just as pretty as you please, right off my arm! I just couldn't believe it!"

"What did you do? Did you report it?"

She looked at him without blinking. "Well, that's what I'm doin' now, sugah--I'm *reportin'* it. I drove over here as fast as I could."

Enrique tried not to let his dismay show. "I meant did you report it in Penster?"

"Yes, to the guard at the mall."

"What about the sheriff in Penster? Did you go see him?"

"No, I came to see you. *You're* my sheriff. Why would I go see somebody else's?"

Enrique, and even Tank, just stared at her in disbelief for a moment. Finally chuckling, Enrique said, "Because, Mrs. Burkas, the theft happened in Penster. I don't have any jurisdiction there, so there's not much I can do for you."

"Oh," she said. "I didn't think of that. What happens now?"

"You said there were three girls?"

"Yeah, they were teenagers. Oh, and one of them was black," she finished and sat back with a look of satisfaction, pleased that she could give them that much.

"And what about the other two?"

"Well, they were white."

"Did you see their faces, then?"

"No, not really, but I did see their profiles and one of them, the black one, looked back as she ran away."

"Could you describe her?"

"Well, it all happened so fast, but I can tell you that she was skinny and short and she wasn't all that dark."

"All right, then, Mrs. Burkas. I'll call the sheriff over in Penster. He'll want to talk to you, so you'll probably have to drive back over there."

"All right, Ricky," she said and everyone in the room could hear the unspoken, *'anything for you.'*

"Tank, give Mrs. Burkas a glass of water or something. I'm going to call Sheriff Johnson," Enrique said and went back into his office and shut the door. Just as he was sitting down, his cell phone rang.

"Yeah."

"Well, is that any way to treat an old friend?" a deep voice said.

"It is if that friend is the one who stuck him in a job in a one-horse town," Enrique said mildly to his best friend.

Charles laughed. "Well, you wanted experience in the field, I got it for you. The governor wasn't too keen on it, you know, considering you the fact that you only have about six months of field experience. But I convinced him that you were the man for the job."

"I know," Enrique said. "And I'm grateful to you." Enrique had gone to law school and had also trained to be an investigator. After several years on the state's bureau of investigation where he mostly worked behind the scenes, he'd wanted some practical, field experience. Charles worked as security liaison for the governor and had gotten Enrique the job in Casaba.

"I called to tell you that I'll be in town soon, but that can wait. I want to know what's got you sounding so riled up today," Charles said. "Don't tell me you've been dreaming of *her* again?" The two had been friends since baby hood and Charles knew all about the dreams.

"Yeah, I've been dreaming of her again," Enrique said as he thought about the conversation he'd heard. Normally, he wouldn't have told Charles about it because it would just be further proof to him that Enrique had a 'functioning' third eye, like his mother said. Charles had always believed it to be true. He'd never questioned it.

Enrique decided to tell Charles. The sense of foreboding was so strong that he felt the need to talk it out.

A long whistle was Charles's first response. "Whoa, that's something, son! What are you thinking?"

"I don't know what to think. A lot of strange things have been happening lately. She's begun to *share* my dreams and, by share, I mean I think she and I are having the same dream."

"No kidding? Has it happened a lot?"

"Not nearly enough for me, but three times so far. The first time it happened, she questioned me about my ability to draw her in. It was phenomenal."

"Yeah, I'll bet," Charles said slowly. "Here's what I think. I think you're about to meet your dream girl, Bubba. As much as you don't want to believe that any of this is real, even you feel that something different is going on. Maybe after all these years, you've finally tapped into some unused gift that she has and that enabled her to share. Maybe your desire was finally strong enough to get through to her or maybe it's just time for you to meet. Whatever it is, she's sharing and she's questioning because she's coming. I advise you to get ready for her, you lucky bastard."

Enrique was quiet as he thought things through. He didn't want to believe it, but it made sense in an illogical, totally unrealistic way. But if Charles were right, and he and his dream woman would soon meet, there was something he needed to tell her and it wasn't just the conversation he'd heard, either. He didn't know how she'd take it. Even as all of this went through his mind, his mouth said, "I don't know, Charles."

"Well, while you're so busy 'not knowing,'" Charles said sarcastically, "Keep something else in mind, too. You sensed that she was in danger and that means that you need to be prepared to protect her from whatever that danger might be."

In spite of the gravity of the conversation, Enrique felt his mouth quirk up in a smile as he thought of her pride and arrogance. "Protect her? Son, *I'd* need protection if I even mentioned the possibility to her."

Charles laughed. "That's right, you've told me how confident she is in her own strength. I keep forgetting things. Tell me about her," he said. "What she's look like again?"

"No," Enrique said mildly. Charles had always liked her description. "No," he reiterated. Charles knew that the dreams could be sexual in nature, but Enrique never shared the details. He knew, however, that Charles suspected that she kept him so busy, drained and satisfied that he couldn't even think about sleeping with other women in real life. Enrique figured that that's what Charles was thinking about now and said, "I don't like that you get your rocks off from *my* dreams."

"Yeah, Bubba, but to you she's just a dream. To me, she's as real as you and I and I tell you what, I wouldn't mind getting even a glimpse of that beauty--in real life or in a dream!"

"Ain't gonna happen," Enrique said and felt pure male satisfaction surge through him at the thought. The beautiful one belonged only to him. "She's mine and only mine.*"*

## Chapter Eight

*"She's mine and only mine."* Edris heard the words as clearly as she would have if he had been standing there whispering them in her ear. *What the?* Was she going crazy? Her face as impassive as she could make it--given that a bolt of lust had shot through her system when she heard the words--she looked at the other people in the room. Everyone's eyes were on the presentation they were being given; no one paid any attention to her. Edris closed her eyes and bit back a moan. She was already wet. *God*, this was almost as powerful as the dreams she'd been sharing with him. She went to bed each night praying that she'd dream of him. And despite her fear that she was going insane, she couldn't help but fervently wish that the words were true.

\* \* \* \*

Traia held a conversation with herself--she did this daily--as she left her seating area to complete a task given to her by her immediate superior. "Idiot's not even my boss, yet I have to do what he says. This is the same man who cheated off me at the academy and now because he got promoted before I did, he gets to push his menial work off on me. Bullshit."

Her complaint was half-hearted at best. She'd been on cloud nine since the Punitive and Corrections Board had handed out her sentence for the hugger she'd destroyed. All she'd gotten was indefinite desk duty and a command to pay for the hugger. She knew that all of the other officers whispered that it had been Edris's doing, but she couldn't believe that, because though she'd apologized to Edris, three weeks later things had not quite gotten back to normal between them. Edris had erected another barrier between them and try all she might, Traia couldn't scale it.

Traia figured she'd just gotten lucky with her punishment and she didn't want to jinx it, so she did everything she was told and tried to keep her head up when she heard the snickers or the snide comments about her being lucky that her sister was Commander.

"Of course it isn't working," she said aloud as she spotted the *Out of Order* sign on the sorting machine. "Nothing ever works in this damned department." She turned towards the other machine and seeing it occupied by another officer, she made a quick decision and turned to leave her department's area.

"I'll use the one over in Traversal. It won't take that long." Technically, all employees had access to the area, but those who didn't actually work in the Traversal Department weren't allowed to linger. "I'll just get Mishka to do it for me," Traia whispered to herself, referring to a friend who worked as a seeker. She walked quickly toward her destination.

"The traversal will happen and it will happen tomorrow." The male voice, though low and whispery, was hard with resolve and made Traia stop in her tracks just as she was about to turn the corner into the department. "We will do it right after the department has closed, as we usually do."

"Sir, I understand your dilemma, but I will need more time to make sure everything runs smoothly." The female voice was subservient and nervous. "I am usually given at least 48 hours to plan, yet you give me a little more than half that time for this mission. I need more time," the voice begged again.

"Nonsense. I will not accept failure. Jenna Pierce will be transported tomorrow at the regular time and I will hear no more of your objections."

Resigned now, the female whispered, "I will do my best, sir."

"I require more than that. We cannot afford any mistakes on this one. You know as well as I the consequences if we are caught."

"Sir, yes, sir. She will be transported at the time you request, sir."

* * * *

"Jesus, they're planning an escape for the Black Widow," Traia mumbled softly to herself as she slowly eased away from the wall, praying that the other two wouldn't notice her. Traia was quite familiar with the case. Jenna Pierce had killed three men within a span of five years. She'd been married to all of them. She was blonde, petite and fragile-looking, but apparently she was also deadly. Her trial was supposed to begin the following week.

Traia's first thought as she walked back toward her own department was that she'd better tell Edris what was going on, an idea she quickly discarded. "She probably won't believe me. I don't even know who's planning the breakout. I'd better figure that out first and then maaaaybe I'll tell Edris," she told herself, knowing full well that she wouldn't. "No, I'm not going to run to Edris with this. I'll do it on my own."

* * * *

Late the next night, Traia made her way through the compound and over to the Traversal Department. "Mishka?" she whispered.

"Are you here?" She'd told him to meet her there one hour after the department closed. Traversals were only supposed to take place between six and eleven p.m., so she knew that any taking place that night would be easy to trace.

"Over here," a voice whispered from out of the darkness. "I don't know about this, Traia," the man said as she walked over to him. He was short and round with curly hair and worried brown eyes.

"It will be fine," Traia assured him. "What could go wrong? All you're going to do is check the portal to find out when the last traversal was and where that traveler went."

"I've already checked," Mishka said. "I left home early before I convinced myself not to come. As a result," he said with a shrug of his shoulders, "I had some time on my hands, so I got started."

"Excellent. Then we're good to go. What do I do first?"

"Well, you just step inside." He gestured nervously to the portal.

"Cool," Traia said, excited at the prospect of her first traversal. "Don't worry, Mishka, I'll be back before you know it and I'll have Jenna Pierce with me. I'll probably get promoted for this," she said with a huge grin as she stepped inside the portal.

"It just seems so risky, Traia."

"It's all right. Nothing is going to go wrong. I have the replicater and you the receiver. You can keep track of me that way. All I'm going to do is grab her and come back. Where did they send Jenna, by the way?"

"To a town called Casaba. It's in Kentucky. You will not appear directly there, you'll appear in the closest remote area, which is a wood outside of town called Hamlin's Woods. It is the same place she appeared. If you're lucky, she went right into town and you can catch her there," he said as he reprogrammed the same coordinates from the previous traversal just to cover all bases. "If not, check the nearest hotel. You have your navigator and it will work in the Sub Parallel, as well. Just show it where you are, tell it where you want to go and it will give you clear directions."

"I know how it works, Mishka. I've used them before," she said and smiled when he looked sheepish. "Thank you for all of your help, hon. Casaba, Kentucky, here I come!" she said and slipped her sunglasses on when she saw him put on his. They were necessary because of the bright light generated by the portal. She waved at him just before she disappeared.

Mishka frowned and removed his sunglasses. The stress of the situation had given him a headache. As he rubbed his temples, he noticed something on the table next to the portal. "Oh, fuck!" he said and picked up Traia's replicater--the replicater that she needed in order to get back. Replicaters fit in the palm of the hand and were created so that travelers could replicate a portal wherever they were in the Sub Parallel and come back home. All they had to do was program it, point and shoot. Without it, Traia was stuck in Casaba.

"Oh, fuck," Mishka said again. This time the words were whiney and resigned. He gathered his things and went to find the Commander.

\* \* \* \*

"She did *what?*" Edris yelled at Mishka.

Mishka stood in her living room wishing for escape. "Umm," he said and cleared his throat. He'd never seen his Commander looking so soft and feminine. She wore a long caftan of green silk and each time she moved as she paced in front of him, one of her long, shapely legs peeked through the front slit. He cleared his throat again. "She went through the portal to Casaba, Kentucky. She is trying to capture an escaped prisoner."

Edris wanted to scream. Why, oh why did Traia have to be so … so … reckless, irresponsible and just simply a pain in her ass! "Damn it!" she said out loud and looked over at the seeker. "Does she at least have identification naming her as being from somewhere in the Sub Parallel?"

"No, ma'am, I do not think so."

"Oh, that little idiot." Edris's words were said between her teeth in frustration. She looked at Mishka again. "How do you know of this?"

Mishka swallowed uncomfortably. "She came to me for help, and uh … I … uh," he broke off, finding it difficult to finish under that hard stare of hers. "I sort of helped her."

"Sort of? Or did?"

Mishka sighed. "I did."

"So you risked your own career to help Traia pull off one of her harebrained schemes. Not very smart of you, Seeker."

"Yes, ma'am. I know, ma'am."

"Very well, so long as you know. You follow me to the portal and program it, so that I may follow my sister."

"Yes, ma'am."

"Sit down while I change into uniform."

"Yes, ma'am." He saluted smartly.

\* \* \* \*

Traia opened her eyes to find herself looking into black. "Duh," she said and removed her sunglasses. The traversal had taken no more than a minute. She looked around in wonder. She had never seen so many trees in her life and even though it was dark as pitch, she could clearly see their shapes and sizes.

She pulled her navigator out, pressing 'on' so that the screen lit up.

"Hello, Traia Perseveranth." She'd programmed the voice to be male and sexy.

"Hello, Navigator. Direct me to downtown Casaba, Kentucky from this location," she said and turned the device away from herself to show it her location. She figured that since it was a small town, Jenna might think she could hide better downtown than anywhere else.

"Processing complete. Directions available on screen."

"Excellent," Traia mumbled distractedly as she studied the screen. She started walking and found herself in downtown Casaba in less than twenty minutes. She was approximately thirty minutes behind Jenna, including the time it took to travel through the portal. She studied the town with a curious frown. "This is it?" she said, looking at the drab buildings. She was sorely disappointed.

She heard a bell ring and looked towards the sound. A woman was walking out of a place called Casaba Diner. Traia smiled. She'd recognize that blonde hair anywhere.

Lucky for me she was hungry, Traia thought as she hurried toward her and met her in the middle of the block.

"Halt, Jenna Pierce." Traia grabbed her arm. "You are under arrest and I'm taking you back to Parallel Plus with me."

Jenna looked at the young, eager face and could have cheerfully spit in it. She'd been minutes from getting away. She only had to walk two more blocks to be at her pick-up point. She tried to bluff her way out of the situation. "Take your hand off of me, young lady! How dare you!"

Traia's grin was unrepentant. "Nice try, Jenna."

Jenna's eyes darted around as she sought a way to escape. She almost cheered as she spotted a huge man lumbering toward them. He was in uniform. "Stop, thief!" she yelled. She thanked God that she'd overheard the gossip in the diner about the teenaged purse-snatchers. "Stop! Officer, officer! This girl is trying to rob me!" She struggled against Traia.

Traia swore. "Be still, Jenna. You know good and well I'm not trying to rob you!" She maintained her grip on the woman's arm.

"You stop it right there, girlie," Traia heard a deep voice say from behind her and turned to see a huge man in a khaki uniform pointing a gun at her.

## Chapter Nine

Edris stormed into the Casaba Sheriff's Office full of steam. How dare they arrest her sister for attempted purse snatching! She too had visited the diner for the latest town gossip and had found out all she'd needed to know. She'd guessed correctly that Traia was 'that strange, little black gal' without any identification who'd been caught trying to rob 'that strange white woman.'

"May I help you, ma'am?"

Edris looked over to see a man with pale skin looking at her from behind a tall, circular security desk that hid everything, except his upper torso and head, from view. She walked over to him. "Yes, you may. I'd like to talk to your superior, please."

Clarence studied the woman carefully. She was dressed just like that other girl in the cell in the back. They both had on black leather pants and jackets and it was at least seventy-five degrees out. He would bet if she took off that matching hat she had on, she'd have the same wavy, black hair as the other one, too. Something strange was certainly going on tonight.

He'd come on shift late to find the girl already locked up and complaining that she was not a criminal, but an officer of the law, and Tank was acting like he'd just won first prize at the County Fair because he'd been the one to lock her up. The girl talked strangely, too. Her speech was formal with a mixture of every-day regular talk. He'd bet his last dollar that the woman standing in front of him spoke in the same odd manner. She sure was a looker, though, he thought as her gray eyes caught his and demanded his attention.

Edris cleared her throat impatiently as the man continued to stare at her. Was every police officer in this parallel as dull-witted and unresponsive as this one? It was no wonder their crime rates were so high. "Officer," she commanded. "I'd like to speak to your superior."

Clarence tamped down the urge to salute and said, "I'm afraid he's unavailable, ma'am. Maybe there's something I can help you with."

"All right, then. You are holding my sister here. I demand that you release her. She is not a criminal."

Clarence scowled. "You demand, do ya? Well, you can *demand* all you want. She's a prisoner and she's not going anywhere."

Edris frowned. "Then I demand to see her."

"I'm afraid I can't allow that. Visiting hours are over," Clarence said and blew a bubble with his gum. "Been over for hours," he said lazily.

"You lie," Edris accused him.

"Beg pardon?" Clarence asked indignantly as he stood.

"You lie to keep me from her. She is my sister and I demand to see her. Now."

"Sister or no, you ain't gonna see her tonight. I repeat, visiting hours are over," he said with seeming unconcern, sat back down and went back to his paperwork.

"You officious, inferior little man! I demand that you get from behind that desk and take me to my sister! Right now!" Edris yelled, her temper completely out of control because she was so afraid--afraid for Traia, who was stuck in a cell without proper identification.

Clarence raised his voice as well. "Why you arrogant, funny-talkin'--"

"What the hell is going on out here?" Enrique asked irritably as he entered the common area from his office. "The noise level out here is ridiculous, Clarence. Who's doing all the yelling?" He hadn't rounded the desk yet, so he didn't see Edris.

Clarence turned around to address him. "It's this woman here, Sheriff. She claims the girl in the cell is her sister and she refuses to believe me when I tell her that visiting hours are over."

Enrique sighed. He had a bitch of a headache and had not only been trying to figure out a way to get to his dream girl to help her, but had also been trying to muddle through all the screwed-up files the previous sheriff had left. "Just let her see her, Clarence. What's it going to hurt?"

"But Sheriff, that little purse snatcher--"

"My sister is not a criminal, you incompetent excuse for a lawman," Enrique heard a strident voice say and he froze. Could she actually be here?

Clarence turned back around. "Look, lady, if you call me a name one more--"

Her voice overrode his. "I insist that you stop calling her one!"

Enrique's heart raced as he slowly made his way around the desk. There she stood, as real as he, so caught up in her argument that she didn't notice him. He studied her. The dark, smooth skin, the long, thin body and the beautiful gray eyes. It had to be her. But he needed to be sure. "Take off your hat," he murmured softly, unaware that he'd spoken aloud. "Take off your hat, *mi bellezera oscura.*"

\* \* \* \*

*Mi bellezera oscura.* Edris heard the words cut cleanly through her argument with the lawman and turned her head with a frown. Her mouth opened, but no sound came out. It can't be, she thought as she studied him. Long, slender, but powerfully built body. Black hair. Blue eyes. It *had* to be him, but it simply *couldn't* be. He didn't exist. Edris held out a hand, as if to ward him off. "Enrique," she mumbled. And then she did something that she'd never thought she'd do in her life. She fainted.

\* \* \* \*

Enrique watched her as she carefully studied him. He totally sympathized with her confusion and disbelief. Her eyes roamed over his features as if she were taking inventory. He saw her hold out her hand, heard her murmur his name and then watched as her eyes rolled to the back of her head. He rushed over just in time to catch her before she hit the floor. He lifted her up into his arms, holding her protectively to his chest as he carried her to his office. "Don't follow me, Clarence," he said over his shoulder and heard, "Well, shit," just before he pushed his door closed with his hip.

Enrique laid her on the couch in his office. He pulled a chair closer and reached over to remove her jacket and boots to make her as comfortable as possible. He stared at the hat, almost scared to remove it. He felt ridiculous thinking it, but he felt like his life's happiness depended upon what was beneath that hat. He took a deep breath, feeling as foolish and giddy as a kid. He reached out, grasped the bill and pulled it off. Wave after wave of black hair spilled out and right in the middle of it--in stark relief--was the most beautiful white hair he'd ever seen.

"It's so beautiful," he said as he sank his fingers into its softness. He watched as her eyelids fluttered open to reveal those gray eyes staring up at him. She smiled at him. He smiled back. "*Hola,* dream girl. Welcome," he said and bent his head to kiss her lips. He lured her tongue into his mouth for a gentle sucking, pleased when her arms lifted to wrap around his neck.

\* \* \* \*

Edris kissed Enrique back, liking the slowness. Something pushed at her consciousness, and she frowned as her memory restored itself in pieces. Traia in trouble … trip to Sub Parallel … argument with incompetent lawman … Enrique … Enrique … *Enrique was real*!

Her eyes widened in shock. She pushed against his shoulders and tore her mouth away. Sitting up, she scooted to the other end of the couch, looking at him in terror. "You can't be real!"

Enrique smiled gently. "I know it's creepy, *bellezera oscura,* but it's true. I'm real and so are you."

"But you are a part of my dreams. You cannot be real!"

Enrique moved to sit on the couch and frowned when she held a hand out as if to keep him away. "You have no reason to be afraid of me. I would never harm you."

Edris ignored him as she brought her knees to her chest and hid her face against them. "It is only a dream," she murmured. "It is not real ... it is not real ... this sofa is not real ... *Enrique is not real!*"

Enrique moved closer and sat near her feet, effectively caging her in. He passed a hand over her bent head, fluffing her hair with his fingers. Encouraged when she didn't jerk away, he pushed his hand between her knees, found her chin and lifted it so she'd be forced to look at him. He held her face with both hands. "I'm as real as real gets, sweetheart. The question is: what're you going to do about it?"

Edris took a deep breath, tears filling her eyes from the sheer potential that the question suggested there was. She let the tears fall as she looked at him. This was too much!

Enrique winced at the tears and swiped at them with his thumbs. "Oh, baby, don't cry." Releasing her face, he offered her his handkerchief. "It'll be okay." He soothingly rubbed her thigh from the back of her knee to her buttocks.

"Thank you." She took the cloth and wiped her face. "I do not know what to do," she admitted. "This has been a banner night for me. First I faint and now I cry--two things I never do!"

"Don't forget the part about finding out your dream lover is real."

"Oh, yes, there is that," Edris said lightly and laughed as he laughed. "How did this happen?" she asked him abruptly.

"I don't know. All I know is that I've been dreaming about you since I was five years old and you were two."

Edris shook her head in disbelief. "That just can't be possible."

"Oh, but it is. I know that you have a scar on your left knee from a fall you took when you were two. I know that you had a clown at your seventh birthday party. I know that some little snot-nosed kid stole a kiss from you when you were twelve and you gave him a punch in the nose for his troubles. I know--"

"But how?" Edris asked.

"I just do, somehow," Enrique said with a shrug. "I also know that you're not from this world," he finished quietly.

## Chapter Ten

Edris froze and stared at him, trying to determine what his next move would be.

"So you see, *mi bellezera oscura*," Enrique said lovingly as he played with the ends of her hair. "I know almost everything about you. Everything except your name."

"It is Edris," she said absently as she thought about this new development. "Edris Perseveranth." Did it matter to him that she wasn't from his world?

"Edris." Enrique let the name roll off his tongue. "I like it. It's beautiful, just like you."

"Thank you. How do you know I am not from your world?"

"I have seen things in my dreams of you that are far too advanced to be from this world--thinking, talking robots, flying cars, and other things. And besides that, I have seen your world. It's so desolate and gray; it looks like something from out of a Sci-Fi movie. You do know what a Sci-Fi movie is, don't you?"

"Yes, of course I do," Edris answered him impatiently and rose to pace. "What are you going to do?"

"About what?" Enrique asked her with a frown.

"About the fact that I am not from your world," she said impatiently.

"Nothing. What do you expect me to do?"

"I don't know, turn me into your authorities, I guess. It is what would happen in my world if one of you from here somehow found your way into it."

"Well, that's not what I'm going to do. All I need is for you to tell me that you're not an alien from outer space with a second head hidden somewhere, or a tail of some sort. I mean, I could deal with either one of those things, sure, but they might be hard to explain to the neighbors."

Edris laughed. "You are a funny man, Enrique. I am as human as you are."

Enrique grinned. "Where exactly are you from?"

"I am from a world that is parallel to this one. We are the plus side, you are the sub side."

Enrique lifted a brow; sure that he and all of his fellow 'sub-siders' had just been insulted. "How do you mean?"

She gave a careless shrug. "I stand in your world. You do not stand in mine."

Enrique grinned at the show of her usual arrogance. "Can't argue with that, can I? So, what are you doing here?"

Edris frowned. "Oh, my gosh! Traia! I almost forgot about her."

"Traia, huh? Is that the little lady we currently have locked in the cell down the hall?"

"Yes," Edris said with a scowl. "You must release her. Are you the one who arrested my sister?"

"No, it wasn't me. That would be Deputy Orwell. He arrested your sister for purse snatching--says he caught her in the act."

"Impossible," Edris said immediately. "Traia would never do such a thing. I demand to see her," she said and sat back down to put her boots and jacket back on.

"Why are you putting that hot jacket back on? In fact, why are you wearing such hot clothing?"

"It is my uniform," she answered as she stood.

"Uniform? I've never in my life seen a uniform like that before."

Edris smirked, knowing that he referred to the simulated leather's tight fit. "Nevertheless, it *is* my uniform," she said.

"Just what kind of work do you do?" Enrique asked.

"You do not know?" Edris asked in surprise. "You did not see it in your dreams?"

"Only once, but I couldn't tell what you were doing. Most of the dreams I've had of you as an adult involved you half-naked."

Edris looked away with an embarrassed smile at the licentious look on his face. "I am well aware of these dreams," she said softly as she felt heat creep up her neck.

Enrique laughed at her. She was such a contradiction. One moment she was so arrogant that she was bordering on rude and the next moment, she was as shy and unsure as a little girl. "It's all right, Edris. We'll take it slow."

Edris looked at him quickly and just as quickly looked away again. "You do not want to make love while I am here in your world?" she asked shyly.

"Do children want candy?" Enrique asked as he approached her and pulled her into his arms. "Do cats want milk? Do dogs want bones?" He looked down into her laughing eyes. "Of course, I want to make love to you, Edris. I'll always want to make love to you."

"Good, then it is settled. We'll make love as much as we want while I am here."

Enrique ignored the last part of her sentence for the moment. "So, you're here to rescue your sister, huh? Did the two of you get here through one of those odd doors I've seen in your world?"

"Yes," Edris answered. "Traia came to try and capture an escaped prisoner and I came to rescue Traia. Please. You must take me to her. She must be terribly frightened."

"All right." Enrique released her and led her out of his office and down a hall to the back of the building.

"Traia?" Edris said as she waited anxiously for Enrique to unlock the cell door.

"Edris!" Traia jumped from the bunk and rushed over to her sister. She fell crying into her arms. "Edris, thank God you're here. They accused me of stealing, Edie, and I didn't have a replicater, and so I couldn't get out of here. Oh, Edie, I've been so scared. I want to go home!"

"I know, Tray," Edris said as she held her tightly. "It's all right, sweetie. I'm going to get you home."

\* \* \* \*

Edris and Traia stood in Hamlin's Woods together as Edris programmed her replicater. "Okay, Tray," she said. "Now remember, your friend Mishka will be waiting for you on the other side. The two of you can't say anything about any of this to anyone or else we'll all get in trouble."

"Right," Traia said. "I'm just so mad that that scumbag Jenna Pierce got away."

"Don't worry about her," Edris said. "Just get yourself safely home once you leave the Compound."

"I'm sorry, Edie," Traia said sincerely. "Once again, I've pulled you into one of

my messes."

"It's okay," Edris assured her and squeezed her in a hug.

"Are you sure you'll be okay here?" Traia asked, glad that they were back on an even keel emotionally. At least one good thing had resulted from her ill-fated plan.

Edris had decided to stay and travel to Chicago from Casaba. "I'll be fine. Don't worry about me." She pointed the replicater toward a stream, pressed a button and watched as a simulated portal appeared. Bright and far from solid, it wavered and shimmered in the night.

Traia kissed Edris' cheek. "Bye, Edie. I love you," she said before she crossed the threshold.

"I love you, too." Edris put on her sunglasses and pressed another button. The area was bathed in bright light for a few seconds and then there was nothing.

"Whoa, that was amazing!" Enrique said as he stepped from behind a cluster of trees.

Edris turned to look at him. "Thanks for staying out of sight," she told him as she took off her sunglasses. "The portals are supposed to be kept secret from this world and I didn't want to put Traia in the position of having to choose between me or the truth if anyone ever found out that I'd showed you." After she'd paid Traia's bail and had gotten her released, she'd told him about the replicater. He'd wanted to see how it worked and had left town before them to find a spot that would keep him hidden from view.

"Happy to do it," Enrique said as he slipped his own sunglasses into his pocket. He took her hand. "So, what do you want to do now?" he asked her.

## Chapter Eleven

They ended up getting food from an all-night burger joint in the next town and taking it back to his place. She'd wanted chocolate and was hungry, so he'd killed two birds with one stone by buying her food to fill her growling stomach and a chocolate malted to satisfy her sweet tooth. Their conversation centered on their careers.

"Your home is beautiful," she told him as they lounged on a navy blue sofa after dinner. It was a large farmhouse on the outskirts of Casaba. She didn't think she could ever get used to smelling such fresh air.

"Thank you, but I can't take credit for it," he said. "I'm renting it from some nice folks who decided that they needed a world cruise. It's perfect because they'll be coming back right after the election for a new sheriff."

"What will you do when you are finished here?"

"I haven't decided yet. I'm kind of at loose ends right now," he admitted. "I like my job in Louisville, but I need more. I'm thinking of opening an investigative and security agency. That's why I wanted field experience."

"Oh, that would be wonderful." She turned toward him, curling her legs under her, the effort made all the easier by the large T-shirt she wore. He'd given her one of his shirts so she could get out of her uncomfortable uniform. "I have often thought of starting my own agency, as well."

"Why haven't you?"

She shrugged. "I have not had the time or the wherewithal."

"Surely, a person in your position makes more than enough."

"It is adequate," Edris admitted. "But things are quite expensive at home." She let out a jaw-crackling yawn. "Oh, excuse me."

"Oh, you poor baby. All that world hopping must have worn you out. What time is it now back in your place?"

Edris looked at her watch. "It is 2:30 in the morning."

"Well, whatever time it is, you're exhausted. Come on," he said as he stood. "I'll carry you."

Edris looked up at him in surprise. "You would do that? I am so tall. It would be quite uncomfortable for you."

Enrique saw the longing in her eyes. She did love to be held.

"Come on," he said again and bent to scoop her up.

Her sigh was deep and content as she curled into him and closed her eyes and began to fall asleep. She soon felt herself being lowered and she opened her eyes. "Will you stay with me?"

"I just have to get undressed."

Satisfied, she settled back into the pillows. A short while later, she felt him climb in behind her. He spooned her and she turned into his arms, sighing again when his arms came around her.

"Sleep well, Edris," he said and pressed a kiss to the top of her head.

"I like it better when you call me '*bellezera oscura*,'" she murmured.

"I like 'Edris.'"

"Yes, but everyone calls me that. Only *you* call me the other."

"Well, I'll use both. After all, I just heard your name for the first time today and I want to say it as often as I can." When the only response he received was slow, deep breathing, he closed his eyes and followed her into sleep.

\* \* \* \*

Enrique awoke to the sun shining, birds chirping and Edris sitting on his stomach. She was gloriously naked.

"I have been waiting forever for you to wake," she told him with an unconscious pout. "Why do you sleep so long, 'Rique?" she asked before she lowered her chest to his and kissed him hard on the mouth.

"Just stupid, I guess," he said breathlessly and tried to capture her lips again, thinking her kiss had been too brief.

"No, no, 'Rique. You don't have the control this time," she said as she bit his chin. "It's my turn."

"By all means," he said.

Edris trailed kisses down his throat, loving the clean taste of his skin. She slid further down his body until her mouth reached his nipple. "So tiny," she murmured and flicked it teasingly with a nail. He flinched and she smiled. She did it again and his hands gravitated to her behind. She opened her mouth and pulled the nipple inside, licking and playing with it between her teeth, making him groan.

She gave his other nipple the same treatment, at the same time sliding her mound up and down on his flat stomach, until it was slick with her cream. She slid further down his body and her vagina slid over his cock. He held his breath as she paused, bit her bottom lip between her teeth, closed her eyes and glided her genitals over his dick several times before continuing downward until she sat on his thighs.

She wrapped her hand around his hard-on, marveling at the full weight and breadth of it, even as she fought the desire to impale herself upon it. "It is so thick and heavy, 'Rique." Suddenly, she removed herself from his thighs, and crawled toward the head of the huge, over-sized bed. "I think I will be better able to do this from up here," she said as she swung her leg back over his body and straddled his chest with her back toward him.

The scent of her arousal invaded his nostrils and he received an up-close and personal view of her mound as she stretched her body over his. He couldn't resist. He pushed two fingers inside her entrance.

Edris cried out in surprise and helplessly began to ride, her backside slapping down against his chest. She screamed when he squeezed another finger inside, the tightness of the fit a bit painful and almost unbearable.

Enrique abruptly pulled his fingers out and slid from underneath her to rise on his knees behind her, holding her steady with an arm around her waist as he slowly guided his shaft into her--penetrating her so fully that she felt every thick, long inch of him.

Edris held onto the bed rail tightly, her eyes closing slowly as she reveled in his possession. "Enrique," she moaned softly and turned her head for his kiss.

Enrique couldn't remember ever feeling so happy and fulfilled in his life. Feelings of tenderness and gratitude for her overtaking his senses, he bent his head and reverently pressed his mouth to hers. His lips sipped tenderly from her mouth and he brought his free hand up to entangle with hers on the bed rail as he forced himself to slowly take her. "*Edris*," he said her name lovingly and longingly against her mouth. "*My woman*."

As his feelings washed over her, making her feel utterly cherished, Edris made a soft, desperate sound in the back of her throat and looped her arm around his neck, wanting to somehow get closer to him. "*Si*, Enrique," she said fervently into his mouth between his voracious kisses. "I am yours. Always and only yours."

At her words, the need to look at her as he possessed her overwhelmed him and he withdrew from her body, placed her on her back and thrust into her wet warmth. A triumphant growl escaped his throat when she moaned, arched her back and wrapped her arms and legs tightly around him. "That's it, sweetheart," he said and kissed her again.

Edris relished his every touch, her mind still marveling at her new reality. Her eyes filled with tears. She was completely awed. She matched his slow movements and let her tears fall. She loved him. She barely knew him, yet she loved him. It was obvious, even to someone as pragmatic as she, that they were meant to be together. She still didn't understand how it had happened, but she determined that she would stop questioning and just enjoy every minute of her time with him.

"You feel so good, baby," Enrique murmured when he felt her slick muscles clinch around his penis. When she transferred her hands to his backside and squeezed urgently, he closed his eyes and quickened his thrusts a bit.

"Oh, yes, 'Rique," Edris moaned. "Do not stop. Please … do not…."

Sweat broke out on his forehead as Enrique did his best to keep it slow, teasing them both and heightening the pleasure. The slow, gentle glide seemed to be enough for her as well and they were soon rocked to completion. He bent to kiss her again just as his orgasm rocketed through him.

Edris screamed softly as her orgasm splintered inside of her, giving her wave after wave of pure pleasure. More tears sprang to her eyes. Saying nothing, Enrique kissed the tears from her cheeks, fell to her side and gathered her in his arms where she buried her face in his neck.

\* \* \* \*

"So what's in Chicago?" Enrique asked her later as they lay in bed. Unable to get enough of each other in real life, they'd made love again, showered and had gone back to bed. For the moment, they were content to hold each other and talk.

Edris debated with herself for less than a moment before deciding to tell him. "As you heard yesterday, criminals are being smuggled from our world into yours. This has been going on for decades. My mother was a victim of the smugglers. She tried to stop them and was murdered for her efforts."

Enrique sat up in bed, bringing her with him. The time had come to share what he knew. Cautiously, he asked, "Murdered? When did this happen?"

Edris didn't understand why he was so interested, but she explained anyway. "My mother was an officer," she began.

Enrique listened to her tell her story, patiently waiting for her to finish. "*Mi bellereza oscura*," he said as he sat up and pulled her up with him. "I don't know how to tell you this, but I saw everything that happened that night you sneaked into your mother's vehicle--well almost everything. I saw your mother get grabbed from behind, I saw you try to run and get away and I even saw how you got this," he said and fingered a strand of her white hair. "But the one thing I did not see," he continued, "was your mother being murdered. I didn't see any blood, but I could have missed that part."

"I do not understand," Edris said. "What are you saying?"

"I'm saying that your mother was not killed. I saw her go through the portal."

Edris jerked away from him. "This can not be. She can't be alive. They said that there was so much blood ... and they found me with her shield and her weapon ... and she never came home ... and ... and...." She tried to convince herself that it wasn't true, but one look at his face and she knew that it was. She burst into tears as the enormity of it hit her. Carma had been alive all this time? "How can this be?" she wailed and went into his open arms.

"It's all right, baby, it's all right," Enrique repeated over and over again as he held her. "I know you've thought her dead for years and I always wished I could somehow tell you what I'd seen," he said sorrowfully and stroked her hair. "I'm so sorry, baby and I don't know what happened, but we'll find out," he promised her.

"But how can she be alive, 'Rique?" Her voice was small and hurt as she looked at him. "She did not come home. She has not seen Traia since she was a month old. Father spent his life looking for her. She did not even come to his funeral. She did not come to see--" Abruptly, she cut herself off and buried her face in his chest again.

Enrique gently finished her thought. "She didn't come to see *you*. Edris, it's okay for you to admit that you needed her," he said as he massaged her neck.

"I cannot need anyone," she insisted softly. "Everyone needs *me*. It is the way it has been since I was ten years old and she deserted us. There has been no room or time for me to need them."

"You may have suppressed the need, but that doesn't mean it wasn't there, baby. We all need someone. It's okay to admit that you do, as well."

She was quiet for a moment and then said contemplatively, "That would be difficult to do."

"But you *can* do it," Enrique assured her. "Now," he said and moved her away from his chest so he could see her face. "Let's put together a plan to find your mother and maybe close the smuggling ring in the bargain."

"You would help me?" she asked him in surprise.

Enrique frowned. "That's the last time I'm going to let you insult me, Edris. You don't seriously think I'd let you do this alone, do you? You *need* me."

Edris grinned and then tackled him. "We will be a team," she said between the kisses she was peppering his face with. "You are wonderful, 'Rique! Wonderful, wonderful, wonderful!"

"Thousands have said so," he said laughingly, surprised at this silly side of her. "Now, let's get started," he said and rose from the bed. Taking her hand, he helped her up. He couldn't help but notice her wince and hiss out a breath. "Sore, baby?" he asked her gently and pulled her into his arms.

"Yes," she said. "My muscles are unused to such activity."

Enrique knew his grin was cocky as he pressed a kiss into her hair. "Well, we'll take it easy. There are other ways to make love."

"I look forward to them," she said seriously, making him laugh and tighten his hold.

Enrique released her and went to pull a fresh T-shirt from the drawer. She was already wearing a pair of his boxers with a safety pin holding them up. "Okay, back to work. You'll tell me all you know and we'll take it from there," he said as he pulled the T-shirt over her head and left her to deal with the sleeves while he pulled on jeans.

"Let's go to the study." He turned and walked out of the room.

Edris followed him, saying nothing. She still marveled at the way in which they'd found each other. Surely, they were two of the luckiest people....

"Come on, slow poke."

She looked up to find Enrique standing in the entryway to another room. He held a hand out to her. She felt like crying again, and in fact, tears did fill her eyes, as she marveled at how eager he was to help her. She smiled as she walked over to him. Stopping in front of him, she placed her hands on his shoulders and leaned up to kiss him. "Did I tell you how wonderful you are?"

Enrique grinned, his hands slipping under the legs of the boxers to palm her butt. "A few measly times, yes."

"Don't let me forget to keep reminding you," she said and slipped into the room.

Enrique followed her. "Okay," he began and grabbed a pad of paper and a pen from the desk in the corner. He sat next to her on the couch. "Start talking. I'll take notes."

"While I was investigating what I thought was the murder of my mother, I kept coming across the sudden disappearances of criminal suspects. Sometimes they'd disappear on the way to trial or on the way to prison, after they'd been convicted. And always, there seemed to be the same few lawyers on the cases. Following that thread, after more research, I noticed that the same judges's names kept coming up, as well.

"Further research led to politicians and yes, even some security and regulations officers and commanders. I did not think that these criminals were all being murdered and it occurred to me that they were being transported out somehow. Well, it was no great leap to figure out that they were sending them through the portals. In my world, it is difficult to travel from country to country because of the scarce resources. No country wants visitors straining what little they have and so intra-world travel is controlled. Controlled, but out in the open."

"So, it's easier to travel to another world than it is to another country?"

"Yes. Traversals are limited as well, but the portals are not out in the open. This makes them perfect for illegal smuggling. However, all I had and *have* is coincidence after coincidence. There is nothing concrete to connect anyone to smuggling. I could only suspect. I then started talking to retired personnel who had worked at the time of my mother's disappearance. I talked to portal technicians, seekers, record keepers and even some retired officers. I was stonewalled at every turn. I believe some of them thought that I was crooked, like many of my predecessors had been.

"I finally met a retired portal technician who was eager to talk to me. He said he'd been holding onto something, waiting for the right person to come along. It is a list of eleven names of people from this world whom he believed were involved. They are all in Chicago," she finished.

"But why didn't the old guy turn the list over before?" Enrique was fascinated.

"He too was afraid of corruption in the system and didn't know whom he could trust. He told me that if I hadn't come to him, he would have had the list delivered after his death."

"How did he get the list?"

"As he tells it, a fellow technician had been in on the smuggling and had kept the list. She had been put in charge of contacting these people in Chicago. She was his lover and he obtained the list when she died."

"All right," Enrique said resolutely. "We go to Chicago."

"When?" she asked after a few moments of silence.

"Today, if you'd like, but first, I have more to tell you," he said as he thought about the sense of foreboding he'd felt for her. "A few days ago, I heard a conversation," he began.

Edris listened, frowning as she turned it over in her head. "You're sure it was about me?"

"Positive. Otherwise, I wouldn't have heard it at all."

"What did the voices sound like?"

"I've thought about that. They were so muffled though; I couldn't tell if they were male or female. All I know is that one person is quite subservient to the other."

Edris studied him. "What is this gift you have?"

"My mother calls it my third eye," Enrique said, having accepted it as true the moment he saw her in the sheriff's office.

"It is a blessing, this third eye, yes?" she asked him.

"Oh, yes," he agreed. "It's through it that I came to know you."

"Can you use it to help me find my mother?" she asked hopefully.

"I don't know, but I can try."

"What will you do?"

Enrique shrugged a shoulder. "Just think about your mother, I guess, and see if I can get an idea of where she is. I've never actually tried to use it before; things would just come to me."

"Perhaps we will be lucky and you will dream of my mother and where she is."

"Perhaps. What do you think about the voices? Is there anyone who wants to hurt you?"

"Oh, yes, plenty. I have been threatened many times in the course of my career. However, I can't imagine who these two people would be."

"Maybe it has something to do with the smuggling ring."

"Oh, most definitely. This is the closest I've ever been to figuring out things, so I'm sure I'm making someone nervous."

"Yeah," Enrique said grimly. "That's what I figured."

"Perhaps they will follow me to Chicago," Edris said with relish.

Enrique laughed when he saw the glee in her eyes. "I guess I shouldn't be surprised that that's something you're hoping for."

"You bet I am."

"Well, we have a little more planning to do before we leave. Let me have the list of names and I'll get the addresses for you."

"Wonderful," Edris said excitedly.

"Don't get too excited, sweetheart. Some of these people may not even be around anymore. Some may have died and you know most, if not all of them, will probably refuse to even talk to us."

"I'm prepared for all of that. I simply want to get started," Edris said and rose. "Oh, but I don't want to have to wear my uniform."

"I don't blame you," Enrique said with a grin. "You'd faint in this heat. Remember how I told you I'd only seen you at work once?"

"Yes."

"Well, that one time was recent. It was when you had three other people in the room with you--an older white couple and a younger black woman."

"Uncle Clay, Aunt Sue and my best friend, Angie."

"You and your friend looked so miserable in those uniforms. You looked sexy as hell, but you still looked uncomfortable."

"Sexy, huh?" Edris asked teasingly as she wrapped her arms around his waist. "Do you think I could look just as sexy in clothes from your world?" she asked him softly as she kissed his neck and chin.

"Absolutely," Enrique said fervently as he gripped her waist.

"Good, because I will need new clothing before we leave for Chicago. Will you take me to some of your stores? And can we leave for Chicago tomorrow?"

"Sure," Enrique said and tightened his hands on her waist when she licked behind his ear. "I'll take you shopping later. In the mean time, let's find some other way to occupy our time, shall we?"

"Yes, let's. Do you have a deck of cards?" Edris asked as she stepped back. She burst out laughing at the look of chagrin on his face.

## Chapter Twelve

"She has arrived in Chicago."

"We knew that she was going."

"Yes, but what we didn't know is that she'd be so quick in finding one of our old contacts. She's already talked to him."

"What happened?"

"He says he didn't tell her anything. He did say that *she* said something, however. He said she asked if he knew where her mother was. She now apparently believes that Carma is alive."

"Damn it. We can't let her find her. It's time to do what you were so reluctant to do. You will have to eliminate both of them."

"Why must *I* do it?"

"Because it is your fault that we are in this mess in the first place. If you had covered your tracks better, we wouldn't be so close to getting caught now. Get ready because we're going to Chicago. Have your contact follow them until we get there."

\* \* \* \*

Edris loved Chicago, but was disheartened by their lack of progress in finding out more about her mother and the smuggling. They'd visited six of the addresses on her list and hadn't met with any luck.

"Cheer up," Enrique told her as he walked onto the wide porch of a Colonial style house. "This is only our seventh person. We may get lucky," he said and rang the bell.

"Yes, I know," Edris said as she stepped up behind him. "Hope springs eternal." A woman of medium height soon opened the door. She was thin and had dark hair, eyes and skin. Edris would have recognized her anywhere. Enrique would have as well.

"Yes?" the woman asked Enrique through the screen door.

Enrique turned to Edris, who just stood there staring at the woman. "Are you all right, sweetheart?" he whispered to her in concern.

Edris looked at her mother. She hasn't really changed at all, she thought. She's fifty-eight and she doesn't look a day past forty. She felt sweat gather in her palms and her heart begin to race. Keep it together, Edris, she told herself as her mother showed no sign of recognizing her. "Well, Enrique," she began in a cold voice. "How odd. She doesn't recognize me. Hello, Mother."

Carma Perseveranth frowned, pushed the screen door open and joined them on the porch. Craning her neck, she narrowed her eyes and looked up at Edris. A harsh breath escaped her mouth. "Oh, my God," she began in a soft, shocked voice as tears filled her eyes and spilled over to flow down her cheeks. "E-baby? Is it really my baby girl?"

Edris flinched at the old nickname and tried not to let it affect her. The woman had left her. "Hello, Mother," she said again.

Carma could tell that Edris was angry, but she didn't care as she threw herself against her and hugged her to her. "My baby! You did get away, you did get away," she said again and again as her tears soaked the front of Edris's blouse. She told herself that it didn't matter that Edris didn't hug her back.

Enrique looked on. He saw the torment in Edris's eyes and wanted desperately to fix things for her. "Uh, ladies," he said and gently separated Carma from Edris. "Why don't we continue this inside?"

Edris let her arms fall back to her sides. She'd been on the verge of hugging her mother back, despite her anger.

Carma wiped her tears with her sleeve, still staring up at Edris. "Yes, of course. Come inside." Afraid to look away from Edris for fear she'd disappear, she reached behind her for the door handle, pulling it open and walking in backwards. "Hank!" She yelled. "Hank! Come quick!" She pulled eyeglasses out of her shirt pocket and placed them on her face. "You are so beautiful," she whispered as she stared at Edris.

Edris frowned. "Hank? Hank Thompkins?"

"Yes," Carma said in confusion. "How do you know his name?"

Edris was even more furious now. "You consort with a man who smuggled criminals? You would stay here with him rather than come home to your family?" Her voice was soft and deadly.

Carma could see from Edris's eyes that she saw no hope for her redemption. She sighed and did not let the panic beating against her chest consume her. "You will let me explain, Edris June Perseveranth. Do not judge until you have heard all."

Edris raised a brow in disdain. "That may have worked when I was a child, Mother, but not now. Twenty-two years have washed away its effectiveness." She felt a hand on her shoulder and turned to Enrique.

"Edris. Let's sit down and listen to what she has to say, okay?"

Edris debated as she stared into his eyes.

"You've come this far. You might as well finish it," he said quietly.

Saying nothing, she marched over to a cream-colored sofa and sat with folded arms. Enrique sat down next to her.

"What's all the racket?" a man asked distractedly as he walked into the room. He was tall, thin and dark, and had gray eyes. The significance was not lost on anyone.

Stunned, Edris could only close her eyes at this latest surprise. Her disillusionment in Carma increased ten-fold and she mourned the loss of what she used to feel for her mother. She heard a low, astonished 'holy shit' from Enrique, but otherwise, he said nothing as he gripped her hand in his. Opening her eyes again, she said nothing as she stared at her mother.

Carma winced at the loathing she saw on her daughter's face. Taking a deep breath, she walked over to sit in the armchair closest to Edris. "Edris, this is my husband," she held out her hand to Hank, who quickly walked over to take it. "Hank, this is Edris."

"How do you do, young lady?"

Edris just looked at him.

Enrique picked up the ball. "I'm Enrique Thomas Rivera," he said. He reached out and shook first Carma's and then Hank's hand.

Hank grabbed the other armchair and pushed it closer to Carma's. Carma gave him a grateful smile when he took her hand in his. "How are your sister and your father?" she asked Edris.

"My sister--*your daughter*--does well, considering she has had no mother. As for my father, I do not know," she said with a stiff shrug and a pointed look at Hank. "You tell me."

"Now just a damn minute!" Hank stood. "I refuse to sit here while my wife and I are insulted and disrespected in our own home!"

"Oh, so you are not my biological father?" Edris asked with studied unconcern as she looked up at him. "My apologies. How odd that we resemble each other so well, but are not related. I wonder how this can be." Her shrug was jerky. "It is a big mystery, no?"

"Edris! That is enough!" Carma said. "I understand you're upset, but we will get nowhere if you continue to act in this way. You have not heard what I have to say and I would appreciate your listening before you judge me."

Edris clamped her lips shut, thinking that "upset" didn't even begin to cover it. The anger, confusion and hurt she felt threatened to explode inside her. She felt Enrique's hand slip under her hair to massage her neck and she wanted to curl into him and cry like a baby. Fighting the urge, she allowed herself to lean into the massage imperceptibly.

Carma began her story. "After you ran, Edris, they forced me to go through the portal. They told me that they'd kill you, your sister and your father if I didn't. So, I went. The choice was not a difficult one to make--I could stay and they'd kill my entire family or I could leave and my family would live. I could choose no other way."

Enrique waited for Edris to say something and when she didn't, he asked, "And what about you, Mr. Thompkins? How do you fit into the scenario?"

Carma answered. "I'd met Hank eleven years earlier on a trip through the portal. I fell in love with him, but was already married to Terrence, whom I also loved. It was not until I came home that I realized I was pregnant with Edris. I didn't see Hank again until the night I came through the portal. I called him because I had no one else. They'd sent me through without a replicater. I had no way to get back."

Edris finally spoke. "I found Mr. Thompkins' name on a list of people from this world who helped to smuggle in criminals. How do you explain that?"

"I can't," Hank said, spreading his hands in front of him in a gesture of helplessness. "Except to say that I was young, foolish and looking for what I thought was easy money. I quit after the second time, when my conscience caught up with me."

"And how did they find you? How did you begin your relationship with people from Parallel Plus?" Enrique asked.

"I was a cop and one day I was approached by someone who asked me if I wanted to make some fast money. It was as simple as that."

Edris abruptly stood. She had to get out of there. Not only was her mother alive, but she was living with the man who could be nothing but her biological father and he was a professed criminal. She'd had enough. "I must leave." She walked back to the front door and turned the knob. Her other wrist was grabbed in a strong grip. She knew who held her and didn't turn around.

"Wait, Edris," Carma said. "Will you come back?"

Edris still didn't turn. "I will tell Traia of your existence when I return home. Perhaps, I will even tell Uncle Clay if you would like."

The grip tightened, so that Carma's nails were digging into her flesh. Edris turned to look at her and was taken aback by the unadulterated fear in her mother's eyes.

"Stay away from Clayton!" Carma said urgently. "He is the one responsible for my having to leave you."

\* \* \* \*

At their hotel, Enrique held her while she cried, and she cried often during the night. She told him that she felt as if her world was falling apart around her and nothing could ever be the same. Everything was a lie. Enrique listened and held her until she had no more tears.

\* \* \* \*

"Are you feeling better, baby?" he asked her the next morning in bed.

"No, but I will," she said.

"Do you want to go back to Kentucky today? Or would you rather go see your mother again?"

Her lips tightened. "I do not think I am ready to see her."

"I understand, but you'll have to eventually. If for nothing else than to tell her that Terrence is dead."

"I do not think she would care. She has moved on. *He* is the reason she did not come home," she said, referring to Hank.

Enrique sighed and cupped her face. He wished he could take away the pain for her. "Edris, that's not true and you know it. Of course, she would care. She loved him. And I'm sure she wanted to come home, even as much as she loves Hank."

"It doesn't matter," Edris said stubbornly and sat up. "I will leave it to Traia to tell. When I go back, I will tell her what I have found and she will decide what to do from there."

"And what about Clay?"

"He will be jailed. Carma has said that she will come back to testify against him and the others. Aunt Sue, of course, will be devastated. She's just another casualty in this awful mess of greed and disloyalty," she finished with disgust.

"Must you go back, Edris?" Enrique asked her softly.

"You would like for me to stay?" Edris asked him and waited with bated breath for his answer.

"Of course I would. What do you think this has all been about? I love you."

"You love me?" her eyes anxiously searched his face. She didn't think she could take any more disappointments.

"Yes. Didn't you know?"

"How was I to know," she began irritably. "When you have not said the words before now?" she finished with an arrogant sniff.

"Oh, so sorry," Enrique said and laughed as he hugged her. "I swear, Edris, only you could manage to still look superior while dressed in a ratty T-shirt and nothing else."

Edris plucked at the covers nervously. "You know, of course, that I love you as well." It was a statement.

"Oh, *of course*," he said seriously. "How could I not have guessed?"

"Do not tease, Enrique. I do not use the words lightly."

"So, what about it? Will you stay with me?"

"But what about my sister and Angie? My job?"

"Both your sister and Angie could move here, too. We'll move to Chicago, since we both love it so much, and we'll open our own agency."

"We would be partners, you and I?"

"Yes. Think about it, Edris. We could have a wonderful life together. You could have my babies," he finished softly and leaned in to kiss her while his hand palmed and rubbed her flat tummy.

Edris' eyes softened as she thought of having little babies with black hair and blue eyes. She made a soft, mushy sound. "Oh, Enrique. Our babies would be beautiful."

"Yes, they would. Especially if they look like you with gray eyes and dark skin."

The mushy sound escaped again and she slipped her arms around his neck. "God, Enrique. I'd love to run away with you and never look back."

"Then do it," Enrique said tenderly as he pushed some hair behind her ear. "Stay here and marry me."

"I will," she said softly, her heart jumping in her throat as she agreed to leave everything she'd ever known. She pulled him down on top of her.

"Oh, baby," Enrique said as he lifted her shirt and slipped inside of her. "You've just made me the happiest man in both your world and mine."

\* \* \* \*

"I am going to visit the bathroom," Edris told Enrique. They'd just finished lunch at a downtown restaurant.

"All right." Enrique leaned back in his chair, a contented smile on his face. He was going to get married soon. His mother would love-- "Shit. I haven't even called Mom to tell her everything," he said aloud. "She's going to kill me--" Suddenly, he sat up in his chair. Something was wrong. *Really* wrong--he felt it. "Edris."

His instincts led him through the restaurant and out the back door and he followed them. Cop instincts took over from primitive male instincts just before he pushed the door open. The primitive male in him wanted to rush out and save his woman, no matter what the consequences to himself.

The cop in him, however, made him take it slow and he slowly pushed the door open a crack, just enough to squeeze through with his gun raised. Edris stood stock-still at the other end of the alley and her 'uncle' stood behind her pressing a weapon into her neck. Shit. Clay held a blaster. Edris had told him that the weapon emitted a powerful laser that could be set high enough to actually incinerate skin and bone.

"I can't believe you're doing this, Uncle Clay," Enrique heard Edris say as he took position behind a dumpster before Clay could spot him. He just needed one clear shot.

"I'm sorry, Edris, but I have to. The money is too good. Hell, it was too good twenty years ago, but it's even better now. I'm sure your mother told you her version of the story, but I bet she didn't tell you everything. Did she tell you that they would have killed both you and her if I hadn't convinced them it was better to just send her through the portal?"

"Am I supposed to be grateful?" Edris asked sarcastically. She was so angry she could barely speak. "Oh, you didn't kill us, but you merely prevented us from being together for more than twenty years. Thank you, Uncle Clay. That was magnanimous of you."

"Shut up, Edris. You're lucky and you should be thankful."

"I will never be grateful to you for stealing twenty years of a life with my mother away from me. Never."

"Well, that's too bad, Edris, because my orders are to kill you, and after you, I'm going to take care of Carma."

Even angrier now, Edris said, "*Your* orders? I thought you were the one giving the orders." she said, just before she used her heel to stomp on his foot, head butted him under the chin and then flipped him over her shoulder.

It all happened so fast that Enrique believed if he had blinked, he'd have missed it. "Magnificent," he whispered with a proud smile. His smile disappeared as another player entered the alley just as Edris was bending to take the weapon out an unconscious Clay's hand. "Shit. I didn't count on this," Enrique whispered and quietly slipped back into the restaurant, rushing through it to the front, hoping he'd make it on time.

"Hold it right there, Edris," Sue Anderson said as she trained her blaster on her. She looked at Clay and shook her head. She knew he'd blow it.

"*Aunt Sue?*" Edris was shocked as she rose slowly from her

kneeling position. "*You're* the one behind all of this and the smuggling?"

"Yep, that I am," Sue said. "I'll go you one better than Clay. It was too easy *not* to do it. I came up with the plan when I was in the training academy and it was brilliant. What better way to make good money as an officer than to work with the criminals? The smuggling started out slow, but once the word got around, I couldn't keep up with the number of people--lawyers, judges, politicians, hell, even other officers--who wanted me to get their loved ones out of the parallel. It was easy money."

"I thought we were in trouble when I heard about that guard over at the courthouse turning snitch, but then I knew I didn't have to worry when Clay was put on the case. We never counted on your mother being so damned tenacious."

"Drop your weapon!" Enrique shouted from the mouth of the alley.

When Sue spun around to protect her back, Edris jumped her from behind, landing a vicious blow on her wrist so that she dropped her blaster. Edris tackled her to the ground and finally just sat on her back when Sue wouldn't stop struggling. Enrique gingerly picked up the blaster.

## Epilogue

"How was your visit with your mother today, *bellezera oscura?*" Enrique asked Edris as she lifted his arm so she could settle against his side on the sofa. He flipped a page in his book and absently smoothed his hand down her hip.

"It went well, I think. We're both still a little uncomfortable around one another."

"What about Hank? Did he come for the visit?"

"No, I asked her not to bring him. I do not want to see him yet."

Enrique left it alone. She seemed to need to blame Hank for something. "Carma could have stayed here, you know," he said instead. "She didn't have to stay in that motel."

"I told her that, but she insisted, saying that she didn't want to get in the way." She was quiet, before saying, "I still can not believe that she was able to live here for more than twenty years and not make one attempt to come home."

"Edris, you're going to have to let it go. She did what she thought was best for her family. She believed them when they told her they'd kill all of you. Besides, without a replicater, how was she *supposed* to get back?"

"I don't know," she said sulkily, her voice muffled against his chest. "I just think if he weren't here, she would have found a way."

Enrique tangled his fingers in her hair to lift her face. "Sweetheart, give her a break. Don't you think it was difficult for her not being able to watch her children grow?" He laughed when her lips moved into a stubborn pout. "You don't give any quarter, do you?"

Edris wrinkled her nose at him and scowled before settling her head back on his chest. She squeezed him when she felt the rumble of his chuckles under her ear. "I talked to Angie today, as well. She said that Sue refuses to talk, but Clay is turning in everyone, including a senator and two commanders."

"Good," Enrique said. While Edris had subdued Sue and tied her hands behind her back, Enrique had placed his handcuffs on Clay. They'd hustled them to the car and Enrique had driven while Edris had sat in the back with her blaster trained on the couple. He'd headed out of town and had driven to a forest preserve. Edris had contacted Angie on the receiver and explained the situation. Angie had been waiting for the two criminals when they'd come through the portal. "When are we leaving for your Parallel?" he asked her.

She'd decided that she'd had to go back just to make sure everything was in order. After all, it had been her investigation. "I should have gone back that first night, but I wanted to be here with you for a while longer. I suppose *I* will leave in a few days." She rubbed his back in an effort to get rid of the tension that had invaded his body. He hated the idea of her going back, afraid that she'd get arrested. He insisted that he go with her. She was still trying to convince him that the risk was too high for him.

Enrique turned his head to press his lips to her forehead. "Okay, then. We'll leave in a few days. We won't be gone long, right?"

Edris narrowed her eyes at him in warning. He only stared at her with a lifted brow. She sighed. "*I* will stay only as long as it takes to hand in my resignation and turn over all of my notes."

"I'm ready when you are," Enrique said in a mild tone and went back to reading.

She sighed again and decided to let it go. For now. "'Rique?" she murmured.

"Yes, baby?"

"When can we move to Chicago?"

"In about four months," he said absently.

She studied the ring he'd placed on her finger just a few days before. "Are you sure your parents will like me?"

"They're going to love you," he assured her. "Has Traia decided if she wants to move here?"

"She hasn't really said. She will be here to visit with Mother soon, though. Angie is going to do the portal coordinates."

"Great. I'll be glad to see her again," he said and went back to his book.

"'Rique?"

"Hmm?"

"I love my new gown. Thank you for buying it for me."

"Well, I know how much you love pretty, soft things. Besides, it matches your eyes perfectly, so I couldn't resist it."

"'Rique?"

"Hmm?"

"I'm wearing the gown now," she said and leaned up to take his earlobe gently between her teeth. "When are you coming to bed, *mi amor*?" she whispered in his ear.

He dropped his book. "Right now, *bellezera oscura*." He stood and picked her up.

She twined her arms around his neck. "Perhaps we can get started on the blue-eyed, black-haired babies now."

# PLEASURE PRINCIPLE

Kimberly Kaye Terry

### Prologue

*Mariana tilted the brim of her straw-hat back a bit on her head and squinted up at the sun before she cast her eyes around the small plot of land. Her garden was in serious need of a little TLC. It had been a while since she'd weeded it.*

*With a happy sigh, she rearranged her long peasant skirt and knelt down in the dirt, shovel in one hand, and shears in the other. She adjusted the volume on the CD player and bounced her butt a little as she happily went to work.*

*She loved this place. She could garden, escape from the world, and* really *listen to music. She was so busy pulling weeds and replanting pansies, she didn't hear the sound of the nearly inaudible steps in the lush grass. She glanced up just in time to see a big hand reach out to delicately finger one of her long individual microbraids.*

*"I love when you do this to your hair," he complimented her softly.*

*She unconsciously ducked her head to hide the blush she felt creep along her cheeks, although she had no idea why he always affected her this way. Cain had been visiting her for as long as she could remember, from the time she was a child.*

*After a few moments of silence, she stole a glance at him from beneath lowered lids. He stood so tall his long body blocked out the sun. She patted the spot beside her in silent invitation and smiled when he immediately hunkered down next to her. When he held out his hand, she reached for the spare pair of gloves and handed them to him. She admired the way he worked the gloves onto his long, strongly sculpted hands.*

*"Where have you been? It's been awhile," Mariana asked as they*

*worked hand-in-hand planting and gardening in companionable silence.*

*He didn't say anything for a moment. When he did, she could hear the weariness that lay just beneath the surface of his deep voice when he answered.* "I had to take care of a few things. I had missions that needed my attention."

*Mariana never questioned these missions of his. Missions that would take him away from her for long weeks at a time. Sometimes months. She accepted that he had a life away from her. Just as she had a life outside of this idyllic paradise also.*

"I wanted to come sooner," *he apologized, and she could feel his intent gaze. Watching her.*

"I understand. You're here now, that's what matters."

"Your brother Samuel needs to go in your place to visit the designer," *Cain spoke without preamble as he often did. He would simply drop one of his sometimes vague comments in the conversation and expect her to follow the flow. Which she always did, she thought with an inward laugh.*

"Arlinda Nyoni?" *she asked, not surprised that he knew Arlinda, nor that she was scheduled to have a meeting with the woman to discuss a fundraiser for her charity.*

"Yes."

*When he said nothing more, she waited. It never worked for her to try and hasten him to speak.*

"Samuel needs to go carefully with her. If he rushes, and accepts what she initially will offer him, he'll lose the greatest reward in the end."

"What's the reward? Is she for Sam?" *Mariana held her breath.*

*He turned dark eyes in her direction and the look in their swirling depths made her breath catch in her throat, before he smiled gently at her.*

"Just make sure you allow Samuel to go in your place, and caution him. It'll all work out as it was meant to. Have faith." *He laughed when she pulled a face at him.*

"Okay, thank you, old sage one, I will duly do as instructed. Now do you wanna know what's going on in my world?"

"That's what I love about you. That irreverence for your elders," *he laughed.* "Yes, please tell me what's going on in your world." *He lightly tapped the brim of her hat.*

*Although she laughingly accepted his suggestions, they both knew that she carefully listened to him and as usual, would take his words to heart. She would speak with Sam.*

*The afternoon was spent in pleasant conversation, and if she thought too carefully on his earlier comment that he loved her, she remembered that he'd been saying the same thing to her from the time she was a child.*

*From the first time that he'd entered her dreams.*

## Chapter One

"Maya, could you please hand me that g-string? No, not the red one, the black see-thru one! How tacky would that be to have a red lace thong with a black sheer bra?"

"Arlinda Nyoni, what difference does it make which color it is? I don't see a red one anyway! Who's going to see it? And if they did would they *really* care that the two didn't match?" Maya grumbled as she half-heartedly fished around the small bin for the requested undergarment.

Arlinda peeked from behind the mannequin she was currently dressing to steal a glance at her irritable friend. She didn't want to laugh at her but Maya had turned into a serious grump the farther she advanced in her pregnancy. At six months pregnant, Maya's general ticked-off-at-the-world disposition had grown in direct proportion to her growing belly.

Maya had recently gotten married and within weeks she'd hesitantly shared the news with Arlinda that she and her husband Mark were expecting. Weeks ago, Maya's obstetrician had informed her friend that she was pregnant with twins.

Maya's husband had been overjoyed but Arlinda could tell Maya was still trying to adjust to the fact that she was going to be a mother, much less the mother of two. Because of Maya's abusive childhood background, she'd unconsciously closed herself off to the idea of having children.

With her husband's love and support, she'd begun to shake off those old beliefs. And it didn't hurt that Mark loved Maya to distraction.

Arlinda stifled an inward sigh of envy.

She loved Maya as the sister she had never had and although the two of them had different upbringings, they still shared a lot of similarities. Arlinda's childhood had been loving and nurturing, unlike Maya's harsher beginnings.

Both were the product of a racial mixture. Maya's mother had been white and her father black. Her parents had died in a car accident when Maya was a child, leaving her in the care of her abusive foster mother.

Arlinda's mother was Puerto Rican and her father was African. Although she'd grown up with both parents, it had been difficult as a child for her to shrug off the meanness of others. Her family had moved from Puerto Rico to New York, and she'd eventually learned to deal with the names and ugly treatment she'd received by using humor as her shield.

Everyone liked the happy girl. The woman who was always up for a party and took life lightly. The one who never shared her true feelings.

She didn't envy Maya for the sake of envy. But she was honest enough with herself to admit she envied her because she'd found that perfect man. If such an animal existed.

She'd found her soul mate, a man who'd been able to look beyond the shield to discover a woman worth fighting for.

Arlinda didn't think she'd ever find that man for herself.

Besides, it was just so much easier to play the flirt role. Therefore when the relationship soured she had little or no emotional investment. She'd leave the whole 'happily ever after' to Maya and Mark.

"Here, damn it, take these!" Maya interrupted her dour thoughts and flung the g-string at her slingshot style.

"Maya, *chica*, you are *so* out of control! What am I going to do with you?" she asked as the panties landed on top of her head. Maya's eyes widened and seconds later giggles erupted.

"Arlinda, I am really sorry! I have no idea what's come over me lately, I promise!" she said, hiccupping around her laughter before promptly breaking down into tears.

"Oh lord, here we go again," Arlinda mumbled under her breath. She caught the demonic look that entered her friend's eyes at her observation. Obviously she'd heard what she'd said.

Arlinda noticed that along with the other side effects of pregnancy such as overall evilness and whims of crying jags for no apparent reason, there seemed to be an unnatural increase in auditory ability.

She hastily got to her feet and removed the pincushion from her wrist. She grabbed the dangling thong off of her head to toss on the floral loveseat next to the mannequin. She walked over to Maya and sat down next to her on one of the tall, leather-backed stools.

"*Es no problema, chica*! And I'm sorry, sweetie. I know you're a ... bit ... emotional. It comes with the territory. Is everything going okay?" she asked, as she tucked a wayward curl behind Maya's ear.

"Yes. Everything is fine, Arlinda." Maya sighed as she sniffed, pushing her glasses further up her nose. "You were right. That seems to be the way it's all going for me lately. Laughing one minute and crying the next! I'm driving Mark insane, I think. He's liable to leave me any minute if I keep up the crazed behavior," she hiccupped.

"*Sure,* Maya! It would take an act of God for that man to go anywhere away from you for any extended period of time. And, girl, even then I could see your man going toe-to-toe with the Almighty! Honey, he's not going *anywhere.*" She laughed as she patted her friend on top of her head.

"I don't know, Arlinda, last week he spent an awful lot of time with Jordan. He claimed the two of them had work to do on a case, but I wasn't buying it. I think he just wanted to get away from me!" She sighed.

Arlinda attempted a parody of a smile but really felt like crying.

Mark and Jordan were detectives and also partners. Arlinda had dated Jordan and they'd recently broken up. The break-up had been hard and although she knew it was for the best, that they weren't really meant for each other, it hurt like hell when he'd been the one to suggest they break things off.

She had to turn her head away at the threat of the tears she felt pricking her eyes.

\* \* \* \*

Maya felt awful.

She hadn't meant to remind Arlinda of Jordan. The break-up was fairly new and although Arlinda went into what Maya privately thought of as her "I don't give a damn" mode, she knew that her friend was hurting.

She glanced at Arlinda and caught the pain in her amber-colored eyes moments before she glanced away.

"Now I'm the one sorry, sweetie. I didn't mean to bring Jordan's name into the conversation."

"That's cool, Maya girl! No biggie. I've been over him for a while now." She laughed it off.

Maya hated when Arlinda did that. Pretended that everything was fine and that she was unaffected whenever she hurt. Even with her, she felt the need to put up a front.

"You know, you can talk to me about it. How you're feeling I mean." She broached the subject lightly. Arlinda once told her she didn't want her to "play psychologist" with her. This was difficult for Maya not to do because she cared for her friend.

That and she *was* a psychologist.

"I know, Maya. But really, I'm fine. Jordan and I weren't meant to be together and we both knew it. He did us both a favor by ending the relationship. You know I have a hard time doing that anyway." She gently patted her on the belly and smiled before she rose from the stool and crossed back to the half-dressed mannequin.

Arlinda deserved more than she gave herself credit for. Not only was she a beautiful woman on the outside, she was just as beautiful on the inside. Maya was still the smallest bit ticked at Jordan for hurting her friend's feelings, although deep inside she knew they really weren't meant for each other. They were too much alike, in Maya's opinion, in areas concerning love and life. Neither one was ready to put their personal shields away.

Arlinda wielded her femininity like a true weapon. She used her petite frame and overly large eyes to give the impression that she was helpless when she thought it would benefit her. Men had a tendency to want to coddle or protect her, never seeing beyond the visage to the real woman beneath. She was a woman with more depth and intelligence than she purposely projected.

But Maya wasn't sure what Arlinda's reaction would be if she shared her thoughts on the subject. Rather than take a chance on her being angry, Maya opted to leave the subject alone.

She sighed. She had things she still needed to work on and feeling comfortable enough to risk her best friend's wrath was on her *to do* list.

\* \* \* \*

As Arlinda finished dressing the mannequin she waited to hear Maya confront her about her feelings on the break up between Jordan and herself.

It hurt, and although she tried to hide the pain, she knew Maya saw beneath the shield she erected. She had to. They'd been friends since college and her friend was very astute.

She continued to pin the leather shorts in place on the mannequin as she waited for Maya to say something. Anything.

She glanced up from beneath her lashes to see Maya staring at her intently.

"Well?"

"Well what?"

"I know you want to say something, so just say it."

She thought for one brief shining minute that Maya was going to finally say *something* and when she didn't, when the moment passed and she saw her shake her head just slightly as though she had something to say but had changed her mind, Arlinda wanted to throw something out of sheer frustration.

"So tell me about this fundraiser you're involved in," Maya asked instead.

Oh well. This was something she was more comfortable talking about anyway. *This* subject didn't make her want to go find Jordan and jack his dusty ass up for leaving her.

Arlinda breathed a deep breath and forced her thoughts away from her former lover. "I spoke with Mariana St. John a few days ago regarding donating some items for her charity closet, and I love the idea of helping with the fashion show and auction! It'll be fun. Yours is the only event I've done like this, but I think this will be great. I'm looking forward to doing this."

"Mariana is such a wonderful woman. She started Mari's Closet a few years ago after she interned with me at Imani House. I like the idea of a place where women can go to borrow suitable clothes in order to go on job interviews."

"Yeah, something so simple is usually overlooked when social service agencies try and help women in job placement. The right clothes can not only make a good impression on the interviewer, but can make you feel so much better about yourself," Arlinda agreed, mumbling around a stick pin clenched between her teeth.

"I'm glad you're excited about it! Mariana and I have been exchanging resources for a couple of years now. She's helped the women of Imani House several times." Maya mentioned her residential facility that helped women escape prostitution.

"We've only met the one time. In fact, she's coming by this afternoon sometime for us to make some decisions on which clothes she'd be interested in using for the show, and also to give me the measurements for the models."

"So you're providing the clothes for the fashion show? How does that work? Mariana mentioned that her brother was financially backing the event and the proceeds would benefit her program."

Arlinda watched in sympathy as Maya grimaced as she stretched her back and stood from the stool, stumbling a bit as she did. Maya was as small in stature as she and Arlinda knew the heavy burden of carrying two babies must be hell on her back.

Yet another reason for her to maintain her carefree existence.

No man, no potential for babies upsetting her balance and equilibrium. If she felt the slightest bit of yearning, she ignored it. Everything wasn't for everybody. At least that's what her mother was always telling her.

"Seems like her brother is some type of real estate magnate. Owns a ton of commercial property. In fact he owns the property in this plaza." Arlinda referred to the small plaza where her business was housed.

"She mentioned her brother. I think his name is Samuel?" Maya asked.

"I make my rental checks out to the Samuel St. John Corporation. So I guess he's one and the same," she agreed as she stood back to admire her work.

"Is this what you have planned for the show?" Maya had walked over to where Arlinda was standing and now stood next to her and both women looked at the dressed mannequin. "Somehow leather and thigh high boots aren't what I think a woman going on an interview would wear." Maya laughed.

The mannequin was dressed in a pair of leather hot pants and matching studded leather halter. Its legs were encased in thigh high stiletto boots and a long leather whip rested in the curve of its hand.

"Um … I don't think this is what Mariana has in mind for this show. This one is for Larissa LeCroix. He was a finalist in the Miss San Antonio Blue Revue Transbeauty Contest! But who knows?" she said. Both women tilted their heads to the side, as they admired the mannequin's ensemble.

\* \* \* \*

"Sam, I really need you to do me this favor! I can't get away right now or I would, and I don't want to stand Ms. Nyoni up. Please?" Mariana begged, as she bustled around her office.

"Mariana, I've already told you I'm on a tight schedule today. I can't do it. I have to prepare for a meeting with my investors for the Atkinson's project tomorrow, or I'd help. Sorry, pooh," her brother said.

Mariana knew she could convince him to help if he called her pooh.

He would unconsciously revert to calling her pooh when he was in one of his more agreeable moods. He'd been calling her that nickname from the moment she'd arrived at his family home with her Winnie the Pooh bear stuck under her arm and her thumb in her mouth.

She glanced over at him as he looked over her financial documents. She smiled as he nudged his reading glasses further up his nose and brushed a frustrated hand through his dark hair, settling it in all directions over his head.

Once a month, Sam would go over the center's accounts for her. He made sure she was taken care of in all areas, and was her advisor as well as one of the major financial supporter's for her social service organization.

Mariana St. John loved her brother. Although they weren't biologically related and looked nothing alike, he was the true brother of her heart. His family had adopted her when she had been only three years old and he'd been ten, and he'd instantly accepted her. He'd never stopped taking care of her and she knew this time would be no exception.

"And it won't take long, just drop off the models' measurements and I'll call her to find a time that we can reschedule our appointment. All you'll have to do is beg and plead with her not to be too angry with me for rescheduling. Come on, Sam, you know you're going to so let's just stop playing around!" She laughed and turned away from him, back to the file cabinet.

When he threw a balled up piece of paper at her, she turned back around and laughed. "What? You know it's the truth!"

"Brat," he mumbled.

"What's that? I can't hear you. I think my hearing aid's battery is low," she teased, fumbling with the small apparatus nestled in her ear.

"Mari, you've been trying that trick for the last twenty-five years and it's not working anymore now than it ever has." He neatly caught the wadded up ball she lobbed back in his direction.

"But, since I love you so much ... I guess I can help you out. As long as it doesn't take too long." He held out a cautioning hand as she did a little dance and ran across the office to hug him. "I'm serious, Mari, I'll deliver the measurements and the message, but that's it ... okay?" He smoothed one of her micro braids behind her ear.

When his sister only laughed and hugged him, Sam hugged her hard, briefly, before he set her back on her feet. "Now go and get me the files on your donations so I can finish this up," he said, suppressing a smile as he did.

## Chapter Two

Why did she always do this?

Why did she always pretend as though she were taller than she was and fall flat on her butt every time? Arlinda thought as she sat amidst boxes in her storeroom.

And why did she feel like crying?

Unbidden, tears filled her eyes and once they started it was impossible to stem the flow. Instead of trying she just went with it and laid her head across her crossed arms and cried.

She felt totally inadequate. Useless *and* inadequate.

Not only could she not reach the hatbox on the top shelf, but neither could she apparently hold on to a damn man. Sure, the two were unrelated but in her current state of depression, they were somehow connected.

When she and Jordan had first started dating he seemed like the perfect man for her. Handsome, funny, intelligent … and good in bed. True, they kept things light, choosing to focus on the things they both enjoyed rather than delving into deeper subjects. But it was how they both liked it.

A few times Jordan would ask about her life growing up or once in a while he would ask her questions about what she envisioned her future to be. When, or if, she thought she'd ever settle down.

On those times when he would venture into unwanted territory, she'd laugh and make some joking comment, turning his attention away from *that* particular line of questioning. She could tell on more than one occasion he'd been ticked at her non-committal answer or joke, although he let it go.

She sighed and hiccupped.

Arlinda stayed in that same position for long moments, feeling sorry for herself and allowing the tears to fall unchecked. The sound of a throat clearing startled her into jerking her head up and turning her body around to see who'd witnessed her lapse into self-pity.

\* \* \* \*

Sam carefully looked at each address as he walked along the plaza until he came upon nineteen ninety-nine. He glanced down at the address on the top page of the sheaf of documents in his hand to verify that he had the correct address for Arlinda Nyoni's boutique,

Designs of Amara.

The small bell trilled as he opened the door to the shop and walked inside. His nostrils flared as he inhaled deeply, his body reacting strongly to the sensual smell in the shop. As he glanced around to see where the smell was coming from his eyes catalogued the simple, yet attractive design of the shop.

One wall held an enormous floor-to-ceiling dark-wood framed mirror. The heavy draperies on the windows were crimson and were tied back to expose cherry-wood thick blinds. The walls of the shop were painted gold, with works of abstract art matted and framed.

As he looked around, his gaze fell on the mannequin that was propped against the wall and he felt his brows rise as he took in tight black leather shorts and matching halter. The mannequin looked to be clutching a whip in its white plaster hand. He hoped to hell this wasn't what Mari had in mind for the charity show or he and his sister were going to have a nice, long talk.

"Hello," he called out as he walked through the shop, his glance falling on the clothes that were scattered on the small red loveseat, as well as the other mannequins scattered throughout the small shop, all in various stages of dress.

"Anyone here?" he murmured to no one in particular.

As he walked closer to the counter he could have sworn he heard crying. The closer he approached the counter, the more he was sure he was right, as he followed the sound through the double doors.

He came to a halt when he saw the huddled small figure in the middle of what looked to be a storeroom, boxes scattered around her as she had her head down on her folded arms, crying as though her heart was breaking.

Sam felt his heart clench at the sound of her tears and cleared his throat to get her attention. When she whipped her small curly head around to stare at him with the largest brown eyes he'd ever seen, more than his heart clenched. As she stared at him with her whiskey-colored eyes, his heart thumped strongly in his chest.

\* \* \* \*

Oh lord.

No, she didn't.

No, she didn't get caught crying her fool eyes out in front of one of the finest men she'd seen in a long time.

Arlinda felt her heart race as her eyes took in the man in front of her in with one assessing glance from the top of his dark, wavy, short-cropped hair to the tips of his well-shod feet.

# WICKED DELIGHTS

Despite any embarrassment over being caught crying, she *had* to admire the way his close fitting dark-ribbed shirt tucked into the waistband of his full-cut, dark slacks. She hiccupped as her gaze settled over the taut plane of his chest and stomach.

Arlinda loved a well-dressed man. And this one knew how to dress.

Her eyes traveled from his chest up the line of his strong throat, to his squared chin which, lord help her--was that a dimple in the middle?--and had just the hint of a shadow in its hollow. She was immediately fascinated by the hard full curve of his mouth, which held just the smallest hint of a smile around its sensual corners.

When he coughed again, she immediately brought her eyes back to his. His eyes were dark and, had it not been for the light filtered in from the windows, she would have thought them to be black. But they weren't. From the distance she was from him, they appeared deep chocolate brown.

She scrambled to her feet, and when he quickly walked over to help, offering his hand in the process, she felt an electric sizzle from the light contact and she literally felt herself get dizzy.

Damn.

She was in trouble.

\* \* \* \*

Damn.

She was fine.

From the moment Sam laid eyes on the small woman, he knew he was in trouble. When she'd been sitting on the floor looking dejected and crying he felt the clench in his heart, but when she turned those pretty brown eyes in his direction he felt more than his heart clench. The moment his hand touched hers, he'd felt as though he'd been sucker punched.

He steadied her on her feet and was hard-pressed not to reach up and touch her hair to see if it was as soft as it felt. Dark thick curls haloed her small head, the curly tips barely reaching the back of her neck. A few short tendrils framed her smooth, cocoa-colored brown skin. His eyes did a quick trip down her short nose, lightly sprinkled with freckles, on to her lush and full lips.

It was her lips that gave him the overwhelming need to adjust his pants, as he felt his cock thump a welcome against his zipper. When she stuck her small tongue out and moistened the bottom rim, he felt like groaning out loud.

Not only were her pretty lips full, but they were just lightly puffed out, giving her a look of having been thoroughly kissed.

His eyes traveled back up to her wide-set eyes and his heart did that crazy lurch thing again when he saw they were red-rimmed from her crying of moments ago.

"Are you okay? Is there anything I can do to help?" he asked. Without conscious thought, he reached out and wiped a tear from the corner of her eye.

He quickly withdrew his hand.

He had no idea what had come over him. He was normally embarrassingly reticent around women. His sister teased him, saying he was shy, but he ignored her teasing.

It wasn't that he was shy; it was only that it seemed to take a lot for him to expend the energy in approaching a woman. And the fact that he was so instantly drawn to this woman, who he assumed to be Arlinda Nyoni, baffled him.

* * * *

His voice was so deep and sexy that Arlinda felt herself grow embarrassingly aroused.

What *was* it with this man?

Or better still what was it with *her*? Was she so pitiful that all it took was a handsome man to smile and offer her a bit of comfort for her to fall apart? Was she that hard up for affection?

As she looked into his chocolate brown eyes she felt his hand brush away a tear. She mentally stopped herself from doing something really dumb by grabbing him by his non-existent collar and hauling him down face level to kiss him.

He'd probably think she was a whack job so she stopped herself from doing something so pitiful. As depressed as she was, there was no telling what she'd do.

"I'm fine," she murmured.

She was caught off guard when he tilted her head up and asked, "Are you sure?"

His deep voice and his touch sparked a flash of electricity that radiated from her chin, where the rough pad of his thumb touched, all the way down to her toes.

"Maybe it would be better if we went back to the showroom, Mr. …" she allowed the sentence to dangle as she realized she had no idea who this man was. She turned back around to face him as she led the way out of the room.

"St. John … Samuel St. John," he filled in and held the swinging door open for her as she walked through to the other side.

"St. John? Did you say Samuel St. John, as in the real estate St. John's Group? The owner of this plaza?" Arlinda felt her heart sink with the instant recognition of his name.

She turned desperate eyes in his direction.

"Yes. One and the same."

He'd casually walked over to her small counter and set his briefcase on top before he looked back in her direction. She slowly walked toward him, her embarrassment flooding her face with heat.

"Oh God! How embarrassed am I?" she moaned, wanting to find the nearest hole to bury herself.

"What for? Because I walked in on a private moment when you were crying? I don't think that's anything to be embarrassed for." He smiled before he lifted his briefcase to the counter.

"Is there a problem, Mr. St. John? Is everything okay? I've just recently moved in. I love the shop and the loft so I hope there's not a problem," she said. One of the main reasons she'd chosen the plaza to open Designs of Amara was because of the availability of the loft that was housed directly above the shop. She'd quickly converted the open room into a cozy residence.

"No, Ms. Nyoni, there's no problem. If there were, to be honest, I wouldn't be the one to contact you." He laughed and she felt ten times the fool. Of course a man in his position wouldn't be there to collect rent or tell her if there was a plumbing problem. But if he wasn't here for the building....

"What are you here for then?" she blurted the question in her thoughts.

What in the world was wrong with her? She wished with all her heart that she could simply snatch her tongue out of her mouth. It would be a lot less painful and much easier in the long run.

"I'm here on behalf of my sister ... Mariana? Mariana St. John. She wasn't able to come today to drop off the measurements for the clothes, so I'm doing her a favor," he said and smiled, one dimple flashing as he finally located the documents he'd been searching for. His smile distracted her for just a minute until she finally made the connection.

"Mariana is your sister? Mariana St. John? The same woman who has contracted with me for this fundraiser?" she squeaked, her voice raising several octaves. His last name clicked as the same one that belonged to her new client. If she thought she was embarrassed before, it was nothing compared to how she currently felt. *Madre de Dios....*

Then she thought about it and was confused. She'd met Mariana and she didn't want to ask, but she wondered if they were biologically related. Mariana was African American, and though he sported a nice golden tan, she didn't think he was African American as well.

But she'd already put her foot in her mouth with the whole crying-on-the-floor-and-nearly-kissing-him thing ... no need to add more fuel to the flame and ask personal questions.

"Yes, that would be my spoiled sister." He laughed and handed her the documents.

"I hope everything is okay with her?" Their fingers touched when she took the folder and Arlinda felt the same electric flash of heat she'd experienced earlier. This time she *knew* he felt it also. His eyes searched hers before she quickly averted hers. She scanned the document and quickly read the jostled notes in what appeared to be a woman's flowing script.

"Everything is fine," he said slowly. "With my sister. She was swamped and couldn't get away," he explained. She felt goose bumps prickle her skin. He spoke slowly, as though weighing his words. She felt crazy as hell but she wanted, no, she *had* to look at him.

When she did, she wished she hadn't. His eyes were trained intently on the curve of her bottom lip. So strong was her reaction that she forced herself not to look around to see if she'd left a window open when she felt her nipples harden.

She was shameless.

It had nothing to do with the breezy San Antonio air and everything to do with her being aroused by this man. Once again, her gaze did a quick visual of his body.

Ummm. She'd love to walk right over to him, lift up his shirt and see if what lay underneath his close-fitting t-shirt, looked as yummy as she thought it would. She was a bit disgusted with herself, but why lie? Men had a distinct purpose. Nice bit of eye candy and a fun time. Nothing more. Nothing less. If she thought otherwise, all she needed to do was recall her recent breakup with Jordan to disabuse her of such happily-ever-after-thoughts.

"Is everything in order? Mariana gave me the folder and I don't really know much else."

"Everything is fine," she said, forcing her attention back to the documents. "These are the measurements of the models who volunteered their time for the show so that I could adjust the measurements of the clothes to fit."

She saw that he'd wandered in the direction of one of the mannequins she was pinning for her transgender client. She held her laugh in check when she noticed his eyebrows rise as he turned back to face her.

"And this would be for the client going for an interview for IBM? Microsoft?" he asked totally straight faced.

"Definitely. I thought, to heck with traditional slacks and blouse. Who needs a boring old suit when a nice pair of leather hot pants and matching halter would say *hire me* so much better? I'm dependable, eager and ready to work!" she laughed. She liked his droll humor.

"Of course you can't forget this." He picked up the leather whip that lay in the curve of the mannequin's hand.

"Of course not! What interview would be complete without a bullwhip? A bullwhip adds just that much more … command to the outfit, don't you think? Just in case the interviewer asks *one* too many personal questions … one whoosh with this baby and all her troubles are over!" she said, swinging the bullwhip back and forth, pendulum style, as they spoke.

They looked at one another and both laughed, no longer able to keep it droll.

\* \* \* \*

Her laugh was so sexy, it was all Sam could do not to grab her and do what he wanted to do in the storeroom. Kiss her senseless.

She had a sexy dimple in the corner of her mouth that came out when she smiled or laughed. He was hard as a rock imaging what she could do with that lush full mouth of hers.

He'd been attracted to women instantly before, but never anything like this. He couldn't remember the last time a laugh from a woman had his dick hard and him randy as hell. But more than that, there was something about her that had pulled at him from the moment he'd seen her crying on the floor. She had looked so forlorn as she sat hunched over with her arms crossed over her bent knees.

He'd also picked up on her awareness of him.

She was a naturally sexy woman and put off vibes she probably wasn't even aware of. The way he'd caught her looking at him, told him that despite whatever had made her cry, she was equally attracted to him.

He allowed his gaze to slide over her, head to toe, as she was looking over the documents. She was very petite; her head barely reached his chest. Her dark hair was close cropped with the curls framing her small oval face. Her eyes were large and amber colored, with a dark fringe of lashes he thought he could individually count from where he stood.

His gaze roamed over her face, past her lush lips without stopping.

He was already hard pressed not to kiss a total stranger and if he kept staring at her mouth he'd end up on the end of a harassment suit when he walked up to her and hauled her close and ground her lips with his.

Behind the small triangle of her brightly colored halter, her small breasts were high and firm looking without benefit of a bra. He could see the imprint of her nipples as they beaded behind the soft material.

The halter ended at the top of her ribcage and he saw a chip of a diamond as it sparkled in the deep recess of her small belly button. He restrained a groan when his imagination took over with thoughts of how it would feel to swirl and dip his tongue in her pretty little bellybutton.

She wore a pair of Capri jeans that dipped in at her small waist before flaring and closely hugging her full round hips. On her feet she wore a pair of pink Nike's without socks. No doubt about it, Arlinda Nyoni was sexy from the top of her short-cropped hair to the bottom of her Nike's. And everything in between.

"These look in order, Mr. St. John," she told him in her sexy, lightly accented voice.

That was the other thing he was drawn to about her. Her voice. It had a hushed quality to it. She also had the slightest bit of an accent that although it wasn't thick, it softly blurred her words together and was sexy as hell to him. Sam quickly brought his attention back to the conversation.

"Good. And please call me Sam," he offered. "Mariana handed the folder to me without any instruction," he said as he walked toward her.

When he drew closer, she looked up at him from beneath lowered lids and for a minute her eyes widened as though she were caught off guard. He saw the way her chest rose

Quickly, the sudden deep breath that she took. Seconds later a sexy smile settled over her mouth and the small dimple in the corner reappeared.

A *deliberately* sexy smile.

"I can give you all the instruction you need. No problems there," she promised. She snaked her tongue out to slowly lick the full bottom rim of her lips.

There was a quiet moment. A moment outside of time while they appraised the other. She was looking at him with a near expectant look on her face. A challenging look that dared him to take what she was offering.

To see if he would.

Her chest rose and fell and from his height advantage, he could see the twin globes of her small breasts as they were pushed together behind the tiny halter.

But as he'd seen the challenge in her eyes, he'd also seen a glimpse of hesitancy. Of vulnerability.

One part of him, the very aroused part said *take it*. She was offering, why the hell not? The other part, the part that knew there was something different about this woman, said no. His instincts told him that if he took her up on what she was offering now, he'd miss out on something more important later.

He felt the tension in the room as they stared at each other for a fraction of a moment, expectancy palpable in the air.

He gave an inward sigh.

"Mariana mentioned that you would have the estimates of cost and your fees available for me?"

She looked at him and he saw the surprise cross her beautiful face. Surprise followed by disappointment. Clearly she'd expected a different reaction.

"Yes, I do. If you'll excuse me I'll get them for you, Mr. St. John." She walked away from him and his eyes went to her small tight butt, cupped so nicely in her jeans. He liked the way her hips swayed as she hastily walked away.

"Please call me Sam," he reminded her. She said nothing in return, only continued searching through the gray metal cabinet for the file. The way she stiffly held her body told him she was a bit off-put at his retreat.

"So you're backing this event for Mariana?" Arlinda asked. She felt heat cover her face in embarrassment. She'd given off enough *come-and-get-it* vibes to attract the entire San Antonio Spurs team and he hadn't been the least bit affected.

Once again, she asked herself what was with this man. Why was she so turned on, and why did it matter that he refused her not so subtle come on? She sighed as she retrieved her cost estimates and turned to face Samuel St. John.

"I am," he answered her question. "As well as a few others." He accepted the folder without looking at the contents. "I'll go over this later."

"Did Mariana tell you when she'd be in contact with me? We have a lot of planning to do before the show in a few weeks."

"Actually there's been a change of plans with that."

Arlinda felt nervousness settle in her belly. "What type of

change?" She was afraid her come-on had been a turn-off. As Samuel St. John was the one paying the tab, she saw the purchase of the bolt of new haute couture fabric from one of her favorite vendors go up in smoke right before her eyes.

"I'm going to be the one working with you directly with this project, not Mariana," he told her with a casual smile.

At the same time that she felt relief at his words, a different type of sensation settled in her stomach when he said he'd be working with her. She quickly glanced at him and the look in his dark eyes, along with the wolfish smile he sent her way, caused a delicious shiver to run down her spine.

\* \* \* \*

"This is a wonderful idea, Sam. To use a few of the women from the organization to model the clothes will make quite an impact. It will give the contributors someone real to connect with. Show them who their money is helping. I should have no problem finding the rest of the models," Arlinda said as she and Sam finished for the evening.

Sam had come to the shop an hour ago, surprising her with take-out from the local deli, saying they may as well kill two birds with one stone by eating and going over the particulars for the fundraiser at the same time.

True to his word he'd been the only one that she'd had any dealings with in regards to the fundraiser. She'd spoken to his sister, Mariana, on the phone a few times over the course of last few weeks but, for the most part, her dealings had been solely with Sam, both on the phone and in person.

She glanced over at him and felt her heart race.

He was so sexy, leaning against the counter like that, elbows propped on the edge. He'd come over directly from his office and had discarded his suit jacket, exposing the fine hairs on his forearms.

Over the last few weeks, she'd tried her hardest to get him to take the working relationship to a personal level. Less than a week ago, he'd surprised her when he'd initiated a kiss that had left her weak and shaky. She picked up the glass of tea and took a sip as she eyed him over the rim. When she noticed a speck of bread in the corner of his mouth, she picked up a napkin, reached across the counter space and gently wiped the crumb away.

"Thank you," he said and she heard the husky catch in his throat before he cleared it.

"It was nothing. I'd like for you to be able to thank me for something a bit more ... substantial ... than that," she daringly said. Although she gave him her patented *come- and-get-it* grin, inside she was shaking and afraid. And uncertain. She'd relied on flirting and teasing playfulness for so long, with both men and women, that she didn't know how to be anything else *but* flirtatious.

"Why do you do that?" he asked quietly as he gathered the remains from their impromptu dinner.

"Do what?" she asked, surprised. She stopped, picking up the remaining trash to glance over at him as he dunked the sandwich wrappers into the small trashcan on the side of the counter.

He turned back around and leaned against the counter, his dark gaze brooding. "Why do you give such flippant answers all of the time?"

"I don't know what you're talking about." She was surprised at his question and turned away. She was even more shocked when she felt his hand on her arm, halting her escape.

"Talk to me," was all that he said. But it was enough. As she looked into his eyes, saw her own reflection in the depths of his deep gaze, she felt as though she were free falling. She wanted, no ... she *needed* to be honest with this man. To try and open up old wounds.

"Growing up, I was picked on a lot when we moved from Puerto Rico." He was silent and she continued. "I got tired of it and decided to put on the comedic '*make em like me, role.*' It's hard not to like the clown. As I matured, I began to get a lot of male attention. I used that to my advantage," she admitted, her voice grown husky with remembered embarrassment.

She cleared her throat and continued. She had nothing to be ashamed of.

"I figured out pretty quickly that the best way to cement my position at the top of the food chain was to take advantage of the fact that I was attractive."

She was silent as she remembered how the other girls disliked her when she started getting all the young boys' attention at school. She remembered the instant fear clutched her heart with their growing dislike. She wasn't ready to be picked on again.

"It was difficult at first. I'd always been the clown, had always made people laugh. But things shift as you get older. Soon the clown role wasn't enough. I needed a new role. I didn't want to go back to being made fun of. It may sound superficial, but being liked and being popular was a hell of a lot better than being made fun of and beat up," she said defensively.

"You're not on trial with me, Arlinda. You did nothing wrong," he said. They were standing close and when he ran a callused thumb down the line of her jaw, she stopped herself from leaning closer into his caress.

She gave a half-smile. "I know that. Thank you." She thought about how she'd walked the tight rope in trying to balance female jealousy and her new desire for popularity with the young men.

"It was always that way for me. The constant need for acceptance. Popularity was a surefire way to prove I wasn't that little kid from Puerto Rico that everyone used to pick on. It became paramount for me to always be liked."

"You don't have to prove anything to anyone. Especially me," Sam said. "I knew you were special from the first time I set eyes on you, and I didn't know a thing about you." With that small statement, Arlinda felt her defenses crumple that much more.

She was right the first time she laid eyes on him. This man *was* special, she thought, as they cleaned up the remainder of the small mess before he kissed her lightly on the mouth. He left her in the doorway of the small shop with an unknowing smile gracing her full lips.

## Chapter Three

"Arlinda it sounds to me like you're sabotaging again."

"I don't think I'd call it *sabotage*, Maya. That seems a little harsh don't you think, *chica?*" Arlinda asked, as she trailed behind her waddling best friend in the kitchen of Imani House, sipping a glass of tea.

"No? Okay what would *you* call it, Arlinda?" she asked, placing her glass of tea on the counter before she accepted a large spoon from a smiling Jorge, the resident chef for the facility.

Arlinda thought about what Maya was saying. She didn't delude herself. She acknowledged her tendency for self-preservation, which was why she'd never felt comfortable opening up with anyone, let alone a man. But in the short time of her acquaintance with Sam, he'd gotten uncomfortably close. He'd gotten underneath her skin. She found herself telling him things she'd never told anyone, with the exception of Maya.

"Ummm, that is so divine! What is it, Jorge?" Maya asked the man, loudly smacking her lips.

"*Es Menudo, especialamente for you, doctura!*" He beamed when an angelic smile spread across Maya's face as she swallowed. From the moment Maya had become pregnant, the smell or taste of any meat, particularly pork, made her gag. Jorge went out of his way to doctor up the menu just for her.

"I added a bit of that soy, meatless chorizo you suggested and *es bueno! ¿Si?*" the small man asked a bit anxiously as she swallowed the concoction. Arlinda knew that Jorge took his duties as chef seriously.

"*Si, Jorge. Es muy bueno! Gracias*, friend," she said, and kissed the small blushing man on his reddened cheek before turning back around to face Arlinda.

"What are you looking at me like that for? It's the truth, Arlinda, and you know it. You sabotage relationships." She returned to their conversation.

"Whatever, Maya! And who says there's a relationship to sabotage, in the first place?"

"Come on. Let's go to my office where we can talk."

"Okay, "Arlinda sighed and agreed and the two women walked

through the large residence, stopping along the way to say hello to several women. Arlinda loved what Maya had done with the house. It had originally been a treatment facility for women in transition from welfare to work. Maya had been able to purchase the rundown building with money left to her by a grandmother she'd never known.

Her grandmother lost contact with her as an infant, when her grandfather found out his only daughter had married a black man and had given birth to a bi-racial child. After the death of her husband, Catherine Rutherford-Spaulding had done everything in her power to locate her daughter and her family.

Unfortunately she'd found out too late that Maya's parents had died in a car accident and she'd been lost in the foster care system. Mr. Callahan, her grandmother's attorney, had granted her last wish and located Maya and she'd inherited Elizabeth's vast fortune.

Arlinda admired the artwork on the walls as they made their way to Maya's office. One of Maya's former residents, Ruby Vallejo, had recently discovered a talent for art and had sold three pieces to an upper-end gallery.

Maya had purchased two others before she sold them to the gallery and proudly displayed one on the wall and the other on a wrought iron artist's easel.

"Hi, Dalia," Maya said as they passed through her assistant's office on the way to her larger one.

"Hello, *Sesute*, there is a message on your desk from a Ms. Mariana St. John. Hello, Arlinda, what a beautiful dress!" The tall, older woman stopped her filing to compliment Arlinda.

Dalia was a former client who'd become Maya's valued assistant at Imani House. She'd emigrated from Lithuania as a young woman and had gotten caught up in the life of prostitution. It had taken years and a lot of determination for her to escape that life.

"Thanks, Dalia! It's one of my own designs." Arlinda did a careful pirouette, fanning the short pleated skirt of the halter dress with one hand as she held her glass of tea with the other, smiling as Dalia laughed.

Dalia was almost six feet in height with a full set of curves and often said totally straight-faced that the only thing she missed about prostitution was dressing up. She said if she did that at Imani House the clients might think it was a residence for current prostitutes instead of former ones. Arlinda loved Dalia's offbeat sense of humor.

"Dalia, could you hold my calls for me?"

"Including Mark's?"

"He shouldn't call, but if he does tell him I'll call him back. Thanks, Dal." Maya turned around and leaned her rotund body against the solid oak door to face Arlinda.

"Obviously, you have something you want to say, so just spit it out, girl! The suspense is killing me." Although she said it jokingly, Arlinda silently prayed that Maya would stop sugar-coating her words with her. They'd been friends long enough for Maya to give it to her real.

Stop mincing words. No more pussy-footing around. She could take it....

"Did you already let him sex you up?"

Arlinda had been taking a drink of her tea and spewed several chunks of ice when Maya asked a question she never would have thought she would ask. And so bluntly. Totally unlike what her normally placid friend would ask.

She carefully placed the tea on the side table and glared at Maya, who'd casually walked to her desk and eased herself down in the supple leather chair.

"What's that supposed to mean, Maya? He and I have known each other for a few weeks! And it's not even that type of relationship!" she denied as she leaned across and retrieved a tissue from the corner of Maya's desk.

She glanced up from wiping ice and tea spit off the small bodice of her dress in time to see Maya raise one eyebrow, with a serious *and so what does this mean* expression on her face.

"*¿Que?*"

"Don't *que* me, Arlinda. You know *what*," she said mildly in her lightly husky voice as she took a sip of her tea and eyeballed her over the rim of the glass.

"No. No, I haven't screwed him yet, Maya. I know you think I'm a total slut, but I usually give it more than a few weeks," she said sarcastically, seriously angry that her friend would even *suggest*....

She glanced over when Maya cleared her throat and this time stared at her with both eyebrows raised so high they completely disappeared into her hairline.

"Well, there was that *one* time," she admitted on a grumble. "But I thought he was special, Maya. Thought maybe he was the one," she admitted thinking of a past love. Arlinda had to look away. She was damned if she was going to cry over any man. No man was worth her tears.

"I know, sweetie. I didn't mean to be so crass. This pregnancy has completely changed my personality." Arlinda heard the instant contriteness in her friend's voice.

"Actually, Maya, you didn't say anything wrong. If you can't tell me the truth, who can? I have a tendency to sleep with a man first and then discover the truth about him after," she admitted in disgust.

"Arlinda, until you stop putting up that shield of yours, how do expect it to be any other way?"

Arlinda didn't say anything.

"Do you remember once telling me that you liked playing roles? That you didn't want anyone to get close enough to hurt you?"

"Yes. I know that's what I *used* to do as a child. But I'm not a child anymore, Maya. I'm a grown woman. I don't need to be afraid that someone is going to pick on me or hurt my feelings. I can take care of myself."

"Yes, you're a grown woman. A very accomplished, beautiful woman. But inside you're still hiding, Arlinda. You can't hide forever," she said quietly.

"I know that, *chica*. I guess I just don't get this man."

"What do you mean? Obviously you're attracted to him. Are the feelings reciprocated?" Maya asked bluntly.

She felt uncomfortable under Maya's close scrutiny, and once again set the tea on the side table and rose from the chair to walk around the spacious office. She walked over to one of the large windows that overlooked the small park across the street.

"That's a good question. Just when I think he is, he says or does something that has me questioning whether or not he's just playing with me. Maybe I'm just not good enough for him," she said in a low voice.

"Arlinda, that's ridiculous and you know it! Of course you're good enough for him. Why would you think otherwise?"

"A few days ago we went to Bentley's to discuss the fundraiser. We were having a really good time...."

\* \* \* \*

"Sam, you are so funny," Arlinda said as she wiped the tears from her eyes. "I already told you there will be no leather or whips in this collection. So just get your head out of the gutter!"

"A man can dream, can't he?"

Their laughter subsided as the waitress placed two steaming plates of food before them and they began to eat.

It was the second time Sam had chosen a restaurant for them to meet after work to discuss the fundraiser. He'd allowed her to pick the first place and when she'd chosen one of her favorite haunts,

Hooligans, she could tell that he wasn't the *least* bit impressed with the nightclub.

However, as she glanced around at the place he'd chosen, she agreed that she liked his choice much more. It was an intimate club that offered food and also featured a small dance floor.

Arlinda's gaze wandered around the assortment of couples and individuals seated around the club. The tables were designed for no more than four to sit comfortably at each table. Most of the men were dressed as Sam, in casual business attire. And a few of the women were dressed as casually as she, in typical lightweight dresses.

The club was dimly lit. The muted lighting came from cast iron tiffany shaded floor lamps that were placed in strategic corners throughout the room, along with the small glass candles on each table and along the bar.

"Do you like it here?" he asked and she brought her gaze back to the man sitting in front of her.

He looked so fine sitting there across from her, with that cute little dimple appearing and reappearing whenever he flashed one of his sexy smiles.

Once again, her treacherous nipples reacted from a simple look from him.

"*Si, es maravillosamente*. Um ... sorry. It's beautiful," she quickly corrected herself. She rarely reverted to Spanish when speaking to non-Spanish speakers. It happened when she wasn't consciously thinking, excited, or nervous. Or aroused.

"You don't have to apologize for speaking Spanish. I've lived in San Antonio my entire life. I'm fairly fluent." He smiled again, before swallowing a forkful of the flavorful rice dish he'd ordered.

"Oh really?" She was surprised. Although San Antonio had a high population of Spanish speakers, not everyone without a Hispanic ethnicity spoke the language. English remained the primary language.

"It's important to me that I'm able to communicate with my clients as well as business partners in the language they're comfortable with. That's not always English," he added.

"Does the rest of your family speak Spanish as well?" she asked.

"My parents aren't as fluent as Mariana and I, but they manage. Mom taught part-time in the public schools for a number of years, as well as at the community college before she retired last year. Many of her students were Spanish-speaking and she had a rudimentary command of the language."

"And your father? Is he retired also?" Arlinda smiled.

She enjoyed hearing about his family. Usually when a man began to speak about his family, she'd shy away from the subject. For some reason it always made her uncomfortable, as unbidden images of going home to meet his family would rise unwanted in her mind. However, the few times that Sam mentioned his family, she found herself eager to learn more.

"My dad still dabbles in stocks," he told her as he pushed his half-eaten plate away and smiled at her across the candlelit table.

He'd told her before that his father had been an investment broker and had been his major investor when he began his real estate business after completing his MBA.

"And what about you, Arlinda Nyoni?" he asked.

She glanced up at him from beneath lowered lids. His voice had grown noticeably husky when he asked the question. She licked the red sauce from her enchilada away with a swipe of her tongue and suppressed a smile when she saw the way his eyes followed the quick motion.

"What about me?"

"I know that you didn't grow up in San Antonio. Your accent is quite different. Where are you originally from?"

"Well…." She laughingly dragged out the word. "*Originally,* my mother and father were from Puerto Rico. But when I was nine years old, the family moved to New York," she answered.

"Both of your parents are Puerto Rican then?" he questioned, and moved away as the waitress cleared their plates away. He nodded his head when the woman asked if they wanted after dinner coffee.

"No. My mother is Puerto Rican but my father is African," she corrected.

"Oh, that's interesting. How did they meet? Your father lived in Puerto Rico?"

"Yes, his family moved to the island when he was a young man. Both of my parents' families lived in *Caguas.*"

"Is that close to San Juan?" he asked.

"It's in the center of the island, about one hour away," she agreed.

"I've been to Puerto Rico once on a business trip. From the plane everything looked so green and lush. But once we landed, and our guide drove us through the streets…."

"It didn't look like the pictures, huh?" She laughed. "I believe people come to the island expecting to see what they've seen on television. Bluer than blue water, palm trees, beautiful island girls…"she drawled out the last words and laughed again when

Sam's face turned red. "And it is beautiful. But like anywhere else, it's gotten polluted. People haven't taken care of the island very well."

"I guess not. The one thing I remember was how diverse the people of Puerto Rico were." Arlinda could tell that he was doing his best to say it politically correct. It was a delicate subject and she'd had more than one person ask her about the diversity of the island.

"Puerto Ricans are a racially mixed ethnicity. The mixture is one third Spanish, one third Indian, or *Tainos*, and one third African. The original island dwellers were a pacific tribe called *Tainos*," she explained without him asking, and saw the relief and curiosity in his dark eyes.

"I'm ashamed to say I never thought about why the Puerto Rican people of today are so diversely mixed. As I said, I was quite surprised when I visited the island. But I do recall enough of my college history classes to know that Columbus was one of the reasons for the mixture," he commented.

"Yes. During his "discoveries" he brought the Africans to the island as he conducted his slave trades and some were left there, along with some of the Spanish men from his crew. Others he brought back from Spain so they could witness first-hand the richness of the island, and rape it as well as the people while they were at it," she murmured around her coffee cup.

Arlinda made no attempt to suppress her grimace of distaste for the man hailed throughout history as an explorer who "discovered" America. He, and many like him, were slave traders and opportunists. The name Puerto Rico was a name given to the island by the Spaniards because of its richness in gold. Gold that Columbus forced the *Tainos* to mine after killing many of their kings.

There was a pause in the conversation as the musicians on the small kiosk began to tune their instruments. Soon a woman stepped up to the microphone and began singing one of her favorite Luther Vandross songs.

"Why did your parents leave Puerto Rico?"

"My father is an art historian and he received an invitation to be the director at the New York Museum of Modern Art and we packed up everything and moved to the Big Apple."

"Wow. That had to be a big change."

"That's not even the word for it." Arlinda didn't like to remember those times. She never talked about it with anyone but Maya, yet with Sam she felt a desire to share with him what it had been like for her to leave her home and face the unknown.

"I was made fun of by the local girls. They made fun of the way that I spoke, called me a *gringo* because my mother appeared white to them because of her light skin. Although *I* was clearly a person of color, they said I thought I was better than they," she admitted in a low voice, embarrassed.

When she didn't say anything else he took her hand across the table, and was surprised when she glanced up at him.

"Come on, let's dance," he said and helped her rise from the table.

Two other couples were on the small dance floor when he took her in his arms and pulled her tightly against his hard body. Sam was no more than six feet tall, but because of her height, or lack thereof, the top of her head barely reached the broad expanse of his muscled chest.

It felt good to finally be in his arms. It felt so right.

As they danced close, she felt him gently rest the side of his face against her hair and rub back and forth before he pulled away. Her heart beat in excitement from the mild affection.

"When they made fun of you, Arlinda, what did you do?" He spoke closely into her ear, and the intimacy it created made her feel as though they were the only two people in the room.

"At first it was difficult," she slowly admitted as she snuggled closer in his arms as they danced. "I wanted so badly to be accepted by them. I think I would have done anything to gain their acceptance. To garner their approval." They swayed back and forth to the music for long minutes without either saying a word.

This close to him, his natural musky masculine smell enveloped her within its heady embrace. Not only did she like a man who knew how to dress well, but she absolutely *loved* a man who also smelled good.

And Sam smelled so good that her nipples beaded beneath her silk shirt as she shamelessly pressed her breasts against his chest as they danced. Arlinda smiled when she felt the hard ridge of his penis behind his slacks as it nudged against her lower belly.

Good.

He was obviously as aroused by her as she was by him. She wound her arms tighter around his neck as they moved slowly to the deep voice of the singer.

When he tilted her head back with his thumb and forefinger she was surprised until she caught the flash of red-hot desire, which couldn't be disguised, in the depths of his dark eyes.

"Let's go," was all that he said and Arlinda felt goose bumps run down her arms.

\* \* \* \*

Arlinda turned her attention away from the window when she heard Maya clear her throat.

"So what happened then? Sounds as though that wasn't the end of the date," she said in her best psychologist's voice, and Arlinda laughed.

"No that wasn't the end, but I kind of wish it had been."

"Hold that thought. It must be an emergency for Dalia to call," she said when her phone rang. After speaking in a hushed tone for a few seconds, she rose from behind her desk and apologized.

"I'll be right back Arlinda; this won't take long," she promised.

"That's fine. I'm not going anywhere." Arlinda heard the dejection in her own voice and didn't really care. When Maya patted her on the back on the way out the room, her thoughts returned to Sam.

## Chapter Four

The drive back to her business and loft was filled with a hushed expectancy. Arlinda felt the tension from Sam's gaze on the back of her neck as she gazed sightless out of the window of his low slung vehicle. She was nervous and felt all of sixteen years old and out on her date with Bobby McFarland, the boy that she'd determined was going to make a woman out of her.

Try as she might, she couldn't stop herself from turning away from the window and glancing over at him in the dark interior of the car. The strong lines of his squared jaw were in profile as he stared straight ahead, pulling to a smooth halt at the intersection. The only light in the dark car was the crimson glow from the traffic light.

When he glanced in her direction, waiting for the light to turn green, his dark eyes assessed her. A queasiness pooled in the bottom of her belly.

"Are you nervous?" he asked, and the sound of his voice in the dark of the car had her squirming in the leather upholstered seat, clenching her legs together in anticipation of what was to come.

But she wasn't going to let him know that a word from him had her wet and aching. She knew how to play the game. Thank God he couldn't see the way his words and voice made her heart leap inside her chest.

"Do I have a reason to be?" She tried for coy, but instead heard the warbling tone of her voice and wanted to kick her own butt. No matter how flexible she prided herself on being, in the small confines of the car, she didn't think she'd be able to manage it.

He only stared at her, his hot gaze traveling from the top of her head and slowly down the length of her curled up legs that she'd tucked underneath her bottom in the seat.

They rode in silence the remainder of the short drive to her business and residence. When they reached the parking lot, he cut the engine and turned around to face her.

"May I come in?" he asked.

Just like that, he asked to come inside with her. No preamble. No hesitancy. No beating around the bush.

For once, Arlinda felt a strange hesitancy. With a mental shrug she brushed it aside, and with a small smile answered, shyly, "Of course."

He reached across and slowly ran his hand down her jaw before climbing out of his side of the car. He walked around the front of the car to help her out of the passenger seat before they walked across the parking lot to the back door of the shop.

He accepted the keys from her and opened the door, and once inside she quickly keyed in a series of numbers to deactivate the alarm. She turned on the nearest lamp and a soft glow tinted the amber room.

"Can I get you anything? Coffee? Tea? Umm … I think I have some…." The rest of her sentence was cut off when he hauled her around to face him, and covered her lips with his.

When he grasped her head with his big hands and kissed her, she almost cried out loud from the flood of sensation when their lips met. Finally.

He licked and raked his tongue across the fullness of her bottom lip before he slowly drew it between his teeth. The sensual scrape had her squirming to try and get closer. He licked and laved her mouth until she didn't think she could take it anymore.

Finally, he pulled away, his breathing harsh in the quiet of the room as he rested his forehead against hers. She could see his chest in the dimly lit room as it heaved when he took deep breaths. "Damn, Arlinda. You taste even better than I thought you would," he admitted huskily.

Without another word, he lifted her in his arms and walked quickly across the room to settle her on her small, red velvet loveseat. He knelt before her, nudged her legs apart, and settled himself between her spread thighs.

He slowly drew her head toward his with one hand as the other went to her butt as he pulled her to the edge of the sofa. He delivered small nibbling kisses to her mouth before trailing them down the soft line of her jaw toward the sharp V of her dress.

Arlinda groaned when he delved one big hand inside the bodice of her blouse and cupped one of her breasts. He carefully fingered her distended nipple as his mouth traveled back toward her lips. His tongue laved and stroked her skin leaving a fiery path in its wake.

"Ummm … you taste so good," he murmured before he found her lips again. He pried them open and delved his tongue inside. When she felt the smooth velvet of his tongue, she opened her mouth wider to give him better access.

The action of his mouth and fingers toying with her had her wet in minutes. She clenched her legs together when she felt the sticky sensation of her own cream between her thighs with each pull and tug of his hand on her nipples.

Arlinda arched her back sharply, the incredible sensation he gave her from his light lovemaking unlike anything she'd felt before.

She tightened her arms around him as she gave herself over to his kiss. To be pressed against his chest, his arms wrapped around her, was divine. Her breasts were achy and tight-feeling as he toyed with her. When he suddenly pulled away, she felt bereft and an involuntary cry escaped.

She licked her lips and felt how they were swollen from his rough kisses as she waited for him to do something. *Anything.*

*He gently pushed her down onto the sofa and covered her body with his and they both groaned when his cock, rock hard and ready, immediately nestled in the V between her thighs. As though it belonged there.*

He bent his head to kiss her again and pulled her tight against his body, leaving no separation between them. She lay pliant against him, her small breasts smashed against his chest.

Suddenly the feel of their clothes was too much for her and when he lifted her blouse from the waistband of her skirt, she almost cried out in relief. She wanted nothing more than to feel bare skin on skin.

"I need to feel your skin on mine," he unknowingly echoed her thoughts in the quiet of the room. "Will you let me?" She simply nodded her head in assent, unable to croak out a verbal response.

He lifted her body slightly as he pulled her shirt over her head before allowing her to lie back against the cushions of the sofa. She saw the fine tremor in his hands when he brushed them against the silk of her bra. With deft fingers, he unhooked the front closure.

"They're as perfect as you are." He leaned down and captured one beaded nipple. He swirled the nub in his mouth, before opening his mouth wide and engulfing a large portion of her tit. His groan was so harsh it sent shivers racing down her body.

He licked and laved one breast as the other hand kneaded its twin in concentrated effort. She arched her aching breasts fully into his mouth and hand. The sensation of him pulling and lapping on her making her so wet and aroused she unbelievably felt the stirrings of an orgasm just out of reach.

He pulled away and stared at her with a look of intense desire and something else that she refused to acknowledge, much less try and name, forcing Arlinda to close her eyes.

"No, baby, I want you to watch me. I want you to see what I'm going to do to you. What I *want* to do for you," he said, before he nudged her legs further apart and lightly kissed his way down her body.

She held her breath when she felt him lift her skirt and ease her thong down the expanse of her legs. She closed her eyes in anticipation of what he was going to do to her.

When she felt his tongue stroke a heated caress down her cleft she arched her back off the sofa in response. She had to bite the inside of her cheek not to scream from the exquisite feel of his talented tongue.

He separated her folds and gently nibbled and laved the inside of her aching channel until she couldn't take it anymore. She lifted her upper body from the sofa and stared down at the sexy image of the top of his curly head as it lay nestled between her thighs.

She was forced to lay back down when he captured her clit in his mouth and drew it deeply into his mouth, swirling and working it until she felt ready to die from the incredible pleasure that he was giving her.

She gripped the edges of the sofa as she willingly accepted his loving torture.

"Oh, this feels so good, I can't take it. What are you doing to me, Sam?" she asked desperately, completely strung out from his oral loving.

Her moan increased and became a scream of pleasure when he eased two of his big fingers into her slit and the walls of her vagina instantly clamped down on them. He played and toyed with her, pumping his fingers in and out of her cream-slicked lips, spreading her own juices over her aching clit.

She cried out and grabbed one of the cushions on the loveseat, holding on for dear life as he continued to lick, eat and stroke her pussy. His face was now buried so deep between her legs that she could only see the top of his head.

As he continued to lave her, stroking her relentlessly, Arlinda could no longer hold back her orgasm and allowed it to break free as she bucked against him, not caring that she ground her pussy into his face as the orgasm ripped through her body.

She closed her eyes and allowed the orgasm to race through her body. It hit her hard. He continued to lick and pump his fingers as the sensation hit her like a tidal wave, forcing her to release her death hold on the pillow and grab the edge of the sofa, while the other hand clutched the edge of the loveseat, as she released, crying, yelling, screaming, from the explosive release.

Entirely spent, she could accept no more and limply lay against the soft cushions as Sam continued to lightly stroke her until all of her tremors had ceased and her breathing was semi back to normal. He came to sit next to her on the sofa and smiled with a look of such tenderness in his eyes that she nearly cried.

"Did you like that?" he asked.

"Did I like it? Oh no. All that screaming and hollering and tears? Oh give me a break! That happens all the time! In fact...." The instant, nervous humorous rebuttal was stilled when he clamped his mouth over hers, and kissed her within an inch of her life. She tasted the essence of herself on his lips.

He slowly drew away from her and tilted her head up with his thumb and forefinger. "Did you like what I did for you, Arlinda?" he asked in his sexy *do me* voice.

She felt the smallest bit rattled and could only nod her head. "Yes," she whispered.

"Good. Because I plan on pleasing you for a long time to come," he promised darkly. She instantly grew wet again with his words and reached up to wrap her arms around his neck.

She was completely unprepared when he kissed her gently on the forehead and lifted away from her. He found her blouse and drew it over her head and she knew she must have looked as confused as she felt.

"What are you doing?" She refused to believe the obvious when he drew her to her feet.

"It's getting late. I have an early meeting tomorrow with some of my investors." He hugged her close for one brief moment.

"I don't understand, Sam," she tried not to sound needy and desperate, but she was thoroughly confused. "I mean, don't you want to ... um...?" She allowed the sentence to dangle.

She wasn't quite sure what to say. She'd assumed that after he'd pleasured her, he would want to continue what they'd so delightfully started. She looked down at the enormous bulge in his pants. "You didn't get anything out of that. Don't you want me to take care of *that*?" she asked.

He saw her glance at his cock and laughed ruefully. "That's okay, baby. That was for you. I'll survive," he said and she saw the grimace on his face as he adjusted himself.

"But you don't have to," she protested. Immediately she felt uncertain. "I ... uh ... I'll take care of you. You don't have to leave like that, Sam."

"I know you would, sweetheart. But that was for you. I need to go now, or I won't be able to leave." Despite the true regret in his deep eyes, she was only slightly mollified. Old feelings of insecurity reared their ugly heads as she followed him to the door.

He must have seen something in her eyes when he turned around. He drew her into his arms and tilted her chin up so that she was forced to look him in the eyes. "I *wanted* to do that for you, Arlinda. I won't lie and say I wouldn't love to take you upstairs to your loft and make love to you. Completely." He forced her head back around when she averted her face.

"It's taking more willpower than I thought I had not to do that right now, Arlinda. Just pick you up and carry you upstairs and make love. But it's not right. Not yet." Despite his tender expression coupled with the regret in his eyes, his words confused her.

"What do you mean? I'm willing. And so are you, obviously," she said and lightly rubbed her hand over the thick ridge of his hard penis. He took hold of her hand within his much larger one and brought it to his mouth to place a small kiss in the center.

"Yes, baby. I know we're both physically ready. But I want more than that," he said and the look in his eyes made her heart race.

"When the time is right, we'll know it and there won't be any turning back for either one of us. I want it all, Arlinda." He leaned down and enveloped her in a tight hug. Despite squeezing her eyes shut, a small tear escaped from the corner of one eye.

"Or nothing at all," he said, pulling away to kiss her stunned mouth. He wiped the tear away, his expression thoughtful, before he opened the door and left her in the doorway as he sprinted the small distance to his car and with a final look back in her direction, eased inside.

As she watched him leave, her hand touched her mouth that still tingled from his kiss, wondering if he could possibly mean what she thought he did.

* * * *

"I am so sorry, Arlinda. I had to take that call. Okay, where were we?" Maya asked, walking back into her office and startling her out of her thoughts.

Arlinda sighed.

She loved Maya, but didn't feel she would understand if she tried to explain how rejected yet curiously elated she'd felt when Sam didn't continue his lovemaking. She wasn't sure that she understood it entirely, herself.

"I don't know, Maya. I guess I just don't have this man figured out, which is new for me. I think it's going to take me a while."

Maya walked up to her and turned her away from her sightless perusal of the children playing in the small play area close to the center.

"Do you remember what you said to me over a year ago about Mark? Not to sabotage a good thing?"

Arlinda remembered when she'd given her friend advice about her husband. She'd advised her to let go of the past and give the relationship a chance.

She nodded her head slowly. "Yes, I remember."

"Well, *chica*, I'm going to give you the same advice. Don't allow the way you've always felt comfortable interacting with men in the past to cloud your vision, Arlinda. This man sounds as though he could come to care for you if he doesn't already. Don't allow fear of what could be, stop you, like it almost did me."

The two women stared at one another, both with tears in their eyes as they thought of their pasts and why they each had the tendency to allow fear to cloud their vision in love.

"Don't sabotage a good thing before it has time to take root and flourish, Arlinda."

## Chapter Five

"Mariana, everything looks good. I think your show is going to be a raging success, little sister," Samuel said, smiling across at his sister as she looked over the myriad of sheets of paper that covered her desk.

She sighed and smiled back at him before she gathered a handful of papers in her hand to stuff inside a blue hanging file folder.

"I think it's more your show than mine, Sam, with all the work you've put into it," she said. "Or should I say all the work that you and Arlinda have put into it?" she teased with a sly look from beneath her dark eyes.

Sam only smiled, refusing to be drawn into her not-so-subtle attempt to garner information on what was happening between him and Arlinda. He nearly groaned out loud when he saw the way her eyes narrowed. Mariana hated when he did that. Not give her information she wanted it about his love life.

"Okay, spill. Let's not even play games, Sam. I want details and I don't want to resort to ugly means to get them," she threatened with a wicked gleam in her eyes.

"Mariana, how about we do this." He closed the cover of her accounting book and gave her all of his attention. "I give up the information that you want when you answer a question for me. Sound fair?" He could tell she didn't like the way he'd turned the tables on her. But he had a few questions of his own.

"I guess...." She dragged out the last word. An uneasy look crossed her beautiful face. She nervously toyed with one of her long, individual braids before she flipped it over her shoulder.

When she stood and slowly walked over to the tall gray metal cabinet in the corner of her office, Sam casually waited for her to turn around before he would ask the question. He knew his sister well. She'd pretend she couldn't hear him if she didn't like the question he asked, and he wasn't going to give her that out.

Once she'd turned fully around he asked, "Why did you send me to Arlinda's, Mariana?"

"I already told you that! I didn't want to reschedule with her and wasn't able to get away that day," she said with a definite sound of relief coloring her voice.

"No, I want the *real* reason, and you know what I'm talking about," he demanded quietly.

Mariana stared at him intently as she worriedly worked her full bottom lip with her top teeth.

He knew what she was thinking.

From the time Mariana was a small child she'd had an ability to tune in to the feelings and desires of others and unerringly find out what they needed. She'd also picked up on strong emotions. Emotions such as anger or violence would give her extreme and sometimes debilitating headaches. It didn't happen often, this empathetic ability, and when it happened, it usually only occurred with those with whom she was emotionally close.

Although his family never spoke about it, no one denied that it was true. Mariana would only talk about her ability with Sam as she grew up, afraid that she'd be laughed at if she told anyone else. Although Sam had never shared what she told him, over the years his mother and father had come to see that their adoptive daughter had abilities that marked her as different. They grew to be careful with whom she came in contact, in order to protect her.

When she continued to bite her bottom lip, he walked over and pulled her into his arms. "Come on, Mari, fess up. It's me. I won't be mad at you," he promised lightly. He sought to put her at ease, not liking the way her eyes had clouded in worry, thinking she'd done something wrong. "In fact, I owe you a debt I don't think I'll ever be able to repay," he said and kissed her on top of the head before he released her.

"Oh yeah?" Her smile was hesitant.

"Yep. Now tell me. It was no accident that you sent me there. What do you know?" He smiled inwardly when her sly grin returned as she sauntered over to her desk.

"Okay. Actually it's pretty simple. When she and I first met, I knew that she was special," she said. When he only nodded his head in agreement, she continued.

"I'd met her friend, Maya, and that's how I was introduced to Arlinda. She'd come by when I went to Imani House and she was so special and her spirit was so amazing that she fairly radiated this bright light around her aura."

Sam smiled. He wasn't into auras and chakras as Mariana was, but he too saw and was attracted to the energy that surrounded Arlinda.

"When I found out she was a designer, and I knew that I had this show coming up … I don't know Sam." Her brows were knitted as she frowned in concentration. "I *knew* that I needed her to be a part of it. And I also knew the two of you needed to meet." She shook her head in puzzlement and glanced at him in question.

"That's it?" he asked quietly. Not because he was disappointed. He had faith in Mariana's gift, and didn't question it. He wanted to make sure she wasn't leaving something out that she thought he might not like to hear.

"Well, there's one other thing...." She allowed the sentence to trail off. He raised one eyebrow.

"I'm not sure how to ask this, Sam," she admitted.

"Just ask, Mari." Sam had eased his body to the edge of the chair, eager to hear what she had to ask.

"You haven't made love to her yet ... have you?" she asked and he saw the flush run along the length of Mariana's brown cheeks.

\* \* \* \*

"Mr. St. John, there's a young lady here to see you, sir. A Ms. Arlinda Nyoni. Shall I allow her to enter, sir?"

"Yes, please do, Brenda. I'm on another line, but that's fine," Sam told his assistant, surprised that Arlinda had come to visit him at his office.

He quickly ended his conversation, his mind already on the woman who stood hesitantly in his doorway. He motioned her in with a wave and a smile and she closed the door and fully entered his office.

She looked absolutely beautiful to him. It was a warm fall day and she was wearing a pretty, nearly sheer blouse and a breezy little skirt that barely reached the end of her thighs. On her small feet she wore a pair of impossibly high-heeled sandals. She'd clipped her short hair back with two butterfly clips on either side of her small ears.

Then, Sam noticed the large picnic basket in her hands and his smile widened as he rose from behind his desk and approached her. She looked adorable, staring at him with those pretty big brown eyes of hers, with the basket hanging over her arm and a smile so sweet he felt his heart clench.

Damn.

He had it bad for this woman after only a few short weeks, he thought with a rueful shake of his head.

"What a nice surprise," he said, as he slowly walked over to her as she stood just inside his office, her back leaning against the door. He leaned down, placed two fingers beneath her chin and gently tilted her head toward his and kissed her softly.

Sam removed the basket from her arm and placed it on the

carpeted floor, before he gathered her into his arms. He parted her soft, lush mouth with his and carefully slipped his tongue inside as he pulled her tight against his body.

While burying one hand in her short curls and placing the other on her round hip, he kissed her gently and thoroughly before reluctantly withdrawing from the nirvana of her lips.

"Hi," she said hoarsely.

Her big brown eyes were wide and unblinking, looking drowsy and her lips were swollen and slightly reddened from his kisses. Her short curls were spiked and all over her head from his hands.

"Hi." He heard the answering huskiness in his own voice and cleared his throat. With a reluctant groan, he pulled away from her to lift the basket from the floor.

"Is this what I think it is?" He took the basket in one hand and her small hand in the other and walked across the room to the small sitting area of his office.

She smiled shyly and nodded her head. "I remember you told me a few days ago that you rarely have the opportunity to go out for lunch. So I thought I'd bring lunch to you," she laughed. "That is, if you have time for me?"

"I always have time for you, Arlinda," he told her sincerely.

He was fascinated with the way she blushed whenever he said things like that to her. He noticed whenever he complimented her or said she was beautiful she'd laugh and flirt, or make a cute comment.

But whenever he said things that had nothing to do with her looks, or made comments hinting that he wanted something more with her, she'd become shy and either change the subject, or not say a word.

He sighed.

"Well, what's in the basket?" he asked lightly. "Whatever it is, it sure smells good."

When she opened the lid to give him a peek, the strong flavorful aroma of fried chicken assaulted his nostrils and he inhaled long and deep. "Ummm, that smells good! Here, let's put this down on the floor and have a real picnic. I'll get us something to sit on," he said and placed the basket at their feet.

"Sounds good to me," she laughingly agreed, as he spread his suit jacket on the floor so that she could sit down.

He lifted the wicker top of the basket and peered inside. He heard her laugh when his stomach growled loudly as he smelled the mixture of aromas from the contents of the basket. She had chicken, fruit and whipped topping, along with an assortment of cheese and crackers inside.

Images of her spread out on the floor covered in strawberries and cream appeared before his eyes and he had to hastily adjust his pants as he knelt beside her on the floor.

Sam allowed her to take out the food and distribute it on their plates, enjoying the moment. After she'd filled their plates, he licked his lips in anticipation before taking a healthy bite of the juicy chicken breast.

"Ummm, baby, this is so good! Did you make this yourself?" he asked. When she didn't answer right away, he glanced at her and saw the look of surprise filter across her face.

"What is it? What's wrong?" he mumbled around the healthy bite of chicken he'd taken.

"Nothing. I guess I was surprised, that's all. It's no big deal, really," she said and he noticed the flush on her face and smiled in question.

"What's wrong, Arlinda?" He was curious as to what had caused her to react as she had. Then he realized what he'd said.

Baby. He'd called her baby.

He'd called her that once before and she'd had the same reaction. He placed the chicken down and wiped his hands with the napkin.

When she tried to avoid his eyes, he turned her back around and *forced* her to look at him as he asked, "Arlinda, is there a reason why it makes you uncomfortable for me to call you baby?"

She wiped her fingers on her napkin also and swallowed her last bite of chicken before she answered. "Not exactly."

"Don't look away," he gently admonished her when, once again, she tried to avert her face from his.

"What?" she laughingly asked, but he heard the nervous tremor in her voice.

That was why, right there, in the middle of the afternoon, on the floor, in the middle of his office, Sam moved the basket of food out of the way and pulled her back against his chest and crossed his arms in front of her small body. He was relieved when she uttered a small giggle.

He leaned down and whispered against the hollow of her ear, "Do you know what I think?" and kissed her small earlobe before propping his chin lightly on top of her of dark curls.

"No, what *do* you think?" she laughed.

"I think that you've hidden behind that barrier of yours for so long, that you're afraid," he said and pulled her body tight against his when she tried to move away.

"What barrier? What are you talking about?" The laughter left her voice to be replaced with a sound of weary trepidation.

"Remember when you told me that your family moved to New York, the other girls didn't accept you. They thought *you* believed you were better than them." When she bobbed her head in agreement, he continued. "Then you said you fell into a pattern of trying to please and hid the real Arlinda behind a mask. Thinking no one liked the real Arlinda, and preferred Arlee instead?"

He knew she didn't like having the topic brought up again. He'd asked several questions about her life growing up, and she'd opened up to him over the weeks, and once laughingly said she often thought she had a split personality.

There was Arlinda and there was Arlee. Arlee was the party girl that everyone loved, the one who was always up for a good time. Then there was Arlinda.

Arlinda was the one who'd worked hard to get rid of her strong Puerto Rican accent, fearing it would further ostracize her from her contemporaries. She was the one who sometimes didn't fit into either community--the black community or Puerto Rican--and it hurt to continue to try. Arlinda was the intelligent woman who'd worked hard in college and opened her own design boutique at an early age and had made it a success.

Arlinda got her feelings hurt when a lover decided that he no longer wanted to have a good time. That he was ready to settle down and find a wife. And she didn't fit the bill.

"When you're ready to believe that someone wants to get to know all sides and personalities of Arlinda, let me know."

She didn't resist when he pulled her back around to face him and kissed her slowly on the lips.

Sam released her lips only to lick and stroke his way down the length of her smooth, creamy brown neck, his teeth nibbling and grazing along the way. He loved the way she practically purred as he caressed her. He eased her body to the floor and followed her down.

As he licked his way down her chest, he nudged aside the gauzy material of her sheer shirt to gain access to her tight little breasts. He moved the miniscule bra to the side and stared with hungry eyes at her.

With his eyes trained on hers, he reached down and cupped one breast in his hand, his thumb caressing the small tightly budded nipple before he licked it slowly. The feel of the tight nubbin in his mouth made his cock thump an eager welcome behind his slacks. It thumped harder when she gave that kittenish purr again.

"Do you like that, baby?" he asked on a groan.

As she lay sprawled beneath him on their makeshift picnic blanket, he quickly flipped their position and laughed when she squealed as she landed lightly on top of his chest.

He reached between them and lifted her skirt so that it fanned over his thighs, positioning her mound over the hard ridge of his slacks. Her mouth formed a perfect O when he lifted her small hips and directly aligned her on his cock as he felt it push aggressively against the suddenly tight restriction of his slacks.

"Ohh, Sam, what are you doing to me?" she moaned. Her head fell back on her neck as she closed her eyes. He could feel the moisture from her vagina through her tiny panties and, with little ceremony, he pulled her head down to his to kiss her as his other hand grabbed her bottom and pulled her mound tightly to him.

"Yessss...." she hissed and moved with feverish disregard against his cock, riding him in tight circular movements, his hand steady against her butt as he allowed her to move.

He knew her orgasm was hovering. He moved his hand between their close fitting bodies and shifted her silky panties to the side. He manipulated and caressed her clit until with a keening moan, she released. He completely blanketed her mouth as he swallowed her cries.

When the last shudder left her body and she lay still and replete beneath him, he felt tension invade her limbs and wasn't surprised. He knew the exact moment when she became aware of her surroundings once more and eased her body off of his.

"I don't suppose you're going to allow me return the favor," she groaned, once again averting her eyes from his.

"I want that more than anything, you have no idea," he ruefully admitted. "But...."

"Whatever, Sam, don't *even* say it or I won't be responsible for my actions." Although his cock was as hard as a rock and he wanted to do her so badly he shook from the effort of restraining himself, he laughed at her grumbled answer.

"May I say just one thing?" he asked.

"What?" she asked warily.

"Sweetheart, what's between you and I is no passing thing. I told you once before that I want all or nothing...." He ignored the way she rolled her eyes at him and continued. "And soon, you're going to have to make a decision. And once you do, what we'll have together will be beyond anything that either one of us have ever had with anyone else. But we can't have that if you don't believe in it. If you don't let down those damn walls of yours."

"I know. I feel more comfortable with you than I ever have with anyone else, Sam," she admitted. He remained silent, not wanting to miss a word of her low voiced confession.

"It feels strange that I've known you for such a short time, yet...." her voice trailed off.

"I feel the same way, Arlinda," he prompted her to continue.

"I want to open up totally. I do. I've never really wanted to before. I've never felt such an overwhelming need to. Not until I met you," she finished.

Sam felt his heart leap at her words.

The rest of the picnic was lighthearted. But Sam could tell that he'd given her something to think about. Maybe enough that she'd finally let him in to get to know the real Arlinda.

\* \* \* \*

"Why did you want to know if I'd made love to her or not Mari?" he asked, after he'd finished his tale.

Mariana knew that although he'd not given her the more intimate details as he recalled his lovemaking with Arlinda, he'd told her enough to know they hadn't consummated the relationship.

She breathed an inward sigh of relief as she recalled what Cain had said to her in her dream. She never questioned Cain. He'd been a part of her life for so long that she naturally accepted that he was real. And although she'd never seen him outside of her dreams, he was as real to her as Sam, or anyone else in her family.

Although of late, she was having disturbing thoughts centered around him. Increasingly, her thoughts were no longer those of a child, hero-worshipping a dreamlike, imaginary friend. It'd been confusing at first, the change in feelings. It had been so subtle. One day she was waiting for a dear, familiar friend to visit and the next ... she was a woman, nervous and antsy, waiting for a visit from her lover.

It was getting to be that she was having a hard time differentiating between the two. Real, imagined, dream ... she didn't know. She sighed and returned her thoughts to her brother and his situation.

Cain hadn't told her anything of more significance that what she'd already gleaned. That Arlinda Nyoni was her brother's soul mate, and that in order for her brother to claim her for his own, he'd have to break through her barriers. Barriers that she'd erected that she no longer was aware of.

"She's the one for you, Sam," Mariana said as she listened to her brother pour his heart out. She ached when she heard the loneliness and love shine through in his voice.

"I know that, Mari," he agreed in a low tone with his head hung low. "I hope she starts to believe it also. If not, I have to leave her alone. I don't want a glimpse of what we could have. I want it all."

Mariana's heart clenched at the sadness that rang clearly in her brother's voice.

## Chapter Six

"Please be careful with that trunk! And just set it right there! And you, why aren't you in makeup? You're in the first set!" Arlinda cried, as she directed movers and models simultaneously in the busy backstage.

"It's thirty minutes before show time and I don't have my emcee," Arlinda wailed to no one in particular as she frantically searched the sea of backstage faces looking for Sam's handsome face.

"Everything looks wonderful, Arlinda!" She jumped when Maya walked up behind her, startling her. She turned frantic eyes in her friend's direction.

"Thanks, Maya. But we have less than ten minutes before this show starts and Sam is nowhere to be seen!" she wailed.

"What do you mean he's nowhere to be seen? Isn't he acting as the emcee for this whole shebang?" Arlinda cast an admiring glance over Maya's husband, Mark, stood behind Maya, wrapped his arms around his wife's expanded belly and pulled her head back for a kiss.

"Yes, he is, which is why I'm about to lose my mind any minute! We drove in together, but he said he had a quick errand to run! I don't have anyone else to replace him, and I can't do it because I have to stay backstage to make sure everything runs smoothly and the models are dressed and ready to roll! And besides that I need a man to emcee the show, and who could I find at this late notice...." Her rant trailed off as both she and Maya turned as one toward Mark.

"Oh no, not me! I don't think so! Baby, don't give me the face. Please, Maya ... anything but the face," Mark pleaded when his wife turned sad eyes in his direction and poked out her lips.

Arlinda looked hopefully in Mark's direction, hoping against hope that the power of Maya's baby face along with the power of her alternating mood swings, which had been increasing daily as her pregnancy advanced, would persuade him.

"Okay," he grumbled and slumped his shoulders forward, sighing with resignation. He looked only slightly mollified when his wife patted him on the back and gave him a toothy, pleased grin.

"Arlinda, I'm so sorry that I'm late, I had to make a quick stop."

All three turned at the sound of Sam's voice as he came rushing toward them.

Arlinda cried out in relief when she saw Sam rush in just as she was going to accept Mark's ... or more accurately, Maya's offer for Mark to stand in his place.

"Well, it looks like everything is in order here ... my services aren't going to be needed!" Mark said with relief. "I guess we'll go out front, Arlinda, and get ready for the show! Good luck, we'll see you later!"

Mark hustled Maya away before anyone could change their minds, the comic look of relief on his handsome face made her laugh as she allowed him to lead them away.

Arlinda didn't notice anyone else when she saw Sam stride across the room toward her. He stole her breath away. She'd seen him in his business attire often over the last few weeks. She'd also seen him dressed casually in jeans and he always looked sexy as hell to her.

But she'd never seen him dressed in a tux. She slid her gaze over him from the top of his close-cropped head to the tips bottom of his shiny black wingtip shoes. The tux fit him as only a tailor made tuxedo could. The shoulders of the jacket had no padding, as he needed no enhancement for his broad shoulders.

As she was admiring him, Sam was doing the same.

He'd never seen her dressed in formal wear. She was so beautiful that she stole his breath. His gaze traveled from the top of her shiny curls, down the length of the form-fitting, long, red beaded gown. The dress fit her tight little body like a glove. It outlined her small breasts and nipped in waist before flaring to hug her nicely rounded hips. The hem of the gown ended near the squared toes of her red stiletto heels.

"Where have you been? I thought I'd have to have Mark go on, Sam! You were supposed to be here over an--" The rest of her sentence was cut off.

He strode up to her, ignored the hustle going on around them, pulled her tight against his chest and smothered her lips with his. He cut her off mid-rant with a satisfying groan as their lips made contact.

The kiss was short yet thorough and when he pulled away he smiled at the way her eyes were glazed and her lips swollen from the light contact. He reached inside his tuxedo jacket and withdrew a handkerchief. Carefully, he wiped her smudged lipstick from the corner of her mouth.

"I had an important stop to make. I'm here now. You know I wouldn't let you down. Don't you?" he asked and smiled when all she did was nod her head in silent agreement.

Sam knew that she'd snap back to her normal self in a minute so he escaped while he had the chance. He placed a kiss on her forehead and said, "I'll see you after the show," and walked toward the stage, leaving a slightly bemused Arlinda in his wake.

* * * *

"You outdid yourself, Arlinda!" Maya said, beaming at her friend. "It all looked so beautiful and effortless."

"Well, looks are deceiving! *Ay Madre*, girlfriend!" Arlinda said with a laugh, easing her sore feet out of her high heels. She leaned down and massaged one achy foot.

"I know it was a lot of hard work, but it looked gorgeous. Congratulations, you did a wonderful job," Mariana seconded. The three women stood onstage and watched the cleaning crew break down scenery, the hustle and bustle of the night's festivities over.

"Well, thank you, Mariana; I appreciate you contracting me for this. The money raised tonight is going to really benefit Mari's Closet. I'm glad that I could be a part of something so wonderful," Arlinda told her sincerely.

"Thank you so much, Arlinda. But honestly, without you and your wonderful designs, this wouldn't have been half as successful as it was."

"I think I need to find Mark. I'm starved," Maya said, looking around for her husband.

"What do you mean you're starved? Wasn't the food good? Didn't you eat?"

Mariana's eyes widened in distress. Part of the night's event had been a fully catered one-hundred-dollar-a-plate meal.

"Don't worry, Mariana, since this one found out she was pregnant? Girl, she's been packing the food away like a linebacker," Arlinda laughed.

"I do not. I'm eating for three! Three meals a day just won't cut it anymore," Maya answered grumpily. Arlinda sighed inwardly in relief as she saw Mark, along with Sam saunter in their direction.

Her back was tired, her feet hurt and she didn't feel like dealing with Maya's crazy mood swings, as much as she loved her.

"Hello, ladies," Sam said when they came up beside them. He leaned over to kiss his sister on the cheek before casually draping an arm around Arlinda's shoulders. "Everything turned out wonderfully, Arlinda. You outdid yourself, baby," he complimented her before he kissed her on the corner of her mouth.

His casual gestures, both his arm around her and the light kiss, made her breath catch and Arlinda glanced up at him from the corner of her eyes.

"Yes, everything was wonderful. Great job, ladies." Mark included Mariana in his greeting. "As great as this has all been, if I know my wife, then I'd say it's time to drop by the nearest taco stand and go home," he said, smiling down at a suddenly beaming Maya.

"Are you ready to go, Arlinda?" Mark asked her, as she'd driven with them to the fundraiser.

"I'll take her home, Mark. You go feed your wife," Sam laughed.

"Thank you for the support, girlfriend! Now go get something to eat before you die of starvation or something! I'll talk to you tomorrow," Arlinda laughed.

When the three were left on the stage alone, Mariana turned to them both. "This was wonderful. I can't say enough. Thank you so much," she said sincerely.

Mariana turned to her brother to include him in the conversation. "I believe that this has accomplished something more wonderful than bringing together beautiful designs, having a great time and raising a lot of money. It's brought together two people who were meant to be together." She hugged them both hard before she released them. "And I see that I'm making my big brother embarrassed, so that's all I'm going to say about that!" she laughed.

"You're not making me uncomfortable at all, Mari. I'm in perfect agreement." When Arlinda glanced up to laugh with him, the smile fell from her mouth. The look he gave her was intense and there was not one shred of humor in his dark gaze. She felt as though they were all alone in the room. She felt naked and exposed, and was unable to take her eyes away from his.

"I'm leaving. I'll see you later, Sam. Arlinda, hopefully, I'll see you soon?" Mariana asked with a smile.

"We're leaving too, Mari. Let's walk out together. It's dark and everyone except the crew has left," Sam said, before he escorted both women by the arms out the backstage entrance.

It was cool, and Arlinda wrapped her arms around her body, huddling closer to Sam's large body as they walked Mariana to her car and Sam helped his sister inside.

As soon as she started the engine and waved from inside her car, Sam tucked Arlinda's hand inside his, guided her to his SUV and helped her inside. She snuggled into the leather interior seat and slipped off her shoes, tucking her feet underneath her bottom.

The trip home was completed in near silence. Arlinda had no idea what Sam was thinking. His silence and the way he'd been watching her throughout the night whenever he'd come backstage had her totally on edge. She glanced over in his direction and studied the strong line of his jaw in profile, wondering what was on his mind, as he drove along the deserted streets.

\* \* \* \*

It was now or never. Sam resisted the urge to turn and look at her in the dim light of the car. He could feel her nervousness. It was palpable. Tonight he'd stake his claim. A claim he'd been slowly staking over the last month.

He made the turn into her business plaza and came to a smooth halt in the back parking lot that led directly to her loft. He cut the engine and turned toward her. She looked surprised that he'd parked in the back.

"Is it alright if I come upstairs?" he asked and caught her surprise at his words. He'd never been inside her loft.

"Of course," she agreed with only the slightest bit of a quiver in her voice.

He quickly eased out of the car and jogged around to the passenger side to help her out. As they walked the small distance to the entry, he lightly grasped her fingers between his and squeezed. He reluctantly let them go when she fished the key out of her purse. She allowed him to open the door.

She led him up the stairs that led to the loft. Once she'd unlocked the door, Sam walked inside, ahead of her, and she followed him inside and turned on the light.

He surveyed the loft quickly. The room was warm and inviting, decorated in rich browns, green and gold. From what he could see, the only rooms that were divided looked to be the kitchen, which was separated from the rest of the room by an Oriental folding door, and her bedroom, which was on a raised dais, the bed circled with sheer netting. An open door off to the side of the bedroom appeared to lead into a bathroom.

"Nice," he complimented, as he removed his tuxedo jacket and laid it over the back of a cream-colored occasional chair.

"Thank you. May I get you anything to drink? I thought I'd make some tea." She'd taken her shoes off as soon as they entered the apartment and padded to the kitchen barefoot. It was then that he noticed she wasn't wearing stockings. The sexy length of her leg and bare foot were now fully exposed.

"No, I'm fine," he said, following her to the airy kitchen.

"Thank you for everything you did tonight."

Sam could tell that she was at a loss for words. Her tension was easy to read. He slowly walked around the butcher-block table until he reached her side. As soon as she put the red kettle on the stove, he turned her around to face him.

"Thank you for everything that *you* did tonight," he said and then captured her mouth with his. He pulled her tight against his body, wanting to get as close to her as he could. Her small body fit perfectly against his.

Soon, the feel of their clothes was something he couldn't tolerate, and he broke the kiss, peering down into her face. "I want to make love to you, Arlinda. Now."

Her small nostrils flared. She lightly nodded her head in assent, and that was all he needed to see. Sam lifted her into his arms and carried her the small distance to the canopied bed before moving the netting aside and laying his small bundle down.

He rose and quickly shed his clothing, his own breathing harsh and heavy in the room as he saw the way she stared at him from beneath lowered lids.

This was it. He wasn't pulling back tonight physically and neither would he allow her to pull back emotionally.

"You're beautiful, do you know that, Arlinda?" he asked. He lowered the straps of her gown slowly down the length of her body, peeling the dress away until it pooled at her feet.

His hands stroked down her bared breasts and toward the springy curls nestled at the juncture of her thighs.

"Had I known you weren't wearing underwear, I would have carried you off that damn stage and taken you home," he said.

"That gown doesn't leave much room for bra and panties, Sam." She giggled when he kissed a line down her neck.

He took both sides of her face in his hands and peered deeply into her eyes before he began placing small kisses over her face. His kisses made her squirm and giggle at the same time, until they became more ardent as he traveled down the length of her body. He stopped when he reached one of her breasts.

He cupped the small mound, fingering the erect nipple before he lapped it gently and pulled it into his mouth. He put as much of her breast into his mouth as would fit and Arlinda moaned loudly.

"You like that, don't you, baby?" he asked roughly around a mouthful of plump breast. She could only nod. What he was doing to her breasts felt so good that speech was beyond her at the moment.

Her breasts had never been handled so well. Because she was small she'd been self-conscious of them during lovemaking with others, but Sam went out of his way to make sure she knew how much he enjoyed them as he lapped and tugged on one while his other hand manipulated its twin.

When he released her breasts, she cried out in protest. Her cry ended in a hissing groan of disbelief when he pulled away from her. He grabbed her by the back of her thighs and pushed her legs up until they reached the sides of her ears. Slowly he shoved his long hard cock deep inside her wet channel.

After he was fully seated, his cock so far in she could feel it touch the back of her womb, they both let out a deep, heartfelt groan.

Then he began to pump into her.

At first his thrusts were slow and methodical; the smooth, slick feel of his penis gliding in and out, in and out. Arlinda bit the inside of her cheek to stop herself from screaming just from the feel of his hard length as he jostled her body with his strong thrusts.

When he increased the tempo, his strokes short and fierce, she cried out, "Yes, Sam! Yes … ummm, just like that. Please, keep it right there." She didn't care if he heard the begging in her voice. It felt good to finally have him deep inside. Her vagina instantly clamped down on his cock in welcome. He felt *so* good. So hard and thick as he plunged deep, steadily rocking into her.

"You feel just as good wrapped around my dick, Arlinda, so nice and tight I don't know how much longer I can hold on," he admitted in a rough whisper in her ear.

His words, coupled with the way he was doing her, had Arlinda going out of her mind as she tossed her head back and forth in sensual agony.

He spread her legs impossibly further apart as he dug into her and rubbed her clitoris at the same time. She was mindless with pleasure.

The close feel of her sweet pussy was driving Sam out of his mind as well. She fit tight as a glove, as though she was made for him.

"Damn, Arlinda, you're so fucking tight I can't get close enough, baby," he groaned. The way her pussy wrapped around his cock was making it damn hard not to come and hold her steady as he pumped into her tight sheath.

As he stroked, he leaned down and captured her lips with his on a groan. He loved the taste of her full plump lips. He could suck them forever, they tasted so good. He was deep enough that he felt her womb touch the tip of his dick and he didn't know if he'd be able to hold on much longer.

"Oh god, baby, I'm coming. I'm coming…." she cried as she felt the orgasm just out of reach begin deep inside her belly. When she felt him stop pumping into her, when she felt the long glorious length of his cock withdraw, she frantically grabbed at his hips to try and pull him back in. "No, no what are you doing?" she whimpered.

"Sshh. It's okay, baby." The bulbous tip of his cock was the only thing inside her vagina. It lay still, barely, inside her quivering lips.

"What is it, Sam? Why did you stop?" Both of their breathing was harsh in the quiet of the room.

"Tell me what I want to hear," he demanded quietly, his breathing labored.

"What? What are you talking about?" She wanted to scream! If he didn't come back inside she'd do more than scream, she'd kill him!

"You know what I mean! Tell me what I want to hear." This time, his demand was fierce and brooked no argument.

She looked desperately into his eyes and saw the steely determination. A determination that he'd pull out and not finish the act, despite the fine sheen of sweat on his brow that she could barely see in the moonlit room. Despite the way his arms were shaking, his chest heaving with the effort that it took not to continue stroking into her. He'd pull out if she didn't say what he wanted to hear.

She knew what he wanted to hear.

"It's too soon for that. I've never said it to anyone before, Sam … please!" she cried desperately, trying her damndest to get him to continue stroking her.

"Tell me, Arlinda. Make a decision, right now," he demanded, looking her in the eyes.

An eternity seemed to pass as they were locked in their sensual battle, but in actuality it was mere moments. Arlinda knew that if she refused to acknowledge what was in her heart, that if she let this man go, she'd be making the biggest mistake of her life.

She was tired of hiding. And damned tired of pretending. She made her decision and the overwhelming relief she felt confirmed that it was the right one.

"I love you, Sam."

"I love you, too," he groaned.

He grabbed her wrists lightly and held them near her head. He pushed his cock into her as far as he could and she didn't hold back the scream this time. He plunged and pumped, holding her hips tightly and she came long and hard. When he reached a hand between them and pinched her clit, a second orgasm hit. Her pussy frantically clamped down on his cock while his fingers pinched and rubbed her clit as she came so hard she was left dizzy and disoriented with the overwhelming intensity of her release.

Her orgasm triggered his and before long, through her haze of tears she saw Sam rear back from her, the muscles in his neck standing out in sharp relief as he grabbed her hips so tightly she knew she'd have bruises in the morning. He delivered four, final, tight corkscrew thrusts that put him over the edge.

For long moments they stayed in that position. His hard, heavy body lay damply on top of hers, his breathing harsh. Eventually he raised his body up and away from her and carefully turned their bodies so that they were facing each other.

He smiled down at her and tucked a curl behind her ear before engulfing her in a hug and resting his chin on top of her head.

"Do we have to move?" she laughingly asked.

"No. I'm fine where I am. I don't want to be anywhere else," he said, his voice deep and hoarse. There was a momentary pause before he continued. "What about you?"

She knew he was asking a question that was much deeper than if she were able to move her body, and despite the anxiety and fear she felt, she also felt a near euphoric feeling of relief.

"I'm happy where I am. I don't see any reason to go anywhere else. For a minute." She held her laughter back when he gave her a light swat her on her butt.

"Oh, just for a minute, huh?" he asked threateningly.

"Okay, maybe a minute or *two*," she laughingly said.

He gathered her close and she felt his smile as he rested his mouth against her forehead before he pulled away from her.

"Where do we go from here?" Arlinda had always been the type of person that once she made a decision went full speed ahead. She'd made the decision to trust this man. To believe that he loved her, and that they had a future together. If that's what he wanted.

Suddenly old insecurities raised their collective ugly heads.

"Hold that thought," he said, kissing her forehead before sprinting from the bed. She loved looking at his tight muscular backside as he leaned down and picked up his discarded tuxedo slacks. He fished in the pocket to retrieve something she couldn't quite make out in the dark of the room and bounded back to the bed.

"How about we start here?" he asked and opened his hand. In his palm was a small velvet box.

Her heart beat wildly. There was no way on God's green earth that he had what she thought he had, no way.... Her mental thoughts came to a screeching halt when he opened the box and inside was a diamond solitaire that shone so brightly it sparkled in the dim light of the room.

"Arlinda, what we have is special. I know it's soon, that we've only known each other for a few short weeks. But the minute I saw you I knew you were the woman for me. I saw behind that mask, that front you put up, to the warm, crazy, beautiful soul of someone that I want to spend the rest of my life with," he told her and reached across to wipe the tear that had escaped and was making its way down her cheek.

"Do you think you could take a chance on me? Take a chance and believe that what we have is special? To finally allow me totally into your heart and know that I'll take care of it and you for the rest of our lives?" There was a small catch in his deep voice.

She wondered if he could possibly be serious. As she glanced nervously from the diamond where it sparkled so brightly in the small box and back to his face, her fears were instantly put aside. It was all there in his eyes.

The catch in his deep voice was what did it for her. That and the honesty she could see shining deep in his dark eyes. She was stunned. Her mind was barely able to wrap around the fact that she'd admitted her love to him and that he loved her in return and now he was asking her spend her life with him.

"Yes," she started and had to clear her throat before she could continue. "Yes, I'll take a chance, any chance with you. I love you so much, Sam." She started to cry.

As soon as she uttered the last choking words, Sam had grabbed her and pulled her naked body tight against his. "I love you too, baby girl."

Tears of joy streamed down her face, but she didn't care. She'd played the flirt, joked and laughed enough. Now it was time to be real. This man was special. She knew without a shadow of a doubt that he loved her with everything he had inside of himself. She didn't question it. She just knew it.

She wasn't going to run away and she wasn't going to sabotage this relationship. She'd found someone who loved her for who she really was and she had every intention of giving them every chance in the world to make it.

The End

Don't miss out on collecting these other exciting Harmony™ titles for your collection:

The Devil's Concubine by Jaide Fox (Fantasy Romance) Trade Paper 1-58608-776-2
*A great contest was announced to decide who would win the hand of Princess Aliya, accounted the fairest young maiden in the land. The ruler of every kingdom was invited--every kingdom that is save those of the unnaturals. When King Talin, ruler of the tribe of Golden Falcons learned of the slight, he was enraged. He had no desire to take a mere man child as his bride, but he would allow the insult to go unchallenged.*

Zhang Dynasty: Seduction of the Phoenix by Michelle M. Pillow (Futuristic Romance) Trade Paper 1-58608-777-0
*A prince raised in honor and tradition, a woman raised with nothing at all. She wants to steal their most sacred treasure. He'll do anything to protect it, even if it means marrying a thief.*

Warriors of the Darkness by Mandy M. Roth (Paranormal Romance) Trade Paper 1-58608-778-9
*In place where time and space have no boundaries, ancient enemies would like nothing more than to eradicate them both, just when they've found each other.*

Clone Wars: Armageddon by Kaitlyn O'Connor (Futuristic Romance) Trade Paper 1-58608-775-4
*Living in a world devastated by one disaster after another, it's natural for people to look for a target to blame for their woes, and Lena thinks little of it when new rumors begin to circulate about a government conspiracy. She soon discovers, though, that the government may or may not be*

*conspiring against its citizens, but someone certainly is. Morris, her adoptive father, isn't Morris anymore, and the mirror image of herself that comes to kill her most definitely isn't a long lost identical twin.*

Labyrinth of the Beast by Desiree Acuna (Erotic Fantasy Romance) Trade Paper 1-58608-782-7
*Offered as a sacrifice to the demons of the Labyrinth, it is Gaelen who teaches Lilith the pleasures of the flesh, and she finds herself succumbing to the lure of security he offers. Too late, she recalls the one thing she knows for certain about demons--they lie.*

Printed in the United States
55635LVS00002B/118-777